KI

"Are you a[...]

"You look a little flushed. Is [...]

"It appears that it is," Dimitri said, fighting the urge to rip the pins from her hair and let it tumble over his hands. "What I have in mind," he whispered, "will not cool either of us. This is all right with you?"

"It is if you want to court me."

Dimitri was taken aback. Were all American women so aggressive? "I—I suppose you could say that, among other things, is what I have in mind."

"What other things?" She tilted up her chin, parting her lips in case he hadn't caught on.

Dimitri lowered his head and brushed his mouth over hers. "Something like that. Do you still approve?"

She was surprised to hear her own voice come out in a breathless whisper. "Mr. Adonis, if I'd known it was going to be so much trouble getting you to kiss me, I would've just sat down and wrote you a letter."

"It never ceases to amaze me how Ms. Ihle can come up with such creative, unique situations. . . . With her sense of the ridiculous, she creates absurd hilarity and tear-jerking pathos that can keep you laughing, crying, and turning pages."
　　—*Heartland Critiques* five gold-starred review

"The humorous dialogue and spicy vernacular will keep you laughing as the tangled web of deceit is surprisingly resolved. . . . A winner from the pen of Ms. Ihle."
　　　　　　　　　　　　　　—*Rendezvous*

Books by Sharon Ihle

Wild Rose
Wildcat
The Law and Miss Penny
Marrying Miss Shylo

Available from
HarperPaperbacks

Harper
Monogram

Marrying Miss Shylo

 SHARON IHLE

HarperPaperbacks
A Division of HarperCollinsPublishers

HarperPaperbacks *A Division of* HarperCollins*Publishers*
10 East 53rd Street, New York, N.Y. 10022

Copyright © 1994 by Sharon J. Ihle
All rights reserved. No part of this book may be used or reproduced in any manner whatsoever without written permission of the publisher, except in the case of brief quotations embodied in critical articles and reviews. For information address HarperCollins*Publishers,*
10 East 53rd Street, New York, N.Y. 10022.

Cover illustration by Jean Monti

First printing: December 1994

Printed in the United States of America

HarperPaperbacks, HarperMonogram, and colophon are trademarks of HarperCollins*Publishers*

❖ 10 9 8 7 6 5 4 3 2 1

For my beautiful daughter, Lisa;
her own Greek god, Panagiotis Kabouridis;
and their adorable son,
Stylianos Joseph Kabouridis;
and, as always,
for my husband, Larry—thanks for filling my
days and nights along the Mediterranean
with so much romance!

Special thanks to
Janice Griffith, director
Old Trails Museum/Winslow Historical Society;
The San Diego Historical Society;
and
Billie Wade for the story of the orphan train and her
great collection of *Arizona Highways* magazines.

Oh, what a tangled web we weave,
When first we practice to deceive.
— Sir Walter Scott

1

New York City, 1888

Awestruck and surprisingly mortified, Shylo McBride stood with her younger sister and stared up at the huge brownstone mansion on the corner of Fifth Avenue. Although she rarely second-guessed any plan of hers once she'd put it in motion, this one suddenly seemed almost too crazy to have a chance in hell of succeeding.

Her knees were nearly knocking, and her throat was dry, parched as if she'd been staked out in the desert for weeks on end. A sense of fear—something foreign to her—whispered that she ought to run away while she still could. But her obsessive need to find her mother kept her in place and urged her to continue her search. Besides, she hadn't come all the way from Kansas just to turn tail and bolt like a frightened rabbit.

Shylo took a deep breath and went over the details

with her sister one last time. "Remember what you're supposed to do and who I'm supposed to be?"

Cassie gave her an exasperated sigh. "For the thousandth time, yes! I'm still a McBride, but now you're pretending to be a Folsom. I'm your traveling companion, not your sister, and have to act like a maid-type female. I'm not to speak to anyone unless spoken to, and then mostly just 'Yes, ma'am'– and 'No, sir'–type answers. And no cussing."

"Especially not that shit word," Shylo amended. "Anything else?"

Cassie thought a minute, then frowned. "I'm not to give in to a fit of jealousy or pout because you're all decked out in that fancy ball gown and getting all the attention while I'm stuck with this plain old traveling dress and purple hair!"

Shylo shook off the residual guilt she still felt over the experiment she'd done on Cassie's hair. "It's not like I knew something could go wrong with the henna. It was a mistake. Now stop worrying so much about it. It'll wash out in time."

But to Cassie, at the age of sixteen—a full five years younger than her sister—even one more day of those hideous locks would seem like a lifetime. "It will probably stay this color until I'm too old to get a beau!"

Though sorely tempted to lecture Cassie about keeping her mind on the main reason they were back in New York—to find their mother—Shylo did recognize that as a dreamer, Cassie lived for the day some nonexistent Prince Charming would come along on a big white steed, sweep her into his arms, and vow to love her forever. Shylo, practical soul that she was, knew such a thing would never happen to either of them, but she kept her opinion to herself, allowing

Cassie the one luxury that didn't cost them a dime: her fantasies.

Shylo tugged her sister's oversize bonnet forward to make sure none of the purple strands showed. "With the pretty face God gave you, you could be bald and still have beaux lined up for miles. Now let's go inside and get this over with."

With a more agreeable Cassie right on her heels, Shylo climbed the elaborate marble stairs and rang the bell as if she had every right to do so. The door opened within seconds, and a butler dressed in the peacock blue livery of the house of Vanderkellen appeared, his right arm positioned carefully across his waist. "May I be of service, madam?"

Shylo lifted her chin to what she figured was an aristocratic tilt and said, "Yes, you may. I'm here on a brief visit, one that came up so quickly, I'm afraid I neglected to bring my calling cards. I have a message for William or Victoria Vanderkellen. Please tell them Miss Shylo Folsom of the Buffalo Folsoms is here to see them."

His frown was almost indiscernible as he glanced from Shylo to Cassie in her drab brown dress, but it was there in any case. If she couldn't get past the butler, how in the hell would she ever get into the party and set her plan in motion? Deciding to parry arrogance with arrogance, Shylo raised her chin to another, haughtier level and arched one sable-colored eyebrow as high as it would go. "Well?" she said, trying to act offended. "Aren't you going to invite us in?"

Uncertainty flickered in his eyes for a long moment, but at last the butler backed away and showed them into a lavish foyer bigger than any home the McBride girls had ever lived in.

"Wait here, please," he said, gesturing for them to take a seat on a gilded settee upholstered in crushed maroon velvet. Then he turned on his shiny patent-leather heels and disappeared behind a pair of huge doors.

Music and laughter, the sounds of gaiety, drifted into the entry before the doors whispered to a close again. Alone and unobserved, Shylo and Cassie took a quick look around. Bouquets of aromatic flowers adorned each of the several occasional tables in the reception area, and tall palm trees with shiny fronds rose up from each side of a curved marble staircase.

Shylo allowed herself a moment of awe. Here she was, a complete nobody, and she'd actually gained entrance inside the Vanderkellen mansion! She'd done it! Filled with more excitement now than anxiety, she turned to see if her sister felt the same way. Cassie was gawking at the richly appointed home, clearly agog over the excesses of marble and oil paintings and the liberal use of gold in trim, trinkets, and figurines.

Shylo elbowed her in the ribs. "Quit looking so damn—darn impressed. Remember that you're supposed to have been in hundreds of houses just like this, one as fancy as another. You're so doggone big-eyed, I'd swear you'd just crossed paths with your first naked man."

Cassie gasped, then giggled into her gloved palm as the doors parted and the butler stepped back into the room. The most elegant woman Shylo had ever seen was standing at his side. The diamonds and emeralds around her neck and on her ears sparkled, setting off her gorgeous strawberry-blond hair, which was the very color Shylo's would have been had the henna worked better on Cassie. The woman practically float-ed as she moved across the marble floor, the train of her emerald velvet gown slithering along behind her like a serpent.

Suddenly unsure of herself, forgetting whether she ought to bow, curtsy, or offer her hand, Shylo slowly rose up from the settee as the woman drew near.

"Miss Folsom, is it?" the matron asked in a haughty tone as she eyed Shylo from head to toe. "I don't believe I recall seeing your name on the invitation list for this reception. Perhaps you've made a mistake."

Jolted as she realized the woman was planning to throw her out, Shylo fell into her role. "Reception? My goodness. Have I come at a bad time?"

"You're not here for the reception?"

"Oh, goodness, no. I have a message for Mrs. William K. Vanderkellen."

The woman's demeanor took on pompous propor-tions. "I'm Victoria Vanderkellen. What is it?"

Never one to do anything halfway, Shylo had figured early on that if she was going to tell one of New York's leading society matrons a lie, it might as well be a whop-per. She smiled broadly and offered her gloved hand. "Let me introduce myself properly. My aunt Frances was a Folsom, and is now—as I'm sure you must know—Mrs. Grover Cleveland." She shook the woman's hand, pleased to see the startled look in her eyes.

"The *First Lady* is your—"

"My aunt Frances. She and the president have been visiting my family upstate in Buffalo." Shylo knew this was true because she'd read it in the newspaper. "When Uncle Grover found out that I was planning a quick shopping trip in Manhattan, well, he just insisted that I stop by and introduce myself to you and your husband."

By now it was the Vanderkellen woman who looked as if she'd seen a naked man. Shylo smiled indulgently. "Please forgive me for barging in on you like this," she said, running another bluff. "I had no idea you'd be entertaining. Perhaps I can stop by again tomorrow if I have time on my way to the train station."

"Oh, no, I won't hear of your going off this way." Victoria reached for Shylo's hands and clasped them between her own. "Please stay. We've having a wonderful reception for the Greek envoy and several of his compatriots." She glanced at Cassie, who was still perched on the edge of the settee. "If your friend would like—"

"Oh, don't worry about Miss McBride. She's my traveling companion, and quite content to busy herself with her little bag of sewing." She turned and smiled at Cassie. "I shan't be long, Cassandra."

"Then you'll stay and join us?" Mrs. Vanderkellen asked.

Shylo's pause was practiced, giving her the opportunity to glance down at her beautiful new dress. She had chosen the outfit carefully, knowing she couldn't afford to waste what little money she and Cassie had left on imported fabrics, velvet, or silk. Her royal blue suit of sateen was stylish yet plain, a lovely little day dress that Cassie's nimble fingers could turn into a ball gown later, if necessary.

She sighed dramatically. "Perhaps I should go. I'm not really dressed for a formal occasion. Had I known—"

"You look wonderful just the way you are. Shall we?"

Shylo smiled sweetly. "If you insist."

As the women walked toward the ballroom, Victoria

told her about the other guests. "You did say you were Miss Folsom, didn't you?"

"Yes, but please call me Shylo."

"And you may call me Victoria, if you like." Dropping her voice even lower, she went on. "You wouldn't believe the assortment of unattached Greek men we have with us tonight. I'm a little jealous of you single ladies—some of these gentlemen are shockingly handsome."

Shylo had been studying the papers well enough to know exactly what the woman was hinting at. It was practically sport in New York for young heiresses to marry Europeans, and the more titled the man, the better. Rich men and their titles didn't interest Shylo, though. Presenting herself to her mother—and in her own highfalutin' territory, no less—did. But she had one other little thing to take care of first.

When they reached the ballroom doors, Shylo bade the hostess to slow her steps. "Excuse me, Victoria, but I wonder if you'd mind doing me a little favor before you start introducing me around."

"Of course, dear. What is it? Would you like to freshen up a bit first?"

"No, but there is something that makes me feel a little, oh, I don't know . . . uncomfortable." She had the woman's attention and hoped she could capture her sympathy as well. Shylo wasn't terribly concerned about the repercussions when the Vanderkellens discovered she wasn't related to the president, but if she could avoid having to explain that little bit of chicanery to her mother, who might not be terribly pleased to see her again to begin with, their reunion would go ever so much better.

"I'd really appreciate it if you'd introduce me as

just plain Shylo Folsom. To mention my connection to the president would make me feel, well, pretentious at the least, but my main concern is those single men you were telling me about." She bit the inside of her lip to keep from laughing. "You'd be surprised how many of them try to take advantage of my position."

Victoria looked dismayed. "Oh, I never, ah, thought of what you must endure as, you know. You're sure?"

"Oh, yes. I'm sure." Relieved to have that out of the way, Shylo reminded herself of the rules of etiquette she'd memorized as Victoria led her toward a small group of guests. A few of those handsome, "unattached" men stood out from the crowd, but Shylo barely glanced their way.

While Victoria Vanderkellen began her introduction into New York society, a distracted Shylo scanned the crowd for the woman who'd abandoned her daughters sixteen years before, shortly after the second, Cassie, was born.

In a corner not far from the doorway, Dimitri Adonis watched as his hostess stepped back into the ballroom. A new guest accompanied her, a simply dressed and rather unassuming-looking young woman who didn't appear to be weighing the bank account of each man her gaze fell upon. She seemed to be a refreshing change from the American females he'd come across during the few days he'd been in the States. Refreshing . . . and intriguing. Perhaps he would seek her introduction instead of waiting for her to make her way through the crowd.

"Dimitri! There you are!" Aristotle Kotsala swept by a tuxedoed waiter, removed two glasses of champagne from the man's silver tray, and never slowed his stride as he offered one of the drinks to his nephew. "How do you think to do business with the Americans if you are hiding in corners? Come, join us."

Dimitri smiled as he accepted the champagne, amazed at the old man's unending supply of energy. Ari, who liked to think of himself as Dimitri's uncle even though the relationship was distant, and by marriage rather than blood, came alive at these gatherings, working the crowds like a fishmonger along the ancient quays of Piraeus. Dimitri, on the other hand, was bored and more than just a little uncomfortable.

Ari's gray eyes glistened, and his nose wrinkled with enthusiasm as he touched his glass to his nephew's. "*Yamas!* Or to be more American, I'll say, 'Bottoms up!' To our successes—mine with the businessmen, yours with the ladies."

Dimitri accepted the toast, though his enthusiasm for either enterprise was slim, at best. There was certainly a need, and a rather urgent one, to stir up interest and procure a goodly amount of capital if the Adonis import business was ever to get back on its feet again.

After what his uncle Niko, his *true* uncle, had done, there was really no choice. On the very day that Dimitri's father died, Niko had raped the business of its assets and fled the country, leaving Dimitri and his widowed mother to pick up the pieces with precious little means at their disposal. It was a business Dimitri had virtually no interest in, but as the only child of George and Anastasia Adonis, putting the company back in order was expected of him. It was his duty.

Uncle Ari knew how much it pained Dimitri to leave the University of Athens, even for this brief trip.

Because of that, Ari had been the first with an offer of help, although because of the man's own adverse financial condition, that help had been strictly of an advisory nature. But he had been unfailing in that capacity. For those reasons, if no other, Dimitri raised his glass to him in salute. "To success, wherever and however we may find it."

Ari downed his champagne in one swallow, grinned, and wriggled his eyebrows. "Come with me, my son. I have three rich young American women who wish to meet you. You must smile on the one you like best, show her your good teeth, and she will be yours, no problem."

Dimitri laughed. "What did you tell them this time, Uncle Ari? That I am a prince, son to King George no less?"

"Would I tell such lies?" Ari smoothed his handlebar mustache. "Hmmm . . . now that I think back, could be yes, I maybe mentioned something about a title. My memory—it is not so good these days."

Again Dimitri laughed. Ari's strategies were so outrageous. "And what, dear uncle, shall I do when one of those American beauties finds out that I have no title or money? What if her father should take it in his head to shoot me as a rakehell?"

Ari shrugged. "No problem. A man as handsome as you just naturally has a way with the ladies. One look at you, and the woman you choose—one who will be richer than God, of course—will forget about all but you. No father will shoot his daughter's love. Come, I show you."

Dimitri was amused, but he held back. He wasn't even slightly interested in getting married to anyone, much less an American woman of "fine breeding."

This was his first trip to the States, and from what he'd seen so far, the heiresses and aristocrats here were spoiled, demanding, and much too artificial for his tastes. Ari might consider a marriage between him and an American heiress as the most lucrative and least difficult way of regaining the Adonis fortunes, but Dimitri was not at all convinced.

"Come," Ari repeated. "You must remember that it is just as easy to marry a rich woman as a poor one. A bride of great wealth awaits you in this room. I feel it in my bones. Come now, you choose."

Dimitri rolled his eyes. He'd rather have pledged his troth to a Turkish peasant than face the rest of his life with one of the women gathered in this mansion, but he decided to relinquish his hold on the corner. After all, they hadn't traveled all this way just for a change of scenery. He and Ari had pooled their assets to make this trip, gambled with what was left of the family business in the hopes that American money would help make the Adonis empire whole and healthy again. The least he could do was pretend to go along with all of Ari's stratagems—even this ridiculous matchmaking idea.

Maybe, Dimitri mused, if he looked as if he were actively seeking a bride, his uncle would turn his concentration wholly on the businessmen, thereby securing the financial backing they sought without an unwanted wedding. After that, Dimitri figured on hiring someone to run the family business so he would be free to pursue his archaeological career once again.

"All right," Dimitri said, sounding resigned as he set his glass on a small marble table. "Take me to the slaughter."

Ari chuckled and rubbed his hands together, but

before they could move toward the center of the crowded ballroom, where most guests were milling around a circular buffet table, she came into view: the lovely, unassuming young woman who had caught Dimitri's eye earlier.

Up close she was even lovelier, her smooth peachy complexion unfettered by powders and rouges. Her manner was surprisingly humble, too, making her seem a little tentative, almost as if she felt out of place or was uncomfortable. The way she looked on the outside was the way Dimitri felt on the inside.

He tapped Ari's shoulder, pointed at the girl in the royal blue, and said, "I choose her."

Ari's bald head swiveled in her direction, then he furrowed his brow. "She does not look so wealthy, my son, nor do we know anything of her. At least wait to choose until I can, how do you say, learn of her assets?"

"I can see her assets, and I like what I see." Dimitri glanced at his uncle and winked. "I choose her."

As she and Victoria Vanderkellen neared yet another group of strangers, Shylo prayed once again that she would finally be looking into the green eyes of the mother she hadn't seen in so long. How could she not be here? Shylo had learned through reading old newspapers that Victoria Vanderkellen and Colleen McBride—now Broussard—were the closest of friends. One would never dream of giving a party without inviting the other. Colleen just had to be here.

Then, out of nowhere, Shylo felt the man's gaze upon her. It was a probing, penetrating stare that made her feel intimidated, exposed somehow. She tried to talk herself into meeting the challenge she felt but was terrified that he might be able to see through her and know her for the impostor she was. As she and Victoria drew closer to the man, Shylo tried desperately to think of a reason to excuse herself.

Then it was too late.

2

"*. . . and these* two gentlemen," Shylo heard Victoria say, "are businessmen from Greece. I'm sorry to say, sirs, that since I've met so many new people this evening, most of them with terribly difficult names, I seem to have forgotten yours."

"There is no need to apologize, Mrs. Vanderkellen." The man's voice seemed like velvet to Shylo, deep and smooth. "My uncle and I can make our own introductions."

"I do appreciate that." Victoria touched Shylo's shoulder. "Will you excuse me, dear? I see that some new guests have arrived, and I must welcome them. I'm sure these gentlemen will keep you entertained, even if I can't tell them what a very *special* guest you are." Then she glided away.

The Vanderkellen woman had been alluding to Shylo's connections since she'd walked into the ballroom, sometimes tossing Washington, D.C., or mention of the White House into her conversations. Although the innuendos embarrassed Shylo, they did have a desirable effect. Most of the guests seemed to be duly impressed with her unnamed "credentials," even though none of them could figure out quite how she fit into political society.

But right now the only thing she gave a hoot about was the impression this man had formed—and why he was staring at her in such a blatant manner. Before Shylo could summon the courage to stare right back at him, that velvet smooth voice caressed her ears again.

"I am Dimitri, and this is my uncle, Aristotle Kotsala."

Not quite prepared for the confrontation, Shylo forced herself to turn to the older, shorter, and far less threatening stranger. "Nice to meet you, Mr. Kotsala. My name is Shylo Mc— Folsom."

Ari reached for her hand and shook it lightly. "It is a pleasure to meet you, Miss McFolsom."

"It's Folsom," she said, quickly covering the blunder. "Shylo Folsom."

"Shylo. What a very interesting name." That voice again, pensive, thoughtful, tasting her name rather than simply enunciating it. "Does Shylo mean something special?"

His tone beckoned her. Shylo suddenly had no will of her own, no thought but to obey him. She glanced up, and for one long, stunning moment she forgot who she was, whom she was pretending to be, and why. He was an aristocrat, that much was for sure. No one could possibly look the way he did and be anything less than royalty. Dimitri's features were godlike, carved in classical Greek fashion with bold, dark sweeps. Topping that perfect face was a head full of blue-black hair that fell in thick waves, then rolled into a mass of curls just below his ears and at the collar of his shirt. Preoccupied by the man's terrifyingly good looks, Shylo forgot all about her previous fears. She dared a glance into his eyes—and froze.

She'd never seen black eyes before, certainly none as dark or luminous as the ones looking back at her, but it wasn't just their color that had her thoroughly trapped; it was what they had to say to her. Those eyes were cool yet hot at the same time, both confident and deeply perceptive, glimpsing through her layers as if their owner knew that just plain Shylo McBride fresh off a Kansas farm lurked beneath the cheap sateen and pile of cumbersome curls.

Seeking relief from his probe, she managed to force her gaze downward to his mouth. This part of him, too, was carved in classic Greek fashion, the bottom lip full, the top finely etched, with an enticing dip at the center. As she stared at that fascinating mouth, wondering briefly how it would feel pressed against her own, those perfectly formed lips spread into a grin.

"Perhaps my question was too personal." Dimitri knew that his command of English was a lot better than his grasp of American manners and mores. Concerned that he'd offended the mute woman, he lifted both of her hands and carefully kissed her fingertips. "I am new to your country, and not familiar with many of your customs. Please forgive me."

"Oh, n-no, there's nothing to forgive." Now that she was finally able to speak again, Shylo's voice sprang up from the pit of her belly, loud and unladylike. She had to get a grip on herself and the peculiar warm way this man made her feel—which was not easy, since his lips had all but set fire to her fingers right through her gloves.

She took a deep breath and softened her tone. "I mean to say that I don't mind your asking about my name. My mother's people are from Tennessee. . . ." Shylo paused long enough to glance around the room in search of that very woman, came up empty again, and went on. "Anyway, she just liked the sound of the word Shiloh, I guess, but spelled my name different, S-h-y-l-o, so I wouldn't be getting confused with a battle."

Dimitri smiled broadly, showing off a pair of dimples as chiseled and perfect as his swarthy features. "Shylo is a lovely name, and if I may say so, you are a very lovely woman."

His pronunciation of "woo-man" added to the melodic way he rolled his *r*'s, had Shylo nearly quivering. She thought Victoria Vanderkellen had been exaggerating mightily when she'd said there were some "shockingly handsome" men gathered in her ballroom, but now that she'd laid eyes on this one and heard him speak, Shylo thought the woman had grossly underrated at least one of her guests.

But whether he was handsome or not, she couldn't afford to be distracted by this man. She was supposed to be thinking with her head, not her fluttering female heart. Hadn't she learned from the way her mother had run out on her father in search of "a better life" that drooling over handsome men or even falling in love with one was a complete waste of time? Of course! Above all else, she had to remember those rules and never let her head be turned, not even by this magnificent specimen of manhood.

Shylo returned his smile and lowered her lashes. "Thanks for the compliment, Mr. er, ah—?"

Beaming over the attraction he saw between his nephew and this possible heiress, Ari pushed his way into the conversation. "Allow me—this is Dimitri *Adonis*."

"Adonis? You mean like in the legend?"

Again Ari fielded the question. "He is Adonis, yes, like the son of Cinyras, king of Cyprus."

Shylo's knowledge of Greek mythology was scant, but to have the same name as a legend sounded awfully impressive to her. She completely forgot the good manners she'd been practicing as she blurted, "Wow! Isn't he the god of good looks or something like that?"

Dimitri laughed, amused by her refreshing candor, but before he could explain that Adonis was simply a surname, Ari took over again.

"The Adonis of legend was a very beautiful man. Some say that Dimitri continues the family tradition very much."

"The family? Surely you don't mean to say that—"

"Excuse me, please." Dimitri's voice had lost its smooth edge. "I must have a private moment with my uncle. I hope you don't mind."

"Oh, certainly not, go on, don't worry about me."

"I shall return shortly. May I bring you a glass of champagne?"

Shylo had never imbibed anything stronger than cow's milk fresh from the teat, but she felt herself nodding as Dimitri inclined his head and walked away. As the two men moved back into a corner, an addendum to her plan materialized in her mind, and Shylo's heart pounded crazily at the thought of it. Her intentions had been to confront her mother in a way that would make her proud—as a polished, well-dressed, and charming enough young lady to be welcomed into her mother's treasured social circles. That way, she figured, there would be less chance of Colleen rejecting her again or, worse, refusing to see her at all.

Wouldn't confronting her mother with this Dimitri Adonis on her arm be like sticking an extra feather in her cap? How could Colleen not claim a daughter who was enchanting enough to attract a man such as this? Any fool could see that if you added the way this Adonis fellow looked to the barrels of money she assumed he had, he probably spent most of his time beating high-bred women off with a buggy whip! She would be the envy of every woman from Kansas to New York if she could get him interested in her.

Shylo tapped her index finger against her chin. Dimitri had clearly been at least a little taken by her, but how in God's name, she wondered, could a plain ole Kansas farm girl go about *catching*—at least long enough to impress her mother—that incredibly handsome Greek? She'd learned one hell of a lot about hunting and fishing during her years on the farm— enough to land the big ones with the best of them as long as she had the right rig. But with a man like this as her quarry? Shylo wasn't at all sure she possessed the proper equipment.

Dimitri, unaware that he was anyone's quarry, spoke his native language in hushed tones as he said to his uncle, "What the devil are you trying to do to me— pass me off as a Greek god? I said I chose her. At least let me conduct my own courtship in my own way."

Ari held out his hands. "Calm down, calm down. I do a little matchmaking, is all. I only thought to sweeten the pot with a taste of honey. Not to worry."

"I'm not the one who's worried, Uncle, you are." Dimitri paused, studying Ari's face. It was round and cherubic by nature, but when he pouted, as he was doing now, he looked downright impish. It was impossible to stay mad at the man. "Why don't you go mingle with a few of the businessmen who might do our company some good, and leave the work of captivating the women up to me?"

"Yes, yes, of course, but you must remember what our hostess said about Miss Folsom. She is a very *special* guest, someone so special, the woman could not even tell us why! Think of what that could mean!"

"The end of our financial troubles, I know." Even though such arranged marriages were commonplace in Greece, Dimitri's expression darkened at the thought of using a woman in such a manner, not to mention using himself as a lure. He forced a smile and shooed his uncle away. "Go now, meet everyone, have a good time."

"Yes, yes, I will go do business over many drinks, and make a few discreet inquiries about Miss Folsom while I'm at it." Ari whirled around, whispering reverently, "God, I love this country." Then he lost himself in the crowd.

Dimitri chuckled over his uncle's antics, but in truth he had quite the opposite opinion of the United States. He'd been distinctly uneasy since his arrival, and not because he was homesick. He hated the fact that he was here on American soil "begging," as it were, for help in restoring the once proud Adonis name. To think that he was also expected to convince one of these snobbish, painfully thin women to return with him to Greece and the far less comfortable world of musty digs, backbreaking work, and blankets tossed on the ground in place of first-class hotels was simply ludicrous. Surely there was a better way!

As Dimitri finally worked his way to the buffet

table, he thought again of Shylo. Along with those big blue eyes and honey-blond hair, he recalled that she had a more robust and healthy nature than most American women. Even her skin seemed less pampered and more earthy, as if it had been exposed to a fair amount of sun, certainly more so than any of the pasty-faced debutantes he'd met so far.

That, if nothing else, made the lady a refreshing sight in this world of wigs and cosmetics. Even so, to think that a woman of her obvious connections and breeding would consider living the way he did was out of the question. Utterly and completely out of the question. But since he had to at least make the appearance of wooing a future bride, Miss Shylo Folsom seemed like an excellent choice.

Two glasses of champagne in hand, Dimitri started back to where he'd left her. His uncle intercepted him midway.

"I have great news!" Ari lowered his voice. "Your choice in brides is admirable, my son. She is none other than the niece of the president of the United States!" He rubbed his hands together, waiting for his nephew to absorb this information. "Imagine the contacts we can make through her!"

Dimitri was not nearly as impressed by this news as Ari. His interest in politics, unlike that of the typical Greek male, was almost nonexistent, even where his own country was concerned. Dimitri cared little whether Trikoupis and his Westernized style of government prevailed over Deliyannis and his traditional followers, or vice versa. Most of Dimitri's countrymen took sides as the two factions alternated in power, but all he really cared about, other than finding his uncle Niko and extracting some measure of revenge, was his commitment to champion the return of the Grecian art treasures that were being held captive by the British Museum in London.

Ari jabbed a finger against his silent nephew's chest. "The shock of hearing about this strong, strong connection has your tongue tied, has it not?"

Dimitri laughed, unable to resist the sparkle in his uncle's eyes. "Good work, Ari. Maybe next time I tell you I have an eye for 'assets,' you will believe me." He held up the champagne glasses. "I'm on my way back to her now. You can join us if you promise not to interfere with my methods to win her hand."

"I promise. Oh, and Dimitri, there is one more thing." He leaned in close, whispering in his native language again. "Say nothing to Miss Folsom about her connection to the president. Our hostess tells me the young lady wishes to keep her relationship to him a secret for some reason."

Across the room, Shylo had finally gotten Victoria Vanderkellen alone again and was just gathering up her courage to come right out and ask the woman why in hell Colleen McBride Broussard wasn't at her fancy reception. Unfortunately her Greek "quarry" arrived before she could even get one word out.

"Mrs. Vanderkellen," Dimitri said, nodding in her direction as he handed Shylo one of the glasses of champagne. He offered his hostess the other. "Would you care for a drink?"

"Oh, goodness, but no, thank you. I've had quite enough already." She turned back to Shylo. "Was there anything else, dear? I really must see to the refreshment table."

Shylo's stomach clenched up good and tight. It was now or never. She took a large swallow of champagne, fought the sudden urge to sneeze as a thousand bubbles exploded in her nostrils, and finally regained her wits enough to say, "There is one more thing, Victoria. I was also hoping to look up the mother of my best friend while I'm in New York, but I can't seem to locate her. I'm told that she is an acquaintance of yours. Do you know where I might find . . ." She took a deep breath before continuing, "Colleen Broussard?"

"Certainly! Colleen and I are very, very close."

Shylo knew all this, of course, but to hear it confirmed made her insides go numb. The earth, her pulse, all that mattered in her world, felt as if it had slowly chugged to a halt. She'd been waiting for this moment for years, almost an entire lifetime, and now that it was here, instead of feeling triumphant, Shylo felt as if she were about to make a blubbering idiot of herself! Her euphoric heart leapt to her throat, crowding the passage and making it nearly impossible to breathe. She swallowed several times in succession, willing the huge lump there to go away, but it didn't move. She took another drink of her champagne.

By then Victoria's perfectly made up face had fallen into the closest thing she ever allowed by way of a frown. "Did you say Colleen is your friend's *mother?*"

Wrestling with a firestorm of bubbles inside her head again, Shylo just nodded. Victoria's frown deepened.

"Odd. I've known Colleen since she was widowed two years ago, and never in all that time has she mentioned a daughter. Are you sure we're talking about the same Colleen?"

"I'm sure." The knowledge that her mother hadn't owned up to the fact that she'd borne two children stung at the least, but Shylo was too close to her now to let anything—certainly anything as useless as hurt feelings—stop her. She smiled sweetly. "Why isn't she at your party? Is she coming later?"

"Not likely, dear." She turned to Ari and Dimitri and gave them a knowing grin. "My husband introduced Colleen to a marvelous Greek fellow he met at his bank last month. The poor man had just moved to New York and didn't know a soul. He and Colleen fell in love immediately in what I guess you could call a whirlwind courtship. They were married just last weekend."

Shylo gasped. While she and Cassie had arrived at the train station, their mother had been getting married for the *third* time? She wasn't sure whether the knowledge sickened her, angered her, or just plain shocked her. She eyed what was left of her champagne, recalling the chapter in her etiquette book that stated ladies should never drink spirits in mixed company. She downed the final sip anyway, partly in defiance, but mostly because she was shaking from her eyebrows to her toenails. Maybe one more swallow would help to calm her runaway nerves. And to hell with the book.

"How nice for . . . Colleen," Shylo finally said. "But I'd still like to say hello to her. Where might I find her?"

Victoria laughed. "She and her Niko are off on their honeymoon."

"Niko?" Dimitri broke into the conversation, which until that moment had bored him mightily. "What is the man's surname?"

"Pappas, but he shortened it as so many do when they come to the States. His real name is long and terribly difficult to pronounce. Something like Pappandup—or Doplass? I can't remember."

The last thing of interest to Shylo was who or what her mother's new husband called himself. All she cared about was where they were! Trying to remain the center of Victoria's attention, she stepped in front of Dimitri. But before she had a chance to say anything further, he spoke over her head.

"I think I might know this fellow." He stuffed his hands in his trouser pockets to keep from making fists. "What does he look like?"

"Oh, he's just adorable, a little like your companion here, but taller." She chuckled lightly when Ari blushed. "Oh, and Niko has the cutest little mole right here." She pointed to a spot at the corner of her bottom lip. "It kind of peeks out from underneath his mustache when he talks and almost makes him look like his mouth is winking at you!"

It was a perfect description of Dimitri's uncle Niko. Who else could it be? In spite of his tight trousers, Dimitri's hands did indeed curl into fists, tight balls of muscle that drove his nails into his palms. The family had assumed that Niko had fled to the westernmost Greek island, Corfu, or perhaps even south to Crete; but unless the man had a twin, it looked as if he'd taken himself all the way to America.

With his jaw taut as his mind spun with thoughts of revenge, Dimitri glanced at Ari. The older man looked stunned, certainly shocked enough to suggest that he was entertaining the very same thoughts about this Niko Pappas. Pappandopolis was a family name, one that had belonged to Dimitri's grandmother before she'd married and become an Adonis. If this was Niko, he apparently had not been ready to turn his back on his past the way he had on his family and surname and must have decided to keep this small link to his ancestry.

Shylo, whose frustration with Dimitri and his interference had grown to monumental proportions, used his moment of introspection to regain control of the conversation. "You said Colleen is on her honeymoon, Victoria. Could you tell me where I might find her?"

"They've taken a trip out west to chase down the partner Colleen inherited from Broussard in some land deals, one Mr. Wyatt Earp."

Ari, an avid student of the American West, leapt into the conversation. "Are you speaking of the legendary Wyatt Earp from the O.K. corral in Tombstone?"

Clearly annoyed to be discussing such common riffraff as a western gunfighter, Victoria turned her nose up as she answered, "The very same."

"This is most impressive!" Ari made a kind of growling sound in his throat. "How far is Tombstone from New York, and how long does it take to get there? I would like very much to meet this American hero."

Victoria sighed. "I'm afraid Arizona is a good distance from here, sir, and the land deals Mr. Earp worked out with Charles Broussard just before he died were made not in Arizona, but in a place called San Diego. That's in California, even farther away."

"*California!*" Both Dimitri and Shylo expressed their displeasure over this locale at precisely the same moment. She turned to him, and he to her, and her clear blue eyes fastened onto his dark black ones, linked by a common denominator neither of them could understand.

Shylo's urgency to find her mother gave her the strength to break away from that mesmerizing gaze first. Slightly shaken, she turned to her hostess again. "Do you have any idea when they plan on returning to New York?"

"Oh, not really, dear, but I don't expect them back for a long time. Charles made a few other investments in San Diego besides the deals he made with that gunman." Victoria laughed. "Of course, I can't imagine that property out there is worth anything, but Colleen plans to sell off as much of it as she can. Between taking care of those investments and the traveling the honeymooners plan to do along the Pacific coast, I'm sure they'll be gone for months and months."

Rendered speechless and far removed from her earlier euphoria, Shylo fell silent. How could this be happening after all her months and years of careful planning? How could her mother *not* be here? She wanted to scream, to stomp the floor or pound her fists against the first available target—Dimitri's chest would do—but mostly she wanted to collapse and die.

But she would do none of those things, of course. She'd survived when her mother walked out the door, and again when her father accidentally drowned at the docks three years later, and even when the Children's Aid Society finally caught up to her and Cassie a year after that and put them in the foundling hospital.

She could survive this, too, and think of a new plan in the bargain. But why, oh, why did her mother have to be in San Diego, of all places? And how in *hell* would she and Cassie—who were practically broke by now—ever come up with enough money for train fare all the way to California?

3

After the music began to play, a few of Victoria's guests took her up on the offer to stroll through her much touted rose garden. Dimitri and Shylo followed along but lagged behind the others, each occupied by matters far more compelling than their hostess's collection of damasks and hybrid teas. As they walked, a heavy floral scent wafted around them and stars twinkled in the moonless indigo sky above. Several wrought-iron lamps mounted high on the gateposts gave off a soft, ethereal glow, but neither of them noticed the heady fragrances or the romantic lighting.

Shylo was too busy hatching and discarding scheme after scheme for making her way west, while Dimitri concentrated on finding an excuse good enough to convince Ari that they ought to spend their time and money on an unscheduled trip to California.

There was no question in Dimitri's mind as to what his uncle would say if he just came right out with the suggestion. In fact, in anticipation of his nephew's state of mind, Ari had already complained loudly about the idea of incurring any needless expenses when all their capital had to be put toward restoring the business. Unless Dimitri could think of a way to justify the trip as a legitimate disbursement, there was no chance of using so much as one drachma of their dwindling funds in such a manner. Even in that unlikely event, Ari would probably accuse him of squandering their capital for a nothing more than a simple taste of revenge. And, of course, he would be right.

"Oh!"

Dimitri turned around to see that Shylo had come to a limping halt. He rushed to her aid and took her by the shoulders to help keep her in balance.

"What happened? Are you all right?"

When she glanced up at him, her bright blue eyes looked filled with pain. "I'll be fine. I just twisted my ankle a little on the pathway."

"Are you sure you aren't seriously injured? Maybe you ought to sit down and let me take a look at it."

Shylo recalled the way the debutantes inside the mansion seemed to flutter over every little thing and, even though she wasn't sure how Dimitri fit into her plans just yet, decided a show of frailty might be in order.

"Oh, my," she said, batting her lashes. "It is a little tender. Sorry to be such a bother. I should have paid more attention to where I was going instead of day-dreaming."

Daydreaming? he thought. Or perhaps concentrating on a little "confidential" work for the president.

Maybe that was the reason for all the secrecy surrounding Miss Folsom's family connections. Maybe, he surmised, finding this Colleen Pappas had more political significance for the young lady than a simple hello. That really was no concern of Dimitri's, but it did seem that the excuse he needed for a trip out west could be standing right under his nose.

Keeping a firm but gentle grip on her shoulders, he decided to find out. "Is it possible that you're distracted over your friend's mother? I couldn't help but notice how distressed you were to discover that she'd gone to California."

"Ah, y-yes, I was—am." Suddenly all too aware of Dimitri's hands and the fact that now they were caressing rather than supporting her, she tried to slip away from him, but he held her fast.

"You'd better let that ankle rest a few more minutes." Now that he'd thought of a plan, Dimitri was determined to have this conversation, and have it while they still had some privacy. "I also overheard the rest of your conversation with our hostess. May I assume that you'll be making plans to leave for California soon?"

She would be if there was any way in hell, but the odds certainly were against making such a trip. Shylo had taken a misstep because she'd been straining her brain, trying to figure out a way to get hold of a pair of train tickets. The more she thought about it, the less likely it seemed, unless . . .

Shylo took a long hard look at Dimitri, wondering why he was so interested in her plans to visit California. Then she thought back to the conversation, recalling with particular clarity how curious Dimitri had been about Colleen's new husband and their honeymoon trip. While she couldn't fathom what his interest in the couple might be, it did occur to her that maybe her way west was standing right beside her.

She grinned, leaned in toward Dimitri just enough to brush against his jacket, and said softly, "You just don't know how much I'd *love* to go look Colleen up." Her head fell back, and she gazed into his eyes. "You see, what I didn't mention earlier is that my dear friend recently . . . died. I'm just sure that Colleen would want to hear about her daughter's last days."

The glow from the lamplight illuminated Shylo's exposed throat as she spoke, drawing Dimitri's gaze to the soft skin between her chin and the collar of her dress. The sight distracted him so, he nearly forgot his objective. After clearing his suddenly husky throat, he said, "Then I really think you should go."

"How I wish I could." Something had changed between them, but Shylo couldn't figure what it might be. Dimitri was looking at her in the oddest way, his ink black eyes impossibly darker than before, and for some reason the little plan she'd just thought out was getting fuzzy. If that wasn't enough to get her off track, a strange, warm little fluttering down low in her belly made her feel like cozying up against him, but she fought the sensation off. "It's not that I don't have the time to go or that I don't have any interest in visiting California, but . . ." She paused dramatically, preparing herself for the final bluff. "I'm afraid such a long train ride through the untamed West could be very dangerous for a pair of unescorted ladies."

Dimitri's hesitation was automatic whenever money was involved, but he paused now to give himself time to regain his composure. How fortuitous!

Shylo had practically served him an excuse to pursue Uncle Niko on a silver platter, and with very little coaxing on his part. How could Ari possibly argue against the expense of making a trip to the West Coast when the main reason for doing so was to protect Dimitri's wealthy "intended"? All it would cost them was two first-class train tickets to California. Naturally they'd have to travel first-class to impress such a woman.

"What would you say"—he reached up to brush an errant strand of hair off her cheek—"if I told you I might have a solution to your problem?"

Shylo shrugged off a sudden tremor. "Th-that depends on the solution, I suppose."

Dimitri smiled, making a great show of his dimples. "My uncle and I are very new to your country, and would like to see it from shore to shore, if time permits. This train ride sounds like a nice, relatively quick way to do it. Is it possible that my uncle and I would make suitable chaperons for your trip out west?"

It worked—it *worked!* Shylo's heart soared, beating out of control again, and for a moment she thought she might even faint. The cause was not only sheer excitement over the plan, but the fact that Dimitri was holding her too close, too tight. The scent of him, the very essence of his maleness, had somehow awakened something that had been dormant within her until now. Shylo realized then that she was quivering right down to her toes—*quivering!* This wouldn't do—it wouldn't do at all! She had to get away from him if she was going to think and talk her way through this latest scheme.

She slipped out from under Dimitri's embrace. "I can't tell you how much your offer means," she said slowly, even though her wheels were turning faster than a westbound locomotive. "And though I am tempted to take you up on your offer . . ."

"There is a problem?"

"Maybe just a tiny one." Actually, more like a huge one, she added to herself. Dimitri's offer was nice, but it didn't go far in getting the McBride sisters to California. She and Cassie couldn't scrape together enough money to buy space in a cattle car, much less seats in first class—where rich fellows like those Greeks would want to sit. She had to run one last bluff.

Shylo glanced over her shoulder and fluttered her lashes. "It's probably silly of me, but I'm very uncomfortable with the idea of going to that Grand Central depot alone. Being a single lady and all, I'm afraid—"

"Would it help if I bought your train tickets when I get mine?"

Shylo hoped that meant what she thought it did— that he planned to pay for them out of his pocket and be reimbursed later. She had to find out. "That's a very generous offer, but I can't accept it unless you promise to let us pay you back the minute we get on the train."

"If that is your wish."

"And you're sure escorting us and all is what you want to do? You're really, *really* sure?"

With his own wheels speeding toward California and a confrontation with Niko, Dimitri didn't even stop to consider what Ari might have to say about buying *four* first-class tickets. He just smiled, dropped his voice an octave, and said, "But, of course."

*   *   *

Later that night in the small hotel room he was sharing with his uncle, Dimitri explained his plan.

"You did *what?*" Ari's booming voice bounced off the walls; he was speaking Greek and therefore not concerned that anyone might hear and understand him. "We cannot even be sure that this Niko Pappas is indeed your uncle Niko! How can you possibly suggest such a trip when it most surely will be nothing but a waste of our time and money?"

As a man who generally believed that actions spoke louder than words, Dimitri's first impulse was to ignore Ari's outburst and let him get his objections out of his system. But since Dimitri was also a straightforward man who knew exactly what he wanted at all times, he possessed little patience with anyone who stood in the way of those goals.

His voice deceptively quiet, Dimitri used his native language as he formed a reply. "Apparently you haven't been listening to me, Uncle. While we're in San Diego, I do, of course, intend to find out if this Niko Pappas is my father's brother, but that is not the only reason I have decided to make a trip to California."

"But I thought—"

"What you think is not at issue here. The Adonis name is mine, and mine to restore as I see fit!"

Dimitri stalked across the room to the window in an effort to control himself, lest his anger get the better of him. Instead of the peaceful view of Gramercy Park he sought, his gaze met a hairline crack in the glass running from the top to the bottom sill. Thick layers of paint, both old and new, curled up along the ledge there, looking like a cheap depiction of white-caps upon the open sea. At finding himself housed in such an inferior hotel when he should be at the university—and through no fault of his own, no less—he grew incensed again.

"If Niko Pappas is indeed Nikolao Adonis," he said, "I intend to see that he shares the burden of putting the family business back in order, at the *least!* If he refuses, I will make certain that he pays for what he's done, and pays dearly."

"And if this man is not Nikolao?" Ari, who knew his nephew well enough to stay clear of him while in such a mood, spoke quietly and without challenge in his tone. "What then?"

"If he is not, I will proceed with my alternate plan." His anger cooling almost as quickly as it had heated, Dimitri turned and smiled at his uncle. "If all else fails by the time we reach San Diego, I intend to propose marriage to the president's niece. If she accepts, I will insist that we wed with all haste."

"Ahhhh." A grinning Ari rubbed his hands together and then reached for the leather satchel that contained their dwindling funds. "*When* she accepts, not if, my son. How much do you think we'll need for our train tickets?"

"I have no idea, but since we're going to have to buy four first-class tickets, you'd better bring our entire bank."

Ari gasped, but before he could comment or object, Dimitri took pity on the man's obsession with frugality and explained the situation. "I promised Miss Folsom that I would pick up her tickets and save her the trouble of going to the station by herself. Once we collect the ladies and get them firmly situated on the train, they will reimburse us for their share. Does that plan meet with your approval, Uncle?"

Ari clutched the satchel to his chest and smiled.

"Yes, and a fine plan it may turn out to be, my son. Just think of it! I get a trip out west and the chance to meet Wyatt Earp, and you get to woo and wed the niece of a great American president. Can you believe the opportunities before us? God, but I love this country!"

From the moment Shylo boarded the train two days later, she had a feeling of uneasiness, almost a sense of impending doom, but for the life of her she couldn't figure out why. Finally, after all these years, it looked as if things were going to go right for the McBride sisters—more than right.

Dimitri had not only purchased first-class tickets for Cassie and her in the parlor car, he'd secured assigned berths for them in the extra-fare sleeping car as well. During their recent, more economical trip from Kansas to New York City, Shylo and her sister had been forced to sit up all night in the day coach and had never even so much as glimpsed the luxurious accommodations surrounding her now. She should have been deliriously happy to have found her circumstances so drastically changed. What woman in her right mind wouldn't be?

The plush armchair she occupied was upholstered in blood-red velvet and mounted on a swivel to allow easy viewing of the countryside as it sped past. In addition to the comfortable chairs, the parlor car featured potted plants, crystal chandeliers, polished wood paneling, and beveled glass in both mirrors and windows. With the exception of the Vanderkellen mansion, Shylo had never seen anything like it. Yet in the face of all that, she had a churning lump in her stomach and felt as if she might burst into tears at any moment.

As the train lurched slowly to life, Cassie let out a squeal of delight. "We're off!" she cried, unable to contain her enthusiasm any longer. "By next week, we'll be sitting on the edge of the Pacific Ocean. Can you believe it?"

"Yes, but I have the good sense to keep my excitement to myself."

Cassie glanced at the Greek men, who were seated across the aisle, their noses pressed against the windows as they took in the sights. She leaned forward on her chair and whispered, "I don't see how in hell you can keep everything inside the way you do, Shylo. Maybe this trip doesn't excite you mightily, but Lordy, if I'da latched on to a fellow like that Greek god of yours, I'd be screaming it from the rooftops! How can you be so calm?"

"I haven't exactly 'latched' on to him, sis. He's just escorting us west."

"He could escort *me* about anywhere he wanted to! I wonder how he feels about lavender hair." Cassie checked to make sure her locks were still hidden beneath her bonnet, then took another glance at Dimitri and let out a wistful sigh. "That's the sort of fellow who rides up on a big white horse in my dreams. I can't believe you got him to buy our train tickets. What are you gonna do when he asks for his money back?"

"Shush!" Shylo stole a quick look toward Dimitri and Ari, but they were still captured by the scenery. "I already told you. I don't think a gentleman would ask. If we just go about our business and act like we kinda forgot about the money, I think maybe they will, too. Now leave me be. I—I'm feeling a little queasy."

Shylo turned her gaze to the window and the disappearing Manhattan skyline. That earlier sense of foreboding was still with her, even though they were finally under way, steaming toward California and the much anticipated reunion with her mother. Yet for some reason, instead of sharing Cassie's enthusiasm or even feeling a glimmer of satisfaction, she felt awful. The lump in her stomach had grown to the size of a large, tight fist; had last night's dinner of stale bread and bruised apples turned on her?

The train's shrill whistle sounded, then sounded again, and something in its tone prompted a rush of emotions so intense that Shylo couldn't control them, much less understand them. What in hell had gone wrong with her? A sudden and completely unexpected onslaught of tears veiled her eyes, blurring her vision. Horrified to find herself coming apart in public this way, especially in front of her Greek escorts, she bolted out of her chair and hurried toward the back door of the car.

Dimitri, who was lounging on a chair directly across from Shylo, caught a glimpse of her white, pinched expression as she passed by him. When he saw Cassie get up as if to follow her, he leapt out of his chair. "Please keep your seat," he said to her. "I'd be happy to go after Miss Folsom and see if she needs any assistance."

Since Cassie had heard rather than seen her sister's departure, and had no idea where Shylo was going or why, she dropped back onto the chair. Her mouth fell open and stayed that way as she stared up at the handsome man. "W-why, ah, t-thank you, ah, kindly, Mr., ah . . ."

As Cassie stumbled over her tongue, Dimitri gave

her a brief nod, then turned to his uncle and quickly said in Greek, "Miss Folsom looks as if she's very upset about something. I thought I'd go see if I can help." If, heaven help him, he found that he had no choice but to employ his alternate plan once they arrived in San Diego, the wooing of his future bride couldn't start too soon. "Maybe you ought to keep her maid occupied so we won't be disturbed."

With a decided glimmer in his bright gray eyes, Ari pushed himself out of his chair. "Take your time, my son, and be sure to show her your good teeth."

The minute Dimitri found Shylo outside at the rear of the observation car, he was pretty sure the last thing she would be interested in was his teeth. Her white-knuckled fingers were gripping the wrought-iron railing that surrounded the viewing deck, and her shoulders were hunched, maybe even trembling. As he approached her, he thought he heard a heart-wrenching sob over the rhythmic clacking of the rails. Was she crying? Now regretting his impulsive decision to follow her—for Dimitri hadn't the slightest idea what to do with a weeping female—he tapped her shoulder lightly and inquired, "Is there anything I can do for you?"

Shylo stiffened at his touch, then fought a wave of nervousness when she recognized Dimitri's smooth voice. Why had he of all people followed her out here? And how in the hell was she to explain her bizarre behavior to him when she still didn't understand it herself? Would he think she'd gone crazy or, worse, that she was nothing more than a cotton-headed piece of dry goods who broke into tears for no damn reason at all?

Struggling to swallow her sobs, Shylo kept her

back to him and muttered, "N-no, thanks. I—I'll be fine."

She thought maybe she would have been, too, if the young woman seated behind her on one of the outside chairs hadn't chosen that moment to shout with glee that she'd spotted the Statue of Liberty. Then she bade all in hearing distance to wave it a fond farewell. With a morbid sense of fascination, Shylo's gaze shifted toward upper New York Bay, and she focused on the towering monument in the distance. In the space of a heartbeat, one that seemed to last a lifetime, pieces of the past and her disturbing emotions of the present came together with a thunderous and terrifying clarity.

The Statue of Liberty had been the last thing she'd seen of New York eleven years ago, the final glimpse of a fading link to her missing mother and the only life she'd ever known. She'd been so excited about returning to her birthplace a few weeks ago, she hadn't felt much of an adverse reaction to boarding her first train in all those years. But now that she was leaving the city again, and by rail . . .

"Oh, my God—that's it!" Shylo turned to Dimitri. "I—I . . ."

But that was all she could manage. In the next instant she was drowning in memories and her own tears. In desperate need of the human touch—a basic need she'd buried, unrequited, for nearly her whole life—Shylo fell against Dimitri's chest and into his arms, crushing her new straw hat beneath his chin.

How long she stayed pressed against his expensive jacket, she couldn't have said, but she knew that she'd remained huddled there long enough to soak the broadcloth through. Dimitri, God love him, preserved her privacy by holding her quietly the entire time, asking and assuming nothing of her, yet giving her exactly what she needed. Someone who cared.

Common sense, not to mention the chapter on decorum in her etiquette book, dictated that she step away from the comfort of Dimitri's arms and explain herself to him. But how could she? Was there a way to explain that she, a presumed society debutante, had reverted to a terrified child of nine? She certainly could not tell him the reason—that she and Cassie had been rounded up by the Children's Aid Society, tossed aboard what they called an "orphan train" along with nearly one hundred other youngsters, and sent kicking and screaming on a frightening journey to the Midwest.

How did one go about explaining that to a man one hoped to charm? He was supposed to think that she was an heiress, an aristocrat. Rich folks didn't throw their children away, and they didn't run off and forget about them, either. To own up to such a past would be to dash her hopes for the future, and Shylo was not about to do that. The only way out of this mess was to come up with yet another lie, one that would gain Dimitri's sympathy enough for him to overlook her inexcusable behavior.

Shylo dried her tears with the back of her hand as she pondered a new story, and finally inspiration struck. She stepped away from Dimitri, kept her head low, and whispered, "I'm sorry for making such a fool of myself. I don't know what came over me, except to say that I was thinking of my friend, you know, the one who . . . died."

Dimitri recalled the earlier conversation. "You mean Colleen Pappas's daughter?"

"Y-yes." She'd counted on him believing her story

but never considered that he might actually exhibit the compassion she saw in his expression or the concern she heard in his voice. The lump in her stomach moved up to her throat. "I was just remembering how my, ah, friend and her little sister were separated from Colleen when they were quite young. After their father died, the girls were put in an orphans' hospital, even though they tried to convince the authorities they had a mother somewhere."

Dimitri's thick dark brows shot up. "How terrible! In Greece, putting a child into an orphanage isn't even considered until every living relative, no matter how distant, has been sought as a substitute parent. Did your government not try to find the mother, or perhaps some other family member?"

"The Children's Aid Society said they searched for Colleen, but when she couldn't be located, they labeled my friend and her sister as orphans and took them away."

"This would never happen so easily in my country. Someone, an uncle or cousin or even a neighbor, would have taken those children in before they allowed the government to do such a thing."

Compassion, concern, *and* understanding? Shylo could see the outrage in her heart reflected in Dimitri's eyes, and for one reckless moment she found herself thinking of telling him the truth, of testing him beyond her impostor status and basking in his commiseration as just plain Shylo McBride. She couldn't do that, of course, so she continued her story about her "friend" and pretended the compassion he offered was meant for her.

"Things are different here, I guess. A lot of folks, especially in your bigger cities like New York, look on orphans as . . . well, less than decent, honorable citizens."

"Less than decent? Please explain what you mean by this."

Shylo lowered her chin, unable to look him in the eye as she spoke of the stigma that had hung over both hers and Cassie's heads all their lives. "A lot of kids start out as orphans because they've never had real families; most folks here call them bastards since, you know, the mother just turned up one day with a baby and no husband?" He nodded solemnly, sparing her the embarrassment of explaining further. "Because of that, decent folks just kinda look on all orphans as bastards, no matter what kind of home they had before they turned up alone."

"That is the way your friend was looked upon?"

Shylo stared up at him, again biting back the urge to say, "No, that's the way I was seen." And again she had to avert her gaze before she could go on. "Yes, that's how they thought of her. She and her sister were adopted by a farmer and his wife who didn't have any children, but since they considered the girls bastards, they didn't treat them like new members of the family. More like servants, I guess, 'cause they never got to go anywhere with their new 'ma and pa,' not to town, and not even to go visiting the neighboring farms. They were adopted to help work the farm. Period."

Dimitri muttered a curse in his native language. "I am sorry for your friend, and for you because you've shared her grief. This young woman was lucky to have someone like you, Miss Folsom. I hope she realized that before she died."

The lump in Shylo's throat swelled, making swallowing nearly impossible. Worse yet, Dimitri was smiling at her in the oddest way, making her feel as if something were amiss, as if she'd forgotten to button her jersey or comb her hair. His expression held the same compassion as before, but now it wavered with a dash of uncertainty or perhaps even embarrassment. When he plucked the handkerchief from his coat pocket and offered it, Shylo—who hadn't even been aware that she was crying again—not only understood his discomfort, but shared in it as well.

"Thanks for being so kind and understanding," she said, taking his handkerchief and regaining her usual firm control of herself. "But I'd just as soon not talk about my friend or her troubles anymore. Why don't you tell me about your life in Greece? How many brothers and sisters do you have?"

Although she tried to listen to what Dimitri said, Shylo heard only a few key phrases as he spoke—that he was an only child, that his family hailed from Thessaloníki—wherever the hell that was—and that he had more than a passing interest in archaeology. She was far too captivated by his smooth yet somehow disturbing voice, by his beautifully carved and increasingly fascinating mouth, and by those wildly expressive eyes to pay attention to anything beyond the very basic information he offered about himself.

Shylo was much too busy looking at Dimitri in a way she'd never considered before to care about anything else. She finally saw him in a more realistic light: not merely as one of the players in her grand scheme, but as a flesh-and-blood man.

A real live flesh-and-blood man. A man who might want to be her gentleman friend if she could figure out how to lead him in that direction. Suddenly she realized she was more intrigued than ever by the idea of approaching her mother with this man on her arm. But how to go about it?

She knew nothing of courtship, the little dos and don'ts between women and men beyond the scant "social requirements" mentioned in her etiquette book. Of course, since Dimitri was new to America and her customs, Shylo doubted that he knew any more than she did. For all she knew, it was up to her to show him, to urge him on. It seemed to her that if Dimitri were interested in her beyond escorting her to California, he should have made some advances by now, maybe even . . . kissed her. Perhaps he was waiting for some sign of encouragement.

Shylo's gaze strayed to his perfect mouth. Something hot and powerful stirred inside her at the thought of touching her lips to his, a feeling so primal, it frightened her almost as much as it excited her. Did all women feel this way around men they hoped to charm? Or was this feeling unique to her, this desperate urge to taste those finely carved lips and to once again crush her breasts against the broad expanse of his chest? She didn't know for sure, but one way or another she intended to find out.

She didn't try to talk herself out of those sudden and completely insane desires. She simply glanced around to make certain they were the only passengers outside on the observation deck—and by now, they were—then quickly pondered what she figured would be the best way to get Dimitri to do his part.

Gathering up all of her scant knowledge of such things, Shylo sidled closer to him, tilted her head until her lips were in line with his, and then closed her eyes, willing him to come to her with all her might.

Kiss me, she commanded silently, peeking through her lashes. *Kiss me now, you handsome fool.*

Dimitri leaned in close, so close she could smell the rich pine scent of his cologne. Any minute now, she thought, her mouth watering over the realization that she was only moments away from her very first kiss. He lowered his head, studying her mouth carefully.

Yes! Now he would do it! His magnificent lips parted, moving ever closer. Then he . . . took her by the shoulders.

"Miss Folsom?" he asked in a concerned voice. "Is something wrong? Do you have a toothache?"

4

Late that night after all the first-class passengers had gone to bed and the train was silent save for the rush of its wheels, the curtain to Shylo's sleeping berth suddenly parted and Cassie popped in beside her.

"Are you awake?" she whispered in the darkness.

"I am now," Shylo grumbled in return.

"Sorry, but I couldn't sleep. I got kinda scared over there by myself. Can I stay with you a while?"

The problem wasn't the size of the bed—she and Cassie had shared much smaller accommodations during their years together—but Shylo had a feeling that her sister wanted to talk. That in itself wasn't the problem, but the hour was. Once they started jabbering in the middle of the night, especially if either of them was nervous or excited about something, it seemed they usually just kept on jabbering until sunup.

"You can stay on one condition," she said, even

though Cassie had already slipped under the blanket as if invited. "No talking. I've just got to get some sleep tonight."

"That's fine with me. I'm feeling as beat as a mudroom rug myself." She hugged her sister and kissed her soundly on the cheek. "Good night, and thanks."

"Good night, li'l sis. Don't let the bedbugs bite." Shylo rolled onto her side and snuggled beneath the covers. After a moment of silence, she heard her sister clear her throat.

"Just one more thing," Cassie said. Shylo groaned. "Did either one of those Greek fellas say anything about my hair? You know, have they noticed what color it is yet?"

"Yes, as a matter of fact, they have." Shylo probably wouldn't have told her if she'd just stayed quiet as requested.

"How in hell did they find out about that? You didn't tell, did you?"

"I didn't have to. Dimitri saw it sticking out of your hat back at the Vanderkellen mansion."

"Oh, shit." Cassie groaned and rolled onto her back.

"I'm not kidding about that word, Cassandra Mary McBride. You've just got to stop using it or we're gonna wind up in a world of trouble."

"Sorry. That's the last time you'll hear it from my lips, I swear!" She giggled at the unintended pun, then asked, "What *did* you tell Dimitri about my hair?"

"I said that you tried to dye it bright red because you were thinking of going to work at Pearly Mae's Bawdy House, but it came out purple instead." Without warning Cassie's pillow came out of the darkness and smacked the side of her head. "I'm kidding!" Shylo cried, both laughing and beating the pillow back.

"Honest, and I didn't really say *all* of that. I told him you tried a little henna and it didn't work right on your hair, but that by the time we get to California it ought to be washed out enough for your regular color to come back."

"It'd better be—and you'd better not be lying again." Cassie tucked her pillow back under her pinkish lavender head and once again settled in for the night. "Sorry if I disturbed you. I won't talk anymore."

Awash with love for her baby sister, Shylo reached out in the darkness and squeezed Cassie's hand. Even though weary, she realized that talking with the one person she'd always been able to trust had made her feel at ease again and more like her usual self than she'd been since her daring foray into the Vanderkellen home. She decided to broach a subject that had been weighing on her mind since earlier in the day.

Shylo leaned in close to her sister's ear and whispered, "Don't go off to sleep yet. There's something I've got to ask you about, and I want the absolute truth."

Cassie groaned. "What in hell have I done now?"

"Shush! You didn't do a thing. I have a question, is all, a curiosity over all that romantic stuff you're always going on about. You know, heroes on white horses, kissing and pawing, all that. Who filled your head with that crap, anyway?"

Cassie was silent for a long moment as she tried to grasp the underlying message in Shylo's inquiry. When she figured it out, and was finally able to speak, her voice was steeped in awe. "Oh, my God—are you getting all mushy over that Greek?"

"*Shush!* I don't want the whole train to know about it!"

"Sorry. But did you get to feeling wonderful around him, and do your insides go all funny on you?"

After muttering the very word she'd insisted that Cassie leave out of her vocabulary, Shylo admitted this much. "I don't know about getting all funny, but I did have some . . . unusual feelings out back on the observation deck today."

"Oh, Lord!" Cassie's head spun at the thought. "Tell me: Was feeling that way just as wonderful as I thought it would be?"

"Hell no!" Now it was Shylo's voice that was much too loud. She dropped it to a bare whisper. "They were as frustrating as all get-out, is what they were, but I don't want to talk about that. I just want to know where you heard about all this nonsense."

"From Ma Anderson, who else?"

Shylo had to bite her lip to keep from shouting her usual retort—"She isn't your ma!"—because Cassie would pout and insist that the woman was the only mother she'd ever known. Even though that much was true, the thought of calling anyone but Colleen "Ma" twisted in Shylo's gut as if she'd eaten a bushel of green apples.

Calm enough now to speak, Shylo asked, "What did Mrs. Anderson tell you about this . . . this funny business?"

Cassie pushed herself up on one elbow and peered down at her sister in the darkness. "Did Dimitri *kiss* you? Is that why you're asking all these questions?"

"*No,* he didn't!" She paused to calm herself again. "Well, not quite, anyway. But I think he wanted to."

Cassie fell back on the bed. "Dear Lord, this is just like a fairy tale come true."

"Quit making more out of what happened than

there was." Shylo's pulse suddenly leapt, making her feel as if it were keeping time with the speeding train. She wondered briefly about the cause but figured she was probably getting all riled up because she was tired of waiting to get a straight answer from her sister. Surely it couldn't have been the subject matter. Or could it?

Shaking off the last thought, she quickly explained what happened. "Me and Dimitri were just talking about nothing in particular one minute, and then in the next, I kinda looked at him and saw that he was looking at me looking at him, and, well . . . it's kinda fuzzy after that, but somehow we got closer and closer to each other, and then . . ." Shylo couldn't stop the shudder that coursed through her at the memory of how close they'd really come to an actual, passionate embrace.

"And *then?*"

"Then . . . he asked me did I have a toothache!"

Cassie, who'd been holding her breath, burst out laughing. "That was all he did?"

"Pretty much, and be quiet about it!" She sighed. "Next thing I knew, Dimitri grabbed me like he thought I was about to faint or something, dragged me over to a chair, and sat me down, then went to get me a drink of water. By the time he got back, half a dozen passengers had come out on the observation deck to watch the country whiz on by, and I never got a chance to get him alone again."

"Sorry." Cassie plumped her pillow and settled down on it once more. "But that don't sound like a romantic escapade to me. Nothing much happened, so I still don't understand what it is you wanted to know."

"What I want to know," Shylo said, nearly forgetting

to whisper in her exasperation, "is why a person with my kind of smarts—you know, someone who doesn't believe in all that love and romance mush—went and got so damn mad because Dimitri *didn't* kiss me!"

Three nights later, after an evening meal of wild turkey and sirloin steak, Dimitri and Ari joined the other male first-class passengers in the smoking car and settled down to enjoy a cheroot and a snifter of cognac.

After taking a long sip, Ari slowly shook his head and muttered in Greek, "I cannot understand the troubles you are having with this American female. I thought you knew all there was to know about courting a woman."

Dimitri was far from excited over this topic of discussion, but he'd brought it up himself in the hopes of finding a clue as to how to proceed with the most exasperating female he'd ever met in his life. "I'm afraid that here in the United States, I am not so sure of myself, Uncle. Sometimes Shylo looks at me as if I'm not even there, and then at other times, I could swear that she seems a little . . ." *Aggressive? Brazen?* "Forward, I suppose. She has practically invited me to take liberties with her person."

Ari shrugged. "If that is so, perhaps you should take them. We are in a wild, uncivilized country, my son. The people and their ways are different here. Perhaps you've gone so far as to offend her by remaining such a gentleman."

Dimitri thought back to the dinner parties he'd attended and to the chivalrous conduct exhibited by the American gentlemen he'd observed. He took a deep puff of the cheroot and let the smoke curl off the end of his tongue as he said, "I don't think I've done anything to offend the young lady, Ari. I just don't know how to proceed."

"My advice, in that case, is to behave as you would at home. Perhaps our cultures are not all that different when it comes to matters of the heart. Proceed as you would if you were courting one of the fair damsels at your university."

Dimitri eyed his uncle, weighing his next words, and then took another sip of cognac. "I suppose that now is as good a time as any to inform you that I don't know how to go about courting one of them, either."

Ari's eyebrows, thick like his nephew's but gray like his eyes and what little hair he still possessed, bunched with surprise. "Surely you jest! There must be at least one serious encounter you can pull from memory."

"Sorry to disappoint you, but no, there is not. The field of archaeology is largely confined to men, and since my main interests lie there, even meeting suitable women is difficult for me." He snubbed out his cheroot. "In fact, the only woman I've ever met who actually seemed interested in such endeavors is Sophia Schliemann, and she, of course, is married to my archaeology professor, Heinrich Schliemann. I'm afraid that my life at the university is rather like that of a monk."

Although he could see how much this information disturbed his uncle Ari, his practically cloistered existence didn't bother Dimitri at all anymore. The entire sum of his experiences with the opposite sex consisted of a few shared laughs and an occasional easing of mutual "tensions" with this one or that one. But even the latter encounters, while usually pleasurable physically, had been largely unsatisfying. There was something in them that Dimitri found demeaning, not just to any woman who agreed to accommodate him, but to himself in the building of a relationship fostered for the simple slaking of lust.

Because of that opinion, which grew stronger as he neared thirty, Dimitri's sex life had all but vanished. Of course, he wasn't going to admit such a thing to Ari, who considered pleasures of the flesh akin to breathing. If he did, the old man would think there was something physically wrong with him. Which there definitely was not.

Ari, who'd been in a state of shocked silence, finally found his tongue—and an angry tongue it was. "You dare to sit there and tell me *now,* after we've traveled halfway to California, that you haven't even conducted *one* serious courtship in your entire life? How did you think you'd find the aplomb to sweep the *president's* niece off of her feet?"

"Let me try to explain again." Dimitri signaled the waiter to bring them another round of drinks. Then he slouched down on his plush leather chair and flashed his uncle an amused grin. "I absolutely loathe the hard-headed, myopic, and thoroughly pompous director of the British Museum, but I believe I can safely say that I have far more of a relationship with him, even by mail, than I've ever had with a female. That is why I am seeking your advice, Uncle. I thought wooing this particular woman would be easy, but now that I find it is not, I am asking for suggestions on how I might proceed in the case of Miss Shylo Folsom."

The drinks arrived, and before Dimitri could even lift his glass from the polished maple tabletop, Ari swallowed his brandy in one gulp. Wheezing as liquid fire burned its way down his throat, he banged his fist on the table. "You have much to learn, my son, and I do indeed have many suggestions of value. We shall proceed, and you shall triumph!"

Dimitri chuckled good-naturedly, for he still believed that an arranged marriage would never have to take place, therefore making his lack of expertise in this area inconsequential. "I suppose you'd best get started with the instructions. I have a feeling I'm a little behind on my lessons."

"Yes, yes, of course." Ready to get down to business, Ari propped his elbows on the small table and leaned in toward his nephew. "I say test the young lady to discover what plans she may have for you. Go ahead, give her a little kiss, and see what happens."

"And what do you suggest I do if she slaps my face? She is, after all, the high-bred niece of the president of the United States. Maybe I should wait a little longer and give her time to come to me."

"No, no! That will never do! Women—even high-bred ladies—like their men to do the courting. You must be aggressive but tender, kiss her gently, saving the hot-blooded advances for your marriage bed." He thought he saw Dimitri frown at those words, but he attributed his expression to impatience. Then Ari issued his final instruction. "Just before you kiss her, remember to whisper a few honeyed phrases in her ear. Oh, and while you're at it, say something like 'By the way, my sweet little kumquat—exactly when did you think you'd be paying me back for those train tickets?'"

Dimitri laughed out loud, a deep, full-throated laugh he rarely turned loose. When he caught his breath, he marveled for a moment over how good he felt inside, then quickly decided it was because of the cognac. "I'll see what I can do about getting our money back later—she probably just forgot about it.

In the meantime, what kinds of honeyed phrases do you suggest I use on her? She strikes me as a very bright young woman, one who won't be easily fooled."

"Ah, yes, I noticed that about her myself." Ari tapped a thoughtful fingertip against the table. "Did you happen to see what color her eyes are, my son?"

How odd, Dimitri thought, that he was instantly able to picture those eyes and their shockingly clear aquamarine color. And without concentrating in the least. He could even see Shylo's long caramel-colored lashes with the remnants of her tears clinging there like a delicate Mediterranean mist.

Most of all, he remembered liking what he saw when he looked into her eyes, and for far more reasons than their brilliant blue color. He saw a goodly amount of independence there, and an unusual measure of candor for a woman, which was a fascinating blend made more intriguing by an irresistible dash of innocence. Dimitri couldn't think of a time when he'd ever noticed such things about a woman.

"Ahh, my son, is this work really so difficult for you?" Ari watched Dimitri for as long as he could, then sighed with frustration. "Perhaps you need more help than I thought, but do not fear. I'm prepared to provide it. The first thing you must do tomorrow is study Miss Folsom's face. Memorize the things you like best, and even those you don't, but take special care to note the color of her eyes. This is most important if you are to make—"

"They are blue, Uncle. Actually, the exact color of the Aegean Sea along the shores of Chalcidice, and so clear she can do little, I think, to hide her thoughts." He grinned as he recalled a few of them. "Most of those thoughts, if I'm not completely mistaken, seem to run a little on the mischievous side. As to her face, she has excellent bone structure, with a strong, square jawline and high, wide cheekbones. A stubborn, but refreshingly lovely face." He thought of their conversation on the observation deck. "I think it's fair to say that Miss Shylo Folsom possesses the face of an angel and the mind of a devil."

"Is that all you've noticed about her?" Ari meant to chide his nephew a little over how much he *did* know, not prompt a further dissertation of Shylo's finer points. But that was exactly what he got, as Dimitri was only too happy to comply.

"If you want more, I can tell you that Miss Folsom's hair is a rich golden color, and may even have a touch of fire to it. I can't be sure because I've never seen it loose or out in the sunlight. Let's see—what else is there?" He hesitated as he tried to think of more details, then remembered an endearing little gesture. "Ah, yes, and when she talks or smiles, she has a tendency to twist her mouth to the left, a cute little habit to be sure, but one that makes her look as if she's self-conscious or embarrassed in some way."

A resolute bachelor by choice, Ari had managed to break a few hearts over the years and even found his own shattered on occasion. From those experiences he prided himself on being somewhat of an expert where matters of the heart were concerned. This made him fairly certain that he saw signs in his nephew that pointed to a far more complicated relationship with Miss Folsom than Dimitri would have him believe. Or maybe he didn't even realize it yet.

Ari was also a man who didn't mince words, so he thought nothing of voicing his opinion on that subject. "Is it possible, my son, that you have taken more than just a little liking to Miss Folsom? Could she have worked her way into your heart so soon?"

Knowing what a hopeless matchmaker his uncle had become over the years, Dimitri laughed the idea off. "You forget, Uncle, that I am trained to observe, required by my profession to notice if even the slightest particle of dust is out of place in a burial chamber which hasn't seen the light of day for thousands of years. I have simply relayed what I observed in the lady."

"We are not discussing the long dead here, but a real, live woman! It is not the same thing."

Unperturbed, Dimitri went on with his excuses. "You're wrong, Uncle, for in many ways it is the exact same thing. I am also trained in physiognomy, the study of facial features as they relate to character or quality of mind. I have employed those abilities along with the others in order to recall everything I could about the lady."

Ari didn't buy this explanation any more than the first. "I think you doth protest too much, my son. If one didn't know better, one might even be inclined to believe that the great, heartless soon-to-be-*professor* Adonis has discovered that he is actually falling in love—and for the first time, no less!"

Dimitri's patience with his uncle had reached an end. "If one did indeed know me well," he said, "one would automatically assume that my observations about Miss Folsom are purely academic. And, of course, one would be correct."

A smug grin tugged at the corners of Ari's mouth, and he couldn't help but issue one final challenge. "In that case, dear boy, I would ask that you communicate your observations about Miss Folsom's traveling companion. What exactly did your well-trained eyes see when you looked upon Miss McBride?"

Caught off guard, Dimitri searched his memory for an image of the woman in question, but he could only remember one memorable feature as he tried to picture her. Finally, with an expression that brooked no further discussion on the subject, he said, "She has purple hair."

Almost a week into the journey, the morning opened to New Mexico's wide, cloudless blue skies and rapidly warming temperatures. The westbound train pushed on, and by noon it had reached the border of Arizona, leaving behind the imposing Ponderosa pines of Colorado's Rocky Mountains, the rushing waters of the Rio Grande, and the dusty little pueblos of Santa Fe. Ahead lay vast stretches of arid desert, the monotonous landscape broken up with occasional formations of red rock, eroded shale, and sandstone sculptures. Scattered among these were clumps of sagebrush, mesquite, and yucca.

Dimitri was utterly fascinated by it all. "Look there!" he shouted, leaning over the back railing of the observation car to point out one particularly strange formation. "Does that not look like a camel to you?"

Shylo squinted at where he was pointing and shrugged. From where she stood, it looked a little like Mrs. Anderson's backside when she bent down to hoe her vegetable garden. "Sort of, I guess."

"It was a perfect depiction of a two-humped camel, I assure you. By the time you looked up, the correct angle for viewing it as such had already passed you by." He stretched his arms and breathed deeply. "I've read, of course, how beautiful and diverse a country your America is, but I had no idea how much each individual state and territory had to offer, or how many different landscapes could be found—and so close together!" The timbre of his voice rising, he added reverently, "You must give thanks every day for the privilege of living in such a land."

A stranger, one of a half dozen men who stood with Dimitri and Shylo to marvel over the ever-changing terrain, assumed the question had been addressed to anyone who cared to answer. And so he did. The man was an easterner, she heard him say, one who'd never traveled west beyond Chicago before. As he spoke it became apparent to her that his enthusiasm over the rugged southwestern countryside was second only to Dimitri's.

Shylo didn't mind being left out of the conversation a bit. It gave her a chance to observe her Greek god, unnoticed. She'd never seen him quite so alive before, or as animated as he was while talking about the land and its history. It made him lose that insufferable aloofness, for once. She wondered if there was a way she could keep him that way. Better yet, would it possible to get him feeling equally worked up over real live people? Over her?

Dimitri was all she'd been able to think about since their "near kiss" the first day out of New York. He was different from anyone she'd ever known, and not just because he was a foreigner. It was something else, something she'd have understood by now if only she'd had another chance to get him alone. Which she hadn't. But he had been friendly enough toward her the past few days, if not terribly romantic, and always said just the right things, treating her as if she were someone special. Still, she sensed he was holding something back, keeping his true self at bay, and she couldn't help but wonder why. Was it because of some lack he'd found in her or some private reason that had only to do with himself?

Maybe, it suddenly occurred to Shylo, Dimitri didn't know how to express himself any better than she did. Maybe, she even dared to think, he might actually *need* someone like her, the kind of gal who wouldn't just say "Yes, sir" and "No, sir" to him all the time but would make damn good and sure he sat up and paid her some attention. Warming more and more to the actual reality of playing lady friend to this man, Shylo glanced over at Dimitri and took an extra-careful look at him.

He was still deep in conversation with the stranger, his thick blue-black hair gleaming under the rays of the hot desert sun. His strong hands were waving as he spoke, drawing her attention to his shoulders as the muscles there bunched and strained against his jacket. Lord, but this man was a pleasure for the eyes!

Dimitri turned slightly then and caught her gaze. Shylo's throat seized up good and tight, making her feel like a prairie chicken caught in a snare. She suspected right then and there that even if he never did loosen up the way she hoped, she'd be happy as long as he simply stayed in her field of vision.

He excused himself to the other passenger and stepped under the car's metal overhang to where Shylo stood just out of the sun. "I didn't mean to ignore you," he said, apologizing. "But I was telling that fellow about the pueblos and ancient artifacts which have been discovered in these parts during recent years. He was most interested in learning about the area Indians."

"Me, too."

Clearly surprised, Dimitri said, "Are you, now. In what way?"

"I'd like to know a little bit more about the way they lived, the Cheyenne in particular, so I can understand what the souvenirs I have were used for."

"You are in possession of Cheyenne Indian souvenirs?"

Shylo nodded at the same moment she realized that she'd trapped herself into another explanation—and another lie. "Yes, but t-they . . . belonged to my friend, who found them out in the fields of the farm she worked in Kansas. There's some broken pottery, a few arrowheads, and some things I think might have been used during the Cheyenne sun dance."

"That's absolutely fascinating." Dimitri wondered if he hadn't accidentally chosen a woman who shared the same interests he did. "You didn't, by any chance, happen to study archaeology in college, did you?"

She raised her chin, defensive about her less-than-thorough education. "No, sir, I didn't. I never got a chance to go to college at all, but I hope to someday."

Hope to? Someday? This from the niece of the president of the United States? Dimitri was astounded, but he tried not to let his surprise show. "As well you should. I would very much like to see your souvenirs, if I may. Do you have them with you, or did you ship them on ahead in your trunk?"

They were with her, of course, in her valise, since the nonexistent trunk was another lie to make him think she and Cassie had a lot more clothing than would fit in their pitifully small traveling bag. But she wouldn't let him see the artifacts. Not today, at any rate, and not until she was damn good and ready to show him. Shylo had *not* missed Dimitri's arrogance or his obvious disappointment in learning that she was not quite his intellectual equal, that she was inferior to him in at least that area.

"The souvenirs are packed in the trunk," she said, unable to hide the irritation in her voice.

"Oh, well. Perhaps you'll show them to me when we reach San Diego."

Dimitri wasn't exactly certain where he'd made his error, but one look into her cold blue eyes told him that he most definitely had. As most of the passengers who'd been sunning themselves filed by him—seeking, no doubt, a cooler spot inside the observation car or a cool drink—he went back over the conversation, looking for clues to his mistake. Nothing of any value came to him, but then he realized that other than the man he'd been conversing with, he and Shylo were the only brave souls left outside in the increasingly uncomfortable heat. Maybe the temperature was the cause of her sharp tongue.

"Would you care to go inside?" he asked, almost certain that's where he'd been remiss. "It's getting a little warm."

Since her new wool jersey was not only suffocating her, but making her itch as if she had a bad case of the hives, Shylo decided to take him up on the offer. Then she noticed the only passenger other than themselves had turned away from the rails and was starting for the door. She and Dimitri would be alone now, and scorching heat or not, she might be looking at the only chance she'd have to go ahead with her newest plan to snag him.

Although her skin felt damp and scratchy and her undergarments clung to her body like wet wash, she gave him a cool smile as she said, "Oh, don't think of going inside on my account. I rather like this weather. Of course, if it's getting too hot for you—"

"Not at all. This is like springtime compared to a steamy summer in Greece. I'm quite comfortable, if you are."

Proud of herself, Shylo smiled at him, batting her lashes for good measure as she quickly reviewed her plan. Dimitri hadn't jumped at the chance to kiss her before, she deduced, because he had no way of knowing whether bestowing such an endearment upon a young lady he was not betrothed to would be considered proper behavior in America. But the way she had it figured, she could tell him just about anything she wanted to, and he'd have to believe her. She might not have any fancy schooling, but she sure as hell could educate him in the ways—*her* ways—of American courtship.

Shylo squared her shoulders and took a deep, determined breath. She would *not* be going to bed mad tonight the way she had before. To achieve that goal, Dimitri's first lesson would have to be blunt, one he couldn't possibly misconstrue the way he had the last time she'd tested her wiles on him.

This time, Shylo vowed, he'd kiss her, by God, or she'd know the reason why not.

5

Since Shylo had left her to her own devices, Cassie moved to the last and most private seat the parlor car had to offer and huddled there, her back to the aisle and the other passengers. Her cheeks were flushed and rosy, a shade even more luminous than the bright purplish pink shade her hair had faded to over the last week. Her nose was buried in Shylo's *Ladies Book of Etiquette, Fashion, and Manual of Politeness,* but Cassie wasn't studying how to conduct herself on the street or in places of amusement. She was deeply engrossed in *Destiny Rode at Midnight,* a ten-cent romance she'd slipped between the pages of chapter fifteen, the section on letter writing. And she'd finally come to the good part.

. . . and as thunder rolled above them, Jesse hauled Elizabeth out of the stream. She fought him, kicking and screaming, but it was no use. He was as strong as

an ox and determined to have his way with her.
"Turn me loose!" she cried into the howling wind.

"Not this time, Lizzy." In one quick movement,
Jesse ripped the front of her dress open. Her wet
chemise met his gaze along with the private treasures
it barely concealed. Jesse licked his lips. "This time,
Lizzy, you're not escaping until you're mine."

She screamed, but the wind tore the sound from
her throat. She arched her back to better strike out at
him, but only managed to excite him more. Jesse
wouldn't stop until he had his way. She understood
that now, and almost welcomed the idea of surrender.
He was going to touch her, to put his hands—

Without warning, the train slid to a screeching halt,
tearing both books from Cassie's hands. Her swivel
chair spun around, smacking the side of her head against
the glass window next to her. When the train finally
came to a stop, she was flung against the back of the
chair in front of her and then fell to the floor with a thud.
All around her women screamed and men shouted,
but no one seemed to have the slightest idea what had
happened.

Using the seat back she'd just collided with for balance, Cassie gingerly pulled herself to her feet and
tested for injuries. Her head hurt, but other than that
she was only shaken. After straightening her bonnet,
which had been knocked askew, she felt the lump
near her right temple, gauging it to be about the size
of a robin's egg.

Then the front door to the parlor car banged open,
and three masked men stepped inside, their pistols
drawn.

One of them, his voice gruff, muffled by a dark

blue handkerchief, shouted, "Listen up, folks! All you got to do is keep your heads about you and no one's gonna get hurt. This here's a holdup."

Out on the deck of the observation car, a stunned Shylo found herself facedown on the floor, the iron leg of an overturned chair tangled up in the folds of her skirt. She leaned up on her elbows, shaking her head to clear it, and realized that her hair had come free and her straw hat had fallen off. Then she glanced up and spotted it tumbling brim over feathers across the desert sands. A moment later it was gone.

"What in hell happened?" she said, forgetting herself again.

Beside her, Dimitri climbed to his feet. "I don't know, but I couldn't have said it better myself." "Hell," an extremely versatile word, had become one of his favorites since coming to America, although to be honest this was the first time he'd heard the expletive uttered by a lady. Dimitri didn't concern himself about the lapse in manners, though. He was far more interested in Shylo's physical condition. "Are you able to stand?"

"I—I don't know." It was the truth. She didn't have to pretend coquettish reticence or fake a helpless demeanor this time. Shylo had no idea why the train had come to such an abrupt halt, how she'd wound up on the floor wrapped around a metal chair, or if she was in need of medical care. She only knew that her bottom was sore and one of her elbows burned as if on fire. Struggling to raise her hand to Dimitri's, she winced in pain.

"Wait! Don't move." He dropped to her side and

removed the chair from beneath her, tearing a wide gash in her skirt in the process, then carefully lifted her to her feet. "Better now?"

Shylo swayed against him, testing her limbs hesitantly. Other than a bruised bottom and an aching funny bone, everything seemed to be in working order. She almost told him so, too, but stopped herself as she suddenly recognized the opportunity before her. For whatever reason, the train had stopped, and because of that, Dimitri was finally where she wanted him—holding her in his arms. There was no way in hell she intended to let him go now.

Tilting her head back just enough to look up at him, she fell into her role as a pampered heiress and lied through her teeth. "I'm afraid I may have sprained my ankle a little, and isn't it just my bad luck that it turns out to be the same one I hurt back in New York?" She leaned into Dimitri's chest, her lashes fluttering out of control. "Maybe if you just hang on to me for a minute, the pain will go away."

He adjusted his grip, holding her up on tiptoes. "Is that better?"

"Tons," she said, sighing heavily. "But now . . . oh, I don't know why, but I seem to be feeling a little dizzy, too." She burrowed her head beneath his chin.

"You *are* hurt." Dimitri lifted her feet off the ground and carried her toward one of the chairs that hadn't fallen over. "I'm going to sit you down and go see if I can't find a doctor on board to come look at you."

"No!" she said, her voice too loud and much too unladylike. Shylo planted her feet, including the one with the "injury," and softened her voice. "I mean, thanks for the thought, but that won't be necessary. I'm feeling a little better already."

Dimitri cocked one thick black eyebrow. "Are you sure?"

"Well . . ."

Her eyes were blinking furiously, struggling to come into focus, he assumed, and Dimitri was sure that she was more badly injured than she admitted. Was she so afraid of doctors or just trying to be brave? Perhaps he should be a little more discreet about rounding one up. "All right. Why don't you sit down anyway. I'm going inside to at least find out what happened to make the train stop so suddenly. We may be in some danger."

"Oh, I doubt that." She slapped his chest lightly. "I'm sure we only stopped to take on coal or water. The engineer probably blew a warning whistle, and we were just too distracted by all this"—she waved her arm toward the barren countryside, frowning as she forced herself to say—"beautiful scenery to notice."

"I won't be a moment."

"Fine!" she snapped, unable to control her temper any more than she could control Dimitri. "Go ahead if you must, but a real gentleman would stay here to help me put myself together."

Until she turned away from him and bent over to retrieve her hairpins, Dimitri hadn't paid much attention to the fact that Shylo's coiffure had slipped loose of its bonds, freeing her tresses to tumble down her back and shoulders. Sunlight highlighted her thick honey-colored locks as she plucked the pins off the deck, confirming his suspicions about the touch of fire he thought he'd once noticed.

He'd been expecting that hint of red, but he was in no way prepared for the impact of observing such a glorious sight. It stirred him to watch her hair fall this way and that, a few lengths covering her shoulders and plunging down to her waist, others curling around the collar of her jacket or draped along her magnificent cheekbones. Even her eyes, now framed by the abundance of those lush, shimmering tresses, seemed to brighten and deepen to a more irresistible shade of blue.

Never had Dimitri seen anything quite like Shylo ringed in sunlight, and the spectacle of her standing there was a match to Aphrodite if ever there was one. He'd thought her reasonably attractive the day they'd met, but now her beauty stunned him, awakening his nether regions with a painful jolt. The sudden physical discomfort was as surprising as it was troubling, but that was nothing compared to the disturbing idea as it occurred to him that he might be losing his careful control—a control he'd worked a lifetime to achieve.

In a voice gruffer than he'd intended, Dimitri said, "I really ought to go find the conductor."

Shylo whirled on him, frustrated over her continuing ineptness when it came to tempting this man; but before she could blurt out something she'd regret, she realized a change had come over him. She had no practical experience in such matters, but something in his dark eyes and in the tense set of his jaw told her he was fascinated with her. Even though he had threatened to go inside, his gaze remained on her face and her unruly curls, and there was a certain longing in his expression, giving her the impression that he wanted nothing more than to touch them, to touch her.

He would come to her now, kiss her, or do anything she asked of him. Shylo was suddenly sure of that, if nothing else. All she need do was ask.

"Looking for the conductor may be a good idea," she

said, slowly turning her back to him. "But would you mind helping me with my hair first? I'd hate to have the others see me in such a state, and it's too much for me to lift by myself." Another lie, but one that worked.

Although he suspected that he would be challenging his control more than he had in a long, long time, Dimitri could do no less than comply. "All right, but I warn you—this isn't exactly my area of expertise. What is it you want me to do?"

"Oh," she said breezily, pleased to hear the strain in his voice, "just bundle it all up and try to twist it into a pile at the top of my head. I'll take over from there."

With hands eager to take on the dangerous assignment, Dimitri plunged into her hair, lifting the bulk of those silken strands, then staring at them as if he'd unearthed a cache of ancient jewels. He had every intention of doing exactly as Shylo had instructed, but once he had her mane in his grasp, he could not resist burying his face in the flame-kissed curls.

He breathed deeply, loving the fresh clean smell, the scent of springtime devoid of the artificial perfumes so overused by most women of privilege. Several of those strands had curled around his fingers, trapping his hands in a silken web, and he impulsively brought them to his cheek, indulging himself with the warm, satiny feel of her hair brushing his skin. Against his better judgment, he imagined what it would be like if he were to wrap those soft locks around his entire naked body.

At the thought, he grew hard, more painfully engorged than he could ever remember being at any time in his life. He doubted this response, or the utterly carnal thoughts he was having about Shylo, were exactly what Ari had had in mind when he'd told him to "test the young lady" and "see what happens."

Digging deep within himself for the strength to drive the lust from his body, Dimitri quickly formed Shylo's hair into a pile, a rather sloppy one at that, and positioned it at the top of her head. Then he held it there, his traitorous body still raging with desire, and waited in agony for her to fasten her runaway tresses into place.

After she slipped the final hairpin into the knot, Shylo turned to face Dimitri again. He still wore that look of fascination, but something else had drifted across his handsome features, darkening them. Something that told Shylo her plan was working extremely well.

"Are *you* all right?" she asked, moving closer. "You look a little flushed and"—she pressed her fingers against Dimitri's brow—"not only warm, but damp. Is the heat getting to you?"

Dimitri clutched her arms, intending to set her away from him again, but instead found himself pulling her up tight against his body. "It appears that it is," he admitted, fighting the urge to rip the pins from her hair and let it tumble back over his hands. "The heat is *definitely* getting to me."

Dimitri's voice had gone all husky, and his rejoinder was rife with unmistakable innuendo. Did it all mean what she hoped it did—that he was as ready for this moment as she? "If I can help cool you off, or something, just tell me how. It's the least I can do after all you've done for me. What do you have in mind?"

"Kiss her a little, test her," Ari had suggested. God knew Dimitri wanted that more than anything right now. So why not proceed with those plans? What the hell did he have to lose at this point? "What I have in mind," he whispered darkly, forging ahead, "will not cool either of us. In fact, the heat may even intensify. This is all right with you?"

"It is if you mean you want to court me."

This, of course, was what he'd hoped for, but Dimitri was surprised. Were all American women so aggressive in matters of courtship? "I—I suppose you could say that, among other things, is what I have in mind. Does this meet with your approval, Miss Folsom?"

"It does." She tilted her chin, offering her mouth in case he hadn't caught on. "What other things did you have in mind?"

Dimitri lowered his head and brushed her lips with his, lingering over them for just a moment. "Something like that. Do you still approve?"

She swayed slightly, her lashes fluttering of their own volition, and was surprised to hear her own voice come out in a breathless whisper as she said, "I—I sure do, and I think it's high time you got around to it. If I'da known it was going to be so much trouble getting you to kiss me, I'da just sat down and wrote you a letter."

Dimitri kind of froze up when she said that, and his expression was unreadable to her. Thinking nothing of it, she took hold of his hand and shook it. "Thanks for deciding to court me. I'll try to make sure you don't regret it." Although she could still feel the spot where his lips had touched hers, she tried not to sound too impressed as she added, "Oh, and thanks for the kiss, too."

Forward in the parlor car, the gunmen split up. The senior member of the gang stayed near the front door, a second bandit made his way to the middle of the car, and the youngest, Buck Dilly, was left to work the back. Due to his age and inexperience, the youth was occasionally referred to as "Dilly the Kid" behind his back and sometimes even to his face. But at seventeen Buck was full of piss and vinegar and more than enough bravado—most of the time—to ignore the taunts.

Today was certainly one of those times. This was his first *real* job, even though he'd ridden with the gang on several other occasions. Before, he'd always been left on the sidelines either tending the horses or sprinting to the other side of town to light fires that would serve as diversions. Never, until today, had he been allowed to take part in an actual robbery. "You're too young to get in the line of fire," his older brother, Bob, would say, "too wet behind the ears to pull a job."

Of course, that was before brother Bob got himself arrested and then hung. After that the gang kind of took Buck under their wing, agreeing to give him his first crack at celebrity by including him in the robbery of a Santa Fe train carrying a huge mining payroll. Six of the men would force their way into the baggage car to seize the payroll, while three others, including Buck, would rob the only passengers worth bothering with: those riding in first class.

Now that Buck was finally a true member of the gang and doing his first real job, his adrenaline was pumping like a brand-new well. As he made his way down the aisle toward the passengers he was supposed to relieve of money and jewels, he spotted a female cowering on the last seat. Deciding she was as good a place as any to begin his illustrious career, he started for her.

When a terrified Cassie heard the clank of a man's boots and realized they were approaching her, she didn't know whether to scream or faint. Then his legs bumped against her chair, and as she slowly raised her wide-eyed gaze to his, she was pretty sure fainting was her only option. And not because of fear, but because of the way the outlaw was looking at her.

He was grinning, staring right into her eyes and *grinning*. Cassie couldn't see all of him, of course, but what she could see, she liked. The bandit wore a denim shirt that matched his tight-fitting jeans, and a shiny brown leather vest. His hat, made of the same leather as his vest, dipped low over one hazel-green eye, making him look a little roguish. His face was mostly hidden behind a bright red handkerchief, but Cassie couldn't help but notice how his big wide grin went all the way up to his eyebrows. Unable to stop herself, she grinned right back.

"Well, well," Buck said, pleasantly surprised to find such a cute young thing riding in first class. "What do we got here?"

Ari, who'd overheard the outlaw's remarks and the tone in which they'd been made, leapt out of his chair to go to Cassie's aid.

Buck heard the man moving behind him and, guessing at his intentions before the old man even stepped into the aisle, he swung his arm in an arc as he turned, his pistol raised high.

The outlaw's gun smashed full force against Ari's temple. He opened his mouth as if to speak, wavered there for a moment, then closed his eyes and crumpled to the floor without ever making a sound.

Cassie shrieked, drawing the outlaw's attention back to her, and as he whirled around, his handkerchief slipped below his chin, revealing his features. She'd planned on screaming again, but once she saw that boyishly handsome face and his playful gaze locked in on hers, she forgot about those plans and wondered once again if she wasn't about to faint.

"Don't go getting all spooky on me," Buck said, still grinning that bad boy grin as he dropped to one knee and swiveled the girl's chair around. Once his back was to the other passengers to keep his identity safe, he used the barrel of his gun to push the brim of his hat back from his forehead, revealing a bank of wavy brown hair. Then he winked one hazel eye and said, "Don't you worry about your friend there. I didn't hurt the old boy none. Just shut him up a little, is all. My name's Buck. What's yours?"

She knew this was wrong somehow, but she couldn't stop grinning at him or think of what to do but answer his question. "It's, umm, Cassie."

"Cassie, huh?" The outlaw's grin deepened, revealing a pair of button dimples, cute little dents that were nothing like the wide, dramatically slashing dimples of that Greek god Shylo had latched on to. These deep little pits gave the bandit an endearingly boyish quality, made him seem harmless somehow.

"Did you know," he went on, his slight twang thickening, "that you're just about the prettiest thing I've ever seen in my whole entire lifehood?"

No one had ever talked to her like that—*no one!* Cassie sucked in her breath, and her eyes felt as if they'd rolled clear to the back of her head. What if she'd been mistaken and hadn't heard him right? Had he said that Cassandra Mary McBride was *pretty?* Yes, yes, he had!

Her heart began to pound, and she had to clutch the arms of her chair to keep her hands from shaking. She gulped and blinked her eyes again. The outlaw was still there, still grinning, waiting for her to reply, even though her brain was scrambled like a Sunday morning omelet.

Cassie said the first thing that came to mind. "I—I have pink hair."

His grin fading to a look of disbelief, Buck pushed the bonnet away from Cassie's face until something resembling a field of spun sugar came into view. He stared at that hair for a full minute and then chuckled softly. "I'll be dogged if this ain't the damnedest coincidence I can recall. Would you believe that *pink* is just about my favorite color?"

So overwhelmed was Cassie to hear those beautiful words that when her eyes rolled back this time, she wasn't sure she'd ever get them lined up forward again. She struggled against a sudden tightness in her chest, renewed her grip on the arms of her chair in order to keep from falling out of it, and tried to come up with a way to thank the outlaw for his kindness.

"You all right, sugar lips?" Buck brushed her cheek with the back of his hand. "You ain't figuring to go belly up on me, are you?"

"Ah, no," she finally managed to say. "I, ah, just wanted to say thanks for being so kind about my hair, and I was also kinda wondering . . . Could I ask you a question?"

"Shoot, sugar, but try not to hurt me any more than you already have just by being so plum easy on the eyes." Buck slipped off his loose handkerchief and mopped his brow with it. "Whew, you are really something, you know it? You're just like a cute little ole lump of pink sugar candy!"

The urge to fall right out of her chair and drown in sheer joy was strong, but using all her might, Cassie willed herself not to swoon. "I was wondering about . . . what color is your horse?"

The amusement never left Buck's eyes, but he was definitely taken back by her question. What in God's blue heaven did his horse have to do with anything? He couldn't fathom her reasons for asking, so he just shrugged and said, "I guess most folks might say he's kinda flea-bit."

"Flea-bit? What's that mean?"

"That he's got some freckles, but that underneath them, he's white."

"Honest? Your very own horse really is . . . *white?*" She practically screamed the last word.

"Mostly, if he ain't been rolling in the mud, that is. Why do you want to know?"

But Cassie was beyond asking or answering questions. Her eyes rolled back yet again, and this time they stayed there as her lids fluttered to a close. Then her rigid hands went limp, releasing her grip on the velvet armrests, and if not for Buck Dilly kneeling directly in front of her, she would have slid out of her chair and onto the floor.

Out on the observation deck, Dimitri had just settled his mouth against Shylo's waiting lips to show her what a *real* kiss was. He halfway expected her to pull back at the last minute, laugh, and run off, for no woman he'd ever known had been quite so vocal about what she wanted from him. Could their cultures really be so different? Or was he holding an exception to the rule in his arms? If she was that, Dimitri thought as her mouth moved freely against his, she was clearly an "exceptional" exception. There was nothing prim or proper about Shylo's kiss, nothing to suggest a great deal of experience, either, but she followed his lead as if they'd rehearsed this interlude a thousand times before.

Shylo was so caught up in the way Dimitri's mouth fit against hers, so content to bask in the sensations as his perfectly formed lips caressed and electrified her in ever so many more places than her mouth—even though he never left it—that at first she almost didn't notice when he deepened the kiss and worked his tongue between her lips to part them. It wasn't until he met her bared teeth and tried to separate them as well that she tore out of his fierce embrace and staggered back a few steps.

"What in *hell* do you think you're doing?" she asked, amazed at his audacity.

"Kissing you, just like you asked." Dimitri wasn't sure where he'd gone wrong this time, but at this point he didn't really care. "Now get back over here and let me finish."

"Finish?" Shylo traced her lips with her fingertips, certain from the tingly, swollen way they felt that he must have been joking. Cassie had been right about this kissing business all along, she decided, because she sure did feel "funny" all over: weak, jiggly, and flushed from one end of her body to the other. How could there possibly be more to kissing than that?

"You demanded that I kiss you, and I have no intention of stopping until you've been thoroughly kissed!" Impatience overriding his gentlemanlike tendencies, Dimitri advanced on Shylo, pulled her back into his embrace, and muttered in a low dark growl, "I *said* I wasn't finished. Now open your mouth and let me continue, woman."

Shylo's mouth did fall open as requested, but not because Dimitri demanded it. She was agape with shock at the sudden change in him, especially by the manner in which he spoke to her and the almost cunning way he was looking at her. Before she had a chance to figure out what had brought about such radical changes, or to decide whether they were signs of encouragement or a bad omen, his mouth came down on hers again, harder this time, more demanding. And this time his tongue gained entrance to the sanctity of her open mouth with no invitation from her whatsoever.

Shylo's first instinct was to fight him off, and to that end she balled her fists and pressed them against the top of Dimitri's shoulders. Then his tongue began to move inside her mouth, first exploring her crevices with infinite care, then sliding up and down along her own tongue in a movement she recognized somehow but didn't fully understand. Then something broke loose in her, an uncivilized urge to respond, and Shylo met his challenge.

With darting, tentative movements, she made a few quick forays inside Dimitri's mouth. Surprised by the groan of pleasure he made, she clung to him, her fists no longer balled, and dug her fingers into the thick black curls at the back of his neck in a desperate attempt to pull herself closer to him—an impossibility, since not even a ray of sunshine could have fit between them now.

So this was the meaning of those "wonderful feelings," she thought, wanting their embrace to go on forever. *This* was the reason women and men had joined together from the beginning of time. How long could sensations such as these last? she wondered. A lifetime?

When gunshots rang out from inside the stationary locomotive, those sensations and the kiss ended right there with an abruptness neither of them could have anticipated.

Dimitri immediately released Shylo, tucked her behind his back, and said, "Get down and don't move, Miss Folsom. I'm going to go see what happened."

More gunfire, this time from outside the train.

Shylo, who hadn't done as she was told, leapt toward the door. "My God! Someone's shooting in there!"

Without hesitation, Dimitri took her roughly by the shoulders, lifted her off her feet, and forcibly seated her on a chair. "Don't *move!*" he said, this time with no hint of his usual melodic tones. Then he slipped inside the observation car.

Shylo decided to give him a few moments. Then she hopped up from the chair, hurried over to the rail, and peeked around the corner of the train. A huge cloud of dust was rolling away from the railroad tracks in a northwesterly direction, evidence of an indeterminate number of horses and riders. Certain those riders were the cause of both the unscheduled stop and the gunfire, and that she'd be as safe inside as she was outside, Shylo started after Dimitri.

She caught up to him in the parlor car, where bedlam reigned. Female passengers were weeping, lamenting the loss of their jewelry and personal belongings, and the men were busy plotting ways of getting their wallets back and bringing the criminals to justice. Dimitri, Shylo discovered, was on the floor, tending to his uncle, who held a bloodied handkerchief against the side of his head.

"Oh, my God! What happened?" she cried as she reached them. "Did they shoot you, Ari?"

Dimitri looked up at her, searing her with a hot gaze. "Didn't I tell you to stay where I left you?"

Shylo didn't like his tone or the insinuation that she didn't have enough sense to make her own decision. "I don't have to listen to you *or* do anything you tell me," she snapped.

"Please, please," said Ari, struggling to his feet. "This is no time for arguments. We have been robbed, and some of us have been beaten. Surely your disagreement can wait for another time."

With a quick, regretful glance at one another, Shylo and Dimitri turned to Ari and almost at the same moment said, "What happened?"

"As I was saying, we were robbed by bandits. I was struck on the head by a gun as I went to your friend's aid, and then—"

"Cassie?" Shylo's gaze shot around the inside of the car. "What happened to her? Was she beaten, too?"

"One of the bandits came at her. I did not like his words, or"—he paused to give his nephew a particularly meaningful look—"the way he spoke them, so—"

Panic overriding what little composure she had left, Shylo elbowed her way between the two men and stared the eldest in the eye. "Explain exactly what in hell you mean by that, and don't be handing me a pile of bull."

Ari covered his shock at Shylo's surprising candor and did the best he could to explain. "The bandit seemed to be a little—how do you say, maybe tempted? . . . by her. I was afraid he would . . . that he might . . . " Ari looked to Dimitri, beseeching him for help.

"I think Shylo gets the idea," he said, taking a cursory glance around the car. "Where is Miss McBride now?"

"Yes," Shylo said, her panic rising again. "Where is

she, and what did that rotten bandit do to her after that?"

Ari shook his head. "I'm afraid his gun knocked me senseless. I do not know."

Shylo picked up her skirts and bulldozed her way through the crowd of passengers in the aisle. "Cassie? Cassie?" she called over and over. "Where are you? . . . Cassie? Are you all right?"

Finally a man who'd been sitting up near the front stopped her progress. "Who are you looking for, miss?"

"My sis—traveling companion. Have you seen her?"

"Is she the one in the big ugly bonnet who sits by herself and reads all the time?"

"Yes, yes. Where is she?"

Dimitri, who was right on Shylo's heels, placed a comforting hand on her shoulder and said to the suddenly quiet man, "Please tell us what you know."

"Sorry, but I thought everyone knew what they done with her by now. She's the one they took."

"Took?" Shylo's mind couldn't accept or digest what he was trying to say. "What do you mean by took, and exactly who are *they?*"

"The bandits, ma'am. They kidnapped your traveling companion, took her along with them as a hostage."

6

Once the tracks were cleared of the debris left by the bandits' barricade, the train continued on its way to the next scheduled stop, Winslow, Arizona. The locomotive didn't even have time to come to a complete halt before Shylo leapt off the step near the doorway of the parlor car and onto the depot platform, where she asked railroad agents where she could find the marshal's office.

Unable to stop her once she had the information she sought, Shylo's Greek escorts dogged her trail as she went down Kinsley Avenue to Third Street, where the marshal's makeshift office was located.

Because they were unfamiliar with American legalities, and Shylo was so overwrought about the kidnapping of her young maid, Dimitri and Ari hung back once the trio reached the log cabin that served as both jailhouse and marshal's quarters, took seats on a wooden waiting bench, and kept their silence as she grilled a startled lawman about his plans for seeing to Cassie's safe return.

Amused, not by the kidnapping or Shylo's distress, of course, but by the lively conversation between her and the deputy, Ari nudged Dimitri's ribs and whispered in Greek, "Would you look at this man's gun? It is as big as a leg of lamb, yet this woman of yours pursues him as if he's unarmed. She will make a fine mother someday, my son, do you not agree?"

Dimitri, who'd been trying to concentrate on what the lawman was saying about his plans for rounding up something called a "posse," found his uncle's statement even more confusing than the heated discussion across the room. He turned to him and asked in his native tongue, "What the devil are you talking about?"

"Look at the way Miss Folsom worries over the young woman in her employ. Can you imagine how fiercely protective she will be as the mother of your children?"

Dimitri wasn't interested in imagining anyone as the mother of his children, not even Shylo, although more and more it appeared as if she might actually be blessed—or burdened—with that honor. He and Ari were in big financial trouble. The bandits had taken the satchel containing most of their funds and had even gone to the trouble of emptying Ari's pockets as he lay unconscious on the floor. Dimitri had a little cash on him, but not nearly enough to see them through their trip to California. If they didn't reach San Diego soon, confirm that Nick Pappas was Dimitri's uncle, and use his assets to refill their coffers, then a hasty marriage to the president's niece indeed loomed as a distinct possibility.

How in God's name had his well-ordered world ever gotten so completely out of control? If not for this damnable money problem, and the fact that his mother had been left virtually penniless, he would probably be sailing to England about now for a long overdue confrontation with the director of the British Museum. He would be doing something of value instead of sitting in a musty old jailhouse trying to understand a conversation laced with words he'd never heard before.

Shylo banged her fist against the pitted wooden desk, commanding Dimitri's attention again, and he listened as she demanded that the lawman do something about this "posse" of his. As she spoke, her voice was lusty with the passion Dimitri now knew lurked inside of her, and Ari's words echoed in his mind: *the mother of your children.*

He'd always assumed that he'd never have children, and although becoming a father still held little appeal to him, there was a plus he could think of should a marriage between himself and the president's niece come to pass and she insisted on babies. Dimitri couldn't recall ever having had such an intense or instant attraction to anyone before. In fact, Shylo had a lot of very desirable qualities in addition to her physical allure; candor and honesty were two of them. Unfortunately, with those good points came several that were not so good.

As he watched her trying to browbeat the man into doing her bidding, Dimitri had to admit that he harbored more than a few concerns about her mental stability and mercurial moods. Whenever in her company, he never knew if he'd be facing the very proper niece of a president or a hellion given to outbursts more suitable to a peasant woman. Shylo was an enigma, a woman of many faces, and as he thought about it, he realized that he wasn't even sure which of them he liked the best. He looked up to see what he thought might be the hellion stomping toward him.

"Will you *puleese,*" she said, "do something to get that marshal up off his duff and outside? He says he's the only law in Winslow, but that he doesn't have the authority to get a posse together. It seems only the county sheriff, whose office is in Holbrook, can do anything about running the bandits down. This, this"—she glanced over her shoulder and glared—"*Marshal* Moss says he already sent a wire to Holbrook asking for help, but that the sheriff may be a while getting here since there's been some trouble down south and he's out of town!"

It was the hellion for sure. Trying to ignore the fact that this side of Shylo seemed to stir his blood one hell of a lot more than the proper lady, Dimitri stood up and took her hands in his in order to calm her. "I'll do what I can," he said, speaking in low, reassuring tones. "But first I have to know what the words *duff* and *possy* mean."

Shylo rolled her eyes. "A duff is, it means . . . " She honestly wanted to think of a better way to put it, but she was just too tired and too upset to think straight. She patted her bottom. "A duff is your behind, and a posse is a group of men, officers like him, I guess, that the sheriff is supposed to gather up to go chasing after the bandits. This marshal"—she pointed to the man—"insists he can't leave the office until the county sheriff arrives from Holbrook, but that even then it might take a while to round up enough volunteers to chase down nine desperadoes!"

"Desperadoes? What are they?"

In abject frustration Shylo raised her hands to the heavens and shook them. "Oh, why do I even bother! No one will take the time to understand or care how important this is to me—no one!"

"Perhaps," Dimitri said, "your vicious tongue puts them off. As long as you are debtor-mined to use it on those who would help you, I think you will find yourself quite without the aid you seek."

"Debtor-mined? What in hell are you talking about?"

"It is an English word, debtor-mined," he said defensively. "It means, ah . . . intending, I think, or maybe stubborn."

In spite of her foul mood, Shylo had to laugh as she figured out what he'd been trying to say. "You mean *determined*."

Dimitri stiffened, for he prided himself on the fact that he spoke five languages fluently in addition to Greek. "Excuse my mistake, Miss Folsom. As I was saying, I think you are de*ter*mined to drive us all away. And so, we shall go." He turned then, gesturing for his uncle to follow as he said to Shylo, "Ari and I are going to go find ourselves a nice hotel. Good luck with your posse."

As Dimitri started for the door, and she realized that he really did mean to leave her behind, Shylo panicked. "Wait!" she cried, hurrying after them. "Please don't go without me."

Speaking in Greek, Dimitri cautioned his uncle not to slow his pace or look back. They kept walking out the door and onto the boardwalk, pausing only long enough to choose a direction in which to travel before resuming their excursion. They headed west, where most of the buildings were located.

Shylo caught up to them and tugged on the sleeve of Dimitri's jacket. "Please stop a minute. I'm sorry for getting so riled up back there, but it's just that I'm worried sick about Cassie. She's about all that I—" Shylo stopped herself before she said too much. "I guess what I'm trying to say is that I think an awful lot of her. In fact, in many ways, I look on her as . . . as a sister."

She'd said the last word so softly, Dimitri almost didn't hear it. Tears shone in Shylo's eyes, and although he wasn't entirely certain that she hadn't conjured them up just for his benefit, he couldn't leave her standing there in such a state.

"Ari," he said, "why don't you go on ahead and pick out the hotel. Miss Folsom and I will be along in a moment." For once, the old man didn't make a comment or raise his eyebrows. He just nodded and continued on his way, leaving Dimitri and Shylo alone under the bright yellow awning of a store. By then her tears were no longer just welling in her eyes, they were rolling down her cheeks. Dimitri took his handkerchief from his pocket and slipped it into her hand.

"I promise to do all I can to help you, but not as long as you insist on doing"—he waved his fingers toward her cheeks—"this."

"This?" She hiccuped. "You mean, crying?"

"Yes. I don't like it, and I don't want you to do it anymore. So please stop it right now."

Sniffling instead of using and ruining Dimitri's expensive silk handkerchief, Shylo swallowed another sob. "All right." She dabbed her cheeks and held her chin high. "I'm through crying. What can we do to help get Cassie back before those, those . . . " *Don't cry! You can't help her if you cry!* She repeated this to herself several times before she could go on. "Before those bandits do something terrible to her?"

"I think I may have an excellent solution, one, I might add, that I'm surprised you haven't thought of."

"Really?" Filled with hope, Shylo latched her fingers on to the lapels of his jacket. "What's the plan? Let's do it!"

This was the woman Dimitri liked best. The enthusiastic lady with just a little of the hellion shining through. He smiled at her, meaning it, and let his gaze fall to the luscious mouth he'd so recently kissed. "The plan is simple," he said, the huskiness in his voice betraying a few other plans he had in mind. "You just have to send a wire to your uncle. If anyone can get a team of good trackers together, I would have to assume, it would be a man with his credentials."

"My . . . *uncle?*" He couldn't mean whom she thought he meant—could he? She'd never so much as mentioned having family to Dimitri, and she sure as hell never told him that particular lie. "I don't think I know who you're talking about."

Dimitri hesitated, wondering if he ought not to divulge what he knew, then decided that given poor Cassie's circumstances, he really had no choice but to tell all. Besides, even if Miss Folsom was doing some secret work for the government, he didn't see how it could possibly matter if he, a Greek national, was privy to the information. Keeping his voice low, he said, "Why, the president of the United States, of course."

"Oh, shit," slipped out before Shylo even realized she was thinking it.

"I beg your pardon?" Surely she hadn't uttered *that* word.

"I said . . . that's it." She paused. "Dimitri," she

murmured in dulcet tones, "may I ask where you got
the idea that the president is somehow related to me?"

"Don't worry," he assured her. "Your secret is safe
with me. I don't even want to know why you can't
speak of your ties to the White House. I just thought
he might be of some help."

"But—"

"Ari happened to be speaking to Mrs. Vanderkellen
at her party, and your name came up. She mentioned
the president and the fact that you are his niece."

That sealed it. There was no getting out of the lie
now, not with Victoria as the gossipy aristocrat who'd
turned town crier on her. Hells bells and dried-up
wells, she thought, recalling a favorite childhood
chant. Now she had not one, but two whoppers to
clear up with Dimitri on down the road. The first, the
fact that she didn't have two pennies to rub together,
she was sure would cause no problem given his
wealth; but the second . . . ah, the second might prove
a tad more difficult.

Greeks, she'd learned at Victoria's dinner party,
set a mighty high store on anything of a political
nature. In fact, now that she thought about it, and
saw herself compared with those New York debutantes, she realized her "political connections" were
probably the only reason Dimitri had agreed to escort
her to California in the first place—or to court her,
the two-faced bastard. When, oh, *when* would things
start to get easier for her? Shylo propped her bustles
against the corner beam of the store, drew in a long
breath, then let it out in a sigh that started from her
toes.

"I'm sorry if this news distresses you," Dimitri
said, not quite sure how to make amends or if they

were even necessary. "I only thought to help the situation here, not add to your troubles."

"You didn't, not really." But Shylo did feel as if she were toting her nonexistent trunk full of clothing across her shoulders. "I can't call on the president for help, that's for sure, and I can't tell you why, not just yet, either. You'll have to, ah, trust me on that."

"Of course I will."

Shylo glanced into Dimitri's devil black eyes, seeking confirmation of his vow, but they looked guarded and aloof as usual. Too tired for any more conjecture, she said, "Well, then I guess there really isn't anything we can do for Cassie but wait until the sheriff gets to town and puts a posse together. In the meantime, I could use a good washing and a little rest. Which hotel do you think your uncle stopped at?"

"The best, of course."

After a few inquiries they quickly discovered that the best Winslow had to offer was the Harvey House Hotel, which doubled as the Santa Fe station where they'd stepped off the train. Situated south of the tracks, even though most of the town was on the north side, the hotel was an impressive two-story structure of red brick and gabled roofs, known not only as the best lodging available in town, but as the establishment that featured one of the finest restaurants in all of Arizona.

Dimitri led Shylo past the well-stocked cigar stand near the entrance to the lobby and deposited her on one of the numerous padded wooden chairs before joining Ari at the registration desk.

"All goes well?" he asked his uncle in Greek.

"We have two rooms, if that is what you mean. If you're asking about money, all is not so well. They want two dollars per day, per room—in advance."

Dimitri whistled between his teeth but dug into his vest pocket and withdrew fifty dollars, half of all the money he had left to his name. "Pay the man, but only for one night at a time. If we're lucky, Miss McBride will wander back into town by morning."

Ari glanced over to where Shylo was sitting with her eyes closed. "And if we're not so lucky?"

Following his uncle's gaze, Dimitri gave a nod of resignation. "I know. It is time to ask for the return of our money."

Ari turned back to the desk. "A good plan. While you're doing that, I will get our keys and see that a hot bath is arranged for your future bride."

Muttering to himself, since that prospect was looking more like "when" than "if," Dimitri went back to Shylo and sat down beside her.

Her eyes flew open. "Oh, you startled me. Do we have rooms?"

"Yes. Ari is getting keys and making sure a hot bath will be waiting for you."

"Oh, thank God." She fanned herself with her only possessions—the etiquette book she'd found lying on the parlor car floor, and something called *Destiny Rode at Midnight,* a book Shylo sure as hell hadn't purchased, but one that somehow had come into Cassie's possession. "Before I get bathed, you'll have to take me to the mercantile and pick me up a few things. A dress for sure, since you ripped this one. It's the only one I own now that those bandits made off with my traveling bag. I can't go around looking like this."

"No, of course not, and I'll be happy to escort you to the shop, but that is all I can do. I'm afraid that because of the robbery, Ari and I are a little financially embarrassed."

"Embarrassed?" *Oh, Lord, not them, too!* "You mean, broke?"

"Not precisely, but the bandits did make off with the satchel in which we kept most of our funds. We were hoping that your resources were still intact, and that you might be able to repay us for the train tickets now."

Shylo gulped and averted her gaze. "I'm real sorry to have to tell you this, but, ah, Cassie wasn't just my traveling companion. She was my, ah . . . secretary, too, and kept all our money in the valise." She gave him a mournful glance. "I guess you know where *that* is."

"With our satchel, I would presume."

Shylo nodded. "I expect so, but maybe things aren't so bad as they seem. Can't you just go wire your bank and tell them to send you more money?"

That would be a last resort as far as Dimitri was concerned. The only funds available to him now were those he'd set aside for his trip to England, a journey that was to have coincided with his doctorate in archaeology. He would have to be in dire straits indeed to even think of touching one drachma of that account. Surely wiring for funds would be much simpler for a woman of Shylo's connections.

"I'm afraid," Dimitri said, careful of his wording, "that is more difficult than you might imagine. There are overseas wires to consider, not to mention international transfers. It would probably be quite some time before I could expect to receive any funds. Wouldn't it be easier for you to wire the president?"

Worn out with all the lies, Shylo sighed heavily. Her life would be so much less complicated if she could just come right out and tell Dimitri the truth—that she was in no way related to Grover Cleveland, and that even if she had her valise, there wasn't enough money in it to cover new underthings, much less a dress. But she couldn't tell him the truth, of course. Not unless she was prepared to face this town and her sister's situation, penniless and completely alone. Which she was not.

Shylo turned to him, making up yet another whopper as she went along. "I wish I could help you, but I'm afraid I can't wire the president or any member of my family, because . . . " She paused, heaving another, heavier sigh as she tried to come up with a plausible reason. "Because the truth is, none of them know that I'm taking this trip, and if they did know, they sure wouldn't approve of it."

"But I don't understand. What about seeing to your friend's mother?"

"Well, you see . . . " Shylo batted her lashes, buying a little more time for her aching brain. "Ah, Uncle Grover doesn't exactly approve of Colleen or her daughters."

"Daughters? She has more than your departed friend?"

"Yes, I believe I mentioned that to you on the train." Shylo quickly weighed the consequences of explaining further and decided that revealing a little more about her sister might even help her cause rather than harm it. "My friend was the oldest child, and her sister, poor Cassie, is the youngest." The tiny sob she sniffed back after that was real.

"Cassie?" Dimitri was confused. "Surely you're not referring to your traveling companion. I thought her name was McBride, not Broussard."

"Did I say that?" If she couldn't keep her own lies straight, she could wind up in a hell of a fix. "If I did, I was only trying to protect her. Her name is McBride, as was Colleen's before she married that Broussard fellow."

"Then Cassie was on that orphan train and sent away to live on a farm?"

"I'm afraid so." Dimitri actually looked distressed at this news, and again Shylo found herself wishing that she could gather up all the compassion she saw in his dark eyes and heap those soothing sentiments on the rejected child inside of her.

To keep focused on her plight and her impromptu script, Shylo had to look away from him before she could go on. "Cassie was the household helper, the one who helped the farmer's wife with cooking, cleaning, and sewing, while my, ah, friend, was put to work outside tending crops and the animals. I guess you could say she was the son the farmer never had."

Angry all over again at the American way of dealing with orphans, Dimitri shook his head. "I cannot understand why your uncle does not wish to come to this poor girl's aid."

"It's a long story, and one I'd rather not talk about, if you don't mind, but maybe now you can understand a little better why I'm so upset about Cassie out there alone with those men. You don't think they'll hurt her, do you?"

If Cassie were even alive, Dimitri couldn't imagine that she hadn't been injured in some way by that gang of cutthroats. Ari strolled up before Dimitri could form an answer that wouldn't reveal this thought.

"Our rooms are ready," said Ari. "Shall we go upstairs?"

Dimitri stood up from the couch, took Shylo by the hand, and helped her to her feet. Then he made what he hoped was the correct decision. She had more than enough worries without concerning herself about where a new dress or the next meal would come from, and since he'd all but pledged his troth to her aboard the train, it was his duty of relieve her of at least that much anxiety. The only way to do that would be to send a wire to the university, asking for a portion of his savings to be sent ahead to San Diego, hoping all the while that he wouldn't actually have to use any of it. In the event those funds were needed, surely Shylo or her uncle would pay him back at their journey's end.

Dimitri held out his hand, palm up. "Please give me Shylo's key, Ari. We have a little shopping to do before she can go to her room."

"Shopping, my son?" Had the desert heat gotten to him? "We are in need of nothing."

"Shylo is." He glanced at her, his smile broad and dimpled. "I'm going to buy her a new dress. Something in Aegean blue, I think."

Some fifteen miles north of Winslow, deep in the sensuously rounded hills and rugged badland canyons formed out of the area's pastel-hued sandstone, three remaining members of the Daggart gang argued about the fate of their unexpected hostage. The other six outlaws had fanned out already, each taking a different route and direction. Over the next few weeks all nine men would converge in the deeply eroded canyons and fortresslike cliffs of southeastern Utah, near where the Dirty Devil River entered the Colorado River.

Fred Daggart eyed Cassie, who was sitting in the shade beneath a ledge carved of russet sandstone. Her mouth was silenced by Buck's red handkerchief, and her hands and feet had been bound with sturdy twine. Daggart slowly shook his head as he addressed the youngest member of his gang. "You'd better think of something fast, kid, 'cause there ain't no goddamn way in hell we're gonna take her to Utah with us and parade her around Robbers Roost."

"I know that," said Buck. "But I don't see a thing in the world wrong with my plan. You fellas split up like the others did, I'll stay behind with the girl to make sure a posse don't pick up nobody's trail, then I'll join you boys in a couple of weeks. What's the problem?"

"You, kid," interrupted the outlaw known as Flat Nose. "Ain't none of us want to run off leaving you behind all by your lonesome. Your brother Bob'd bust right out of his coffin and gut the lot of us if'n we was to leave off without you. Tell you what: how about you ride out with Fred?" He cast a gaze toward Cassie. "I'll stay behind and take care of the girl and the posse."

"No, dammit!" Buck had never so much as raised his voice against the members of the gang, let alone stood up to them. But in this he was dogged. "I'm the one thought of the hostage plan, and I'm the one gonna see it through. You two ride on out. I can find my way to the Roost from here, and I'll see you a coupla weeks down the road."

Flat Nose elbowed the boss's ribs. "I told you we shoulda run that boy down to Nogales to let off a little steam before we ever trusted him with a real job. He's got his head so far up that girl's skirt, he can't even think straight."

"Ease up on the boy a little, Flat Nose." Daggart

took a long time mulling over the options before he finally said, "Even if the kid's pants are egging him on, I think maybe he's trying to make a man of himself in more ways than just the one. Ain't you, boy?"

"Yessir."

Daggart shot another quick glance at Cassie. "All right, kid, if you really think you can handle that little bundle of fluff, *and* a posse, the job's yours."

Buck swallowed the urge to whoop with joy. "I can handle the both of them real good."

"Both of 'em, Dilly?" Flat Nose laughed and leaned in close. "Just how good do you think you're gonna be the first time out? Or don't you figure on telling that gal you're a virgin?"

Buck flushed and ground his teeth. "Shut your big goddamn mouth! Ain't none of your business what I do or what I say."

Daggart stepped between the men and issued his final orders. "Mount up, Flat Nose, and do what the kid says—shut up." As the outlaw complied, laughing a deep belly-roll kind of chortle, Daggart took the kid by the arm and pulled him up tight. "This here's serious business, kid, and a business where we can't afford to take chances. When you're done with the girl, what did you figure on doing with her?"

"Doing? I ain't exactly sure what you mean."

"I already told you I don't want her at Robbers Roost, and you can't hardly turn her loose to go giving our descriptions to the law or telling where we went." He narrowed one eye. "I'm asking you again, kid. What do you figure on doing after you've finished with her?"

Buck hadn't thought that far ahead, but he knew exactly what Daggart meant. And what he had to do.

Fingering the leather sheath at his waist that contained his Bowie knife, he said, "I'll be leaving her *body* behind as a message to anyone who tries to follow us."

"You sure you can handle that part, too?" Daggart refrained from adding, "Since you've never killed anyone before?"

"'Course I can." Buck's gaze flickered to Cassie, but he didn't really look at her. "I could do it right now, if I had to, but I'd rather keep her around another day or so." He laughed. "Now you two get on out of here. See you later."

Daggart punched the kid's arm. "Later, Dilly. And be sure to keep an eye on your back."

As the outlaws rode by the spot where Cassie sat trembling, Flat Nose spat a stream of tobacco juice in her direction, splattering the hem of her dress. "You be sure and do what the boy tells you, darlin'. He's some mean varmint." Flat Nose threw back his head and laughed. "That there's none other than Dilly the Kid."

Her eyes bright with fear, Cassie watched as the pair of bandits rode away and gradually faded from view. She'd been stunned, to say the least, when she'd awakened to find herself atop Buck's white horse, galloping across the desert at an alarming rate. Now she was nothing short of terrified. *Dilly the Kid?* As in Billy the Kid or Jesse James? And what did the outlaw mean when he asked Buck if he could he handle "that part, too"?

A shadow fell over Cassie as she contemplated her situation, startling her. Her head snapped around and her gaze shot up to meet the hooded eyes of Buck "Dilly the Kid." His legs were spread, his expression grim. Nothing in his manner or appearance eased her worried mind.

Buck stepped forward, drawing her attention to an object he held in his hand. Sunlight reflected against metal, blowing her a sparkling kiss from the blade of his huge knife. Then he dropped to his haunches, brandishing the weapon in one hand and reaching for her with the other.

7

Later that night after sundown, a spectacle that included a sinking fireball that turned the sky into a blood-colored landscape to match her mood, Shylo stared at her menu at the Harvey House Restaurant with unseeing eyes. She couldn't seem to compose herself even though she felt more refreshed and comfortable than she'd been since the day they'd left New York.

The dress Dimitri had bought for her was made of printed lawn combined with frothy organdy in shades of yellow, not Aegean blue, and accented at the waist by a wide sash of bright lemon-colored satin. Not only was the gown lightweight and far cooler than her ruined traveling suit, she also had brand-new underthings, including *two* crinolette petticoats with matching chemise and lacy drawers trimmed with powder blue ribbons. Her underwear, she'd noted sardonically, was prettier than any dress she'd ever owned as a child or during all her years on the farm.

Between the new clothing and refreshing bath, she ought to have relaxed at least enough to make a choice for her supper, but she couldn't seem to concentrate on her menu. The Harvey House offered a huge assortment of food, more entrées than she'd ever heard of, much less had the opportunity to sample. There were bluepoints on the shell, whatever in hell they were, and an assortment of lamb, beef, duck, and fish, all presented in French sauces or manners of cooking Shylo didn't understand—and there wasn't one plain vegetable listed anywhere. Potatoes were française, peas were marrowfat, and the asparagus was in some kind of cream sauce. She glanced briefly at the dessert menu, then looked away. The only thing she recognized there was "assorted fruits and cheeses."

Since a Harvey Girl was standing beside him waiting for their order, Dimitri finally said to an unusually quiet Shylo, "Would you like me to order for both of us?"

"Yes, I would. Thank you." Not interested in the choice he made for her, Shylo let her trancelike gaze drift over to the window.

Frowning to himself, Dimitri placed their order. "The lady will have pork with applesauce, and I'd like lobster salad with salami of duck."

After the waitress collected the menus and went on her way, Dimitri thought of catching Shylo's attention again but decided it would be of no use. She was lost in another world, one that didn't include him. Ari, who'd left them to dine alone so they might get better acquainted, might as well have joined them, Dimitri thought, feeling hungry for conversation in addition to sustenance.

Then again, he suspected there might be another, more compelling motivation for his uncle's absence. Like many other Greek men his age, Ari had a fondness for gambling. That fondness—or weakness, depending on how you looked at it—was the main reason the old man's funds were so low at a time when he should have been enjoying his retirement without financial cares. Surely the old man wouldn't squander what little money he had in his possession on games of chance—or would he? On his earlier excursion around town, Dimitri hadn't missed the vast assortment of saloons and houses of ill repute dotting Winslow's notorious Front Street, and he was certain that Ari hadn't, either. It was entirely possible—probable, now that Dimitri considered it—that Ari was at this very moment trying to drum up a little game of backgammon. Hoping that luck would be on his uncle's side if he should try to parlay some of their money into a bigger stake, Dimitri heaved a heavy sigh.

"Pardon me?" Shylo said, brought out of her daze. "Did you say something?"

He could have said "Yes," he supposed, and made something up, but Dimitri knew it wouldn't make much difference. Shylo still had that "not of this world" look about her, so he just smiled and shook his head, hoping that she would make him believe that she realized he was there. She didn't. Instead she turned back to the window, leaving Dimitri with a surprising revelation: he missed her crooked little smile, a gesture he hadn't seen since their kiss at the back of the train. And he missed their casual and sometimes heated conversations. He missed *her*.

The food arrived, and since she hadn't eaten a bite since breakfast, the sight of it alone should have brought Shylo's stomach to growling and mouth to watering, but her usually robust appetite was gone. All she could think of was Cassie. Was she warm enough out there in the great desolate unknown? Was she in pain? What would *she* be having for supper tonight? Or would that gang of cutthroats even bother to feed her? Everything, no matter what she tried to think or do, revolved around Cassie, the bright-eyed girl who in many ways was more daughter to Shylo than sister. The knowledge that she'd somehow failed in that responsibility weighed heavily on her shoulders.

Shylo glanced at Dimitri, who'd fallen on his food with vigor. She couldn't even concentrate well enough to enjoy his company tonight. When he spoke, his voice seemed distant, garbled, as if a great veil of water separated them. Even his image, as much as she loved to look on his classical Greek features, seemed blurred and indistinct. Shylo rubbed her tired eyes and forced herself to focus on him.

Dimitri looked up to meet her gaze then, sympathy and a bit of confusion shining in his dark eyes. She sensed that he wanted to share in her sorrow but didn't understand it. Was it possible that he'd never cared for anyone in his life the way she cared for Cassie? Maybe, she thought, touched by a finger of sadness, he'd never loved another at all. And then again maybe that wasn't such a bad way to live. If nothing else, life must hurt less that way.

Shylo glanced back out the window, wishing she could feel as detached as Dimitri always seemed to be, but it was no use. She closed her eyes, and in her heart she believed she felt Cassie's terror. When she listened hard, she swore she could almost hear her heart-wrenching screams.

* * *

At that very moment, in the cave Buck had stashed her in after he'd cut her free of her bonds, a frightened Cassie flattened herself against the wall at the deepest point of the den. Something moved. She screamed into the darkness, the sound echoing off the sandstone ledges like a cat chasing its tail.

Near the entrance, a man, lupine in appearance, moved swiftly toward her. She dropped to her knees and crawled soundlessly in the opposite direction. Glancing toward where she'd last seen his shadow, she caught the mottled silhouette of a creosote bush near the mouth of the cave, but no sign of the man.

Then, with a suddenness that took her breath away, came a savage cry. He leapt out of nowhere, leapfrogged onto her back, and threw his arms around her waist. Before Cassie could cry out again or catch her breath, he rolled her onto her side, then tumbled with her firmly in his grasp, to the center of the den.

"Gotcha!" he said, out of breath. "And that's the third time today."

"Oh, Buck, you fool!" With her fingers splayed against his chest, Cassie locked her elbows and shoved. "I *knew* it was you the last time you snuck up on me. This time, I couldn't see who it was, and you scairt hell out of me."

"Sorry, sugar, I didn't mean to scare you. It took me a little longer than I figured it would to get my horse settled for the night, and it went and got dark on me before I could get back." He rolled over to where he'd fashioned stones into a fire ring earlier and struck a match to the sagebrush and tumbleweeds he'd gathered there. Then he rolled back toward Cassie, shifting his body until he was lying beside her, and propped himself up on one elbow. Grinning, he licked his lips and said, "But I am back now, and happy to be here. Damned if you aren't one fine-looking woman. I must be the luckiest human being in the whole wide world tonight."

Looking up at him in the glow of firelight, Cassie couldn't help but feel the same way. Buck's craterlike dimples seemed bottomless, and his eyes, whiskey-colored in the semidarkness, shone like those of a cuddly little puppy. "Oh, Buck," she murmured. "You don't really mean all that, do you?"

"You know I do, sugar." He reached over, tugged the ribbons loose on her bonnet, and slipped it off her head. "Let me see that hair of yours—all of it, you little peppermint drop, you."

Blushing, Cassie sat up, took the pins from her hair, and let it fall free. It wasn't as long or thick as Shylo's, and where her older sister had curls, Cassie had almost indiscernible dips, but viewed through Buck's glowing eyes, she felt as if she had the lushest, most gorgeous tresses of any woman anywhere— even if they were pink. She shook her head, spilling those luminous locks down her back and across her shoulders.

"Damn," Buck muttered huskily. "If you ain't some sight. Tell me how you got that pink hair, sugar lips, and don't go leaving nothing out."

Toying with the length hanging off the tip of her left breast, Cassie blushed again as she said, "My sister done it. She's always trying experiments on me to make sure they're safe for her. Why, just before she done this to my hair, she put pomegranate juice all over my cheeks to try and rouge them up like those fancy high-bred ladies. I looked like a clown by the time she got done with me."

Buck laughed. "Why the hell does she do all that to you, and why do you let her?"

"'Cause she was trying to look like one of them society debutantes." She wondered briefly if she ought to keep their plans a secret but couldn't think of a good reason not to tell him. "We're searching for our mother. She ran off with some rich French fella right after I was born, leaving us girls and our pa behind in her dust."

Buck scratched his head. "Don't make much sense to me why you'd want to go looking for a mother who run off from her babies, and you ain't seen your whole entire life. I'd say good riddance."

"It was Shylo's idea—that's my sister—but no one's supposed to know it 'cause she's pretending to be someone else. Anyway, she's the one decided we ought to go after our ma. She and I got adopted by a farmer a long time ago, and when he dropped dead in the middle of harvest last fall, his wife give us part of the money she made after she sold the farm, and set us free. First thing Shylo did was study up the New York newspapers until she found a picture of our real ma with her rich husband. That's when she decided it was time to go pay her a visit, and that we had to look as rich as her, too."

Buck, who'd taken the length of hair from Cassie's fingers and wound it around his own, continued to play with the lock, occasionally brushing the back of his hand against the nipple of her left breast in the process. "And did you find your ma?"

"No, not yet." Cassie shuddered as Buck's hand grazed her bodice. Did he know what he'd done, or how it made her feel inside? Her cheeks grew hot as she admitted, "I don't much care one way or another if we never find our mother, but that's all Shylo ever thinks about. I'll bet if we do find her, she won't even want to see us."

"And what do you want, sugar?" Buck's voice was soft and low as he coaxed her back down on the blanket he'd arranged near the fire ring. "Are you hungry? I got us a nice fat rabbit in the snare. I could cook him up in no time."

Something in Cassie's throat began to quiver, but she answered him anyway. "Ah, n-not yet. Maybe later."

"Thirsty?" Buck went on, still fondling that lock of hair and the breast beneath it. "I got a canteen full of water, but I also got some whiskey and a little mescal. I could warm you up from the inside out." He shivered as he realized what he'd said.

Cassie missed the innuendo. She was too caught up in the way Buck's fingers felt as they skimmed her bodice time and time again and the way those caresses, in turn, made her insides feel. "I—no thanks. I don't want anything right now."

"Well, I sure as hell do." There. It was out in the open, bold and forthright. Since he had no idea what he was doing to start with, Buck proceeded in the same manner. "Listen, sugar—I ain't got much time, two, three days at the most. If I don't head out by then, I'm afraid my horse will drop dead from starvation. Ain't much out here for him to eat, you know."

Cassie looked him straight in the eye, knowing he was asking something of her, not entirely sure what that something might be. "What are you trying to say to me, Buck?"

"I want you to be my girl." He took off his hat and

flattened it across his heart. "I love you, Cassie, I do. I've loved you from the minute I set eyes on you aboard that train. I want you to be mine, all mine, for whatever time we got together. Whaddaya say? I need you, girl, I need you *real* bad."

Buck looked distressed, and he was breathing hard enough to have chased down their supper rabbit on foot. Then Cassie realized that she was short of breath, too. Could it mean what she hoped it did? Could it be that Buck "Dilly the Kid" was her own true Prince Charming, bad boy grin and all? He *had* come to her riding a big white horse, swept her into his arms as she lay unconscious, and then carried her off into the sunset. Who else *could* he be?

"Oh, Bucky," Cassie said through a breathless sigh. "I—I think I love you, too. W-what is it you want me to do?"

Buck slipped his hand beneath the nape of her neck and lifted her head until her lips practically met his. "I ain't exactly sure, sugar face, but I have a feeling that between the two of us, we'll get it figured out."

On the third morning after her sister's kidnapping, Shylo's nerves were stretched tighter than her last dollar. Nights were the worst, when she could almost swear she heard Cassie crying out and moaning . . . and dying, she feared. She couldn't take it one more day—or night. After slipping out of her room fully dressed, she crept down the hall to the room Dimitri shared with Ari and knocked softly. She waited a few moments, then knocked again. Finally, as she raised her fist to tap on the door one more time, it opened a crack.

His eyes smarting from the glare of the hallway lamp, Dimitri squinted to identify his late-night visitor. "Shylo! What are you doing up at this hour?"

"It isn't that all-fired early. Sunup's only about an hour off." She glanced up and down the hall. "Are you fellas decent enough for me to come in a minute?"

Dimitri glanced down at himself. "Give me a second."

The door closed, then opened again a few moments later. He'd slipped into a pair of black trousers and was still hastily buttoning a white dress shirt as she stepped inside the room. She couldn't help but notice that he quit the task before he reached the top two buttons, leaving his shirt to gape open at the throat. Between the glimpse of ebony curls that covered Dimitri's chest and the intriguing sight of his sleep-tousled hair, Shylo almost forgot why she'd come to him in the first place. She quickly looked away and glanced around the room. That's when she saw that Ari's bed was empty and made up.

"Where is your uncle?" she asked.

"I don't know for sure. Gambling, I think," he said, but Dimitri was far more concerned about the reasons for Shylo's visit and the impropriety of his entertaining her alone in his room. "Is something wrong? Why are you here so early?"

"I—it's . . . " Anxious to get on with it and get going, Shylo didn't waste time. "I can't take it anymore. I can't stand all this waiting for sheriffs that never show, and wondering if Cassie's all right or if she's . . . dead."

Once she'd finally put words to her worst fear, it was like kicking a hole in a beaver dam. Shylo burst into tears. "Oh, God, Dimitri! What if she *is* dead? I can't take the not knowing, the wondering about what's happening or already happened to her. I can't take it anymore!"

Dimitri pulled her into his arms, in spite of the way it might look should Ari burst into the room at that moment. "Don't do this to yourself, Shylo," he whispered, calling her by her given name for the first time. "You're worrying yourself sick over what *might* be. Since we're pretty sure the bandits took your friend to use for bartering in case the law caught up with them, she probably hasn't been harmed in the slightest. For all we know, she's perfectly safe."

As he spoke, Shylo allowed herself the comfort of Dimitri's strong arms and even felt herself being lulled by the warmth of his chest and the rhythmic sound of his heart beating against her cheek. When she digested what he had said, she pulled away from that calm shelter. "Safe? A lone woman in the company of nine gunmen? Even you don't believe that!"

Spinning away from him, for she never could think straight when Dimitri was too close, Shylo went on. "I didn't come here to guess at what's happened to Cassie, or argue with you about it, either." She faced him again. "I came to tell you that I can't sit around waiting for the sheriff to show up any longer. I've got to go *do* something."

"I couldn't agree with you more. If you're ready to wire the president, I'm with you one hundred percent. Just give me a minute to get my boots on."

"The pres— No. That's not what I had in mind. I'm on my way to the livery to rent a horse. I've got to go see what happened to Cassie for myself."

Dimitri was in the midst of tugging on a sock, and he paused there, balancing on one leg as he said, "That's ridiculous! Not only would such a foolish trip be a waste of time and money, it's a very dangerous idea." He jerked the sock fully over his foot, then stood with his hands on his hips. "Have you looked at the countryside around Winslow? There's nothing for miles and miles in every direction."

"That's exactly my point." Shylo began to retreat. "What if the bandits noticed there's no posse after them, turned Cassie loose once she was no use to them, and left her wandering around in the desert by herself? What if she's out there dying as we speak?"

Dimitri moved closer. "That's an awful lot to assume."

"But it could be true! Don't you see? I *can't* not do something, and I won't!" Shylo took another step backward and bumped against the door. Reaching behind her, she felt for the knob. "Nothing you can say or do is going to keep me from going. I only came by to ask you if you'd care to meet me at the livery. I'd just as soon not have to go alone." She tugged the door open.

"Wait!" Dimitri bought a moment for himself, weighing the consequences of what he was about to do against his better judgment. Then he realized it didn't make a damn bit of difference what he thought. He'd been around Shylo long enough to know that one way or another, with or without him, she was going to make the trip.

With a sigh of defeat, or maybe even admiration, Dimitri rubbed his hands across his sleepy eyes and said, "Go down to the kitchen and ask them to prepare us a big basket of food—enough for all day. And lots of strong coffee. I'll meet you there in one minute."

"You'll . . . go with me?"

"I hope I'll live to regret it, but yes. I'll go with you."

Beside herself with gratitude, Shylo rushed back into the room and threw herself into Dimitri's arms. Tears sparkled in her blue eyes, but this time they were tears of joy. "You won't regret it. I swear to God you won't." Then she pulled herself up to his surprised mouth and kissed him with all her might.

It took them better than two hours to round up the supplies Dimitri insisted they bring along with them: a pick, a shovel, and a barrel of water were among the essentials, along with the picnic basket and coffee. Instead of a horse, they rented a sturdy mule and well-made wagon to transport their supplies and, should they come across her, Cassie. The liveryman, sympathetic to their cause, tossed in a pair of thick horse blankets to use as padding for the wooden seat Shylo and Dimitri shared and lent them his rifle for protection should they happen upon trouble.

After a quick stop at Rand's Mercantile, where Dimitri bought a large sunbonnet for Shylo and a pair of rugged denim work pants and a Stetson hat for himself, they were finally on their way out of town.

At Shylo's insistence they started their journey by traveling east, to the location where the train had been disabled. Using that spot as a landmark, she was able to make a better guess at the precise direction in which the gang had ridden off. Within four hours of leaving Winslow, they reached a dry river valley leading into the windswept mesas and isolated buttes that made up the outlying regions of the Little Painted Desert.

Concerned about the mazelike appearance of the softly contoured slopes ahead, Dimitri brought the mule to a halt. He glanced up at the sky, noting the willowy-wisp clouds skating across the harsh noonday sun, then looked back out at the badlands. The barren landscape summoned him, promising ancient discoveries the equal of any of the treasures he'd unearthed at Mycenae, but he knew he couldn't answer the call. Although he felt more relaxed than he'd been since setting foot on American soil, more comfortable with his clothing and more excited by his surroundings than he could ever be as a "merchant of means," he had Shylo to think about. He'd allowed all the risks with her life he intended to.

"It's taken us almost half the day to get this far," he said. "If we go any farther, we might get lost and never make it out before dark."

Shylo, who was grateful for the company, not to mention fascinated by this new "westernized" Dimitri, kept her wits and her patience as she turned to him. She could hardly believe the change in him since he'd donned his new hat and Levi Strauss denims. The hat, black with a turquoise-and-silver band circling the crown, made him look less aloof and, incredible as it seemed, even more handsome than before. If she hadn't been so preoccupied by her sister's plight, Shylo thought, she might even have picked up with this man where she'd left off aboard the train, with another kiss.

But Cassie came first. "Let's at least go in far enough so I can climb to the top of one of those mountains and have a look around. I could call out Cassie's name a few times, and who knows? She might be out there lost and hear me."

Dimitri shook his head. "I'm afraid if we go in, *we* might be the ones who'll be lost. I don't think we ought to take that chance."

Fighting the urge just to fling herself off the wagon and forge ahead on her own, Shylo forced a soft tone as she touched the sleeve of Dimitri's shirt and said, "Please. I can't go back now that we've come this far. Let's just go in a little ways, far enough anyway for us to find a vantage point so I can at least look for signs that she's even been here. Please?"

Again spurning logic and his better judgment, Dimitri sighed, cracked the buggy whip over the mule's back, and guided the rig into the narrow valley. As they passed within touching distance of striated cliffs of russet, beige, and smoke gray, he couldn't help but feel a tremor of foreboding.

Three miles into the heart of those badlands, Cassie and Buck were in the cave, resting from a bout of fervent lovemaking. Cassie's traveling suit was covered with sandstone, her petticoats ragged and torn, and her body felt bruised and tender, raw from one end to the other. She'd never felt better in her life.

Yawning loudly, she turned on her side and caressed Buck's bare chest. "You sleeping again?"

He patted her hand. "Just resting, sugar. You plumb wore me out."

"Do you still love me?"

"You know I do, girl. What do I got to do to prove it?"

That was an easy enough question. Cassie pouted as she said, "Stay with me forever. That'll prove it."

Buck groaned. "You know I can't do that. I got to meet up with the gang to get my share of the loot. Besides, if I don't show, they'll think something's happened to me. A couple of them might even come looking for me. I can't let any of the boys take that kind of risk with a posse coming for us sooner or later."

"But you *can* let me go just like I never meant nothing to you?" Her pout grew more pronounced. "Well, the hell with you, Buck Dilly, and the hell with your stupid gang. I hope you all get caught and thrown in jail!"

Cassie sat up as if to leave, but Buck pulled her back down beside him. "It don't have to be like that, sugar lips. We just got to make us a plan for meeting up again."

Her expression wary, she said, "What kind of plan?"

"Well, let's see." Buck rubbed the stubble of his sparse beard. "I've got to clear out of here by morning, ain't no two ways about that. I'll ride you out of these here hills and get you as close to Winslow as I dare without getting spotted."

"What's in Winslow?"

"The sheriff, for starters, and I'd guess your sister. She wouldn't have gone on to California without you, would she?"

Cassie considered that a moment. "I don't think so, but she is awful set on finding our ma. If Shylo is in Winslow, do you expect me to *walk* all the way to town while you ride off to Utah?"

She was pouting again, so Buck tickled her under the chin as he said, "I told you I'll get you as close to Winslow as I can without being seen. You'll be all right."

"Maybe. But what about you and me meeting up again?"

"I'm thinking on it, I'm a-thinking." He scratched his head, then shot Cassie a big grin. "You're going on to San Diego no matter what, ain't you?"

She shrugged. "Sure. We still got train tickets supposed to take us there, and I expect that once I'm found, we'll be heading to California again. Why?"

"I ain't never been west of Flagstaff." His grin deepened. "Would you like it if I was to meet up with you at San Diego in, say, three or four weeks?"

Cassie squealed. "Really? You'd come all that way just to get me?"

"I sure would, sugar face." He captured her chin and pulled her up close for a kiss. "You begin marking the days tomorrow, and at the end of three weeks' time, you'd best start moseying on down to the San Diego post office every day to check and see if there ain't a letter addressed to Miss Cassandra McBride. General delivery, of course."

"You're gonna write me a letter? What for?"

"For you to read, cotton-head. I'll write down the name of a spot and a time for us to meet. I'll be there every night until you show."

"Oh, Buck!" Cassie's heart felt aglow with the romance of it all. "That's the best plan I've ever heard."

"You think that's good, wait till you hear the rest of my plans." At her look of bafflement, he gave her a broad wink. "We just got today and tonight to last us for a month. I don't know about you, but I don't *plan* on wasting the little bit of time we got left on talking." Then he took her into his arms and kissed the remnants of her pout right off her lips.

Less than two miles from the cave, Dimitri was pacing alongside the disabled wagon, his concerns about being able to repair it growing as each minute ticked by. The front left wheel had fallen into a deep fissure, a rut he hadn't seen because Shylo had distracted him with another of her "sightings"—a ruse, he suspected, to get him to drive deeper and deeper into the badlands. Now the rig was buried up to its axle at an impossible angle, and if the loud *crack* he'd heard when the road gave way was any indication, they had a broken wheel to contend with as well. All because of Shylo's constant insistence that they move farther into this forbidding desert in search of her friend.

Dimitri turned to her, his frustrations and fears for their safety rising, and said, "Are you happy now? Even if I use the mule, it will take me hours to get this wheel free, and when I do, I think we'll find at least one broken spoke."

"So what?" she snapped in response to his tone. "Can't we just fix it?"

"With what? Look around you, Miss Folsom." He swept his arm in an arc to encompass the smoothly rounded hills, which showed few signs of vegetation. "If spokes are broken, I'll need some sturdy wood to repair them. Do you see any trees around here? Hell, no!"

Wiping her brow with the edge of her sleeve, an overheated, overwrought Shylo could think only of continuing her search. In frustration she kicked the buried wheel, then winced as a sharp pain shot from her big toe to her shinbone. "You don't know that it's broken for sure," she snapped at him again, "so why don't we dig it out first and worry about fixing it later?"

"Whatever you say, Miss Folsom, but I know not why I should listen to any more of *your* great ideas. If

I hadn't listened to you in the first place, we would not be in this, this ... unhappy ... "

Dimitri turned and started for the rear of the wagon where the tools were stashed, trying to cool his temper. His command of English was good enough that he could usually think as clearly in the foreign language as he did in Greek—unless, of course, he was flustered, highly excited, or downright angry. And right now he was all three.

Dogging his heels, Shylo said, "Are you blaming me for getting the wagon stuck? *Me?*"

Dimitri reached over the low side of the wagon, grabbed the shovel, and flung it toward the front wheel. "Yes, I am," he said, losing the battle with his temper. "I wanted not to go in here, but you insisted we search this, this God-hates-it desert. I can't believe I am idiot enough to let you talk me into coming all the way out here!"

"And I can't believe you were *idiot* enough to drive the wagon over a rut as big as the Grand Canyon!" She picked up the shovel. "What in hell were you thinking of, anyway?"

With the pick in his hand, Dimitri stomped to the front of the wagon. Leaning his face in close to hers, he said, "I think if I'd stayed in Greece, maybe where I belong, I would not be here!"

Although his words didn't make a lot of sense to her, the tone did. Jutting back her shoulders, Shylo said, "Well, I sure as hell won't try to argue you out of that. I'd be better off if you'd stayed in Greece, too!"

The veins in Dimitri's neck bulged, and his olive skin took on a deep red flush. He knew he was over-reacting, and that worry over their circumstances was the major force driving him on, but he couldn't seem to stop himself or find his usual control. That, in turn, made his English even worse.

"And I," he said, his tone blistering by now, "should not know a stubborn, sass social woman like you! I would not to accompany across the street this female, but never to California."

Shylo almost laughed over the way he'd slaughtered the sentence, but he'd said it well enough for her to understand what he meant. "Then why *did* you accompany me out here, you two-faced son of a— It wouldn't have anything to do with the fact that you heard the president of the United States is my uncle, would it?"

Dimitri should have collected himself right then, defended himself against her accusation—even if she had touched on the truth—and gone to work on the wagon wheel, but the last of his control unraveled when Shylo pointed the tip of her nose toward the sky, uttered a self-satisfied grunt, and twirled away.

"Yes!" he shouted, his words bringing her to a skidding halt. "Now you have truth! I would not think of to bring you anywhere with your mule head. But of course I did because of your famous uncle! But of course!"

Although she'd believed that herself, it hurt her to hear it. Suddenly all her recent training as a refined lady was shot to hell. She turned back to him. "Why, you miserable, no-good, two-faced bastard!"

"This is not good talk." Dimitri narrowed one eye. "For that, you should eat wood!"

"Huh?" Shylo knew she had offended him by mouthing off that way, but the rest baffled her. "What does 'eat wood' mean?"

Beyond frustration, Dimitri simply couldn't think

of an English translation to make it clearer, so he showed her. Raising his right fist, he drove it into the palm of his left hand. "Eat wood. *Katalaves?*"

Shylo gasped and backed away from him. "I hope my *uncle Grover* never finds out that I let myself be escorted to California by a madman like you. Why, you're no gentleman at all, let alone a Greek god. You're nothing but a goddang Greek—period!"

The woman's eyes were bluer and hotter than the blazing Arizona skies overhead, and her breasts were rising and falling with the force of her anger. Between her statement and the wild, savage look of her, Dimitri couldn't have stopped himself from forcefully taking her into his arms if he'd wanted to. He jerked her up against his body, his voice a low, dark growl as he said, "And don't you or your uncle ever forget it, because that's exactly all I am, woman."

She tried to shrink away from him then, a shadow of fear crossing her exquisite features, but Dimitri's grip remained firm around her waist and shoulders. His eyes glittering with equal parts of rage and sudden, painful desire, he became fully aware of Shylo as a woman—a woman he wanted so badly, he could almost taste her, even though thoughts of wrapping his fingers around her throat and squeezing seemed almost as intense a need. Aware finally that he'd gone way beyond the limits of decorum, Dimitri set her away from him.

"It is getting late," he said, his voice harsh. "I think we should not worry who is in blame for our troubles, but better if we try to find a way to get that wheel fixed." He glanced at the sky, noting that the slowly sinking sun was already draping the pastel mountains in glorious shades of purple and crimson.

Then he lowered his head and pinned her with a heated, purposeful gaze. "It will be dark soon. Believe me when I say that you do not want to be left out here alone with this 'goddang' Greek for the night."

8

Much to their mutual chagrin, by the time Shylo and Dimitri managed to free the wheel and repair two of the three broken spokes with the branches of a creosote bush, the hour had moved beyond dusk, leaving them with no choice but to spend the night where they had broken down. Dimitri's temper had cooled considerably by then, too, and after assuring Shylo that she really had nothing to fear from him, they finished the fried chicken the hotel had prepared for them and settled down for the evening. Although neither of them was particularly pleased by these arrangements, they decided there would be less danger if they slept in the back of the wagon and left the warm desert sands to the more hostile creatures of the night: rattlesnakes, gila monsters, and scorpions among their numbers.

As the moonless sky progressed slowly toward

dawn, releasing its grip on the utter darkness, Shylo drifted in and out of sleep, aware not only of the man lying beside her, but of how indecently close she'd gotten to him while she slept. When they'd bedded down, the gap between them had been as wide as the rig's walls would allow, but sometime during the night Shylo figured she must have gravitated toward Dimitri, most probably seeking his warmth. Even though temperatures during the daylight hours had been blazing, the desert was surprisingly chilly after the sun went down. What other reason could there be for her to awaken and find herself snuggled up against this otherwise unapproachable man, her head nestled into the crook of his arm?

Dimitri stirred then, tugging her hair in the process, and Shylo realized that her braid had slipped loose of its bonds—and that one of Dimitri's hands was tangled in her tresses. Another accident of the night? she wondered. She breathed deeply, inhaling the essence of a man who'd toiled without rest until darkness kept him from completing his task. Surprisingly enough, his scent did not offend her, but rather beckoned her, prompting her to wriggle even closer to him, to slide her hand up to the center of his chest, where her fingers lingered, tracing the outline of the dark curls just beneath his shirt.

At these exploratory caresses, Dimitri stirred again. He rolled toward Shylo, swung the hand that was not tangled in her hair across her hip, and tugged her close to his body in a very possessive, intimate embrace. Yet he did not seem to be awake. He inhaled deeply, let out his breath in a long, sleepy sigh, then murmured something far too low for her to understand. The impact of this whispered prattle, however, was no less potent. The sound of his melodic voice, coupled with his clean, honest scent and sensuously warm embrace, collided within Shylo, striking a match deep in her belly, a flame that grew hotter and blazed a wider path through her body with each passing moment. Could these be the sensations she'd been seeking as she'd edged toward him in slumber?

Impossible! Until the moment she dropped off to sleep, Shylo had still been furious with Dimitri, blaming him for everything from Cassie's plight, to the broken wheel, to the fact that she had only a scratchy woolen horse blanket with which to cover herself for the night. Between the loose equine hairs clinging to her nose and mouth and the pungent, unrelenting aroma of stale horse sweat, she'd almost opted to sleep directly on the wooden floor of the wagon, with only her thin lawn dress to protect her from the elements. Of course, that was before the noises had begun.

Just as Shylo finally had started to drift off to sleep, an owl had punctuated the quiet with a series of queries, bringing her fully alert again. Shortly after that, the mournful barking of coyotes had begun echoing off canyon walls, some yelping in such high-pitched tones that she'd wondered if they weren't tearing each other to bits. Finally, adding the most frightening sound of all to the cacophony, the shrill, ominous cry of a killdeer, night bird of the desert, had filled the air.

She'd been truly frightened then, more so than at any time during their journey, but had managed to fall asleep in spite of her fears. Perhaps those sounds combined with the chill in the air had driven her to seek Dimitri's embrace—though Shylo still couldn't understand how she'd wound up in his arms. She knew only one thing for sure right now: a deep sense of belonging had come over her as she lay enveloped in Dimitri's embrace, a feeling akin, she supposed, to this imaginary thing called love.

Whatever it was, she couldn't remember having felt anything like it in her entire life. She'd experienced almost the same sensations in his room when he'd pressed her so tenderly against his chest, making her think that he cared just a little bit. Of course, that had all been a part of an act, a way of impressing the president's niece. What would he do if he knew the woman he'd performed for was nothing but an impostor? Not a socialite or debutante, but a penniless orphan? She had an idea he would loathe her for the terrible lies she told, and that the fit of anger she'd witnessed in him yesterday would seem like a minor irritation.

As that deep sense of belonging gave way to her usual loneliness, Shylo stared up at the cluster of stars high overhead. Even the mood of the desert as dawn approached seemed to reflect her empty existence. All was still, too still. The animals of the night were quiet now, burrowing into dens to sleep through the blistering day, while the sun-loving creatures remained hidden in slumber, the air too cold yet to venture out in the open. Nothing stirred, not even distant memories of a mother's love.

An eerie calm had claimed the land around her, as if sound didn't exist at all. Maybe, Shylo thought, she'd been right all along. Maybe love didn't exist, either.

Just an hour later Cassie sat at the mouth of the cave and watched the sky change from gray to pale peach as a big red sun appeared, casting fantastic shadows on the surrounding mountains. Buck had

gathered up his saddlebags and her valise, then gone
off to collect his horse. Soon they would be on their
way to Winslow, where Shylo would probably be
waiting, worried sick by now. It troubled Cassie to
think of her sister fretting over her safety, but she
couldn't seem to stop trying to work out a way for her
and Buck to stay together a little longer. Even one
more night would help ease their parting and take this
awful hurting out of her chest.

When he finally rode up a few minutes later, then
hollered at her to climb down to him, Cassie admitted
the truth to herself at last. It was over for the time
being, maybe even forever. Her heart breaking, she
followed his instructions and gingerly made her way
down the side of the hill, careful not to drag the hem
of Shylo's pretty blue dress along the colorful sandstone path.

"Hot damn!" said Buck when she came into view.
"Where you been hiding that getup?"

Cassie blushed, as she did whenever he compli-
mented her. "It's my sister's, and the only decent dress
we got between us. I was hoping when you saw me in
it, you'd just naturally want to keep me around a little
longer, or maybe even come with me to California
now."

"Aw, sugar face, you know I cain't do that." He
leaned down, stuck out his hand, and tugged her up
to the front of his saddle. "But now that I see what I'll
be missing, maybe you ought to check that post office
in about two weeks instead of three or four. I don't
know if I can wait any longer than that to set eyes on
you again." He laughed deeply, nuzzled her behind
the ear, then spurred his big white horse.

They rode away from their little cave, Buck's hands

full of leather reins and a squirming Cassie, who was busy showering him with kisses, and headed due south. They stayed mostly in the washes, following the natural curves of the land, but occasionally Buck would guide his mount up the side of one of the numerous hills in order to scan the horizon for signs of riders. It was as they crested the third peak that he saw movement in the distance. After spurring the horse back down the hill, Buck slipped his spyglass out of the saddlebags and belly-crawled up the side of the mountain again.

He brought the scope to his eye, scanned the countryside, then gestured for Cassie to join him.

"What is it?" she asked breathlessly.

"Get down, dammit!"

"But I can't ruin this dress, too. It ain't even mine."

Buck reached up, grabbed Cassie's hand, and jerked her off her feet. Never had he spoken to her in such a harsh manner, much less treated her so roughly. "You're hurting me, Buck," she cried, "and you—"

"I'm truly sorry about that, girl," he cut in, "but do you think that dress won't get ruint or you won't get hurt even worse if someone was to put a bullet hole through your gizzard? You were a-standing there in broad daylight like first prize at a turkey shoot!"

She gasped and scanned the horizon. "You mean the posse's caught up to us?"

"Somebody has. I cain't tell how many's out there for sure, but I can see two of them, and one's wearing a big ole sunbonnet and a dress." He handed her the spyglass. "Take a look and see if that ain't your sister."

It took Cassie a minute to adjust the glass to her eye, then find the exact spot Buck was telling her to look, but when she finally brought the intruders into view, she cried, "Oh, it is! It's Shylo . . . and Dimitri, too!"

"Hush your mouth, girl! Or are you looking to get me shot and kilt?"

"No! Oh, no." Cassie threw her arms around his neck. "I love you, Buck, you know I do. I'd die if you got killed."

"Well, I love you, too. That's why we got to get moving, and fast."

She pulled away from him. "But can't I just sit in the middle of the wash and wait for Shylo and her Greek fella to come across me?"

"I don't think so, sugar pie. Looks to me like they're packing up and heading south, away from the badlands. We're gonna have to circle around them and do it in short order before they make it out to the flats. Otherwise you're gonna have one *hell* of a long walk ahead of you."

Because there was really no other option, Buck didn't wait for Cassie to agree with the plan. He just gave her a shove to get her started down the sandstone hill in tobogganing fashion. The sled beneath her bottom was Shylo's pretty sateen dress.

"About last night. I, ah . . . "

Dimitri cleared his throat and tried again. "It was never my intention to keep you out overnight in the first place, and I surely didn't mean to compromise your reputation by . . . What I'm trying to say is that I never thought to—no, I didn't expect to wake up and . . . Oh, the *hell* with it!"

Dimitri had been working on a long overdue apology to Shylo, ever since she had disappeared a few minutes ago in order to accomplish her morning ablutions in private. She hadn't reappeared yet, but she might as well have. He was pretty sure he could stand in the middle of this wash all day and still never come up with just the right phrase to make everything all right again. He, a man who'd experienced no difficulties in coming up with enough words to fill a hundred-page master's thesis, couldn't seem to find a way to say "I'm sorry. Please don't demand that I marry you because of this."

Of course Shylo had every right to do just that, and he could do no less than make the offer. Through his own carelessness, he *had* placed her in a scandalous situation that might do irreparable damage to her reputation. Even if he couldn't be held responsible for the accident or the nasty remarks he'd made to her yesterday, apologies were certainly in order for the compromising position he'd wrestled her into as she slept.

He'd somehow managed to drag Shylo into his arms during the night, cradled her against his body, and worked his fingers into her glorious hair, freeing it from the braid she'd fashioned the previous evening. It was bad enough to wake up and find he'd taken such intimate liberties with her as she lay helpless—not to mention his body's lightning responses to her soft curves—but when he met her wide-eyed gaze and realized that she'd awakened before him, Dimitri had realized his fate was pretty well sealed. She'd known what he'd been up to during the night, and now he had no choice but to marry her. Assuming, of course, that she would even have a scoundrel like him.

Glancing over his shoulder once again, Dimitri saw that Shylo was coming his way, looking like a fresh-picked daisy among the barren hills. "Are you ready to go now?" he asked as she drew near.

"All set," she said, brushing past him on her way to the front of the wagon.

Shylo had fluffed her new yellow dress and petticoats to make them look less bedraggled than before, tucked her hair up under the wide-brimmed bonnet, then pulled the hat down low to hide as much of her face as possible. She wasn't about to risk eye contact with Dimitri—not before she absolutely had to, anyway, for she wasn't quite sure what had gone through his mind when he'd awakened to find her sprawled across his chest this morning. God only knew what he thought she'd been up to, and since she wasn't quite sure herself, she wasn't about to risk a conversation that might lead to a discussion about her shameful behavior.

So they traveled in the same awkward silence they'd awakened to, speaking to each other only to agree on the direction to take each time they came to a fork. Other than that, Shylo dwelled on the steady clop, clop, clop of the mule's hooves against the soft sand and imagined that she heard the phantomlike sound of Cassie's voice calling her name over and over, as she'd done in her sleep so often of late. With her mind fully on her sister again, Shylo was close to breaking down over the thought that she might never see her again when Dimitri abruptly reined in the mule.

"Listen!" he said. "Do you hear that?"

Trying to ignore the familiar sound of Cassie's sweet voice ringing in the back her mind, Shylo strained to pick out another sound. Other than the howling wind, nothing met her ears. "It's just the wind," she replied.

"But I was sure there was a woman's voice. I

thought . . . I don't mean to get your hopes up, but I could have sworn I heard her calling your name."

Shylo whipped her head around. "You mean you heard it, *too?*"

"A woman's voice, yes. You heard this as well?"

Staring out at the wash ahead of her, Shylo listened hard, this time trusting her ears. When she heard Cassie's voice again, she cried, "Oh, my God! It *is* her! I thought I'd imagined . . . "

She didn't give herself time to finish the sentence but leapt off the side of the wagon and dashed head-long down the wash, calling, "Cassie! Cassie, where are you? It's me, Shylo! Cassie . . . *Cassie!*" Over her rapid breathing, she finally heard an answering cry.

"Over here, Shylo! Can you find me? I'm over here."

Following the sound, Shylo zigzagged up the side of a small mountain, then scanned the sandy valley below. Up ahead at the fork, she caught a flash of bright blue material. "Don't move!" she said, hollering at the top of her lungs. "I'll be right there."

Behind her Shylo could hear a man's voice—a very angry man's voice—shouting at her, but she paid it no heed. Without so much as a glance back, she raced down the hill, the hem of her new dress catching on her shoes, and stumbled toward the point where she'd seen the flash of blue.

A moment later the sisters met in a collision of ribbons, petticoats, and bonnets knocked askew. When the initial hugs and kisses were over, and she could finally bear to tear herself away from the sister she loved so dearly, Shylo held her at arm's length, tears streaming down her face, and looked her over carefully.

Choking back a sob, she said, "Are you all right? You don't look too worse for the wear."

"I'm fine," Cassie said, even though guilt over the way she'd let her sister worry had twisted her belly into a painful knot. "They didn't hurt me a'tall."

Not believing her for one minute, a more collected Shylo took Cassie's face in her hands and turned her head first this way, then the other. "No bruises. What about the rest of you? Are you bleeding anywhere?"

Cassie fiddled with the hangnail on her thumb. "I already told you—they didn't hurt me a bit. They just kept me a while, then turned me loose. I'm fine."

But Shylo knew her sister better than that. She was hiding something. "You can tell me anything, and you know it. Tell me what they done, and I'll see that they pay for it with their lives." Cassie's gaze fell to the ground, and Shylo was sure then that there was a *lot* she wasn't telling. "Did they make a grab for you, or try to, ah . . . mess with your nuptials?"

Her cheeks hot and glowing, Cassie had to bite her lip to stop a secretive grin from popping up. Keeping her head and eyes down low, she said quietly, "I told you once, and I'll tell you again. They didn't hurt me none."

Shylo probably would have kept at her no matter how hard Cassie tried to reassure her if she hadn't heard a tremendous roar from overhead at that moment. Someone had shouted a word that sounded a hell of a lot like her own name. She turned, glanced up at the mountaintop, and saw Dimitri planted there. The morning sun was at his back, making him look like a large, dark shadow. She could see that he held the blacksmith's rifle high in one strong hand, while the other, fist clenched, was raised to the heavens.

"Can you *never* listen to what I say to you, woman? I am responsible for your safety! What of the bandits?"

Bandits? Shylo had forgotten all about them in her joy at spotting Cassie. She quickly glanced around. "There's none down here," she called back, then whispered to her sister, "They are gone, aren't they?"

Resisting the urge to look back to where she'd last seen Buck, Cassie said, "They lit out of here days ago."

When Shylo looked up to Dimitri to report this news, she saw that he was scanning the surrounding mountaintops, still holding the rifle with one hand, the butt tight against his hip as if he'd brandished a weapon in such a manner before. She cupped her mouth to call out to him, but he held up his free hand, silencing her, then waved to her and Cassie, beckoning them to join him.

"I thought I heard a horse riding off in the distance," he explained when the women reached the crest of the hill. "Let's get out of here so we're not quite so vulnerable in case they return." With that he led them back to the wagon, helped them aboard, then joined them on the bench seat and cracked the whip over the mule's back.

After they were under way again, Dimitri leaned forward, caught Cassie's gaze, and directed his questions to her. "Did you say the bandits left you here by yourself *days* ago?"

She nodded.

This made absolutely no sense to Dimitri. "Why did they take you in the first place if they meant to leave you behind?"

Prepared for this interrogation, Cassie gave him the answers she and Buck had worked out. "They just took me along as insurance in case the sheriff lit after them. Soon as they got this far, they stuck me inside a cave with enough food and water for a coupla days, then rode off and left me be. I run out of water last night, so I started for Winslow early this morning."

Shylo turned to her sister in surprise. "You *knew* to go to Winslow?"

"The bandits told me I ought to go there, and where to pick up the trail and such. I probably should have left for town yesterday when it looked like I was going to run out of water, but I was hoping a posse would have come along by now and saved me the trouble."

The girl's story still didn't make a lot of sense to Dimitri, and he suspected there was a lot more to it than she was willing to tell. Assuming her ordeal was probably too horrible to discuss in mixed company, he decided not to press her further. "I'm glad we found you when we did. I'm not sure you would have survived the walk to town."

"I'm glad you come along, too! I got scared out here by myself. You should hear the strange noises around here at night!"

Shylo was able to commiserate with her on that point, even though she was sure there was more to Cassie's abduction than she'd let on. "I think I heard those same noises just last night, and I don't mind telling you—they scared the living hell out of me."

"Last night?" Cassie cocked her head, looked from her sister to the handsome Greek, then gasped. "Alone? Just the two of you?"

Dimitri sat back out of Cassie's view and turned away from the women. That observation had pretty well slammed the door to any hopes he still entertained about not having to make an offer of marriage to Shylo. Now there was a witness who could attest to their night alone—one who, he decided as he heard her chuckling to herself, would take great delight in seeing that he paid for the injuries to her mistress's reputation.

His voice grim, he explained the situation, even if it wouldn't do him much good. "We had an accident with the wagon while looking for you yesterday, Miss McBride, and were forced into staying the night. Believe me when I say that no harm came to your employer on my account. Of course, I do intend to make these unfortunate circumstances right somehow when we get back to civilization."

Cassie wasn't quite sure what he meant by "make these unfortunate circumstances right," but she was fascinated by the idea that perhaps her sister had found true love in the same way she had. Grinning, she leaned in close to Shylo. Her expression reversed itself, and her train of thought derailed when she caught a whiff of her. "Pee-*hew,*" she said, holding her nose. "Do you know that you smell like a horse that's been rode hard and put up wet?"

That comment made Shylo feel almost as happy as she had when she saw the trail of brick-colored stains all over the back of the blue sateen dress Cassie was wearing; but just having her sister back safe and sound made even those things seem trivial.

"You don't smell a hell of a lot like a rose yourself."

The women shared a hardy laugh over that, and Shylo draped her arm across Cassie's shoulders, squeezing her with a renewed burst of enthusiasm. Everything would be all right now. Soon they would resume their journey to California to reacquaint themselves with their mother, and nothing would ever trouble them again. Nothing, Shylo thought, could upset her now that the McBride sisters were together again.

Absolutely, positively . . . *nothing.*

9

Even though they cut several miles off the distance to town by taking a direct route from the badlands, it still took the tiring mule better than four hours to reach Winslow. After returning the rig and paying for the damaged wheel, a nearly penniless Dimitri insisted that Shylo and Cassie accompany him to the marshal's office, where they could relay the story of the younger woman's abduction and release, as well as provide a description of the outlaws to aid the authorities in their search for the men.

The marshal, who'd been napping on his chair, nearly fell out of it when Dimitri and the ladies stepped into his office and slammed the door behind them.

"Morning, folks." He blinked up at them, rubbing his eyes. "What can I do for you?"

"In case you've forgotten," Dimitri began, irritated

to think that the man didn't remember them or their troubles, "Miss Folsom and I were relieved of our capital while traveling on the train that was robbed, and her companion, Miss McBride, was taken hostage by those same bandits. Miss Folsom tried to convince you to round up a . . . a—"

"Posse," Shylo supplied.

"Thank you. A posse to go look for her friend, but if you'll recall, you wouldn't do it. This"—he gestured toward Cassie—"is Miss McBride. We went after her ourselves and thought you might be interested in her story. Who knows? Once she gives you their descriptions, you may even think of going after the bandits yourself—if you're not too busy, of course."

Filled with sudden admiration for Dimitri, Shylo gave him a broad smile. Perhaps he wasn't quite as indifferent to those around him as she'd thought.

The marshal, obviously filled with something other than admiration, jumped out of his chair, adjusted his holster, then spat an angry stream of tobacco juice into a bucket near his feet. "Like I said before, the sheriff from Holbrook is gonna take care of getting a posse when he gets here! As for the lady's ordeal"—he glanced at her and flicked his finger against the brim of his hat but didn't attempt to remove it—"I'm terrible sorry to hear about your troubles, ma'am, but it don't look to me like you're in too bad a fix now."

Dimitri bristled, looking as if he might just leap across the desk and take the man's head off. Shylo might have encouraged him to do it, too, if not for a deepening sense of urgency over resuming her long anticipated journey. As much as she'd have liked to see the smirk wiped off the marshal's face, she couldn't let Dimitri jeopardize the reunion with her mother. If he attacked the lawman, he'd probably wind up in jail, leaving her and Cassie without escorts—or money, for that matter.

She slipped her hand into the crook of Dimitri's elbow. "Let's go," she said, forcing a light tone. "This man is not interested in catching the outlaws. Maybe we can wire a description of the bandits to Holbrook."

"There's no point in doing that," said Cassie. "They never took their masks off. Folks on the train saw them as well as I did."

Sighing heavily, Shylo gave Dimitri's arm a tug. "Like I said, we might as well go." Thinking they could be on their way without further incidence, she took a step toward the door.

"Hold on a minute, folks." The marshal's nasal twang stopped Shylo cold in her tracks. "You ain't going anywhere just yet."

Dimitri took Shylo's hand from his arm, preparing for the scuffle he thought he heard in the man's tone. "And why not, if you don't mind my asking?"

"As it turns out, I don't mind a bit." He hooked his thumbs in his belt and rocked on his heels. "You're another one of them foreigners, ain't you? I can tell by the funny way you talk."

"I am visiting here from Athena, if that's what you mean."

"Athena?" He scratched his head. "Where in tarnation is that?"

"Athens." The man still didn't understand, and even though Dimitri was rapidly losing what little patience he had left, he explained further. "Athens is the capital of Greece, which is in the Mediterranean, as is Italy, Egypt, Turkey—"

"I get it!" The marshal scowled, then relaxed a little as his expression spread into the lazy grin of a hungry coyote. "You traveling with that other Greek fella, by any chance?"

Dimitri's spine stiffened. "You mean Ari?"

The marshal glanced down at the papers on his desk. "I'm talking about one Aristotle Cotsomething—Ari, I guess. You with him?"

Although Dimitri had the distinct impression that this was not a good time to admit the relationship, he said, "Mr. Kotsala is my uncle. What's happened, and where is he?"

The marshal threw back his head and laughed. "That old man is where he's gonna be a good long time if you don't come up with the two hundred bucks he owes Murphy Springer over at the Red Dog Saloon."

"Two hundred dollars!" Dimitri and Shylo echoed the words at precisely the same time.

"A-yep." Marshal Moss cocked his thumb over his shoulder. "Got your uncle locked up in the back room. He tells me he ain't got no money, so that's where he'll be staying until someone pays up for him. If no one does, I expect when the sheriff gets here, he'll haul him off to Holbrook with him."

The weary, frustrated trio let out a collective sigh. Then Dimitri, who could hardly believe that yet another misfortune had befallen them, said to the marshal, "I'll be back to discuss the reasons you felt you had to detain my uncle shortly. Then we'll see if we can't figure out a way to settle his bill. First, I think it'd be best if I saw the ladies to their hotel."

*   *   *

Fifteen minutes later Dimitri joined his uncle in his makeshift cell, a tiny room connected to the marshal's main log cabin featuring rough-hewn walls, a cot, and nothing else. No windows, no chairs, and just one door that led to the marshal's office. Ari was sitting on the edge of his narrow bed, his aching head hanging almost as low as the miserable excuse for a mattress.

Dimitri, who'd already explained his excursion with Shylo into the desert, was still venting a considerable amount of spleen over the tale his uncle had just told him.

"How *could* you," he said, speaking in his native language, "have believed for one minute that you would become proficient at this poker card game in one night? It took you years of practice to become an expert at backgammon. What made you think this western game would be any different?"

Ari shrugged and, like his nephew, spoke Greek. Unlike his nephew, his voice had a decided nasal tone because of a badly broken nose. "I met some American cowboys, men who work for the Aztec Land and Cattle Company raising Texas longhorn—"

"I'm not interested in them. Tell me what happened to you."

"I am, my son, I am." He gingerly dabbed a handkerchief beneath his constantly dripping nostrils. "These men, Hashknife cowboys, they are called, invited me to join their game. The card parlor offered no other games of chance, so I accepted when these Hashknifes said that poker was a simple game to learn, and that they would teach me all the rules."

Dimitri stopped pacing and drew in a deep breath. There was no point in going over the details again, for each time the story came out the same. Ari either had

misunderstood those rules or had been misled by the
cowboys. Then, when it became apparent that he'd
been duped, he'd complained loudly that he'd been
cheated out of what little money he'd had on him. The
cowboys, who didn't take kindly to being called
cheaters, had taken Ari to task over the insult.

Although he had put up a good fight, when the
ruckus finally ended Ari had been pinned to the floor
by a pair of burly Hashknife cowboys. Now his nose
was broken in two places, and his knuckles looked as
if he'd sharpened a pair of sheep shears with them. It
certainly explained why the old man hadn't returned
to the hotel by the time Dimitri and Shylo left for the
badlands, but that was about all it did. Now they had
to come up with two hundred dollars to pay for "damages" done to the Red Dog Saloon—and do it by
morning or they'd miss the next train to San Diego!

His temper flaring anew, Dimitri began to pace the
stifling cubicle again as he went over in his mind all
they'd been through.

"This entire trip to America has become a bigger
challenge and even more puzzling than the Pyra-
mids!" He shot his uncle a narrow gaze. "You do realize, don't you, that if we miss the train tomorrow,
we'll have to wait four more days for the next one?"

Nodding carefully, for the slightest movement
jarred his swollen nose, Ari said, "I know, but there
doesn't seem to be much I can do about it except say
I'm sorry again."

"Sorry won't get us out of this predicament. We
barely have enough money to cover our hotel rooms
for the night and one good meal. Do you realize the
position you've put me in?"

Ari frowned without thinking, then winced with

pain. "I don't know exactly which position you're referring to."

Coming to a halt directly in front of his uncle, Dimitri hunkered down so he could look him in the eye. "The very position I'd hoped to avoid. Between the unchaperoned night I was forced to spend with Miss Folsom and the needless expense you've incurred for us in the name of gambling, it looks like the only way out of this mess is a rather hasty wedding. *Mine!*"

Ari tried to smile, but it hurt too much. "I can think of worse positions, my son. She will make you a lovely wife, not to mention that you will be regarded as a very important man both here and at home."

Uninterested in either a wife or his own stature, Dimitri grumbled as he wondered how Shylo would react to his proposal—and, later, to life in Greece. Then he recalled how she'd responded to their accident in the badlands. He couldn't help but admire the way she'd hiked up her skirts and joined in to help dig the wheel out with no encouragement from him whatsoever. No complaining about the actual labor or circumstances, she had just wielded that shovel as if she'd been doing manual labor all of her life.

Even when it became obvious they'd have to spend the night in the desert, Shylo hadn't complained, worried about appearances, or made a fuss over her hard "mattress." An interesting enigma, this woman, but confusing at any rate. How could someone of her caliber and upbringing be so well suited for such inconveniences?

Then he suddenly realized that she might also be a woman who would not object in the least to working alongside him at archaeological dig sites. This thought, as attractive as it seemed, wasn't quite good enough, however, to keep him from brooding over the troubles at hand.

Dimitri stood up and shook his head incredulously. "I still cannot believe that I've managed to get myself into such a hell of a mess since coming to this country!" He went on, talking more to himself than to Ari. "My uncle is in jail, owing hundreds of dollars in a town run by dishonest cowboys; we have less than ten dollars between us, yet I am expected to convince the woman I've compromised—through no fault of my own, I might add—to become my bride. And *if* this woman should agree to the marriage, I have to assume that her beloved companion—a young lady who, in case you haven't noticed, sports *purple* hair—will also become a part of our lives."

"Ah, all sad but true," said Ari, "but you forget the bright side—part of Miss Folsom's dowry includes a close connection to a United States president and, I would guess, a large amount of money. You may not need to worry about chasing down the funds your uncle stole from the business after this match is made."

Dimitri had forgotten all about Niko, but now that he'd been reminded of the reason for making the trip to California in the first place—a confrontation with a man who might or might not be his uncle Niko—it seemed insignificant in the face of all that had happened since he'd left New York. In fact, Dimitri wasn't even sure that settling the score with his father's brother mattered anymore. All he really wanted to do now was go back to the university and reclaim his well-ordered life.

"Dimitri?" Ari snapped his fingers to recapture his

nephew's attention. "Since we have so little time left if we even hope to clear up matters here before tomorrow's train arrives, don't you think you ought to get right over to the hotel? Even with your considerable attributes, I'm afraid that convincing the young lady to marry you on such short notice may not be as easy as I once thought."

In the time it took Dimitri to convince Shylo that what he had to say needed to be discussed in private, and that Cassie would be quite all right if left alone for a little while, he was pretty sure he had used up all of his powers of persuasion. Now that he finally had her sitting with him in a secluded corner of the hotel lobby, he absolutely couldn't bring himself to begin the proposal. If he'd had a choice, apologizing for unintentionally assaulting her as she'd slept in the wagon suddenly seemed like the easier task.

Shylo drummed her fingers against the arm of her chair. "I'm going back to my room to stay with Cassie if you don't start talking this minute. You know I didn't want to come down here in the first place."

"All right, all right." Damn! Why couldn't Ari be here instead of him? Dimitri cleared his suddenly dry throat, reached for Shylo's hand, and sandwiched it between his own. Anything else? he wondered. Should he drop to one knee? Two? Or remain where he was, seated beside her? Opting for the less embarrassing solution, he stayed put, cleared his throat again, and began the one assignment all his years of schooling had not prepared him for.

"A lot has happened to us in the last few days, most of it terribly unexpected and unfortunate."

"I know that," she said. "I was there. Tell me something I don't already know."

Adaptable and blunt, too, he thought. Certainly not the best combination for a wife of his to possess, but something he would have to work out with Shylo later. Right now he had to convince her to become his wife in the first place.

"I've been thinking about this for some time, since we left New York, actually. . . . " Dimitri paused to loosen the collar of his shirt. "After what happened, I speak of our . . . impossible, no, I think *improper* night alone together, not our fault, in the desert. We must take ourselves and correct it, soon, and not because . . . " His thoughts weren't falling into the right pattern—at least not for English—and Dimitri was pretty sure his words were coming out every bit as mixed up. He sighed heavily. "Swiftness is, I think, what I'm saying, and what I hope you understand."

Shylo stared at Dimitri as if he'd suddenly grown an enormous wart between his eyes. "Pardon my language, please, but I have no idea what in *hell* you are talking about."

Outspoken, too, yet another character deficit to be dealt with. "I will try again." Dimitri heard himself gulp, unaware that he'd even swallowed. "I'm talking about courtship—yours and mine—and not to have one."

"Our courtship?" Had her behavior in the desert disgusted him so much that he planned to leave her behind? Feeling shocked, and disappointed somehow, Shylo tried to tug her hand out of his grip, but Dimitri held her fast. Tears filled her throat, not only surprising her but drowning her with horror. She couldn't burst into tears in front of Dimitri, not now, and not over something like this—his rejection of her!

Leaning heavily on her anger, she snapped, "Maybe you're the one who misunderstood! I never wanted you to court me. In fact, I hope I never see you again, you big-headed, overblown—"

"Is you misunderstood," he said, cutting her off. "I sometimes have trouble with English when I'm nervous or upset. I am both of these right now. Please excuse me."

"Well . . . maybe. That depends on what you're trying to say."

Thinking of yet another task ahead of him—the curbing of her volatile temper—Dimitri inched closer to Shylo, bringing her within kissing distance, and finally got to the proposal. "I say that I think it could be very profitable for us to combine our assets."

"Combine our assets?" This made less sense to her than anything he'd said so far. "You mean like go into business with each other?"

"In a manner of speaking, yes." Dimitri tried to swallow again, but by now his throat felt as if it were lined in lamb's wool. "Forgive my awkward presentation, but I have never done this before. In fact, if we were in my country, I wouldn't have to do it at all. A matchmaker, someone like Ari, would be speaking to you, not me."

A little tickle of alarm raised the hair on her scalp. "A matchmaker? Why on earth would one of them be talking to me?

"He would be asking you, and I would hope, in much finer words, if you would become my wife." He gulped. "Will you please to do this?"

The hand Dimitri wasn't holding flew to Shylo's throat. *His wife?* Of all that she'd imagined when he'd first come to her room, none of her suppositions even came close to this! She was thrilled, to be sure, for not only was this her first proposal, but to have it come from a man such as this was sweeter than fresh-cut clover. Imagine that! But her euphoria quickly gave way to suspicion. Why ask *her,* of all people? She'd let down her guard around Dimitri often enough of late that he most certainly knew she was not quite the polished lady he'd met back in New York. Surely this Greek god could have his pick of women, debutantes who fit into his esteemed circles and understood him when he got to talking in fancy words. Selecting an impostor like her simply didn't make sense.

But then that thought prompted Shylo to remember something Victoria Vanderkellen had mentioned back in New York: if there was one thing a Greek man couldn't resist, it was politics.

Her tone ringing with sarcasm, she asked, "This sudden urge to marry me wouldn't have anything to do with my dear uncle, would it?"

Dimitri knew he could hardly lie to her about that—especially after the things he'd said to her in anger when the wheel broke. And since he wasn't familiar with American customs or how she might view the Greek method of matrimony—as much business as pleasure—he tempered the truth a little with a slight distortion.

Caressing the back of her hand with his thumb, he said, "Your uncle's esteemed position does, of course, carry a certain attractiveness, but Ari and I believe a union between us would be of benefit in many other ways as well. What do you think?"

Shylo didn't know whether to believe him or not, but she did know this much—courtship, engagements, and marriage were areas in which she had almost zero knowledge. And the little she had learned was enough to convince her that Dimitri's proposal seemed a little cold. She still couldn't understand why he'd want to hitch his wagon to hers.

"I—I don't know what to say or think, Dimitri. This is a real surprise to me, and . . . frankly, it sounds more like you're proposing a business deal than a marriage."

Relaxed again, he chuckled softly, still stroking her hand. "Yes, I suppose it does, since my culture is so different from yours. In Greece, romantic love, or whatever you want to call it, is not a requirement when arranging a marriage."

"You mean Greeks don't believe in love?"

"Of course they do, but to have a perfectly sound marriage, this sentiment is not a requirement." Recognizing an obstacle he hadn't thought of, he said, "Is marrying for love so very important to you?"

"*Me?* Oh, goodness, no!" The minute the words were out, Shylo could almost taste the lie in them. But she laughed it off and went on. "I'm not even sure love exists, to tell you the truth."

Immensely pleased to know she wouldn't require a heavy emotional investment from him, Dimitri joined her laughter. "If love didn't exist, I believe many of our lives would be far less complicated." Then he added boldly, "May I assume that we have an agreement?"

Shylo glanced into his dark eyes, then quickly averted her gaze. She could hardly believe that if her next word was "yes," she might actually become Mrs. Dimitri Adonis! She gave herself a moment of fantasy, imagining the look on her mother's face if she were to show up in San Diego with this man as her husband and not simply as an escort. How pleased Colleen would be to see what her daughter had done for herself! Surely she would not be able even to think of rejecting her again.

But there were drawbacks to accepting as well. Marrying the man would mean the end of her independence. She would have to play "wife" in every aspect imaginable, she supposed. Was ensuring her mother's acceptance worth the sacrifice she would have to make—the giving of herself, of her very *life,* to Dimitri? Weighed down with indecision, Shylo sighed.

"You have doubts?" Dimitri asked. "Tell me what they are, and perhaps I can ease your fears."

"Well . . . " She hedged, trying to find just the right way to express her concerns, then did what usually worked best for her. She came right out with it. "I was wondering exactly what's in it for me if I say yes."

She was so very, *very* blunt. But he chuckled as he said, "For one thing, the respected Adonis name and the import business that goes with it." He considered telling her the financial difficulties the company was having but decided against it. He was trying to further his cause, not weaken it, and he doubted she'd be interested in a discussion about money in any case. Searching for added inducements, he recalled Shylo's reactions to his embrace on the train. He smiled deeply. "For another, I believe we are well suited to one another in at least one very important area."

Before she could ask what he meant, Dimitri glanced around the hotel lobby to make sure no one could see them in their corner. The clerk at the cigar stand was reading a magazine, and other than that, the lobby was empty. Releasing the fingers he'd been caressing, he slid his hand along the side of her cheek, stroking the even softer skin there with the pad of his thumb. Then he lowered his mouth to hers.

The kiss was gentle but brief, a lure, a promise of things to come. When Dimitri pulled away from her mouth and his gaze lingered there, Shylo's lips followed his automatically, hungry for more.

Pleased by her reaction, not to mention his sudden and very intense response to the slick, satiny feel of her mouth beneath his own, Dimitri's voice plummeted to a low, dark whisper as he said, "We make a very *good* match, I would say. What do you say?"

Her gaze riveted to his lips, to the deep, entrancing cleft of the upper one, she echoed, "A good match."

"Then you have no further concerns about a marriage to me?"

If she did, Shylo couldn't think of what they might be. She couldn't think at all. "I . . . " She shrugged.

Dimitri was all set to pronounce them man and wife right there on the spot, but one other consideration crossed his mind. In all fairness he really had to give her some idea of the kind of life she would be living. Again he took her hand.

"Before we strike an agreement, I think I should make it clear to you that I have no intention of running the family business once we return to Greece." If the idea of moving to another country shocked her, she gave no indication, so he went on. "My true calling is archaeology, and I plan to spend most of my time at the University of Athena. I hope that will not be a problem for you."

This snapped her out of her fugue. "University? Are you going to college?"

"Yes," he said with a laugh. "I have been going to school for some time now—most of my life, in fact. I expect to get my Ph.D. within six months, and after that, I plan to teach at the university."

"When you say teach, you mean to say that you're gonna be a college *professor?*"

"Yes. Through the doctorate program, I already teach a small group of students." Or at least that's what he should have been doing instead of crossing this strange country of America.

Shylo was agog. Never in all her life had she known anyone smart enough to be a college professor, much less dreamed that a person of such great intelligence would ask her to be his wife. Her mind spinning with possibilities, she dared to put words to her second fondest dream.

"If I was to marry you, do you think you could teach me like you do your students?"

"You mean see that you get a college education?"

She nodded enthusiastically, the hunger for knowledge shining bright in her eyes. Viewing Shylo this way, Dimitri found yet another reason to admire her, to think that perhaps, on a more personal level, this match wouldn't be such an ordeal after all. "But of course I will. If an education is what you want, I can promise right now that I'll do everything I can to see that you get the best one available."

Shylo wouldn't have been surprised if she'd just spiraled right off the sofa and gone twirling across the floor like a whirligig gone wild. This was too good to be true! A marriage to a prestigious and handsome man who also intended to get her the education she craved—all without so much as blinking an eye?

Perhaps, Shylo thought, tossing a little cold water

on her joy, it was too good to be true. If she did agree to become Dimitri's wife, she really ought to let him know that she had no ties to the president. It wouldn't be fair to him otherwise. But if she did confess the truth, would his offer still hold? He *had* admitted that her connection to the White House was a factor in his decision to propose.

If he did withdraw the offer to marry her, she had to assume that he would also withdraw his services as escort, leaving her and Cassie penniless in Winslow, Arizona. Even if she and her sister boarded the train tomorrow and went on to San Diego alone, they had no way of letting a room, feeding themselves, or, most important of all, impressing their mother, a woman to whom impressions were everything.

Almost certain now of what she had to do, Shylo looked into Dimitri's eyes again. He wanted her. It could be that simple. So where was the harm in not telling him who she really was—at least until she established herself on firm ground with her mother? It would serve him right after all the rotten things he'd said to her yesterday.

He would be angry when he found out that she'd lied, of course, but he'd get over it. Besides, other than the social prestige she assumed it would bring, just how much could being related to the president of the United States matter to Dimitri, anyway? This was a business arrangement, like he said. It wasn't as if she'd be breaking his heart when he found she'd been less than truthful.

Her confidence restored, Shylo offered her hand. "I think we have ourselves a deal."

"Splendid!" With a dimpled smile on his face, Dimitri accepted her handshake. Then he broached a subject so sensitive that he hadn't dared mention it until he'd struck a bargain with her. "There is one more thing we need to talk about. As you know, Ari and I are pretty much without funds right now, and will be until we reach San Diego, where I directed the bank to wire my money. I noticed that the bandits allowed Miss McBride to keep her valise. I don't suppose they were kind enough to leave your money in her care as well? We could certainly use the train fare you owe us."

It was all she could do to keep from groaning out loud. Would he *never* forget about that damn money? No wonder he was so blasted wealthy! If there was one thing she'd learned from Mr. Anderson during her years on the farm, it was that rich folks got that way by hanging on to their money so tight, they practically squeezed the feathers right off their Indian-head pennies. This fiancé of hers could probably stuff a mattress with the feathers he'd squeezed from his coins—a bad habit she would have to work on changing the minute they were wed.

Doing her best to look dejected, not vexed, Shylo said, "I'm sorry, but I'm afraid they took every cent."

"In that case, I suppose we can wait until after the wedding to put our finances in order." He stood up from the couch, extended his hand, and pulled Shylo to her feet. "In the meantime, if we're going to accomplish everything we must and still make that train to San Diego tomorrow, we don't have a moment to waste."

"I'm afraid I don't understand. Are we going somewhere?"

"Yes, we are." Laughing softly, Dimitri chucked her under the chin. "To a wedding, I believe. Before I went to collect you from your room, I took the liberty of asking the marshal to help me find a preacher. I engaged one who is prepared to marry us within the hour. Will that be enough time for you to make your preparations?"

10

"Hold still a minute. I'm almost finished," said Cassie to her fidgety sister as she snipped off the thread holding the new lace polonaise to the yellow lawn gown. Once Cassie got over her shock at hearing Shylo's news, she'd dashed off to the mercantile with the last of their money and bought enough lace to turn the simple day dress into something resembling a wedding costume. After tying the tails of the flimsy material at the back of the gown, then draping them over Shylo's bustles as a makeshift "train," she stood back to admire her handiwork.

"You look"—Cassie burst into tears—"b-beautiful."

Trying to ignore this latest round of sobs—her sister had been alternating between bouts of weeping and hysterical joy since hearing about the upcoming wedding—Shylo reached for the sunbonnet Dimitri had purchased for her. Cassie had covered the crown of the hat with a wide strip of lace, leaving the ends extra long to use as ties. She fit the bonnet over her hastily arranged coiffure, tied the lace ends into a large bow beneath her chin, then stepped in front of the full-length mirror.

"Good God," she said over her sister's wails. "I look like Little Bo-Peep. All I need is a staff!"

"D-don't say that!" Cassie blew her nose. "You really are beautiful, Shylo, a lovely bride. I—I'm so jealous."

Although they'd already used up the hour Dimitri had given them, Shylo turned to her sister and gave her a hug. "You don't have anything to be jealous of, sis. Just keep looking for that prince of yours to come riding up on his big white horse. He's bound to show up one of these days."

She'd meant to calm Cassie enough to get her down the stairs, not stir her up even more, but for some reason her words brought about a regular downpour. Cassie wept even harder than before, soaking the bodice of Shylo's thin dress, and there wasn't a thing to be done about it until she'd cried herself dry.

At last Cassie backed away and blew her nose again. "S-sorry," she said through a hiccup. "I guess I'm too danged sentimental to be anyone's maid of honor. Maybe you ought to just go on without me so's I won't ruin your wedding."

"Don't be ridiculous. If you won't come with me, then I'm not getting married at all."

"I don't know why you'd say that. Look at me! My eyes are all swollen and red, I got dirt ground into the back of your pretty blue dress, and I can't even think about you getting married without blubbering all over the place. Why would you want a big ole baby like me at the ceremony?"

"That's easy enough. I love you." She pinched Cassie's cheek, then went over to the bed and picked up the huge black bonnet. "Now no more talk about staying behind. If we don't hurry and get over there, the groom might change his mind." She reached up to place the hat on her sister's head, but Cassie ducked out of the way.

"Please don't ask me to wear that bonnet. I can hardly breathe with my head stuffed into it, and besides that, it's too damn ugly to wear at a wedding." She set her chin and pushed out her bottom lip. "I've pretty much decided that I ain't gonna wear it anywhere else again, neither."

This surprised Shylo, for Cassie's locks, while no longer purple, were still far from their natural color. "But we don't have anything else big enough to cover your head. You have to wear it if you expect to keep your hair hidden."

"I don't expect to do that again, neither." A secretive smile drifted across her face. "Some folks actually *like* pink hair. I figure those that don't can just keep their eyes off of me."

Because it had taken nearly a full day to convince Cassie to go outside at all when her hair had first turned out purple, even wearing the bonnet, Shylo could hardly try to talk her out of her new attitude. In fact, she took it as a sign that her baby sister might even be growing up.

"Damn right," she said. "And just for the record, I think you're the prettiest maid of honor a bride ever had, swollen eyes, stained dress, pink hair, and all. Now let's go get me a husband! We were supposed to be there twenty minutes ago!"

As they crossed the railroad tracks and headed

toward the marshal's office, Shylo realized that so far during their stay in Winslow, she had yet to see a church. Was that why Dimitri had asked her to meet him at the marshal's office? she wondered, continuing on her way. Surely if there was no church in Winslow, he could have found a better place for their wedding than a jailhouse!

When she and Cassie reached the marshal's little log cabin, Shylo was prepared to insist that her fiancé find a more suitable spot for the ceremony, but Dimitri lit into her the minute she crossed the threshold, robbing her of the chance.

"You're late! Have you no concept of time, woman? I am waiting, and the preacher, too!"

Laughter from a booming voice in the corner plugged Dimitri's tirade. "Now don't go getting yourselves frothed up over nothing. It's not like y'all are keeping me from anything else."

Shylo turned toward the big y'alling Texan and saw that he was stretched out between two chairs, his backside planted firmly on one, his boots propped on the other. As she stared at him, her mouth agape, he kicked the chair out from under his feet, stood up, and came toward her. He was tall, at least as tall as Dimitri, but probably eighty pounds lighter, his black frock coat hanging down from his body as if from a wire hanger, his flat-brimmed hat riding low on his long forehead.

"My dear lady," he said, bowing slightly as he approached her, "would I be correct in assuming that y'all are the bride-to-be?"

"Yes, she is," said Dimitri, his impatience still ruling his tongue. "Shylo, this is the waiting Reverend Bill Tucker, our preacher. He is the one who travels on something of a circuit—"

"I know what a circuit preacher is." Vexed over the way he'd greeted her at the door, Shylo cut Dimitri off, then ignored him in favor of the preacher. "Nice to meet you, Reverend. This"—she turned toward Cassie—"is my maid of honor, Cassandra McBride."

Cassie sniffed back a tear. "Pleased to make your acquaintance, Reverend Tucker."

"'Reverend Bill' is what most folks call me, little lady." With an incredulous gaze pinned to her head, he gave her a broad smile. "My, my—that's a very . . . interesting shade a hair y'all got there. Were you brought into the world that way, little lady, or were you struck down by lightning?"

Dimitri, who'd barely noticed that Cassie had walked in the door along with Shylo, let out an audible groan as he took a good look at her. Why had she'd chosen today of all days to leave her hat behind, exposing hair that was no longer purple, but pink? *Pink!*

Shylo replied stiffly, "Cassie had a little . . . accident with some dye, is all. Her hair will be back to its normal blond color in no time."

"Accident," the preacher echoed. "Yes, I would certainly say so." He looked to Dimitri. "If we're all here now, I think we'd best get started."

"Yes, of course." He glanced at the lawman, who was keeping a lazy eye on the proceedings from his desk. "Deputy Moss? Would you mind collecting the best man for us?"

He yawned, then said, "I expect not."

Moss rose from his desk, lifted the keys from their peg, then unlocked the door to the back room and disappeared inside it. A moment later, and much to Shylo's surprise, out stepped a battered-looking Ari.

His suit was rumpled, his nose was swollen, and he sported two black eyes. She couldn't help but notice that he also wore a shiny pair of handcuffs and that the barrel of Deputy Moss's .45 was pressed firmly against the center of his back.

Stunned by the sight, Shylo whispered to Dimitri, "My God! What happened to him, and why is he still under arrest?"

Unable to look her in the eye, he shrugged and said, "He had a little trouble with some gamblers. It is nothing to worry about now. We'll work on getting him released after the wedding."

But Shylo wasn't so easily put off. How could he call it "nothing"? She glanced back to Ari and the marshal. The lawman hadn't relaxed the position of his pistol an inch and was looking as if he'd just as soon pull the trigger and blow a hole through Ari as not. Why hadn't Dimitri thought this development important enough to mention to her before now? Or hadn't he known when he proposed? In either case, should she still go through with the wedding as planned?

Unaware the bride was having second thoughts, Reverend Bill took Shylo by the shoulders. "Now then. Since I b'lieve we're ready to begin, I'd like you to stand here." He moved her a few feet to his right, then directed Dimitri to stand beside her on the left. "Let's have the maid of honor come right up alongside the bride, if y'all please, and Marshal, you fetch the best man up next to the groom's elbow."

When he was satisfied the wedding party was in proper alignment, Reverend Bill began the ceremony. "Dearly b'loved! We-all gathered here today to bring these two fine folks together in holy matrimony."

Cassie began to sob, drowning out the considerable resonance of the preacher's voice.

Reverend Bill leaned in toward Shylo and said, "What's the matter with her?"

"She's, ah . . . happy for me."

"I see." He stepped back, frowning at the still sobbing Cassie, but went on with the ceremony. "If y'all don't mind my saying so, it seems fitting that I make mention of the fact that this wedding has all the earmarks of becoming one of the most . . . unusual of my long career. Not only is this one decidedly more *colorful*," he said, directing a meaningful gaze Cassie's way, "but while I have officiated at a fair share of weddings where the bridegroom and . . . ah, a shotgun were featured, I do b'lieve this is the first ceremony I've performed where the best man was being held at gunpoint!"

Ari, whose nose had started to bleed, held a handkerchief to it as he looked at Shylo and said, "Sorry for the trouble."

She shrugged but gave Dimitri a narrow, sidelong glance. He shifted his feet restlessly and continually folded and unfolded his arms, but he did not hazard a look in her direction or say one word in his uncle's defense. She was missing something, she decided, some little detail or secret between the Greeks that was purposefully being kept from her. How could she go through with the wedding while suspicions such as these were running through her mind?

"Listen up, y'all," the reverend went on, his voice rising to fever pitch. "It is my duty to ask if there is anyone heah who objects to the joining of these fine folks before me. Speak now if y'all dare, or forever hold your peace, 'cause we're about to get on with the serious part of this heah service."

Shylo was ready by now to call a halt to the entire affair, but as the preacher lapsed into his well-rehearsed wedding speech, she faltered. How could she explain her way out of it without giving herself away as an impostor? She could hardly complain that the best man was held at gunpoint or that her maid of honor's hair was a very disrespectful shade of pink. How could she criticize anyone in the wedding party when she, the blushing bride, looked more like a character right out of a Mother Goose rhyme than a New York debutante about to be wed?

Besides, there wasn't really anything for her to worry about. Dimitri had assured her that he would be getting Ari released as soon as the ceremony was over, hadn't he?

Less troubled now, Shylo listened carefully to what the reverend was saying and realized that he was speaking directly to her.

"And now do you, Miss Shylo Folsom, take this man, Dimitri Adonis, as . . . "

Warning bells went off in her head, drowning out the words *love, honor,* and *obey.* Miss . . . *Folsom!* God in heaven, why hadn't she thought of that little complication before things had gotten this far? And how could she go through with the wedding now that she had? It didn't strike her as particularly legitimate for her to marry Dimitri or anyone as Shylo Folsom, a person who didn't exist. In fact, she was pretty sure such a deception would be considered downright illegal. She had to think of something to stop the ceremony—and fast.

"Ahem." The reverend cleared his throat. "Miss Folsom? Do you or do you not take this man as your husband?"

"Huh?"

"Say, 'I do,' Shylo," came Dimitri's melodic, velvety voice.

She looked up at him in utter confusion. Even though he was frowning, looking tight around the mouth and eyes, he was still the most handsome, mesmerizing man she'd ever laid eyes on. Dressed in his best suit of black broadcloth and a high-collared shirt complete with ruffled bib, he was not only terrifyingly handsome, but regal and princelike. Could she find the strength to walk away from a man like this, even though logic told her she had to?

Beside her, Cassie's sobs increased in volume, startling Shylo into action. There was really only one way out of this mess at this stage, she figured, and that would be to reveal all her lies. And she wasn't even close to considering going to such extremes.

Her mind made up, she hid her hands in the folds of her new lace polonaise, crossed her fingers, and turned to the reverend. "Yessir, I believe that I do."

"Praise be and hallelujah, little lady. I thought I'd gone to all this trouble for nothing." The reverend gave her a broad grin, then directed his remarks to Dimitri. "And do you, Dimitri Adonis, promise to love, honor, and keep your lovely bride by your side for as long as y'all shall live?"

Without hesitation he said, "I do."

"In that case, I b'lieve it's time for the ring ceremony. Y'all do have a ring, don't you?"

Dimitri hadn't prepared for this. With just a moment's hesitation, he nodded, turned to Ari, and held out his hand.

The old man looked puzzled for a moment. Then, as understanding sank in, his expression slid into a frown.

Her new husband, ashamed of himself when he saw what he'd been doing to his bride's hands—crushing them—released her and turned to the window. Gripping the windowsill now instead of his wife, Dimitri took several deep breaths in an effort to calm himself.

"That's better," said Reverend Bill. "Now then. Why don't y'all tell me what's going on between you two—one at a time, starting with the lady."

"I—I don't know." Rage was still crowding her throat, making it impossible to talk beyond that.

"How about you, sir?" the reverend asked, directing his inquiries to Dimitri's back. "Can you shed some light on the problem?"

Dimitri turned to the man and tried to summarize their bizarre conflict. "The president of the United States happens to be my wife's uncle. I am trying to convince her to wire him on my uncle's behalf since we can't seem to strike any kind of a bargain with the law in this town." He shot the marshal a particularly vicious look. "As you may have heard, my wife refuses me this favor."

From over his shoulder the reverend asked, "What's the man done, Moss?"

"Busted up Springer's saloon a coupla nights ago. Owes two hundred bucks for damages."

His speculative gaze back on Dimitri again, the reverend said, "Y'all look to be pretty well fixed. Why don't y'all just pay the man and be on your way?"

"Because," Dimitri said, tired of explaining their situation over and over, "the four of us were unfortunate enough to be on the train that was robbed. So we are quite without the funds to pay for Ari's mistakes. To that I should add that I believe my uncle was tricked by a group of cowboys called knife bashers, or something like that."

"The Hashknife cowboys?"

"Yes, that would be them."

Turning in a slow circle, Reverend Bill addressed the marshal. "That true, Moss? Was that poor little Greek fella set up by those boys?"

The deputy shrugged but couldn't look the preacher in the eye.

"Hell's fire, Moss. You want the president of these heah United States brought in on this?" Again the marshal shrugged. "How do y'all think Commodore Perry Owens, county sheriff of these heah parts, is gonna like it when he gets here and finds out that you wouldn't let these esteemed folks go on their way—especially when he finds out those ruffians over at the Aztec Cattle Company were involved?"

Lowering his gun, Moss finally said, "Someone's got to pay Springer's bill. We can't just forget about that."

"No, I don't reckon we can."

Seeing a ray of hope, Dimitri said, "I already made the offer to send money to cover the damages after we arrive in San Diego, but the marshal would not accept those terms. If he'll reconsider that offer, I can sign some sort of document if my word isn't good enough."

Reverend Bill nodded slowly. "What do you say, Moss? That sounds like an excellent idea to me. Just excellent."

The marshal, who'd already unlocked Ari's handcuffs, said, "His word's good enough for me if it's good enough for you."

Enormously relieved to have that problem out of the way, Dimitri sucked in a huge breath, intending to

let it out in a long sigh. The breath froze in his lungs
when he caught Shylo's deadly gaze.

It didn't take a full doctorate's worth of education
for him to figure out that the battle he'd won here
with the law had been but a minor victory. Now that
he'd seen the hostility in his new wife's expression,
Dimitri had a pretty good idea that his troubles in
Winslow had been nothing more than a minor incon-
venience compared to what was in store.

After spending a considerable amount of time nego-
tiating with both the marshal and saloon owner Murphy Springer, Dimitri not only secured the man's
agreement to the IOU, but convinced him to reduce
Ari's share of the bill to half of what he owed—$125—
leaving the Aztec Cattle Company responsible for the
rest. After that, the wedding party returned to the Harvey House Hotel for a celebration supper at the establishment's acclaimed restaurant. Although the dining
room had only a handful of patrons, and the seats at
the counter were empty save for one old man, Dimitri
instructed the waitress to seat them at the back of the
room in the most private corner possible.

They settled at a table spread with Irish linen, fine
china featuring Native American motifs, and Sheffield
silver from England. It was an atmosphere fit for a
king, at a surprisingly reasonable price of seventy-five
cents per diner. Knowing to the penny exactly how
much money he had left, Dimitri figured they could
dine in style and he'd still have two dollars and fifty
cents in his pocket—more than enough to book a
third room for him and Shylo to use as their bridal
suite. Looking forward to the night with surprising

eagerness, since he'd yet to lose his earlier anger, he waved over the waitress and took it upon himself to order for them all.

"We'll start with bluepoint oysters all around," Dimitri said to the waitress in a crisp black-and-white uniform.

"Very good, sir." She jotted down the order. "And for the entrée?"

"How's the roast sirloin of beef au jus today?"

"Excellent. It's fresh from a fine local herd of Texas longhorn cattle, and comes with creamed asparagus and Yorkshire pudding."

Very familiar by now with the brand those cattle would carry, Dimitri chuckled as he said, "That sounds fine. We'll have four orders."

As the waitress scurried away, Dimitri rested his forearms on the heavy walnut table and glanced across the floral centerpiece to where his bride sat, her eyes downcast. She had yet to look at or speak to him since their argument in the marshal's office, and the rest of the wedding party was curiously silent as well. To his left, Ari had stretched back against his chair and tilted his head toward the ceiling to ward off yet another bloody nose. To his right, the usually chatty Cassie wept quietly into her handkerchief. A casual observer would have thought the gathering more a wake than a wedding supper.

"Wake up, everybody!" Dimitri said, suddenly in the mood to celebrate. "This is no way for Shylo and I to begin our life together. Let us forget what's happened in the past, and look toward the future."

Ari, a cloth pressed firmly against his nose, picked up his silver spoon and banged it lightly against his crystal water glass. "Yes, yes! A marriage has taken place today. We must celebrate with much joy! Waitress?" he called, waving his free hand. "Oh, waitress!"

When it dawned on Dimitri what Ari was thinking, he slid his foot to the left and kicked his uncle's ankle with the toe of his boot. He connected with the table leg instead. As he drew back his foot to launch another attack, the waitress arrived.

"Yes, sir?"

"Wine!" Ari shouted. "We must have wine for a wedding celebration! Bring us a bottle of your finest!"

"Ari . . ." Dimitri started to protest, but there was no point in going on. He'd neglected to inform his uncle just how short they were on cash, and there was no delicate way to explain his plans for the little money he had left. His only hope was that the restaurant was as conservative with the wine prices as it was with the meals.

When the waitress returned with the wine, she set it near Ari's elbow and said quietly to Dimitri, "That will be one dollar and seventy-five cents extra, sir."

He sighed heavily. "But of course."

From there on, as far as Dimitri was concerned, the "celebration" evolved into a circus, with Ari as a most zealous ringmaster to an audience of one—Shylo. The rest of the wedding party showed a decided lack of interest in the proceedings. After only one glass of wine, Cassie dissolved into yet another bout of tears and rambled on about princes, horses, and lost loves, gibberish that made no particular sense. As for Dimitri, his mood had darkened considerably, and he no longer felt like celebrating at all.

Shylo, on the other hand, positively glowed from within as the spirits warmed her and enthusiastically encouraged Ari to tell her all about Greek wedding customs. Her eyes were sparkling, alive with laughter and that thirst for knowledge Dimitri so admired in her, but they were only for Ari. She had yet, he noted sourly, to favor her new husband with anything other than an accusing glare. To have, to hold, and to by God look him in the eye, he thought, vowing to set up a few rules between them before the night was over. He'd done his duty by marrying her. The least she could do was take her duties a little more seriously. He was, after all, her husband. She ought to be showing him a little more respect. A lot more, in fact.

When the meal was finally over, an even surlier Dimitri escorted the ladies upstairs, leaving Ari to drool over the vast assortment of cigars at the stand in the lobby. When they reached their room, he stepped between the two women as he opened the door.

"Shylo is coming with me. Good night, Miss McBride," he said as he showed her into her quarters. Then he closed the door and turned to Shylo. "Let's go."

Even though the wine had mellowed her considerably, Shylo had prepared herself for the moment when her husband would demand his "husbandly" rights. "I'm not going anywhere with you, and furthermore, I don't have a thing in the world to say to you but good night." She reached for the doorknob, but before she could turn it, a strong hand circled her wrist.

"You don't have to say a thing," he said, tugging Shylo away from the door. "But you will listen."

"L-let go of me!" She planted her feet, but Dimitri just lifted her off them and dragged her alongside him, not slowing his stride until he'd reached a small viewing alcove at the end of the hall. The second he set her back down, Shylo doubled up her fist and took a wide swing at his head. She missed him entirely and would have fallen to the floor if Dimitri hadn't grabbed hold of her again and pinned her arms to her sides.

"I said, you will *listen!* If you don't, I'll be forced to . . . to . . . " He couldn't think of the correct English word for what he was thinking—apply a little persuasion to her backside—and as he paused to consider an alternate threat, she filled in the blanks for him.

"What? Make me eat some wood? Why don't you just divorce me instead? In fact, please do, because now that I know the real you, I don't think this business arrangement is going to work out so good! And while you're at it, *let . . . me . . . go!*"

But he didn't. Dimitri continued to hold her imprisoned between his arms and body, and as she struggled against him, rousing parts of him that would get no relief on this night, he increased the pressure of his grip to try to still her squirming hips.

"Believe me," he said, his voice a low, silken warning, "what we've been through today is definitely *not* what I had hoped for on the day I wed, either, but I have no intentions of seeking a divorce from you." She relaxed a little, so he went on. "To tell you the truth, Shylo, I never wanted to get married to anyone."

Taken aback by this confession, she looked up at him and became lost, as usual, in his devil black eyes. Her anger gone for reasons she didn't understand, she laughed as she admitted, "That's the first thing you've said since 'I do' that I agree with. Truth is, I never figured on getting married myself."

"Really?" Dimitri was stunned, for he had assumed all American debutantes spent their formative years in preparation for the day they wed. He eased his grip but continued to hold her in his arms. "May I ask why not?"

"I never thought about it much, I guess. I always had more important things on my mind." Realizing that she'd left the door open for him to question her in areas she had no ready answers for, she added, "Things like that college education I want."

"That's very admirable, and something we'll start planning as soon as our 'honeymoon' trip is over." Shylo favored him with a smile, so Dimitri let one hand slip to the small of her waist and brought the other to her throat. Stroking the soft skin there, he said, "And speaking of honeymoons, I'm afraid that due to our financial condition, I must leave you with Cassie and go back to the room I share with Ari this evening, delaying the beginning of our marriage at least one day."

A reprieve! But what did he mean by "at least"? "Oh," she said, acutely aware of his fingers as they caressed her neck. "That's all right with me. We have lots of time to get started after we hit San Diego."

"I doubt we'll have to wait that long." His voice grew deeper, huskier. "Assuming that we'll still have private berths on the train, we should be able to consummate our marriage and truly begin our life together by tomorrow night."

Until he had spoken those words, until he thought of her that way, naked beneath him, offering up her innocence like some sacrificial symbol, Dimitri hadn't truly understood the meaning of desire—or the sheer agony of denial. Giving in to both the urge to claim

her and the need to lessen that agony if only for a brief
moment, he took her surprised lips with his own,
branding her with a heated promise of things to come.

Because Shylo was truly his wife, even if in name
only, Dimitri raided her unprotesting mouth, plunging deeper and more intimately into her than before,
staking his claim in the only way possible on this most
impossible of nights. Freed of the restraints of yesterday, when they were but acquaintances, he let his
hands roam down his wife's back to her bottom,
where he caressed her beneath the pile of petticoats
and bustles. Driven on by a fierce surge of lust, he
abruptly pulled her tight against his hips, grinding her
soft curves against the rigid planes of his hard body,
wanting and needing her with an intensity that shook
him as much as it fired him. Nearly out of control,
feeling almost reckless enough to take her right there
where they stood, Dimitri finally tore his mouth from
Shylo's and set her away from him.

His groin aching with desire, his hands shaking
with need, Dimitri stood there a long moment, staring
at the bride he should have been claiming in a private
suite by now. They would be good together, he decided, very, very good, if her response to him was any
indication. Shylo was panting and breathless, her lan-
guid blue eyes as dark as a stormy sky, her crooked
little smile more sideways and innocently provocative
than ever. Even in the murky hallway lighting, he
could see that she was trembling from head to toe,
alive with need. Tomorrow, he thought with deepening frustration, would be a long, long time in coming.
If it ever dawned at all.

His voice husky with desire, Dimitri said, "I'd better get you back to your room now."

Then, without another word between them, he took her by the hand and escorted her to Cassie's room. Afterward, as he headed for the stairs with the six bits jingling in his pocket, Dimitri wondered just how far seventy-five cents would take him at the bar.

Inside the southwestern-style hotel room, Shylo stood flush against the door, unable to make her legs move. In truth, the door was holding her up, for she was pretty sure if she tried to walk on her own, she'd fall flat on her face. She was on fire from head to toe, her knees fluttering like little wings, and the peculiar warmth Dimitri's kisses usually started in her belly had spread to all her nerve endings, intensifying into a firestorm that seemed big enough to consume her. How long could she fight him off when his touch rendered her so completely helpless, so utterly brainless?

"Shylo?" said Cassie. "Do you need something?"

She blinked, trying to clear her rattled mind. "Huh? Oh, maybe a glass of water."

"I didn't mean that kind of thing. Did you stop by to pick up your brush or something?"

"No, I came to stay with you."

"*Me!* You should be with your husband. I don't need a keeper."

"My hus—" Shylo laughed, and the force of her chuckles freed her body from Dimitri's curious hold over it—temporarily, at least. "Weren't you at the ceremony today? Shylo *Folsom* is the one who got married, not me. I don't really have a husband, so I don't really have to be a wife."

"Oh, but you must! I mean, you two think you're married, so that ought to be good enough for you to act like you are, too." She giggled. "Why if I'd said 'I do' in front of a preacher, and to a man like that handsome Greek of yours, it would sure be license enough for me to hop in his bed. I'm surprised your drawers haven't just slid right down to your knees from thinking about it!"

On the strength of that comment, Shylo charged across the room to where Cassie sat brushing her hair at the vanity. "Where in *hell* did you get a notion like that? From reading that cheap little romance story I found on the train?"

Cassie blushed at her own intimate knowledge of men and their ways, but she held her ground. "Maybe a little, but mostly I got it from watching the sparks fly when you and Dimitri are together. I truly think you ought to just skedaddle on down to his room and make a real wedding night out of it."

"What?" Shylo could hardly believe her baby sister thought of such things, much less gave voice to them. "I can't go sleeping with a man I'm not married to! Why, if I did such a thing, it'd make me no better than a common saloon whore."

As Cassie thought of the long blissful nights she'd spent with Buck, she hung her head in shame. How horribly unfair it all seemed! Here she sat, pining away for a man who should be her husband, while her sister, who technically was married, balked at the idea of spending even one night with the man she'd wed. It was not fair at all.

Shylo, who hadn't noticed Cassie's distress or her shame, made one last observation on the subject. "Since I'm not about to let any man turn me into his whore, Dimitri can try to get me into his bed all he wants, but nothing he does will work." Silently she amended her vow: As long as I don't let him kiss or touch me again, anyway. "That's all there is to it. There's no way I'm gonna let that man put a hand on my nuptials. No way in hell!"

A little inaccuracy sometimes
saves a ton of explanation.
—Saki

11

When Dimitri and entourage finally arrived at the terminal at the foot of D Street on the thirtieth of June, San Diego's weather patterns were running true to form, despite the circulars he had read. Not only did they tout San Diego as a "Cornucopia of the World," they described it as "a sun-drenched community with a mild climate, even in January and February." To the contrary, the dirt streets were sodden from recent rains and the skies overcast and dreary.

But the gloomy weather didn't bother Dimitri in the slightest. In fact, it matched his increasingly sullen mood. His only concern was for Shylo, who, dressed in her flimsy lawn gown, shivered in the damp, cold city. He could think of several ways to warm her, none of them mentionable in public, but there were at least as many chores to take care of first. He could only hope that the main cause of the foul mood he was in—unrequited lust—would finally "be put to bed" at the end of this long day.

Due to the fact that the extra-fare sleeping berths had all been booked, Dimitri and his new bride had been forced to sleep on their first-class seats the past two nights, chairs that converted to comfortable sleeping cots but were hardly private enough for the beginning of a honeymoon. He'd been a married man for over three days now and had yet to find a private moment alone with his wife.

If that wasn't frustration enough, once they disembarked in San Diego Dimitri had gone to the baggage department to collect Shylo's trunk, only to be informed that it had not arrived, and there was no record suggesting that it was on its way. Apparently, the baggage handler informed him, it had been sent elsewhere by mistake. Since Shylo told him her claim ticket had been lost during the robbery, there was no way to trace it, either, so once again she was left with only the clothing on her back—a situation he would have to remedy before she caught her death of cold.

The first bright spot in the day came when they stopped by the telegraph office. Dimitri's funds had arrived from Greece, so they were financially set for a while, anyway. Next up on the list of things to do was the search for a suitable hotel. Several townsfolk they asked—from the baggage clerk at the depot to the teller at the California National Bank, where he'd collected his money—insisted that the finest lodging in San Diego could be found under the red roofs and crisp white walls of the newly opened Hotel Del Coronado.

Dimitri balked at that idea. The elaborate structure was located across the bay on the island of Coronado, and the only way to reach it was by ferry boat. That would be a time-consuming, needless expenditure, especially because he hoped to accomplish their goals quite quickly.

Dimitri had no desire to spend more than one night in this barren burg—a town whose lone claim to charm was its picturesque little bay, as far as he could see. Looking east, inland San Diego was nothing but a panorama of rolling hills almost bare of vegetation save for drab clumps of sagebrush. Beyond them in the endless haze lay a high range of dark blue mountains separated by stony slopes and ragged gullies. The place was hardly Dimitri's idea of a honeymoon in paradise.

After he obtained grudging agreement from his travel-weary companions—Shylo, in particular, who was sure Colleen would be staying at the Hotel Del Coronado—they sent Ari to book their rooms at the first decent-looking place Dimitri saw, the very elegant Horton House Hotel. Located across the street from the bank they'd just left, the palatial inn filled an entire block and had been considered San Diego's finest until January, when the hotel on Coronado Island officially opened.

While Ari took care of securing the lodgings, Dimitri took Shylo and Cassie a couple of blocks down the city's main street, Fifth Avenue, to the George W. Marston Dry Goods Store and bought them each a warmer suit. Shylo's, a bargain at $10.75, was made of pale pink sateen trimmed with dark rose lace and black velvet and even came with matching hat and handbag. Cassie chose a plain muslin wrapper of soft peach and a cute little straw bonnet trimmed with hyacinths.

Finally, after a quick supper at the hotel restaurant, the foursome headed upstairs to their rooms. Ari, who already had his key, bade them good night and disappeared down the hall. Dimitri and the ladies continued on to room 210, where he opened the door and handed Cassie the key. Then he took his wife by the elbow and started toward the bridal suite, whistling all the way.

Shylo balked before they'd taken two steps. "Dimitri, stop a minute, please. I— Oh, my. I don't feel very good."

"You are sick?" Concerned, he brushed his lips across her forehead to test her temperature. Her skin was cool. "Where are you ill?"

"It's my stomach, and I have a dreadful headache." She dramatically wrapped her arms around her middle. "It's probably nothing, but you know that I've hardly slept the past two nights. I know that I won't be very good company tonight, and I don't want to start our marriage out like that. If you don't mind, I think it's best if I stay with Cassie."

Of course Dimitri did mind, but he could hardly force her to join him for their first night together. "I can make you comfortable and see that you get the rest you need as easily as your maid. I think you should come with me."

"Dimitri, please." She rested her hand against his chest, then looked up at him with what she hoped was a perfectly pitiful expression. "I really prefer things this way tonight. Tomorrow I'll be refreshed and, I'm sure, feeling much better." Once she found her mother, she would be. Then she could end this charade of a marriage. "Good night, and thanks for understanding."

Dimitri sighed heavily and with another chaste kiss to the cheek bade his bride good night. Then he headed back down the stairs to the bar. This time he had enough money in his pocket to last him as long as *he* would last.

The following morning after breakfast, Dimitri and Shylo strolled across the street to Horton's Plaza, a small oval-shaped park bounded by a neat row of hedges. A fountain at its center was surrounded by three rows of steps, and eight wooden benches were situated between clumps of tall junipers and low-lying flower beds. Shylo was much too nervous to sit or even to enjoy the hazy sunshine peeking through the overcast skies. She was worried about approaching her "husband" with her plans for finding Colleen Pappas, and he didn't appear to be particularly approachable this morning.

A dark shadow covered Dimitri's handsome face from his cheeks to his throat, and his lusterless eyes were sunken, highlighted by dark smudges just below them. Shylo didn't know where he'd been last evening, but she had a pretty good idea that if he'd gone to bed at all, it hadn't been until the wee hours of morning. Between the black cowboy hat and his rough-edged, unshaven appearance, he looked dangerous, more like an American outlaw than a Greek god. A little shiver coursed through her at the thought.

Shaking off the sensation, Shylo steeled herself for the coming battle and said, "I got the addresses for Mr. Earp's gambling halls from the reception desk this morning. I think it would be better if we went there now instead of later, don't you?"

Dimitri turned to her with a scowl. "I also got the

addresses, but *we* are not going to look them up now or later."

"Oh," she said breezily, "then you want me to go alone?"

"Of course not." Dimitri sank onto one of the benches. "Try to remember that you are a married woman now. You must listen to me and obey my wishes. I do not wish to take my wife into the part of town known as the 'stingaree.' I was told last night that only an idiot would do such a thing."

She laughed, trying to lighten the mood. "I don't see why you should be worried about taking me with you, in that case. You were idiot enough to take me into the desert and get me stuck overnight, and that turned out all right. This will, too. You'll see."

"In Greece, a wife never questions her husband, but always obeys him. Please remember that and do what I say."

Although she'd promised herself to remain calm, Shylo blurted out, "In case you haven't noticed, we're *not* in Greece."

Dimitri pushed back the brim of his hat and looked up at her with a particularly annoyed expression. "Perhaps you haven't noticed that you married a *Greek* man. You will do as I say, and what I say is that I will go, and you will stay here. *Katalaves*—understand me?"

Between the look in his eye and his obvious exhaustion, Shylo knew better than to argue with Dimitri any further. He would just get louder and increasingly difficult to understand as he got angrier. She had no choice but to agree to his terms, and then she would do as she damn well pleased.

"All right," she said, strolling over to one of the

benches and sitting down. "I'll wait right here in the plaza for you, but please hurry."

"As you wish," he said, climbing to his feet. "I'll return as quickly as possible."

Giving him a prim smile, Shylo waited until Dimitri was a safe distance away before standing up again. Then she followed him, careful to keep him in sight, as he worked his way into the raunchy, hell-raising area encompassing several square blocks between First and Fifth Avenues. The better parts of San Diego she'd seen featured three-story brick buildings, giving the streets a more modern look, but the rest of the town was comprised of the wooden false-front shops and the same warped boardwalks so common to the other western towns they'd passed through.

Still, Shylo didn't feel terribly out of place or threatened when Dimitri disappeared inside the Earp gambling hall on Fourth and E Street. In fact, she'd just about decided to follow him inside when he came back out and continued down the boardwalk. It wasn't until he had moved deeper into the "stingaree" that she began to regret her impulsive decision to follow him.

She became increasingly uneasy as she passed by various bawdy houses, gambling halls, opium dens, and saloons with names like the Seven Buckets of Blood, the First and Last Stop, One-Eyed McInery's, and a place called Till A. Barnes, where she was forced to sidestep the unruly "pet" bear the owner kept chained outside on the boardwalk. By the time Dimitri finally reached the next Earp gambling hall, Shylo was but one step behind him.

"Dimitri—wait," she said, her voice quivering.

Hardly able to believe his own ears, Dimitri turned

on her in shocked surprise. "Shylo! What are you doing here?"

"I . . . well, that is, I thought—"

"You did not *think* at all! What of your promise to me?"

"I'm sorry, but this meeting is just too important for me to sit around and hope it all goes well." She glanced over the saloon's door. "Is Mr. Earp in there?"

"It matters not." He clamped his fingers around her arm. "This place is filled with drunks and louds, and you will not be going inside. We will return to the hotel at once."

The doors to the saloon behind them flew open then, disgorging a pair of drunken sailors onto the boardwalk. Shylo canted her head in their direction and said, "I think it'd be just as easy to take me inside. We're both here now, so why not get this over with?"

Glowering at her, Dimitri saw with horror that the drunks had gotten to their feet and were staggering toward Earp's place. With rage choking his voice, he said, "You will pay for this, this, not listen later, but come with me now."

Then, gripping her arm roughly, Dimitri pushed open the doors and marched Shylo through the crowd of noisy gamblers, some whistling as she passed, others shouting ribald comments or hooting their catcalls. Wondering if he hadn't gone completely mad to bring his wife into a place such as this, he spotted a man at the bar wearing a suit with matching vest and an expression vastly superior to the lowly crowd he surveyed. Dimitri decided he would most likely be the manager.

When he reached the bar, Dimitri pulled Shylo in front of his body, shielding her from view of the others in the room. "I must see Wyatt Earp this minute. I come on a matter of extreme urgent. Please at once to me bring him."

Biting back a grin, Shylo patted Dimitri's arm, which was wrapped possessively around her waist. "My, ah, husband is new to this country, and his English gets a little sloppy when he's upset. Could you please tell us if Mr. Earp is in?"

His piercing blue eyes flickering between her and Dimitri, the man answered in a deep foghorn voice, "You're talking to him. What's so important?"

Shylo nearly gasped. She'd heard of Wyatt Earp, of course, especially after the bloody battle at the O.K. Corral and the indictment for murder he'd gotten for slaying the man who'd killed his brother, but she'd never seen a photograph of the famous marshal before. He was as tall as Dimitri, though not as broad and muscular, and russet-haired with a thick handlebar mustache in a darker shade of auburn. His cold-eyed gaze aside, she supposed that the former marshal was probably the kind of man most women considered very handsome—had they not seen the Greek god standing directly behind her first, of course.

Dimitri was very aware that his wife was gawking at Wyatt Earp, a lawman who'd already become an American legend at the age of forty. And he didn't like it one bit. His tone more brusque now, he stated the reasons for his inquiry.

"We have come to San Diego to find some friends of ours, and were told that you might know where they can be found. We seek Colleen and Niko Pappas."

Earp adjusted his string tie and rested an elbow against the bar. "If I was to know these folks, what's your interest in them?"

While Dimitri was unaccustomed to most American rituals, he did recognize both the challenge and the attempt to downplay that dare in Earp's calculated yet casual appearance. One wrong move, and he was pretty sure the legend would blow a hole in him. His grip tightened around Shylo's waist as he replied, "Niko is a fellow countryman and an old family acquaintance. Mrs. Pappas is the mother of one of my wife's dear friends. We only wish to say hello to them since we are in the area, and bring them news of home and family."

"Is that so?" Earp's free hand moved toward his hip. "I've never heard Colleen mention that she had any kids."

"Well, she does!" Shylo blurted out.

Earp straightened, pinning her with a frigid gaze, and at that same moment Dimitri practically squeezed the breath right out of her. Realizing belatedly that her reaction had been too obvious, too defensive, she laughed and said, "Colleen has—*had* two daughters. They're grown now, but I've known them since . . . since they were born."

"That's probably why she didn't mention them," said Dimitri, determined to take control of the conversation again. "Do you know where we might locate the Pappases, Mr. Earp?"

"As a matter of fact, I do, but I'm just a mite curious about why you call 'saying hello' to a pair of old friends an 'extremely urgent' matter. That don't sound quite right to me."

"The urgent of matter, sir"—Dimitri paused to take a breath, calming himself—"is the fact that my wife insisted I bring her along with me. I want her out of here as soon as possible so she won't have to listen to any more of . . . of—" He simply couldn't think of a

correct word for the situation other than a profanity
he'd picked up in New York. "Surely you can understand that I'd like to get her out of here as quickly as
possible."

"I suppose I can see your point," he said, his gaze
roaming the dress of pink sateen and the curves
beneath it. "I sure wouldn't bring my Josie in here,
and I own the place."

Not the slightest bit happy over the way Earp was
eyeing Shylo, Dimitri muttered, "That's why I'd like
the information we seek now, please."

"And sinners want whiskey in hell."

Dimitri had been frustrated and upset by the fact
that he'd been fool enough to bring his wife into such
a sordid atmosphere, but now, thanks to this famous
gunman who seemed to be enjoying his discomfort,
he was embarrassed and humiliated as well.

Seething, mad at everyone including himself, he
gripped her elbow. "Let's go, Shylo. This donkey back
has no intention of helping us find our friends."

Dimitri turned with her still wrapped in his arms,
but before he'd taken a step, Earp's burst of laughter
brought them both to a halt. Then he said, "I've been
called a lot of names in my day, most of them unmen-
tionable in a lady's presence, but I do believe that's
the first time I've been referred to as a donkey's back.
Is it best that I don't know exactly what you mean by
that?"

His jaw rigid, Dimitri nodded, since he had indeed
tried to find a decent way to call the man an asshole.
"I would say it is best. If that's all?"

"Not quite." Earp laughed again, then relaxed
against the bar, this time for real. "Colleen and Niko
were staying at the Belle View Hotel at Fourth and G

where me and Josie live, but I'm not sure if they plan on going back there when they return to San Diego. Colleen was mighty interested in having a look at that new hotel over on Coronado."

"Come back from where?" said Shylo. "And when?"

"They took a little honeymoon trip to Mexico." Earp showed her a meaningful smile. "They caught a coastal steamer for Ensenada, and figure on going even farther south if they like what they see there. They'll either be back by packet a week from this Saturday afternoon, or next."

One or two weeks more! Shylo slumped against Dimitri's chest. Would this nightmare of chasing her mother never end?

"Thank you for the information." Dimitri offered his hand, although he'd rather have doubled his fist and popped the lawman in the mouth. After the men shook hands, he added absently, "Perhaps we'll meet again when our friends return to San Diego."

Earp gave him a tight smile. "You can bet on it, partner. My Josie and I have gotten real friendly with Colleen and Niko. I wouldn't want anything to get their feathers ruffled." He narrowed his cold blue eyes. "Know what I mean?"

The rest of that day went by in a blur of conflicting emotions for Shylo. Not only was she deeply disappointed to learn her long anticipated reunion was delayed yet again, but now she had to face a very real concern. Putting off Dimitri and the consummation of their "marriage" had been relatively easy up until this point, but how in the hell could she possibly manage to avoid him for another week or two?

If she told him the truth—all of it—he would most certainly pull his support of her and Cassie, and where would that leave them? Out in the cold, damp streets of San Diego, a town that wasn't nearly as civilized as she'd hoped it would be. They wouldn't survive two days, much less two weeks, given their financial situation.

If she continued with her lies—which naturally included pretending that she'd actually wedded Dimitri—sooner or later he would demand that she perform her wifely duties. And she wouldn't have a leg to stand on in refusing him. Shylo's head was swirling with all that and more by the time supper was finished that night, but she'd managed to come up with an excuse that she hoped would buy her just a little more time and keep her out of the marital bed for at least another day.

Dimitri had been consumed by his own thoughts throughout the afternoon and evening as well, but his concerns revolved around the night ahead and the proper way a gentleman ought to go about seducing his bride. In his previous and limited experiences, he'd never been privileged—or, perhaps, challenged—to make the intimate acquaintance of a virgin. Certain his new bride was still innocent in that way, he was determined not to hurt her; that was the last thing he wanted to do. From what he understood of these things, however, if he proceeded with the *first* thing he wanted to do, she would suffer some pain no matter how he went about his lovemaking. He'd thought more than once of seeking Ari's council but just couldn't bring himself to discuss such a private concern.

As he saw the ladies upstairs after their meal was finished, Dimitri was still absorbed by the variety of ways he might go about accomplishing the pleasant task ahead of him. He absently bade Cassie good night at the door to her room, then slipped his arm around Shylo's waist for the walk down the hall to their suite.

As she had the night before, she balked and pulled away from him. "Oh, Dimitri. I know that you've been very patient with me so far, but I have to ask you to remain that way for a little while longer."

Quite sure that he didn't want to hear what she had to say, he asked the question anyway. "Are you trying to say that you're not planning to come to our room with me *again?*"

"I really can't. I hope you'll understand."

"Well, I don't! Please explain yourself."

She took a backward step, alarmed by the feral look in his dark eyes. "I—it's Cassie. She hasn't been herself since those outlaws kidnapped her. Sometimes I find her just staring out the window with tears running down her face, and when I ask her what's wrong, she says, 'Nothing,' in a flat kinda way, and then stares out into space again. I'm worried about her, and don't think I should leave her alone." She laughed nervously. "Why, that girl doesn't even have enough sense to lock her door. I'm always reminding her, but she just can't seem to think of it."

Shylo reached for the brass knob and turned it. "See what I mean?" After swinging open the door to Cassie's room, she stepped inside, turned to Dimitri, and said, "Thanks for understanding. I'll see you in the morning at breakfast." Then she closed the door in his face.

At first he just stood there, absolutely still, like a perfect imitation of the marble statue he hoped to restore to Greece. When he realized exactly what had happened, and that once again he was a groom without his bride, a sudden cold fury seized him. He clenched his fists, raising them as if he planned to pummel the door until it fell, then lowered them to his sides and started for the staircase instead.

He thought he had a grip on himself, and that he would descend to the bar two floors below as he'd done the previous evening, but when he reached the top step he hesitated.

"Hell if I'll spend another night alone," he muttered to himself. "The *hell* if I will."

Reversing direction, Dimitri stormed back down the hallway to Cassie's door and quietly tested the handle. As Shylo had suggested it would be, the room was still unlocked. To give the women a small warning—as little as the law might allow—he beat on the door as he opened it, then took a quick glance inside. Both ladies were in shock, but decently dressed.

Strolling toward them, he said quietly to Cassie, "Do you think you are feeling well enough to manage alone in here?" She looked at him as if he'd truly gone crazy. He rephrased his question. "Can you possibly stay by yourself for the night so that my wife and I can have a few moments to ourselves?"

Cassie burst out laughing. "Of course I can, silly. I'm not a baby all scared of the dark, you know. I'm a full-grown woman."

"Good. I'm glad to hear it." Dimitri glanced at his bride and held out his hand in invitation. "Well? Shall we retire for the night?"

Shylo's eyes widened as they darted from Cassie to Dimitri. Hedging as once again she tried to find a plausible rationalization, she backed away. "Umm, well . . . "

"You're quite out of excuses, my little kumquat." He advanced on her. "And I'm quite out of patience."

Then, before Shylo could say a word or understand what he was about to do, Dimitri swept her off her feet and heaved her over his shoulder. He strode to the door, carrying his speechless bride hanging off his back like sack of wool, and paused long enough to give Cassie a warning from over his shoulder.

"Be sure to lock the damn door when we're gone so Shylo won't be worrying about you all night. I'll wait outside until I know you've done it."

A moment after he'd pulled the door shut behind him, Dimitri heard the metallic click he'd been listening for. "Good night, Cassie," he said. Then he started toward the bridal suite.

Finally locating her voice, Shylo clung to the back of his shirt and protested loudly, "Dimitri! Stop! I—I can't go with you."

"In case you haven't noticed, you seem to be going anyway."

"B-but—" She was frantic to think of an excuse. "But I don't even have my nightgown with me!"

"That's not going to be a problem, Mrs. Adonis. You won't be needing it."

12

   Once inside their suite, Dimitri headed
straight for the bedroom, where he deposited his bride
none too gently onto the mattress. As she thrashed
about trying to regain her balance, he lit the bedside
lamp but left the flame low, illuminating little more
than the center of the bed and the brass headboard.

   "How . . . dare you treat me like that!" Shylo cried,
regaining both her feet and her senses.

   "I don't see why you are so upset—it is traditional,
is it not, for a man to carry his bride across the threshold?" Dimitri flashed his dimples and laughed.

   "I don't think you're one bit funny." Shylo tried to
straighten her bonnet, which had slipped to the side
of her head, then tore it off in frustration instead. "In
fact, you should be ashamed of yourself! Why, if I
were a man—"

   "If you were a man, I wouldn't have gone to the

trouble of collecting you." Dimitri gave her an indulgent smile, then took off his jacket and draped it over a chair. "And if you had tried to be a better wife to me by now, none of this would have been necessary."

Shylo had no ready answer for that, so she turned, showing him her profile, and raised the tip of her nose to a properly insulted tilt. He laughed at her again, but when he spoke she heard little amusement in his tone.

"That's a very cute expression, Mrs. Adonis, but cute is not what I'm after tonight." Now his voice was heavy with meaning, but she dared not look at him. "You have two choices; either you can begin undressing yourself or I'll do it for you."

Shylo whirled around. "Y-you—you wouldn't *dare!*"

"But of course I would." Dimitri swiftly unbuttoned his shirt and tossed it over the jacket. Then he reached for his belt buckle. "You have done nothing but avoid this moment since we arrived in San Diego. Your disobedience earlier today and your reluctance to join me in our bridal chamber has done little for my male pride, I can assure you of that. By the time this night is over, I intend to have it restored again. You can help—or not."

The last thing Shylo cared about was Dimitri's male pride—the removing or restoring of it—but she kept her silence, watching him the way a rabbit observed a coyote from its hiding spot in the tall weeds. How would she ever get out of this one? His belt was open, he'd removed his shoes and socks, and now he was in the midst of sliding his trousers down over his hips. He really was going to strip in front of her! Shylo quickly averted her gaze.

"Since you've yet to begin undressing," he said, his

voice more velvety and melodic than before, his accent thicker, "may I assume that you'd prefer I did it for you?"

"I—no!"

Forgetting the state of undress he might be in, Shylo turned back to him and, in spite of her fears, found herself feasting on the sight of Dimitri's bare chest. The dark curls scattered there rose and fell gently as he breathed, leading her gaze down a narrow path of those same coils until they stopped at the waistband of his drawers. Her eyes skimmed the pouchlike protrusion at his groin, then returned there again and again. Something was amiss. That pouch of light blue lamb's wool seemed to be swelling and changing shape before her very eyes. When it finally occurred to her what must have been happening, Shylo couldn't contain a gasp of surprise.

"Thank you for the compliment," he said, starting for her. "Now if you'll be so kind as to afford me the pleasure of reacting to your charms . . . "

He reached for the top button of her sateen jersey, and Shylo's hands flew to his fingers. "Don't," she said, gripping them tightly. "Please, don't."

Dimitri released her immediately. "What's wrong?"

He searched her eyes, concern reflected in the black core of his gaze, and his handsome face was so close to hers, she thought she might die from the pleasure of looking on him. She opened her mouth to answer him, but nothing came out except a slight croak.

"Surely you're not afraid of me, are you?"

"Afraid?" she echoed, so mesmerized by the nearness of this incredible man, she almost didn't recognize the escape route he'd offered. "I—yes! That's it. I'm flat-out terrified of all this!" Once she started,

Shylo couldn't seem to stop talking, rattling on with words that didn't even make sense to her. "I'd appreciate it if you'd just let me be. Besides, I'm pretty sure I won't be much good at this sort of thing, and honestly, I mean, if you've just got to do this with somebody, I don't mind—"

Dimitri covered her mouth with his, swallowing the rest of her sentence along with the little bit of sanity she still possessed. Her throat, her stomach, even her hands and feet, felt as if they'd been invaded by swarms of butterflies, and Shylo reached up to try to save herself. Groping for a way out, her fingers slid over the very chest hairs she'd ogled only moments ago, and before she knew it she was exploring those sooty black curls and the man beneath them. She found rock-hard muscle, but also areas of surprising softness—and, to her surprise, a pair of firm nodules much like her own nipples. Wondering if they were as sensitive as hers, she rubbed them with the tips of her fingers. With an abruptness that startled her, Dimitri set her away from him.

His black eyes were luminous, and a mysterious flame burned at their very core. He looked as if he wanted to speak but couldn't come up with the proper words. Stunned into silence herself, Shylo licked her lips.

Dimitri's eyes hardened and he shivered.

So did she. From her head to her toes.

"It would seem," he finally said, the words, thick, "that I've managed to put your fears to rest; at least I hope I've convinced you of that, *kouklitsa.*"

Her jersey fell to the floor along with her skirt, startling her. She hadn't even realized he'd undone the fastenings.

"I'm your husband," Dimitri said to his strangely silent wife, "and I want to make love to you. Do you understand what that means?"

Shylo thought of her years on the farm and the nasty Hereford bull who forced himself onto any cow who wandered into his path. She understood all right. She gulped. "It means breeding."

"*Breeding?*" Dimitri laughed as he gathered the hem of her chemise into his fists and slipped it over her head. "That seems an odd and clinical way to put it. I do not know the more romantic way to describe to make love, but I think you'll like it better if I show you instead." Dimitri smiled at her again, this time adding a little wink as he leaned over the bed to pull back the big puffy white quilt, the sheet, and the blanket. Then he patted the mattress. "Come. Sit down."

Her knees wobbling, Shylo did as he asked, but her mind was still racing with thoughts of escape. Somehow she would have to get out of this before things went any farther! She glanced down at herself, amazed to find that she wore only her new camisole and drawers, then realized that Dimitri had dropped to his knees before her and was in the midst of taking off her shoes. When he finished that task, he rolled down her stockings and took her bare feet into his hands, warming them just before he gently kissed the instep of each. This time when she shivered, it began at her toes and traveled up the length of her body.

"You are relaxing at last," Dimitri said, still smiling as he rose.

He turned away from her and paused before the lamp, making up his mind, she assumed, whether to leave it burning or blow it out. Shylo's gaze fell in line with the front of his drawers. The fabric there was so stretched by now that all traces of the "pouch" she'd noticed before had vanished. He'd swollen up even bigger than ever, impossibly huge! With a gasp that was more of a groan, Shylo fell back on the bed and pulled the covers over her head. In the darkness of her little cocoon, she heard Dimitri chuckling lightly. Moments later she felt the weight of his body as he slid beneath the sheets beside her. Then his voice came to her again, the sound magic, black velvet caressing her from within.

"If it is darkness you prefer, so shall you have darkness."

He reached for her, pulling her close, and found her lips with his. The kiss he bestowed now was hotter than before, more urgent, but it didn't frighten her as much as the feel of his searing palms against her skin. How could she be lying here practically naked? How had it happened, when? His fingers, even hotter than his palms, tugged at the tight buttons of her new camisole, and before she knew it all six of the little glass beads had slipped loose of their moorings. Next thing she knew, she was naked from the waist up, with only fuzzy recollections of how she'd lost her clothing.

Dimitri folded her in his embrace, squeezing her tighter and closer than ever before, then suddenly he ended the kiss, gasping for air as he pulled away from her mouth. Shylo felt as if she were suffocating, the atmosphere beneath the covers stifling, depleted of oxygen. Using her arms like a swimmer, she exploded up through the surface of bedding. Dimitri popped out beside her in the next moment, and then the two of them were laughing together, wrapped in each other's arms. Acting, she thought with alarm, like a pair of lovers.

"Sometimes," Dimitri said when he'd regained his breath, "too much darkness is not a good thing." Then his dimples receded and his expression grew solemn. "It's time, *kouklitsa*. Time that I made you mine."

He was looking at her in the strangest way, his features bathed in a thin sheen of perspiration, his gaze liquid fire, pinned to her breasts. It wasn't until then that Shylo realized her torso was completely uncovered, exposed to him. Her first instinct was to cross her arms and hide herself, but instead of fleeing or diving back under the covers, she found herself fighting the impulse. What had she become? She actually *liked* the way he was looking at her. And the way that, in turn, made her feel.

Dimitri removed the few pins still holding the remnants of Shylo's coiffure together, then fanned out her disheveled tresses along her back and shoulders. "I love the color of your hair," he murmured, "especially the way it looks in the sunshine with little sparkles of red in it. It is beautiful and different, like you."

Shylo had to swallow the urge to laugh over that as she thought back to the disaster she'd made of Cassie's hair, trying to achieve just that affect. Had she really possessed what she'd been looking for all this time but had been too blind to see it? Dimitri gathered her in his arms, and as he fit her body beneath his, she forgot about vanity and hair disasters as a sudden wave of new sensations swept her away.

He nuzzled the spot behind her ear, his hot breath blowing through the hair he'd said he loved so much, and Shylo nearly cried out, so intense was the pleasure of his touch. She shouldn't let him do this, she knew that this was wrong, but she couldn't bring herself to say the word *stop*. She struggled to find the strength, but now Dimitri was spreading hot kisses down the side of her throat, touching her breasts in a way that made her feel funny inside, wicked like the kind of woman who'd let a man do just about anything to her.

God forgive her, thought Shylo, she liked Dimitri's touch even more than the way he'd been looking at her, no matter how wrong it might be. Besides, even if she wanted to, she no longer had the strength to resist him—and if it meant she'd rot in hell for the rest of her days, so be it.

Dimitri raised up on his elbows. "For such a talkative woman, you're very quiet. Do you still have reservations?"

"I—no. I trust you, Dimitri." Her mind was chaos, but she managed to toss something she figured a real lady of high morals might say. "Just leave my nuptials out of it, if you can."

The moment the words *I trust you,* were out—the sweetest phrase he'd ever heard from anyone—Dimitri had all the permission he needed to consummate his marriage, at last. Shylo's final words, something about nuptials, rang in his ears as he worked her drawers down over her hips, but he couldn't make much sense of them. Was she talking about paperwork? A marriage license? How could she be interested in legal documents at a time like this? He wasn't. He *sure* as hell wasn't. In fact, he thought with a full measure of panic, if he didn't join with his new wife soon, there wouldn't be much reason to try.

Driven on by almost unrestrained lust, Dimitri tore off his own drawers, then flung back the sheet that had covered their bodies. Shylo didn't seem to notice. Her eyes were closed, her arms outstretched as if waiting for him. He drank greedily of her nakedness, a sight worth all the treasures of Rome, then fell on her mouth for one passionately deep and satisfying kiss. Using his hands as guides, he followed them down the curves of her body, strewing kisses across the mounds of her breasts and down the gentle slope of her navel. Shylo began to writhe beneath him then, calling out his name through her moans, and when he kissed the tender flesh at the backs of her knees, she nearly bucked him off the side of the bed.

Chuckling huskily over the lust he'd unearthed in his reluctant bride, Dimitri slid his fingers up the inside of her thigh, halting just before he reached the apex of her legs to stroke the ultrasoft skin there. His mouth followed as he raised his hand higher, his fingertips barely skimming the thick sable curls between her legs. Then he moved to the other thigh in search of that most exquisite softness there.

Half out of her mind with need, Shylo arched her back and looked down the length of her body to where her husband lay between her legs. He glanced up at her, the devil shining in his dark, dark eyes, and lightly kissed her where she ached the most. Shylo's head fell back on the pillow with the sharp, exquisite pleasure of it all. "All right, all right," she said, panting so hard, she could barely breathe. "Forget everything I said about not touching my nuptials. Just do it—do it *now.*"

Although he still didn't understand what she was talking about, Shylo's suddenly eager body was all the encouragement Dimitri needed. He pushed her legs apart and fitted himself between them. The groan Shylo uttered as he stroked her most sensitive self was hoarse and guttural, a siren that called his own lusty juices to life with a vengeance.

Raising his hips, Dimitri slowly eased his way inside of her, fighting against his release every inch of the way. As he broke through Shylo's maidenhead, Dimitri could almost swear he heard the strains of the clarion trumpeting the "Hasaposerviko," a wedding song that started out slowly and sensuously, then built to a rapid and resounding climax. He fought against the urge, tried to think of other things, but Shylo's body egged him on, her sweet voice crying out with pleasure. When she called his name in ecstasy, it was the final push that sent him over the edge. A tremendous shudder passed through him along with his seed, and he roared with an impulsive and savage triumph. Then he collapsed against his wife's soft body.

Shylo, who was just getting the hang of this lovemaking business, didn't know what had gone wrong. But something had. She tapped her husband's shoulder, trying to rouse him. "Dimitri? Are you all right? What happened?"

Stricken as he realized how truly out of control he'd become, he glanced up into Shylo's wide blue eyes. "Don't worry," he said. "I'm all right. I just need to have a short rest."

"Oh."

He hadn't been entirely truthful with her, Shylo knew that without a doubt. Something *had* gone wrong. Was it something she had done—or hadn't done? Had he hurt himself physically? Lord knew it hadn't exactly been as smooth or painless for her as his kisses had been. In fact, he'd hurt her a little, and she still felt some tenderness between her legs.

Also, she had to admit, there was this delicious ache, a swollen sensation that made her want to move her hips and rub herself against Dimitri some more. Made her want to be a nasty wicked woman all over again. Was this what became of women who gave themselves to men they weren't really married to? Would she truly rot in hell for the sins she'd committed here in this bed? Or was she paying already?

Shylo turned her face toward Dimitri's to check his breathing. He'd calmed down considerably, but his breath was still coming in erratic gasps. Lord, what if she'd almost killed her make-believe husband with her wanton and completely unladylike behavior? Dimitri had hardly been able to move since she'd screamed like some wild thing and twisted beneath him like a common barn cat! Oh, God, what if that was it? Tears rolled down her cheeks at the thought of how badly her sins might have hurt him. Shylo sniffled, struggling to hold them back, and then he spoke to her, his voice a warm caress.

"Don't cry, *kouklitsa.*" Even though he hadn't quite recovered yet, remorse brought Dimitri out of his lethargy and up to her side. "I'll make it up to you. I promise."

Make it up to her? What in hell did he mean by that? "I'm afraid I did something wrong. I'm not exactly sure what, but I know that I—"

He pressed a fingertip against her mouth, then replaced it with his lips. Dimitri nuzzled her more than kissed her, speaking against her skin as he tried to reassure her. "If you did anything wrong at all, it was that you felt too good to me. This time is for you. Only you."

Shylo still didn't know exactly what he meant, but she never got a chance to ask him about it. When she opened her mouth to speak, his fingers found that most sensitive place again, the wicked part of her that would have promised him the moon and more if only he'd keep stroking her there. Then he lowered his head, moving his mouth down the column of her throat, and wrapped his lips around the crown of her breast. When the tip of his tongue began to tease the nipple beneath, matching the ever-increasing rhythm of his fingers below, Shylo thought she'd go mad from wanting something, anything, to release her from the sweet agony of this terrible desire. A low, guttural oath reached her ears, a forbidden cuss word she was pretty sure had come from her own mouth, but even that didn't stop her from shouting or from begging Dimitri to do something for her, anything, but to please just *do it*.

He pushed up between her legs again, this time thrusting into her with abandon, and Shylo welcomed the relief of the new sensation, the easing of the fierce ache inside of her. Her respite didn't last long. The moment Dimitri began moving rhythmically again, with ever longer and deeper strokes, Shylo leapt to a new level of desire, one that lifted her to the very peak of fulfillment, then left her dangling there, frustrated and half out of her mind.

"Oh, God!" she cried. "I don't know what's happening to me. Help me, Dimitri, *help me!*"

With whispered words in a language she didn't understand, he drove his hand between their bodies, working his fingers into her damp curls, then dared her with both his voice and his touch to let go, to fly over the edge. The world exploded inside of Shylo after that, raising her higher and farther than she'd ever dreamed was possible. Her body seemed to melt at the core, merging and uniting with Dimitri in a union so perfect, so pure, the experience was almost ethereal.

As Shylo slowly tumbled down from those dizzying heights, her nerves, her mind, her heart, all tingling with a euphoric kind of joy, she felt as if she'd captured the moon and the stars deep within her, the answer to the universe and all its puzzles. When the last falling star inside her body finally flickered and died, she owned the darkness, too—and a sense of peace she'd never known before.

Late the following morning, as Dimitri slumbered through his second "rest period" in as many hours, Shylo leaned up on one elbow and took her first real glance of their room. It was huge, and so lavishly furnished, she could hardly believe it was real. Although she'd yet to venture out there, she vaguely remembered passing through a wide foyer and living room containing several puffy white chairs and couches. Here, in the separate bedroom, his and her dressers, washstands, and other Victorian furnishings were made of walnut and topped with imported marble. A small settee nestled in front of the fireplace was upholstered in snow-white velvet, and the canopied four-poster bed was draped in Nottingham lace accented with gold threads.

If all that weren't enough to dazzle a farm girl from Kansas, the bridal chambers featured a completely separate dressing area and bathroom, the latter offering cold *and* hot water piped right into the room, a sparkling enameled tub with gold fixtures, and a private privy! Shylo was impressed by her surroundings all right, but as she stared down at her husband, his features illuminated by the light filtering in through the lace curtains at the bay window, it all seemed terribly trivial. The real riches in this room, she realized with a start, were lying right beside her.

The sheet hung low on Dimitri's hips, exposing most of his flat stomach, all of his torso, and every handsome angle of his flawless face. Waves of his tousled hair, its ebony color stark against the soft white pillow, dipped down over his forehead to cover one eyebrow, making him look boyish and innocent, the exact opposite of what she now knew him to be.

All that and a Greek god, too. He was a man any woman would be proud to call husband or even . . . lover. A man who could warm even the coldest heart, coaxing it to blossom with love. He'd done that much to her, Shylo thought, even though she didn't truly believe in such nonsense. But there was no denying by morning's light that she loved him, if only just a little.

She giggled at the thought, then reached across Dimitri's chest and picked up the silver platter of fruit he'd ordered for them earlier. Along with the other appointments in the bridal suite, the hotel offered a bell that was wired directly to the manager's office. If they were hungry, or thirsty, or just wanted a copy of the *San Diego Union* or *Daily Bee,* all they had to do was push the buzzer, and moments later a member of the hotel staff would knock on the door to their suite and see to their needs. Feeling wickedly spoiled, Shylo plucked a fat orange slice from the still bountiful selection of fruit and dragged it slowly across her husband's mouth.

His tongue darted out, and as he licked his lips Dimitri said, "Grapes, woman. If you're going to seduce a Greek man with fruit, you must use grapes. Or kumquats."

She laughed and popped the orange slice into her own mouth. "Umm, I feel so wicked lying here with

you, naked, eating in bed. Wicked and nasty. Do you
suppose I'll go to hell?"

"How can you go to hell for lying with your husband?" He sat up and helped himself to a bunch of
grapes. "And as for eating in bed, I think it's allowed—
especially on a honeymoon."

Husbands and honeymoons. Shylo could claim neither excuse for her behavior, which meant she probably would go to hell, but she shrugged off the thought
and the shame that went with it. She was here now,
Dimitri's bride for the time being, and by God she
was going to enjoy herself. Lord knew that wasn't too
difficult—especially if he touched her again.

"It seems to me," she said as she nipped off the tip
of a ripe strawberry with her teeth, "that married legal
and proper or not, it's as wicked as all get-out to be
lolling around in bed when the sun's up and shining." She thought of her years on the farm and the
cows she'd have milked by now, not to mention the
hogs she'd have slopped and chickens she'd have fed.
Again she laughed. "Wicked and just about the best
morning I've ever had in my entire life."

Dimitri pulled her across his chest and kissed her.
"Me, too, *kouklitsa,*" he murmured. "Me, too."

"What's that you've been calling me?" she asked,
toying with a curl on his chest. "Coo-oo?"

"*Kook-leet-saw.* It means 'little doll.'" He chuckled, then tapped the tip of her nose with his finger.
"That's what you are. A *wicked* little doll—the best
kind." She giggled softly, her cheeks glowing with a
still innocent blush, and settled into the crook of his
arm. "And by the way, that reminds me of something
you said last night. Why were you so concerned about
our wedding papers?"

"Huh?" She raised her head and looked into his eyes. "I don't know what you're talking about."

"Last night you mentioned something about not touching our nuptial agreement, I believe. Did you think I would tear it up if you didn't let me make love to you?"

Shylo burst out laughing, then blushed at the memories. "Oh, that. It's just a word Cassie and I made up for, you know, the, ah . . . nether regions."

Her cheeks were bright red, and that crooked little smile he adored was more twisted than ever. Her expression telling him all he had to know, Dimitri reached beneath the sheet, coaxed her legs apart with his fingers, and then caressed her lightly. "You mean the nuptials you were talking about are right down here?" She nodded, and her breath came out in a halting sigh. "Ahh, I see. I'm afraid that I misunderstood you last night. Please accept my apology for the error."

"You're . . ." She shuddered. "F-forgiven."

By the time Dimitri bestowed all the apologies he could manage upon his wife, and she had given him a wealth of forgiveness in return, she was sitting on the plate of fruit she'd carelessly left lying beside her, and three perfectly beautiful strawberries had been ground into the white linen sheet beneath her. After another brief rest, Dimitri felt relaxed enough in her company to broach a few new subjects—namely those of a financial nature.

"*Kouklitsa?*" he called, blowing her a kiss. "Are you awake?"

"Uh-huh," she murmured. "I was just lying here wishing this day would never, ever end."

It was a thought he shared, but Dimitri knew he really had no choice but to move on to more serious things. "I'll do my best to keep to you feeling like today has never ended, but I'm afraid we must take some time out of that fantasy to talk about things of this world as well. I refer to your dowry."

Sudden anxiety turned her daydream to dust. "My . . . dowry?"

"Yes. I think perhaps it is time we sent a wire to your father informing him of our marriage. I need to know the terms of your dowry and when we might expect to see at least part of it. I wasn't able," he added, trying to explain their circumstances without alarming her too much, "to solicit much of my money from Greece. We'll be needing more funds soon."

"Oh . . . *hell!* " Shylo covered her face with her hands, forcing herself to clear her mind. She had to think—*think!*

Dimitri would not be put off. "Is there some problem with wiring your father that I should know about?" he asked.

Hell, yes, she thought to herself, it's all a big fat lie! It was a considerable problem no matter who was looking at it or from what angle, but she couldn't tell him the truth—not yet. So out slipped another lie.

"You can wire my . . . father if you want to, but it won't do us a damn bit of good. If you're expecting money by way of a dowry, I guess I'd better tell you now that my family doesn't have any. Not even two nickels to rub together."

"No money?" Dimitri could hardly believe it. "But what about your ties to the White House, and what about—"

"My uncle Grover—" She paused to swallow, the taste of her lies suddenly bitter on the tip her tongue. "The president has plenty of money, I suppose, but my family is certainly not entitled to any of it. Neither am I."

With a heavy sigh, Dimitri flopped over on his back and stuck both hands beneath his head.

Sure that she'd gotten past another barrier, Shylo concentrated on Dimitri's reactions to her news. He was disappointed, naturally, but he seemed almost *too* disappointed. Why? "Dimitri," she began, careful of her wording, "I'm sorry about the dowry, but it doesn't really matter too much—does it?"

"Well, no," he said, hedging, "but Ari and I did assume that you were, well . . . "

"Rich?"

He nodded, adding yet another piece to the surprising puzzle. She, at least, had a good reason to be looking for money from him, but why on earth would he want money from her?

"I, ah, thought *you* were rich enough for the both of us. What difference does it make if I'm not?"

He groaned, his hopes for hiding the truth dashed. "I'm not rich, my sweet little kumquat. Far from it, in fact."

Her eyes bulged. "B-but what about your big fancy business back in Greece, your imports and exports and all that stuff you and your uncle went on about back in New York?"

He decided right then to tell all, to clear up any misunderstandings he—and particularly Ari—may have initiated. It would feel good to have everything out in the open, the way it should be between husband and wife.

"Adonis Imports is failing. That's why Ari and I came to the United States in the first place—to get financial backing from American investors or banks. If

that didn't work out, we figured I could always . . . "
He gave her a sheepish grin.

"Oh, Lord—marry a rich debutante?"

"Yes," Dimitri admitted. "Such an arrangement is common in my country. I told you that back in Winslow."

"But you didn't tell me you were broke, or that you were only marrying me to use me!"

Dimitri sat up abruptly. "It wasn't that way. There were other reasons I asked you to be my wife, even though perhaps the main one was to replenish my bank account with your money. I have been honest with you. There is nothing to be so upset about."

"No? What about this?" She rose to her knees, oblivious of her nakedness. "You can't have married me for my money, because I married *you* for *yours!*"

"What?" English and Greek collided in his brain as he tried to make sense of what was going on. "I'm not to understand!"

"Well, I do—you pretended to be rich, so I figured you were. You tricked me!"

"No more than you tricked to me!"

They sat staring at each other for a long, awkward moment. Then the corners of Dimitri's mouth began to waver and he started to laugh. Shylo, who was unable to find any humor in the situation, became even angrier and let off steam in another way.

"Oh . . . *shit!*"

Pleased to see the startled look on her husband's face—not to mention the fact the oath had cut his laughter short—she threw herself back down on the pillow, muttering under her breath about Greek gods, money, and matrimony. The man she'd married was no better off than she was, and no more an aristocrat, either! How had she managed to delude herself so badly and bungle everything all at the same time? She had thought she was smarter than this!

A shadow suddenly came over her. Shylo opened her eyes to find Dimitri hovering over her, staring down into her face like a great vulture.

"What did I just hear you say?" he demanded.

She didn't care for the look in his eye or his attitude. She gave him a flippant reply. "Nothing."

"Hah! You said *shit.* I heard you loud and clear."

She thought of lying again, but what did his opinion of her matter now, anyway? In a tone as insolent as her mood was black, she snapped, "So what!"

"I won't have a wife who speaks such filthy words, is what. Now apologize and promise you'll never say it again. Such words are not becoming on you."

Shylo was sorely tempted to tell him that he didn't have to worry about having a wife with a filthy mouth because they weren't really married, but then she would be back where she'd started—alone and penniless. Not that she was a hell of a lot better off than that now. Lord, what should she do? How could she present this man to her mother and still claim wealth and success?

She cocked her head, studying him, and said, "I'll do my damnedest not to cuss in front of you or anyone else, if you'll make a little promise to me."

Although Dimitri didn't consider this to be an area for discussion or barter, he nodded. "Perhaps. What is it you want me to do?"

"You've done a pretty good job of it so far—can you at least keep up appearances and pretend to be rich until after Colleen and Niko get into town—until I say that it's okay not to pretend?"

This made Dimitri madder than her foul language had. His lip curled at the corner as he rolled off the mattress and onto his feet. What a fool he'd been to think that Shylo was different from the other society darlings! How could he have thought for one minute that she had a head that couldn't be turned by wealth and status? He really was an idiot, he decided as he climbed into his clothes. An idiot and a fool.

"Did you hear me, Dimitri?" she asked as he finished dressing. "Will you agree?"

"I'll do the best I can." He stalked to the bedroom doorway, then glanced back to where his wife lay. "I think my best should be good enough. After all—I fooled you, didn't I?"

Then he left the room, the echo of his angry footsteps filling Shylo's ears long after the door had slammed shut.

13

Downstairs in the hotel bar, Dimitri had just finished telling his tale of woe to his uncle, who'd immediately ordered cognacs for them both, and doubles, no less. After the drinks had been served, they moved to a more private table in the corner of the room, where the stained-glass windows looked out on Horton's flowering plaza across the street.

Dimitri decided it was a far better view than gazing upon Ari, who hadn't completely recovered from the injuries he'd received in Winslow. Though the old man's nose was no longer dripping or overly sensitive to movement, it was still swollen and misshapen. His eyes were clear save for a small clot at the corner of the left, but the puffed flesh beneath them had faded from midnight blue to a ghoulish shade of green. Despite his physical appearance, Ari's mind seemed unharmed as he offered his thoughts for solving their newest problem.

"To learn that your bride has no dowry is indeed a blow, my son, but all may not be lost." As usual, he spoke his native language when alone with his nephew. "Just the fact that you are now related to the president should be enough to help Adonis Imports find the backing it needs after we return to New York."

There was wisdom in those words, but they didn't solve everything. "And what do you suggest we do for money in the meantime, dear Uncle? Between meals for four, clothing for my wife, who has no trousseau and no way of finding her old trunk of clothes, two rooms at this hotel plus a suite, and passage back to New York and Greece, I think you'll find that we aren't going to last much longer with the funds I have left at my disposal."

"You have a definite point, my son." Ari tossed down his brandy, then shook his head with robust enthusiasm. "As I see it, we have only one choice. We must return to New York with all due haste, and forget about confronting this Pappas fellow, whoever he may turn out to be."

Dimitri hadn't considered this, but now that his uncle suggested it, the idea really did seem like the only plausible solution. Besides, he'd done enough foolish things of late. Spending his last drachma in San Diego while waiting for a man who might or might not be the person responsible for the downfall of Adonis Imports seemed the most foolish of all.

After downing his cognac, Dimitri banged the glass against the table. "I agree. We must head back to New York on the first available train. Then, on to Greece."

"An excellent decision, my son." Ari wriggled his eyebrows. "Now on to more interesting matters. How was the night with your new wife? Did all go well at last?"

Dimitri glanced across the table at his uncle, who eagerly awaited an answer, then turned his gaze toward the window. To say that things had gone well would have been a gross understatement, he realized with a start. He never would have believed it possible, but his wedding night turned out to be one of the most, if not *the* most, profoundly intense experiences of his life—including its rocky beginning. He'd been embarrassed at first to have lost control, but Shylo was so responsive to him, so innocent and eager to learn, that his chagrin, if that's what it was, hadn't lasted any longer than he had.

That, along with the many wonders the night had to offer, had been an enormous surprise to Dimitri. Since he'd been anticipating the consummation of his marriage for so many days, he'd expected a tremendous feeling of relief—and in that way he hadn't been disappointed. What he didn't expect was the overwhelming sense of responsibility that came with the consummation of his marriage or the dredging up of new emotions, confusing emotions.

The union between himself and Shylo was supposed to have been a business deal, one that, as it turned out, wasn't quite as lucrative as he'd hoped. That fact alone should have kept his mind clear and his concentration where it belonged—on his studies and on the committee he headed back in Greece—but it seemed that all Dimitri had to do was hear Shylo's name, and he became consumed by thoughts of her instead.

Even now, as he found himself wondering how she was doing upstairs alone in their room, his chest tightened and his heart pounded, making him feel weak all over—a strange and unwelcome sensation for a man as emotionally guarded as he. Perhaps, he thought, he was coming down with a terrible American virus. But somehow he knew that was not the case.

Ari's impatient nature could wait no longer for an answer. "You look distraught, my son. Surely there were not problems with this part of your marriage, too?"

"No. No, of course not." Still troubled by his thoughts and the odd way they made him feel, Dimitri forced a grin. "Everything between us is fine."

"Then we have much to celebrate!" Ari signaled the waiter for another round of cognacs. "We must drink to good fortune, which surely will be just around the corner!"

Since Shylo had lolled around in her bed about all she could stand—especially now that she was alone— she decided to dress and then headed up the hallway to check on her sister. Testing the doorknob as she always did when Cassie was alone in a room, she found it unlocked—as usual.

Shylo, already in a foul mood, let her anger race out of control as she burst into the room and shouted, "Have you no brains at all? How many times must I tell you to lock up after yourself!"

Cassie, who'd been leaning back on a nice soft Queen Anne chair with her feet propped on her bed, flung the magazine she'd been reading into the air, then tumbled over backward, chair and all. With the breath knocked out of her, she lay on her back, her petticoats inverted over her face, her legs sticking straight up in the air.

Filled with instant regret, Shylo rushed to her aid. "Oh, my God!" Pulling Cassie by her hands, she dragged her away from the chair. "Are you all right, sis? Talk to me!"

Cassie looked up at her, batted her lashes, and groaned.

More panicked now, Shylo gripped her sister beneath the armpits and pulled upward. "Come on, test your legs a little and you'll see—you're just fine."

After Cassie finally got to her feet and regained her breath, she tore herself loose from Shylo's gasp. "W-why in God's green earth did you come in here hollering like that? You went and s-scairt hell out of me!"

"I'm sorry, truly I am." She reached for Cassie, who sidestepped her embrace. Following her sister around the room instead, Shylo tried to explain. "I was worried about you after leaving you alone for so long last night, and I got kind of upset when I found you'd left your door unlocked—again."

"So? Nothing happened to me, and near as I can figure, nothing ever will in this godforsaken, falling-off-the-end-of-the-world town."

"Don't talk like that—if you dare bad luck, it just might come your way."

"I'll dare bad luck if I want to!" She flounced away and headed for her dressing table. "I'm tired of you telling me what I can do and can't do. I'm a grown woman now who can do what I damn well please without a big sister who thinks she's my mother telling me what to do all the time!" Out of breath from her tirade, Cassie fell onto the tufted vanity stool.

Surprised to see this new side to her sister, Shylo held back a retort and approached her from another angle. "I'm sorry if I seem too motherly at times, but I'm only repeating what my husband said to you as he carted me out of here last night. Don't you recall hearing Dimitri give you strict orders to lock this damn door?"

Cassie remembered all that and more. Her mood considerably brighter, she swiveled on her little stool and offered her sister a somewhat less than remorseful expression. "I'm sorry about the lock. I took care of the door last night like Dimitri said, but I went downstairs for some breakfast this morning and must have forgot to lock up after I got back." Grinning, she stood up and sashayed over to her sister. "Speaking of your husband . . . "

"He's not *really* my husband," Shylo reminded Cassie, but once the words were out, they felt like another of her lies. It was odd, Shylo thought; was she more like her sister than she realized? She was beginning to believe her own fantasies!

"So tell the truth," Cassie said. "Being trapped alone in a bedroom with a handsome man like that wasn't near as bad as you thought it'd be, was it?"

Shylo blushed and averted her gaze. "I stayed the night in his bedroom and lived through it, if that's what you mean."

Giggling softly now, Cassie said, "If all you did was survive the night, how come when I mentioned you getting trapped in Dimitri's bedroom, your cheeks went all bright? You look like you rubbed pomegranate juice all over your *own* face for a change!"

"I, ah—" Distinctly uncomfortable with this line of questioning, as well as with the role reversal between her and her sister, Shylo pressed her palms against her cheeks to cool them. "I'm a little sunburned is all. Nothing to worry about."

Wrapping her arms around her tummy and holding on, Cassie turned away from Shylo and fell onto her bed. Doubled up with laughter, she finally managed to say, "H-how in t-tarnation did you get sunburned? We haven't even *seen* the sun since we left Winslow!"

"I just did, and that's all there is to it!"

Finished with the ridiculous conversation, Shylo marched across the room, picked up the fallen chair, and positioned it next to the bed where Cassie lay, still howling. When her sister's chuckles ebbed enough for her to get a word in edgewise, Shylo said, "That's enough talk about last night. We've got troubles again."

Cassie wiped the tears from her eyes, then rolled onto her side so she could see Shylo's face. "What kind of troubles?"

"The usual. Money. Dimitri told me this morning that he's as broke as we are."

Cassie sat bolt upright. "But I—I thought, I mean he *looks* as rich as any man we ever met. Are you sure he wasn't just kidding around with you?"

"I'm sure." Shylo leaned forward and touched the back of her sister's hand. Finally she managed to smile over the irony of the whole mess. "You're gonna love this part—Dimitri also admitted that he married me for—guess what—*my* money."

"You're kidding!"

Shylo pressed her lips together and shook her head solemnly.

"Oh, shit!" Cassie fell back on the bed. "What are we gonna do now?"

"We're going to have to do a little thinking, but first I'm going to ask you one more time to please stop cussing and saying words like 'shit.'" At the sound of the expletive coming from her own mouth, Shylo cringed. "It's not becoming on you."

Cassie's initial reaction was to defend herself, but

she realized that Shylo hadn't been tossing orders about as usual, so she quietly agreed. "I'm sorry that I keep forgetting about that cussing business, and I promise to do better from now on. But what are we gonna do?"

"There isn't much we *can* do right now but sit tight and hope that our mother is on that packet this Saturday. If she isn't, and Dimitri runs out of money . . . "

The sisters regarded one another, each gripped with a panic of a different kind until a knock sounded at the door, breaking their trance.

"I'll get it!" Cassie yelled.

Ever hopeful that Buck might have decided against rejoining the gang and caught the next train out of Winslow instead, Cassie was desperate to get to the door before Shylo. She rolled off the bed, caught her foot in the hem of the quilted coverlet, and fell to the floor. After quickly getting her feet under her again, she ran across the room, brushing past her sister.

Cassie opened the door a crack and peered out nervously into the hallway. "Oh . . . it's you."

Slightly offended by the young lady's odd reception, Dimitri still managed a warm smile. "Good afternoon. I hope I didn't disturb you. I'm looking for Shylo. Have you seen her?"

Cassie flung open the door and stepped out of his way. "She's in here."

Shylo had started toward the door, but when her husband walked into the room and her eyes met his, she froze.

"Shylo," he said as he closed the gap between them, "I've been looking all over for you."

The velvet caress of his voice, which had always been enough to upend her thoughts, seemed more intimate now, almost as if it had the power to make love to her on its own. At the thought, memories of their night together filled her mind and body, and Shylo shivered with sudden desire. When Dimitri reached her, took her gently by the shoulders, and then lightly kissed her forehead, those shivers became tremors. Unable to stand on her own any longer, Shylo leaned heavily against his chest. Had she ever before felt so helpless, so alive? Or so utterly and deliciously female?

"I've been worried about you," Dimitri murmured against the curls at her temple. And that much was true, in spite of the fact that she'd lied to him or, at the least, led him astray. Now he felt only relief over having found her unscathed. "When I came back to our room," he said, caressing her shoulders, "and you were gone, I thought I might have frightened you off—or made you so mad that you ran away."

Stunned by this confession, Shylo leaned back and looked into eyes darkened with passion. He cared. He really cared. Her heart in her throat, she took her share of the blame. "But you were so angry when you left, I thought *you'd* never come back. I didn't know where else to go but in here with Cassie."

"Your place is with me—never forget that, no matter how many mistakes I make along the way." Dimitri wrapped a possessive arm around her waist, then traced the outline of her upper lip with the index finger of his free hand. "My bad temper is to blame for what happened between us this morning. I'll try to do better with it and you in the future."

The future. My God, she thought with alarm, he expects a future. And why shouldn't he? He believed they were man and wife by law, and as such, he was living his life with the future in mind—one that included her by his side. She hadn't considered this complication before, but now she saw that what she'd concocted here was much more than an elaborate plan to locate her missing mother. She'd figured on inventing a husband for herself, a convenience no more real than Cassie's fantasy prince riding up on a white horse. Now the truth hit her full in the face, and she finally saw Dimitri for what he was—a real live flesh-and-blood man. One who actually seemed to care about her. Shylo clung to him, and to that thought as well, and held him tight in an effort to muffle a sudden sob.

Dimitri heard the sound as he picked up a vague movement out of the corner of his eye. Too concerned over Shylo to investigate what he thought he saw, he said, "Please forgive me, if you can, for walking out on you this morning. I had a lot to think about, a lot of plans to make."

"Oh, of course I forgive you," she said, swallowing her tears along with her feelings of guilt. She thought back to Dimitri's proposal, to the businesslike proceedings and his declaration about not believing in marrying for love. What was there to feel guilty about? When this charade was over, the most her deceptions would cost him might be a bit of trouble and a little money. It wasn't as if she'd be breaking his heart.

That thought went a long way toward easing Shylo's conscience, but it also made her wonder if she'd taken enough steps to protect her own heart—if it wasn't already in jeopardy.

Something moved; maybe it was a shadow, but Shylo couldn't possibly look away from Dimitri. She had to let him know that she accepted at least part of the blame for the argument she'd had with him. Hell, if the truth were known, she was pretty sure he couldn't be held responsible for any of the blame. And she didn't want to feel guilty about that, either.

"I'm the one who's sorry, Dimitri. I shouldn't have cussed at you the way I did this morning. I guess I was just upset, you know, about all the things we talked about."

"Then you haven't run away from me, *kouklitsa?* We can start fresh?"

His dimples were like deep caves, his eyes the darkest raven color imaginable. And he was hers, at least for a short time. Hers anytime she wanted him. Another shiver coursed through her, and Shylo returned his smile tenfold. "I told you—I only came here to check on Cassie. We can start fresh any time you like." She hadn't thought his dimples could get any deeper, or his smile any wider, but she was wrong.

"In that case, my little kumquat . . . " Dimitri lowered his head. "What would you say if I were to suggest something like this?" He captured her mouth with his, then whispered against her lips. "Or this . . . " And parted her teeth with his tongue.

"I'd say," came a loud, exasperated voice from nowhere, "that if you two don't stop carrying on this minute, I think I might have to throw up all over this pretty rug."

Dimitri and Shylo sprang apart, each of them horrified to realize they'd forgotten that Cassie was in the room. Shoving his hands in his pockets, Dimitri said, "Forgive my manners. I seem to have left them in the bar downstairs." Then he strolled toward the window, his back to the women, and willed his heated body to cool off.

Shylo, her cheeks aglow, gave her sister a wan smile. "I guess we kind of forgot about you."

"That's all right." Tears sprang into Cassie's eyes. "Everyone else has, too."

"Oh, honey—please don't cry." Shylo threw her arms around her sister, sure that her tears were prompted by thoughts of the woman who'd abandoned her as a newborn babe. "It's going to be all right. I promise. Everything will be all right."

After overhearing the last part of Shylo's conversation, and feeling in control of himself again, Dimitri turned toward the ladies. "She's right, Miss McBride," he said. "Once we get a few things straightened out between us, everything will be just fine."

He glanced around the small room, looking for a suitable spot for a quiet discussion. The narrow bed and a vanity with a matching stool tucked beneath it were the only items of furniture other than a large dresser and the Queen Anne chair. He pulled the stool out for himself, offered the chair to Shylo, and said to Cassie, "Why don't you have a seat on your bed for a minute. We might as well get this over with now."

As Dimitri straddled the stool directly across from her, a suddenly suspicious Shylo sank onto the thick cushion of her chair. She didn't like his tone or the fact that he thought he had to "get something over with." And she had a pretty good idea what "it" might be.

Narrowing her eyes, she asked him, "What's going on? And leave out the flowery words and phrases. I'd like to hear this straight."

"Then straight you shall have it." Dimitri shifted his gaze from Shylo to her traveling companion—a much safer place. "Ari and I had a long talk about finances this morning. We've decided that we must leave San Diego on the next eastbound train."

Both women leapt to their feet, shouting in unison, *"No!"*

Surprised to learn that her sister was every bit as determined about the matter as she was, Shylo didn't follow up her refusal with an explanation. She just stood there, pleased beyond measure, and listened to Cassie plead their case.

"I ain't leaving San Diego—not now, and maybe never! You might think you can toss Shylo over your shoulder and drag her off anywhere you want, but you got no rights with me. You can't make me do nothing I don't want to, neither."

Which was fine with Dimitri. Cassie could stay here, pink hair and all, for the rest of her life as far as he was concerned. But for Shylo's sake, he had to at least offer to keep her in their employ. He gave her a magnanimous grin. "I have no wish to force you into doing anything, Miss McBride. You're free to come with us or to stay here. The choice is entirely yours."

That was good enough for Cassie. "Thank you. I'll be staying, in that case." Then she sat back down on the bed.

Shylo dropped back onto her chair. "I'm staying here, too."

Dimitri took a deep breath and directed his comments to his wife. "As I already said, we're very low on money and can't afford to remain in San Diego another day, much less another week. Miss McBride will have to welcome her mother on her own. You've accompanied her this far—surely that's enough to show your appreciation for all she's done for you."

"No, it isn't."

"But I told you in New York that I only had time for a quick trip out west. I have wasted enough time in this country—I must get back to Greece immediately."

Tears blurred her vision, and although she knew her reaction might stir Dimitri's suspicions, Shylo went on, "I'm sorry about that, but I'm not leaving San Diego until Colleen arrives. I—I've got to see Cassie through this thing. I promised I would, and I will. She needs me." She turned to her sister. "Isn't that right?"

Knowing how much the reunion with their mother meant to Shylo, and knowing too how it would break her heart to have come this close and not seen her, Cassie turned to Dimitri, tears rolling down her cheeks, and said defiantly, "That's right. I'm counting on her to be with me when Ma gets here."

Both women turned on Dimitri then, a couple of stubbornly set chins and two pairs of flashing blue eyes brooking no argument from him. For a moment he thought his wife and her friend looked enough alike to be twins—or, at the least, sisters. He would have laughed over the idea if not for the gravity of the situation, and he worked up an extra-vicious scowl to make certain that he didn't. His expression must have been fierce indeed, Dimitri decided, because when he turned it on them, Cassie and Shylo fell into each other's arms, effectively freezing him out as they sought consolation from each other.

Since he was so new—and obviously inept—at handling one woman, Dimitri knew he could never manage two. He threw his hands up in air, rose from the stool, and ambled over to the small window. Pulling aside the curtain, Dimitri stared out at the horse-drawn street cars trudging down the center of the dirt road, then glanced up to the row of tall arch-light towers lining the avenue. False-front stores, boardwalks, and saloons littered this section of town, yet the area was illuminated by electric lighting. The old enhanced by the new, the future edging out the past.

Dimitri couldn't help but liken the changes this wild town was undergoing to the reorganization of his own life. How had his goals gotten so turned around after his arrival on American soil? His return to Greece and his life's work were paramount and always had been—enough so that those goals had cost him the respect and friendship, if not the love, of his father. He hated the idea of anything getting in the way of those interests now that he'd invested so much in them both emotionally and financially, but Dimitri did see that as a married man he might have to alter his plans just a little.

Besides, he thought, finally able to see a bright spot, if he went along with Shylo's quest to bring about a reunion between Cassie and her long-lost mother for just a little bit longer, he stood at least a slim chance of finding Niko and maybe even getting back some of the funds that had been stolen from the business in the bargain.

As Dimitri turned back toward the women to offer a new version of his plan, he could hear them whispering—plotting, he imagined, the many ways in which they might coerce him into agreeing with them. He couldn't help but wonder then how much of himself he could surrender to Shylo and her schemes and still remain true to himself.

His voice shadowed with this new worry, he broke into their murmured conversation. "Ladies, I've thought your problem over, and have come up with another solution." Once he had their full attention he proceeded. "I've decided that we can stay in San Diego until the packet arrives this Saturday."

Shylo leapt up from the bed. "Oh, Dimitri! That's wonderful news. You won't be sorry you changed your mind. I promise you you won't!"

"I promise you I won't, either." He winked at her, then spelled out the terms of his compromise. "Make no mistake about what happens after Saturday, however. If the woman you're looking for is not on that ship, we'll leave for New York immediately."

Cassie opened her mouth to protest, but Shylo silenced her with a sharp glance. If Colleen hadn't returned from Mexico by Saturday, they would just have to figure a way to stay another week in San Diego. There was no sense in dealing with another problem before it even existed.

Shylo gave her husband a broad grin. "Thanks for understanding, Dimitri. I—we really do appreciate it."

He strode over to her, took her by the hand, and said, "Then maybe you ought to show me a little of that appreciation. On the way upstairs earlier, I ordered some food to be sent up to our room: a little bread, some cheese, a few strawberries in thick, sweetened cream. Interested?"

Shylo glanced up at him. "Strawberries in . . . cream?"

Dimitri licked his lips and rolled his eyes.

"See you later, Cassie!" said Shylo as her husband pulled her toward the door.

After they stepped into the hallway, both Dimitri and Shylo glanced back inside the room and said in one voice, "And this time, don't forget to lock the door!"

14

Saturday morning dawned bright and clear, the first fog- and mist-free day since they had arrived in the little seaside town. Between the beautiful weather and sparkling sapphire-blue bay, Shylo couldn't help but get her hopes up as she strolled arm in arm with Dimitri along the steamship wharf at the foot of Fifth Avenue. Today, if all went as expected, she would see her mother again at long last.

Briefly indulging in the scenario she'd envisioned over and over through the years, Shylo pictured the look on her mother's face as she gazed upon her fully grown and very successful daughter. Colleen would be overwhelmed with joy at first, then would welcome her with open arms, crying buckets of tears over all the time they'd been apart and promising never to let her out of her sight again.

Today, Shylo thought, barely able to contain her

excitement, that dream would finally come true. Nothing would go wrong this time, nothing. How could it after all she'd been through to bring about the reunion?

She and Cassie had planned this moment down to the last detail—including the fact that Shylo would greet their mother alone. The reasons were twofold: first, they figured if they were to shove two daughters at the poor woman instead of one, the shock might send her scurrying in the opposite direction—again. Second, and more important to Shylo, was the fact that she wanted desperately to welcome the mother she remembered so well with nothing to distract them or intrude on the moment. There would be plenty of time later for Cassie to become acquainted with the mother she'd never known.

The fact that both Dimitri and Ari had accompanied her to the dock wouldn't be a problem—Shylo would make sure that Colleen didn't take any notice of them until she was good and ready to introduce her mother to her "rich" husband. As for extracting herself from such a blatant lie—both the rich and the husband parts—she would simply have to worry about that after she and Colleen had become close enough that nothing could tear them apart.

"Look! Look!" cried Ari, who'd been staring across the bay at the castlelike turrets and red roofs of the magnificent Coronado Hotel. "I see smokestacks. The steamer will be arriving soon!"

Following his gaze, Shylo scanned the horizon and glimpsed a small ship slipping between Coronado Island and the tip of Point Loma. Her breath caught in her throat. The moment was almost upon her. From over her shoulder she heard Ari and Dimitri muttering to each other in Greek, and a couple of other voices joined them as well, but she paid them no mind. Her stomach was churning wildly, and her pulse was pounding in her head so hard and fast that it drowned out the cries of the scavenging seagulls above. A few moments later she did manage to hear Dimitri say something about his wife just before he took her by the hand and pulled her up beside him.

"You've already met Mr. Earp, Shylo. This is his wife, Josephine."

"Josie," the woman said, her nose set about one degree higher than even the most haughty New York matron. "Nice to meet you. I understand you've come down to the wharf with us to welcome Niko and Colleen back to town. Have you known them long?"

With us? "I—I knew Colleen when I was a young girl. I've never met her new husband."

Josie gave her the once-over, and then, as if exchanging pleasantries with Shylo were the only courtesy required of her, she turned away and listened in on the conversation among the men.

Shylo had taken an instant dislike to Earp's wife even before her obvious snub. Josie's big brown eyes and voluptuous beauty would have been reason enough to draw out any woman's fighting side. That, combined with the fashionable way Josie had dressed her slender frame, conjured up feelings of envy and self-doubt in Shylo and made her want to push the woman into the bay. Her elegant walking suit, made of gorgeous aquamarine silk and royal blue velvet, looked as if it had come straight off the pages of *Harper's Bazaar*. Standing beside her, Shylo felt insignificant, as if she were still wearing the rags and hand-me-downs of her youth. How would she ever be able to impress her mother in her common sateen suit with this picture of perfection alongside her?

Unaware that his wife was thinking of kicking Josie off the dock, Dimitri studied the affable exchange between his uncle and the former lawman. "I didn't realize you'd met Mr. Earp before, Ari. When did this happen?"

The old man grinned. "Since I discovered that my friend Wyatt owns three gambling halls that feature *twenty-one* games of chance—backgammon among them."

Dimitri groaned, then quickly chided his uncle in Greek. "Did you learn nothing of Americans and their gambling ways back in Winslow?"

"We are not in Winslow," Ari muttered in his native language, "and this man runs an honest house. Do you forget who he is, my son?" Then, in English, he faced the Earps and loosely translated his conversation with Dimitri. "It seems my nephew fears that I will lose my entire life savings in your parlors should I venture into one of them again."

Earp let out a rare chuckle. "That's not likely to happen. You're an exceptional backgammon player, Ari. Better than any I've seen. If you ever need a job, you've got one with me."

Shylo, whose nerves were stretched tighter than the laces on her corset, couldn't bear any more idle chatter or disdainful glances from Josie. She edged away from the group of gamblers and began pacing along the wooden dock, which was shared with the railroad. Just what she needed—Wyatt Earp and his wife to come along and spoil her private reunion. How would she ever manage to get Colleen off by herself with this arrogant woman intent on welcoming her back to town? Maybe she *should* trip the stylish Mrs. Earp and "accidentally" bump her into the bay. It would serve the woman right after snubbing her so rudely.

She closed her eyes against the bright sunlight, and her mind against her wicked thoughts, and let the fresh aroma of tangy salt water soothe her jangled nerves. By the time the steamer finally hissed its way alongside the dock and lowered its gangplank, Shylo's concentration was back on the imminent reunion, but her stomach was still twisted in knots. So intent was she on the purser as he lowered the rope, allowing the first passenger to debark, that when Dimitri came up behind her and slipped his arm around her waist, she let out a yelp of surprise and lurched forward, nearly falling into the bay herself.

"Take it easy, *kouklitsa,*" said Dimitri as he hauled her back a safe distance. "Why are you so nervous? If I didn't know better, I'd think this meeting was between you and your own mother."

When she heard Dimitri's astute observation, Shylo nearly broke down and spilled the truth—all of it. After forcing herself to take several deep breaths, she managed to calm her jittery nerves as the passengers began to file down the gangplank.

It took a full twenty minutes for the packet to clear her decks of voyagers and another ten before Shylo could even begin to accept the obvious. Her mother had not returned to San Diego aboard this ship. As she finally acknowledged that her reunion had been postponed again, a horrible ache seized her chest, leaving her short of breath and slightly dizzy. She thought she'd grown used to the "empty" sensation that always accompanied thoughts of her mother, that hollowed-out part of her that started in her breastbone and reached the pit of her stomach, but now it had grown in proportion, as if it had expanded into a bottomless well.

Shylo swayed and might even have fainted then if not for Dimitri, who pulled her away from the ship. "Come on, *kouklitsa,*" he said quietly. "You've done the best you can for your friend. Ari and the Earps have gone back to town, and so must we."

She glanced up at him with unseeing eyes, then went along with him wordlessly. Dimitri didn't care in the least for Shylo's white, pinched expression or blank look in her eyes. Again trying to console her or at least get her to snap out of this trancelike state, he said, "Do not trouble yourself further with Cassie's affairs. Think instead of the adventures before you—and the challenge you'll encounter when we get back to our room."

Confused, she glanced at him. "Challenge? I don't understand."

"I was just thinking how tricky it might be for you to pack my clothing *and* yours into the small traveling bag we'll have to share for our trip to New York today."

Later that night—much later than Dimitri had anticipated—they still hadn't gotten around to packing so much as a pair of drawers. And he knew the precise reason why. Shylo, his formerly innocent little bride, had spent the better part of the day seducing him. The minute he began to stir after each encounter and the brief nap that followed, she was all over him again, kissing and fondling him to complete and utter distraction. He had a pretty good idea that this suddenly insatiable wife of his had ulterior motives for her amorous behavior.

Testing her, Dimitri yawned and stretched his arms high over his head. Shylo slipped her hand beneath the covers, then brushed his body with her fingertips.

"I know what you're doing," he said, surprised to find he still had a flicker of desire left in him. "But I'm not carved of marble, you know. I'm just a man—and a very tired one at that."

"That's funny." Shylo gave him a sidelong look as she increased the pressure in her fingers from feathery caresses to bolder strokes. "It seems that at least *part* of you is made of marble."

Drawing in a sharp breath, Dimitri reached down and tore her hand from his body—while he still could. "We're leaving San Diego first thing in the morning, Shylo, and all of your considerable . . . talents won't prevent our departure."

She threw herself down on her pillow. "I can't leave, Dimitri, and I won't."

"Yes, you will. You promised you would go *today* if I agreed to stay until the steamer arrived. Even if I wanted to remain here another week—which I don't, since I *must* get back to my work immediately—you know we don't have the funds to support us that long. We simply have no choice but to go."

A brilliant idea suddenly hit her. "What if we come up with the extra money we need for our rooms? Cassie can sew like the wind, so she could pay her own way from now on."

Although he had no intention of staying another night in San Diego no matter what schemes his wife thought of, Dimitri said, "That's a lovely plan, Shylo, but we still would have to pay for two rooms and meals for an entire week."

"We'll cut back on expenses!" Shylo sat bolt upright.

She and Cassie had literally survived on bread and water for weeks on end during their rougher years. They could do it again if it meant buying the time they needed for their mother to return to San Diego. She pushed out her stomach to make it appear bloated. "I've been eating like a pig since we got married. Doing without some of that rich food ought to do me some good."

"It won't do you any good at all." Dimitri had to admit that he loved the glimmer of excitement in his wife's eyes, but this little game of "do we stay or do we go" had gotten completely out of hand. "Even if you starved yourself for the rest of the week—which I would never allow—it still wouldn't be help enough. We're leaving and that's all there is to it."

"But we can do more than cut down on food to save money! I'll move back in with Cassie, and you and Ari can share a room like before in Winslow. You'd only have to pay for your one room!"

"No way in hell, Mrs. Adonis."

In spite of the fact that she was thinking frantically of ways to persuade him, Dimitri's comment and the glimmer of desire she saw shining in his eyes gave her pause enough to make her feel all warm and cuddly inside—and more adored, if not loved, than she'd ever felt in her entire life.

Feeling ridiculously coy, Shylo grinned. Then she said, "All right. We'll keep three rooms, but you and I don't need a suite. We can take a less expensive room, and maybe even go to a cheaper hotel. What do you say to that?"

Hardly able to believe that he was even considering her request, Dimitri studied her long and hard before he answered. It was that crooked little smile, the one that made her look like a naughty little girl and a sensuous woman all at the same time. That *had* to be it, the reason for his hesitation. But he wasn't ready to cave in over just an expression, no matter how irresistible. Not quite, anyway.

"I cannot understand why this reunion is so damned important that it takes precedence over my wishes. Does it really mean so much to you?"

"Oh, God, yes." She leaned across Dimitri's chest, pressing her breasts flat against his nipples, and looked directly into his eyes. "I don't know exactly how else to put it, and I can't really explain it, but this . . . meeting Colleen next Saturday means more to me than anything has in my entire life. You've got to believe that, and to try, if you can, to understand how strongly I feel about it."

"If you're talking about an obsession, I believe that I do understand."

"An obsession?" Shylo tasted the word, likening it to a child's craving for chocolates and sweet cakes, and found that the flavor fit. "I suppose you could say that I'm obsessed by the idea of bringing about a reunion between . . . a mother and her daughter. Can you understand that?"

Dimitri slid down until his head was on his pillow, then tucked Shylo into the crook of his arm and gently kissed the top of her head. "Yes, *kouklitsa*, I would say that I do. I am, as many would say, obsessed with my work. Namely, my chief goal of soliciting the return of the Parthenon frieze, which is a series of marble sculptures, and the caryatid Lord Elgin stole along with them."

"Carry a—what's that?"

He chuckled softly and kissed her again. "You have heard of the Acropolis in Athens and its great temple, the Parthenon?" She nodded, brushing her hair against his lips, and he breathed deeply of it, loving its fresh, unspoiled scent. Then he returned his mind to the subject.

"There is a lesser temple to the west of the Parthenon called the Erechtheion. This temple features a porch comprising marble statues. The models for these sculptures were six of the most beautiful women who lived in Greece over two thousand years ago. These are the caryatids. Today only five of the statues remain on the Acropolis. The sixth is in the British Museum of London."

"Where Lord Elgin took her?"

"Correct. You are an excellent student, Mrs. Adonis. I can't wait to see how you perform in a real classroom."

"Me neither." She toyed with the curls on his chest. "So now the museum won't give the sculpture back to Greece?"

"Correct again. Different groups have tried to reclaim it over the years, but to no avail. I am in charge of the newest committee assigned to the task."

"Wow. That sounds like quite an honor." Shylo raised her head to look up at her husband. "I'm very impressed."

"And well you should be." Playfully he ruffled her hair, then tucked her head back down on his chest. "Reclaiming that caryatid is far more significant than the simple return of a marble statue. She represents the heart and soul of my countrymen, and has even spawned a legend for herself during her absence from the Acropolis."

"A legend? How exciting—tell me about it."

Dimitri supposed that's what he'd intended to do all along, since he'd brought the subject up, but he usually didn't like to perpetuate the myth. It was a silly story, completely illogical. But for some absurd reason it touched him in a place he'd rather not have acknowledged, even to himself. In any case, he found himself telling the tale.

"Many think the caryatids are sisters. It has been said that each day around dusk, as the British Museum closes its doors for the night, this stolen statue, who is dreadfully lonely for her five sisters, begins to cry for them. These teardrops, or whatever they are, splash down upon her marble bosom and leave visible stains for the next day's tourists to see." He paused, giving Shylo a moment to absorb this and himself the opportunity to shake off the emotions the story always roused in him.

"This phenomenon, the crying caryatid, has supposedly been observed by respectable scholars of impeccable reputations, but I have never been able to learn their names or substantiate their claims."

"Oh, but Dimitri, why should you?" Again Shylo raised her head, revealing damp lashes and glistening blue eyes. Reminded of the nights her own sister had been missing in the desert, and the lifetime of nights she'd wept for her mother, she felt an instant kinship with that lonely statue—and believed in it. "It's an absolutely beautiful legend, the kind of story that asks not for proof that it exists, but for blind faith."

With those words Dimitri knew exactly why he'd brought up the subject and told his wife the tale in the first place. As he'd hoped deep inside, she understood—both his obsession and a little part of him he'd always kept entirely to himself. How could he possibly offer her anything less than what she'd given him?

Taking Shylo's sweet face between his hands, he said, "I would say that we've come to understand each other a little better through our obsessions. Because of that"—and only that, he convinced himself—"I intend to have a little talk with Ari in the morning. Wyatt Earp offered him a job in his gambling hall, and I believe my uncle would enjoy that line of work very much. If he's as good as everyone says, perhaps what he makes there will be enough to stretch our funds through to next Saturday."

"You mean . . . " Shylo could hardly say the words, so afraid was she that she'd heard him wrong. "We can stay?"

"If that is your wish, of course we can."

"B-but what about getting the lonely sister back? I understand now why you have to return to Greece as quickly as possible."

Dimitri had been watching her expressions, loving her enthusiasm over the things that mattered most to him, and suddenly he couldn't wait to feel the satiny texture of Shylo's soft mouth beneath his. He pulled her closer, then kissed her with a tenderness he hadn't known he was capable of before. When he released her, he wiped a tear off her cheek with his thumb and said, "That lonely sister has been weeping for almost eighty-seven years. I suppose if your friend can wait another week for her reunion with her mother, so can my marble lady."

Tears ran freely down her face after that, and Shylo seemed helpless to stop the flow. Dimitri understood this, too, he thought, and cradled her in his arms long after she'd cried herself dry.

*   *   *

The following morning Shylo awakened as something hit the mattress beside her. She cracked her lids and saw a large package lying next her.

"Wake up, my little kumquat. The honeymoon is over."

Shylo stretched, rolled onto her back, and glanced up at her husband. He was freshly shaved and dressed from toe to head, including the black cowboy hat he'd purchased in Winslow. "Why are you up so early?" she asked.

"I can't just lie around here day after day—even though you are a very tempting reason to do just that. I don't know when, or if, I'll ever come back to San Diego again, and I don't want to miss the opportunity to study the area a little. I was hoping you'd like to accompany me to what promises to be some very interesting tidepools." He opened the package and pulled out a riding skirt with divided trouserlike legs. "I thought you'd be more comfortable in these since we'll be climbing around on some pretty slippery rocks."

"W-why, thank you." Would he never cease to amaze her and surprise her? Filled with a new kind of excitement, Shylo snatched the garment from his hands, then tore back the covers and climbed out of bed. "I didn't know the study of sea life was part of archaeology."

"I suppose it isn't, not really, but I'm interested in all things old."

As she slipped into her drawers, Shylo gave him a sly grin and said without thinking, "Does that mean you'll still be interested in me when I'm old and gray?"

"What do you think?"

That was all Dimitri had to say. His look gave her

the answer she needed—his expression was incendiary enough to set fire to her from across the room. It was then Shylo realized, with a jolt, that after this week he would never be interested in her again, never more to look at her the way he was now. Gazing upon each other when they were old and gray was never, ever going to happen to them.

All at once she wanted to scream, to cry, to tear open her chest and rip out the pieces that hurt so much. This was not supposed to happen, not a part of her plan! All the hurt and pain she'd endured through the years was to have been behind her by now. Damn it all, she thought, she deserved a little happiness! When would it ever come?

Careful to hide this newest anguish from Dimitri, Shylo turned away from the face she'd grown to love and finished dressing.

15

Over the next five days Shylo and Dimitri took a variety of buggies and local steam lines to the tidepools located in Pacific Beach, La Jolla, and their personal favorite, Ocean Beach. That area was served by the Ocean Beach Motor Railway, which more often than not got stuck in the mud. When it did run, it went from the eastern banks of San Diego Bay across its headland, Point Loma, then on to the shores of the Pacific Ocean. The little steamer dropped passengers off near a nice flat, sandy beach, but Shylo and Dimitri preferred to take the short but incredibly beautiful walk south to a long expanse of majestic sandstone cliffs.

Shylo likened the view of the ocean there to sitting on top of the world and always insisted that she and Dimitri stop for a spell before descending the treacherous cliffs. Twice now they'd been privileged to view truly awesome sunsets from that spot, with the sky tinged in colors ranging from canary yellow to pumpkin to crimson, all within the space of a few minutes. If the clouds were just right, as they had been the night before, an incredibly beautiful shade of pink began the display, filling the sky with streaks of color not unlike the shade of Cassie's hair.

Perhaps, Shylo thought as she removed her shoes and left them lying on the sandy beach, they could all come back tonight for one last sunset, Cassie and Ari included. Tomorrow the packet carrying Colleen Pappas would arrive from Ensenada, and after that opportunities like this would be rare, if they occurred at all. In fact, everything would change—including the role she'd been playing as Dimitri's "wife."

Her heart suddenly heavy, Shylo glanced over to where Dimitri was already poking around in a group of rocks carpeted with bright green surfgrass. How she would miss him! Dimitri had taught her much over the past two weeks, and not simply in the bedroom. She'd experienced more of the world and its wonders during this period than throughout her entire life. More than she'd ever dreamed was possible. And all because of him.

As she started for the water's edge to join him, she thought back through the last few days. She and Dimitri had acted like a pair of carefree children, romping together and delighting in each day as it dawned with nary a thought for tomorrow or the possible heartbreak it might bring. They spent their daylight hours combing San Diego's endless tidepools, venturing into dark little sea caves, and cavorting on her pristine beaches; the nights, exploring each other. During that time, the vast emptiness inside of her had quietly closed up somehow, shrunk to the size of a little ball. Maybe, she dared to hope, after the packet arrived tomorrow, that vacuous hole would disappear altogether, and at last she would feel whole.

"Hey!" Dimitri called to her over the ocean's roar.

Shylo glanced toward the rocks and saw that he was waving his arms and pointing at her legs. She glanced down at herself, amazed to find that she'd waded into the ocean way beyond the surf line and was standing in chilly seawater up to her knees!

"Oh, Lord," she cried, pulling her hems out of the foamy brine as Dimitri made his way to her. "I've gone and made a mess out of my new riding skirt—again. I think the salt water has ruined it this time!"

Unconcerned about his—or her—clothes, Dimitri waded out to where Shylo stood. Laughing, he gathered her into his arms. "You are a very silly *kouti* to worry so over a dress."

"A cootay?" She could see by the glimmer in his dark eyes and the depth of his dimples that he was teasing her, so she faked a pout. "There you go calling me bad names again, and I can't even understand what you're saying."

"I am saying that you are . . . " Dimitri tapped her forehead. "*Kouti* means like you are having no brains—but only in the kindest way, of course."

"Saying that I have no brains doesn't sound very kind to me." She slapped at his chest. "I said that I'm sorry about the dress. I really didn't mean to ruin it."

"No, no, you misunderstand. I don't care about dresses. When we return to Greece, I'll buy you a hundred more dresses if that is your wish. What *I* care about, what *I* wish for, is to see you smile and the enthusiasm you have for everything—even when it is my work, not yours.

"*Katalaves?*"

"Katalaves," she whispered back, using a Greek word for the first time. "I understand very well."

Loving the sound of his native language spoken from Shylo's lips, Dimitri cupped her sun-kissed cheeks between his palms and stared deeply into her sky blue eyes. The briny aroma of summer-baked seaweed and ocean flotsam swirled all around them, and from behind, waves crashed down in rhythmic sequence, slapping foam against the backs of his jeans. Seagulls and cormorants fought noisy battles overhead, struggling for the best morsels of crab, mussels, and tube snails that inhabited the rocks he'd been investigating earlier.

But Dimitri didn't feel, hear, or smell anything but Shylo. He saw nothing but her and in every way imaginable. Not only was she here in his arms, but now he could actually picture her at primitive excavation sites, not simply as a helper or a wife at his side, but as someone who would share his enthusiasm for the work. Someone who might possibly come to love the somehow comforting aroma of dank earth and ancient dust as much as he did.

Shylo tapped his shoulder, interrupting his train of thought. "I think we—"

"Shush." He wouldn't let anything so earthy as words interfere with his deep thoughts or the sublime way he was feeling at this moment. "Don't talk right now."

"But, Dimitri—"

Determined to preserve the mood, he silenced Shylo with a surprise kiss, a display that was filled with as much hope as passion. A split second later something huge and powerful slammed into the middle of his back, taking both him and Shylo on a headfirst somersault into the surf.

Lost and confused at first, Dimitri opened his mouth to cry out—only to have it filled with salt water and sand; when he surfaced, he was choking and sputtering. "Sh-Shylo! Shylo—where are you?"

Another wave hit him, this one far less imposing but big enough to bury him once again beneath a mass of water and kelp. This time when Dimitri got his legs under him, he dug his bare feet into the sand and waded through the strong current until he was out of harm's way. He would be no use in saving Shylo if he drowned! After wiping the sting from his eyes with the backs of his hands, he spotted her sitting on a dry stretch of beach just ahead. She was laughing so hard, she had to hang on to her tummy.

"So then," he said, gasping and out of breath as he reached her. "You think the fact your husband almost drowned is funny?" He shook his dark head, sprinkling Shylo with the excess water, then dropped down beside her.

"I tried to warn you," she said, still laughing. "I saw this really huge wave building up behind you, but when I started to tell you about it, you wouldn't listen. You kissed me instead."

"In that case, I would say my near death was worth it." Dimitri glanced out at the churning ocean, saw a black dot floating away to infinity beyond the incoming waves, and added, "Except for the hat."

"Hats." Shylo pointed to the formerly attractive straw bonnet lying beside her, now resembling a cross between an enormous sand dollar and a soggy pancake.

Dimitri burst into laughter, then took stock of Shylo's wet clothes. Because the morning was unusually warm, she'd left her jacket behind and wore only a plain white blouse with her riding skirt—a garment, now that it was soaked, that had become almost transparent and revealed more of her than it covered.

"We're in a hell of a mess," he said, still chuckling. "I can't take you back to town looking like that, so I guess we'll just have to sit here until we dry out." His gaze raked her breasts, particularly the way her taut nipples jutted out, and his amused expression evolved into something far more carnal. "I can sure think of a lot better things to do to pass the time than just sit. Too bad this is a public beach."

"We're not very far from that sea cave we found the other day." She gave him a coy grin and started drawing figure eights in the warm sand. "Want to go . . . exploring?"

Not entirely certain what she was suggesting, he asked, "And what are we looking for?"

She shrugged but kept her grin. "I thought we could examine the boulders scattered around in that dark, *dark* cave."

"Oh, yes," he said, his groin springing to life. "The very dark cave. Now I remember it. And what did you say about the rocks inside?"

"I was just thinking that if we were to find a boulder, oh, about yea high"—she held her hand up and measured off a foot—"and I stepped up on it, that ought to bring my hips up level with yours. I could slip out of these wet things, and then we could . . . " Shylo ran her tongue along her bottom lip. "Well, ah . . . you know, in the dark."

"In the dark," he repeated.

"Umm, yes, and standing up like that, we wouldn't have to worry about getting all sandy, either."

Although by now he was burning with need, Dimitri managed to keep an impassive expression. "I think you were right the other day to have called yourself a wicked, nasty woman. If you're suggesting what I think you are, you most surely will go to hell for it."

Shylo wasn't certain that he was kidding. "You think so?"

He nodded solemnly. "Oh, yes. You will absolutely go to hell. You're just lucky to have married a true gentleman like me."

"And why is that?"

"Because I would never allow you to go to such a terrible place unaccompanied. Now where did you say that cave is located?"

Later that afternoon, after their clothes had dried and they'd found what they needed in the cave, Shylo and Dimitri returned to the Horton House Hotel. He'd insisted that they keep the honeymoon suite, and since Ari had been quite successful in his new venture thus far, the extravagance was no longer beyond their financial means.

As they walked down the hall toward their room, a supremely happy Shylo swung a bucket filled with treasures she'd collected during the day—a dried-up sea star, a perfectly formed sand dollar, and shells of every description. Thinking she heard a high-pitched squeal, she suddenly came to a halt in midswing.

She glanced at Dimitri. "Did you just hear a scream or something like that?"

He paused and cocked his head. "No. Perhaps you—"

Again came the sound, this time louder.

Recognizing something in the tone, Shylo dropped her bucket. "My God! That's Cassie!"

Then, before he could stop her, she ran across the hall, yanked open the door, and rushed inside the room. Dimitri followed right on her heels, into utter chaos.

Cassie was lying on her back in the center of her bed. She was fully dressed but struggling with a man who was obviously trying to relieve her of that attire. Dimitri intended to beat the stranger to a bloody pulp, but before he could make a move he saw Shylo *fling* herself onto the assailant's back.

"Get off her!" she screamed as she wrestled with the man. "Get off, you dirty bastard!"

Shylo clawed at his face, then clamped her knees around his hips as if breaking a wild mule. "Let her go, you son of a bitch, or I swear, I'll kill you!"

One of her fingers found the corner of his eye, and she gouged at it, drawing a bellow of pain from the man. He abruptly rolled over, trying to dislodge his "rider," but Shylo remained strapped firmly to his back. When he rolled again, the two of them fell off the bed and hit the floor with a bone-crunching thump.

Shylo groaned, but even though she'd banged her head against the bedpost and the man had landed heavily on her right knee, she continued to pound on him with both fists and kick at him anywhere she could reach. Through the din of Cassie's sobs, the stranger's howls, and her own shouted curses, Shylo picked out Dimitri's voice—and he didn't sound happy at all.

"God damn it, Shylo—if you don't get off that man this minute, I swear I'll make you eat wood!" He hunkered down and wrapped his big hand around her arm. "Now go off!"

Suddenly more afraid of her husband than the man she'd pummeled so thoroughly, Shylo loosened her hold on the stranger and crawled away from him. Her hair had come unbound and stuck out in every direction, one of the sleeves on her blouse was torn at the shoulder, and she was gasping for breath.

But all and all, she figured as she glanced behind her, she looked pretty good compared with the son of a bitch who'd attacked her sister. Her fingernails had clawed three grooves down the side of his face, leaving bloody trails, one of his eyes was puffed shut, and both his hands were holding on to his crotch for dear life. Dimitri grabbed the man by the collar of his shirt then and hoisted him to his feet. When the stranger winced with pain, Shylo even managed a little smile. Served the dirty bastard right, she thought. Then Cassie's cries caught her attention, and gaining revenge on her sister's attacker didn't seem so important.

"I'm here, Cassie," she said, gingerly getting to her feet. "Everything's going to be all right now."

Her knee throbbing, Shylo hobbled toward her sister in order to comfort her, but as she reached the edge of the mattress, a sobbing Cassie rolled to the other side and leapt off the bed.

Then she darted to where Dimitri held the man pinned against the wall and cried, "Oh, please don't hurt him! He didn't do nothing wrong!"

Assuming the girl was hysterical and didn't know what she was saying, Dimitri increased his grip around the man's throat and said, "How would you like your face in the wallpaper, you son of the biggest bastard?"

The pressure against his Adam's apple was so great, all Buck could manage was a strangled gurgle.

"Oh, God in heaven!" cried Cassie as she finally glimpsed the damage visited on the man she loved. "What have they gone and done to you? You're all bloody!" Her wails increased. "Oh, Bucky, I'm so-o-o sorry!"

Dimitri shot her an incredulous look. *Bucky?*

Shylo, who'd joined them by now, had heard

Cassie as well. *"Bucky?* You *know* this fella, Cassie?"

"Yes, I do!" She tugged on Dimitri's sleeve, pinching the flesh beneath it. "Turn him loose this instant! You're killing him."

Dimitri removed one of his hands from the boy's throat, reached into his holster, and "borrowed" his gun. Then he released the young man and stepped back but kept the weapon level with "Bucky's" navel.

His voice impatient, Dimitri said, "Somebody better start to explaining, *now!"*

"That's a hell of a fine idea!" Hands on hips, Shylo looked directly at her sister. "Why don't we start with you?"

Cassie and Buck exchanged worried glances, then she dropped her gaze to the floor. "This here's Buck Dilly. He's a . . . a good friend of mine."

"Yes," Shylo agreed. "I would say from the looks of it when I saw you two together on the bed, that you and Bucky-boy here are very good friends!"

More defiant now, Cassie looked up at her sister. "We wasn't doing nothing wrong—just horsing around a little, you know, playing catch-me."

"Nothing wrong? 'Catch me'?" When—and *how*— had Cassie possibly come to this? Shylo wondered. And right under her very own nose, no less! "How long have you known this fella?" she demanded. "And while we're on the subject, exactly *where* did you meet him?"

Again Cassie glanced at Buck. "He, ah, we've known each other for . . . a spell, I guess."

"A spell." Shylo's temper was rising like a high tide. "What's that mean? Back in New York? On the farm? What? When? Where?"

Cassie began to cry.

Buck, ready to sacrifice anything for his sweetheart

if need be, took the burden of answering from her. "We met on the train."

Dimitri narrowed his gaze at the young man. "I don't recall seeing you in the parlor car."

Buck swallowed hard, rattling his Adam's apple. "No, sir, you did not. I wasn't exactly a passenger. I was working for the, uh, fellas that, uh . . . well, they robbed the train."

Dimitri muttered a curse in Greek.

Shylo gasped and clasped her heart. "You—y-you're saying that you're one of those no-good *outlaws?*"

"Yes, ma'am, but I want you to know that I've done quit the life."

"That's right," said Cassie, her confidence restored enough by Buck's bravado for her to walk in front of Dimitri's weapon and put her arms around her lover. "But you'd better watch out how you talk to him, retired or not, 'cause this here's none other than Dilly the Kid. Once he gets work of a more legal-type nature, we're going to get married."

Dimitri, who felt more foreign than ever, wasn't quite sure what was going on, but he suddenly felt foolish training a gun on the girl and her intended. He slid the barrel of the weapon into the waistband of his jeans and glanced at Shylo. She was staring at the outlaw, her mouth agape and her eyes wide with horror. Odder yet, her lips were moving, but no sound could be heard.

"Perhaps," Dimitri suggested, feeling awkward and intrusive, "we should go and leave these young people to themselves."

"No!" Shylo faced her husband. "I think it'd be better if you and . . . " She could hardly force herself to say his name. "*Buck* went downstairs and left me and Cassie to talk about this, ah, woman to woman."

"And what," asked Dimitri, none too pleased by any of the goings-on, "do you suggest I do with this outlaw downstairs? Haul him off to the sheriff—or perhaps take him to see our new friend, Wyatt Earp?"

Buck's good eye bulged. "Wyatt Earp is, is . . . *here* in San Diego?"

"Yes, he is." Dimitri smiled. "He is my very good friend. I'm sure he'd like to meet a train robber so famous as Dilly the Kid."

Releasing her grip on the man she loved, Cassie spun around to face Dimitri. "But you can't turn Buck in! He didn't do nothing wrong 'cause he never got around to no actual robbing! He was too busy carting me off the train."

"Cart—" Shylo could hardly believe her ears. "You mean to tell me this is the very man who *kidnapped* you back in Winslow?"

Cassie shrugged. "Sort of, but not really. He didn't force me to go 'cause I was passed out at the time."

Shylo staggered backward a step, reeling with the shock of it all. She had an overwhelming sense that not just her plans but her entire life was crumbling down around her shoulders. As these sensations washed over her, they nearly knocked her off her feet as effectively as the wave had earlier in the day.

After taking a deep breath to gather herself, she turned to Dimitri and said, "Please take this man out of here now. I've just got to talk to Cassie alone."

Dimitri glanced at his troubled wife. "Are you sure? This man has admitted that he is an outlaw. Since Miss McBride is his woman, you may not be safe alone with her."

Shylo sighed heavily. "Believe me, Dimitri—I'm a lot safer around Cassie right now than she is around me. Take her, her *intended* downstairs to the bar and buy him a beer, please." She took another hard look at the young man. "Better make that a sarsaparilla— he doesn't look old enough for beer. Just keep him down there until I send someone after you, all right?"

Dimitri still wasn't crazy about the idea, but he agreed. "We'll go, but you be careful." Then, as he ushered Buck toward the door, he told him, "We will go to the saloon as if we are great friends, but if you try to escape me, I will shoot you, no problem. *Katal*— Understand me?"

"Don't worry about me causing any trouble, mister." Buck waved at Cassie. "I ain't going nowheres without my girl."

After the men had left and she was sure they were out of earshot, Shylo glared at Cassie, who'd turned her back and retreated to a corner by the window. At least now her sister's odd behavior made a little bit of sense, she thought, holding herself back a moment. This in part explained Cassie's amazing survival alone in the desert, her insistence that she hadn't been hurt in the slightest, and her irrational fits of weeping ever since the train pulled out of Winslow. Yes, now it all began to fit into a very disturbing puzzle.

Stalking across the room, Shylo unleashed some of her shock and outrage. "How could you have tossed your good name away on a no-good like that outlaw? Have you gone absolutely *crazy?*"

Cassie hung her head. "I don't know what you're talking about."

Inches from her sister now, Shylo spoke in a low, guttural growl. "You know exactly what I'm talking about. I also think you weren't alone for one minute during the three nights you were stranded in the desert!"

Picking at her fingernails, Cassie shrugged. "You're not my mother, and I don't have to answer to you."

Fueled by her growing anger, Shylo took her sister by the shoulders and shook the pins right out of her hair. "No, I'm not your mother, and it's a damn good thing I'm not, either!"

"Then leave me be—get out!"

"Oh, no. You're not getting off that easy. We've got one more day to get you straightened out before you have to face your real mother, and that's what we're going to do! Now tell me what happened out there in that desert!"

Slowly raising her chin, Cassie gave Shylo a defiant glare. "What happened isn't any of your business."

Although she'd known somehow in her heart that it was true—that Cassie had experienced a lot more than a girl her age should have—hearing her all but admit her indiscretion nearly broke Shylo's heart. She wasn't Cassie's mother, she knew that intellectually, but since she'd done so much of her "raising up," she couldn't help but act a little motherly toward her. And feel a mother's pain and disappointment over a child gone wrong.

"How in God's name could you have given yourself to a disgusting outlaw?" she asked. "Have you no shame?"

"There's no shame in what I done with Buck, because I love him!" Cassie shouted back. "I love Buck, and that's all the reason I needed in the world to bed down with him! Now let me be about it."

So upset was Shylo over this admission, she shook from head to toe. "That's all the reason you need to be called a whore, too, or didn't you think of that?"

Her sweet face twisted with sudden hatred for this condescending sister of hers, Cassie blurted out something she knew would hurt Shylo in return. "I think loving my man is a hell of a good reason for bedding down with him—you, on the other hand, don't even have that reason. If I'm a whore, then you're a bigger one!"

Shylo drew her hand back, but until Cassie flinched and ducked, she hadn't even realized that she'd intended to pop her sister alongside the mouth. Ashamed of her violent reaction, disturbed to think it might have been prompted by something as ugly as a certain amount of truth in what Cassie had said, Shylo willed herself to calm down.

"You know," she began, hating the cornered look in her sister's pale blue eyes, "I was pretty much forced into sleeping with Dimitri. I wasn't out looking to get myself in the kind of fix you're in—it just happened. So it's *not* the same as what you've done—not even close."

Her fighting side up, Cassie fired another salvo. "You don't think bedding a man just to *impress* someone—your mother, for God's sake—isn't whoring? I sure as hell do."

"Leave me out of this! It's not me got tangled up with an outlaw, it's you!" Again Shylo had to calm herself. "Face the fact that you've shamed yourself—shamed the entire McBride family name."

Cassie's lip quivered over those words, but she fought the urge to break into sobs. "That's right—I forgot that you're a 'Folsom' these days. I guess that does leave me to shame the McBride name alone."

"Cassie, for God's sake—"

"Know what else I think?" Tears were dripping off her chin, but she ignored them. "I think you're jealous, that's what! I love Buck, and he loves me—and you can't stand that it never happened to you!"

"That's not true!" Shylo wanted to shake some sense into her, shake her until her pink hair fell out, but she controlled the urge. "And you're wrong about me and Dimitri, wrong—do you hear me? I do love him! Understand what I'm saying, I . . . Oh, God, I—I *do* love him."

The moment those words were out, Shylo nearly collapsed from the surge of emotions that swept through her. How could that have happened? When? And to a woman who didn't even believe in love? Why now, of all times, the day before her big reunion with her mother? Why in God's name could any of this be happening just as everything was looking so bright for a change? A tear rolled down Shylo's cheek before she even realized she was sobbing. Wiping her face with the sleeve of her blouse, she turned away from her sister.

"Oh, please don't cry," said Cassie, suddenly feeling contrite and remorseful. "I didn't mean all them hurtful things, honest I didn't. I just wanted you to know how much I loved Bucky."

Choking back her tears—she couldn't fall apart now, not *now*—Shylo spoke softly, although she couldn't face Cassie yet. "I'm not crying. I just wish you'd have told me all this before when it happened. I so wanted everything to go smooth with our reunion tomorrow, but it seems the more I wish for that, the more messed up everything gets."

Certain from her sister's tone that the worst was over now, Cassie said, "I guess I wished I'd listened to you about locking my door. If I had, none of this woulda happened, and you wouldn't be all upset like you are."

"Oh, I think it would have happened." Shylo finally turned to face her again. Cassie's expression was sheepish, and she was still fiddling with her fingernails, but the defiance and hatred were gone from her eyes. "I just wouldn't have caught you. Isn't that what you meant to say?"

Cassie giggled and shrugged.

"Well, it's done, and now we got to figure out how to make everything all right again." With a start, Shylo thought of Buck and Dimitri downstairs at the bar, of the conversation they might be having at this very moment. "My God—how much does this Buck know about us and our plan?"

"Pretty much all of it, but if you're worried he'll talk to Dimitri about us being sisters and all, don't be. He knows how important this reunion is to you."

"Oh, does he now? How can you be so sure he'll keep quiet, especially after what I did to him?"

Cassie frowned. "That was mean of you, Shylo, but I trust Buck. He won't talk."

"That's very . . . *comforting.*" Shylo's voice was ragged with sarcasm and fatigue. She pushed her fingers through her hair and tried to sort through the newest complications to her plans, but it seemed hopeless. "I don't see any way in hell that you can present yourself to our mother tomorrow dragging that outlaw along with you. You're just going to have to tell him to stay away, or better yet, to go back to Winslow."

"I guess you haven't been listening to me. I don't care if I never meet our ma—I just care about Bucky."

Done with all the nonsense, Shylo reached for her sister, took her by the shoulders, and forcefully sat her down on the edge of the bed. Peering down at her with a narrow-eyed gaze, she said, "You don't mean that—say you don't mean that, after we've spent our whole lives waiting for this day."

With Shylo hovering over her like a vulture, Cassie couldn't help but cringe. Her voice lacked substance, but she found it in herself to declare, "It's not *me* who spent my life waiting for this day! Finding our ma is *your* dream, not mine!"

"You don't mean that, either. I know you want to see Ma as much as I do."

Cassie was getting scared now, especially at the desperate look in Shylo's eyes. "You've got to listen to me, Shylo. I don't even *know* Colleen McBride. I have no memories of her, and I don't care if I never do."

Shylo released Cassie's shoulders and straightened her spine. "I don't see how you can say that after all we've been through to find her again."

"I'm only here because you didn't give me a choice in the matter. And you know what else? I think it wasn't me that was the dreamer all these years—*it was you.*"

That stung Shylo's pride, but she couldn't ignore the dollop of truth in her sister's words. "I suppose in some ways I was, but at least my dreams stood a chance of coming true. They were real, a lot more realistic than your fantasy of Prince Charming riding up on a big white horse—especially now that I've seen your prince."

"Yeah, well . . . " Cassie's pout became more pronounced over the insult to her lover. "Buck is all the prince I'll ever want or need, and by the way—he *did* ride up and carry me off on a white horse!"

"He did?" Cassie nodded, and in spite of their argument and her general turmoil, Shylo found herself chuckling. "Well, I'll be damned."

Joining in with her sister's chuckles, she said, "I expect the both of us will be damned over the way we've been carrying on of late, don't you?"

Feeling her usual love for her sister blossom inside her again, Shylo stroked Cassie's colorful hair. "I expect you're right." She glanced down at herself, noting her soiled and torn garments. "I also expect we've said about all we can to each other for now. I'd better go to my room and get myself washed up. Ma *is* coming in on the steamer in the morning, and I want to look my best."

One glance in her sister's hopeful eyes told Cassie what she had to say next. "I'll make sure that I'm cleaned up good and proper by the time you come back here with her tomorrow, too. And Shylo—I won't let Buck hang around here then, neither. I'll save that little surprise for later."

"Thanks, sis." Shylo bent over to kiss her forehead, then said as she started for the door, "Just because I'm done hollering about Buck for the time being, don't think I'm happy about you and him—you're too young for a serious beau."

"I am not," said Cassie as she followed her sister to the door.

"We'll discuss this later, but in the meantime, I don't want to find that outlaw in here again." Raising one eyebrow, Shylo issued a tongue-in-cheek warning. "I'm telling you if you don't keep him away from you, I swear I'll send for Wyatt Earp—and I don't think that man will bother to give your train-robbing, kidnapping Dilly the Kid a trial."

Cassie giggled as Shylo stepped into the hallway. "You wouldn't *dare!*" she said, and closed the door.

Of course she wouldn't, and Shylo had only been kidding around with her sister, but as she headed for her room, it occurred to her that telling Wyatt Earp about the baby-faced outlaw might not be such a bad idea after all. In fact, she was willing to bet her gaudy, eye-popping wedding ring that after the former lawman had a little talk with him, Bucky-boy would turn tail, jump on his big white horse, and ride out of town like his pants were on fire.

16

Shylo had a troubled, restless night after that. Even though Buck had agreed to sleep in Ari's room so that someone could keep an eye on him, she was still concerned about his relationship with Cassie, and she agonized over what she could do about it without alienating her sister. In the back of her mind was the idea of having Wyatt Earp talk to the young man, but she decided not to pursue that option just yet. Cassie would never forgive her if Earp actually *did* haul Buck off to jail or to the hangman.

If Shylo wasn't worrying about Cassie, images of her fiery-haired mother stepping off the steamer in the morning would come to mind, and she'd become so excited, she could hardly lie still.

But most disturbing of all was the realization that she'd somehow allowed the impossible to happen— she'd fallen in love with Dimitri. That alone would have kept her tossing and turning all night. She'd trapped herself in a web of her own lies, tangled her deepest emotions with a man who could never truly be hers. How could she have dug such a miserable hole for herself? She'd always known that after she and Colleen were reunited, Dimitri was bound to learn the truth about her. Once he uncovered her lies and realized that he was not her legal husband or responsible for her in any way . . .

Shylo could hardly bear to think about it. When she did, she saw Dimitri running right over Buck and his big white horse in his haste to flee the scene of his "inconvenient marriage." What would she do if he hated her so much that he wanted never to see her again? How would she ever live through the pain? Just thinking about him leaving her behind crushed her so, Shylo could scarcely draw a breath.

Dimitri's deep, easy breathing soothed her in the darkness, and the somehow comforting sound of his light snores allowed her to think there might be a small drop of hope. What if he didn't hate her when all was said and done? After all, she had already told him the truth about most of her lies, and he'd even admitted to a few inaccuracies of his own. Didn't that make them about even in the deception department, down to the pot calling the kettle black? Other than the one little fib about being related to the president—and Shylo really couldn't imagine how that could be important to a man from Greece—she didn't see how her lies could have affected his life too much. Not enough to hate her, anyway.

Knowing that dawn was close, Shylo clung to those last few thoughts and snuggled next to her snoring husband, hoping to catch at least one hour of sleep.

Moments later worries about her sister returned, and the image of Cassie alone in her room with Buck brought her fully alert again.

"Dear God!" Something she might have overlooked suddenly struck Shylo, jerking her into a sitting position. "Oh, Lord."

"What?" came Dimitri's groggy voice in the darkness. "What's wrong?"

"I—I don't know for sure. I was just wondering— doesn't Ari work *nights* for Mr. Earp?"

He rolled onto his side, murmuring, "Uh-huh."

"You mean to tell me it's possible that Buck has been alone in that room all night with no one to keep him from pestering Cassie?"

He took a long time answering, and when he did, Dimitri's voice was clear and sharp. "Could be—but we've interfered with them enough for one night."

Without any warning, Shylo tore back the bedcovers, grabbed her robe off the bedpost, and dashed out of their room.

"Shylo!" Dimitri called, but she was too far away by then to answer. Muttering in Greek, he climbed out of bed and stumbled after her, realizing just before he reached the still open door that he was naked. Cursing in his native language, he slammed the door shut, then quickly lit a lamp and yanked open a dresser drawer in search of some clothes.

Still adjusting the sash to her robe, Shylo raced up the hallway to Cassie's room; when she reached the door, she twisted the knob and, as usual, continued her forward momentum without slowing down. This time there was no give, and she smashed into the door face first.

"Ow!" she cried with the little bit of breath that

hadn't been knocked from her lungs. She twisted the knob again and found—for the first time ever—that the door was locked. *Locked!* Sure now that her fears had not been unfounded, she began to pound on the door with both fists.

"Cassie! Open up and let me in! Do you hear me? It's Shylo, open up!"

This went on for several minutes, and just when she thought she was going to have to find a way to break the damn thing down, the door finally opened.

"Shylo?" said Cassie, rubbing her eyes. "What in hell are you doing here in the middle of the night?"

After craning her neck to see into the room, Shylo pushed her sister aside and walked in. Then she turned the lamp up high and said, "I, ah, was worried about you. Is everything all right in here?"

"Sure. What could be wrong?"

Shylo strolled around the room, checking the bed, each of the corners, and even sat down at the vanity table so she could stick her foot under the draperies and check the hollowed-out space between the drawers. There was no sign of Buck. She glanced into the corner by the door again, noticing that the valise she and Cassie shared looked bloated, as if it were still packed. That was strange. They'd emptied it of all their belongings the day they'd arrived in town. Was Cassie planning on taking a little trip? Intending to check the bag more carefully on her way out, Shylo dropped down on all fours and lifted the coverlet to have a look under the bed. That's when Dimitri stormed into the room.

He'd donned a pair of pin-striped dress trousers but topped them with one of his blue denim work shirts— an item he'd buttoned so hastily, the left side of his collar was a full two inches higher than the right. And, Shylo couldn't help but notice as he stomped toward her, he was barefoot.

"Get off!" he demanded.

Since there was nothing under the mattress, Shylo complied with the order she assumed he was trying to give and got to her feet. Then she favored her angry husband with a sheepish grin. "I didn't mean to get you out of bed, Dimitri. I just wanted to make sure Cassie was all right."

"I'm fine, as you can see," said Cassie, her hands planted firmly on her hips. "Were you thinking you'd find someone in here with me? Is that why you're here?"

Dimitri answered the question. "She was *not* thinking of her brain very much. Forgive us if we disgusted your rest." He took Shylo by the hand and dragged her toward the door.

Since she was in no position to argue or do otherwise, she called to Cassie from over her shoulder, "Best lock up again. Oh, and wish me luck at the dock this morning."

"Good luck, Shylo. And . . . good *night.*" She firmly twisted the lock behind them.

Cassie waited several seconds after she heard a door close down the hallway before moving. Then she quickly retrieved Buck's clothes and boots from her valise and crept over to the window. After pushing aside the beige linen curtain, she shoved up the heavy wooden window frame, stuck her head outside, and whispered, "It's all right now. They're gone."

A moment later a white-faced, wobbly-kneed Buck inched his way along the narrow ledge until he was just outside her window. The only item of clothing he'd had time to grab was his red woolen drawers, but they hadn't been able to keep the bone-deep chill of the damp night air from settling into his slender body. Shivering uncontrollably, he leaned on Cassie's shoulder for balance and finally managed to climb back inside the room.

In spite of the cold air, beads of sweat glistened on his brow. Wiping them away with the back of his hand, Buck said, "Whew! I hope to hell I don't ever have to do that again, sugar lips. I don't mind the cold or even taking a dip in a frosty pond now and again, but there's something you got to know—I'm plumb scared shitless of heights."

Just like last time, Wyatt Earp and his wife joined Shylo, Dimitri, and Ari as they stood at the steamship wharf the following morning, awaiting the packet's return. Although Josie wore yet another smashingly gorgeous walking suit, this one fashioned in shades of russet and brown, Shylo was decked out in her only presentable costume—the same pink sateen outfit. Today, however, she really didn't mind the other woman's presence. She was far too eager for the reunion that was about to take place to let this woman dampen even one moment of her excitement.

So it was with unfettered joy that Shylo stood alongside the steamer and watched as the purser dropped the rope gate to usher the first passengers down the gangplank. The long anticipated moment when she would glimpse her mother again ended just ten minutes later when Colleen Pappas and her swarthy husband appeared at the top of the steps. Even though she'd aged a little, Shylo would have known her mother anywhere—she was simply the most beautiful woman she'd ever seen.

Colleen's flaming red hair was darker than Shylo remembered, almost auburn now, but coiffed stylishly with a neat little row of curls ringing her hairline like a fluffy band. She couldn't see her mother's eyes from the distance, but she knew they would be grayish green "Irish eyes," as William McBride had been fond of calling them.

As Colleen neared the bottom step and a hungry-eyed Shylo could see her more clearly, she gazed on her mother's wide cheekbones and slightly squared jaw, surprised to see that those features were so very like her own. In the next minute Colleen was standing not two feet away from her, hugging and kissing both Wyatt and Josie Earp.

Suddenly surrounded by passengers and those who came to greet them, Shylo was momentarily lost in the glut of laughter, chatter, and strange voices. A man, his voice rife with a thick Greek accent, called out, "Dimitri! Is it really you? And Ari, too? What a surprise!" Other heavily accented voices joined his, Dimitri's among them, and the conversation gradually evolved into their native language, shutting Shylo out entirely.

Of course, her gaze never left her mother, who was standing so close now, Shylo could almost reach out and touch her. Frozen with both excitement and a fair amount of fear, she stood rooted to the spot and listened in as they laughed over something to do with *posadas* and *tortillas,* whatever the hell those were. Ignored by Colleen and Josie on her left, and the Greeks and Earp on her right, Shylo began to feel as if she were isolated on a lonely little island, and that the bits and pieces of the excited conversations were coming at her from underwater. Then, suddenly, while she was still in a state of "not really being there," the women finished exchanging pleasantries, and Colleen dropped a surprisingly cool glance on Shylo.

She didn't know exactly what she'd expected of this moment, but the last thing Shylo imagined when her eyes met Colleen's was the instant chill that skittered through her, freezing her to the bone. The fleeting thought that her father had erred in calling those eyes "Irish" flashed through her mind, for Colleen's gaze didn't in any way capture the warmth and gaiety generally associated with the Irish. Of course, thought Shylo, her mother didn't have any idea whom she was looking at, and a woman in her position must have learned long ago to keep a safe distance from jealous strangers.

Through the mélange of conversations and her own buzzing mind, Shylo finally realized that Josie was trying to present Colleen to her.

" . . . and says that she is one of your friends from some time ago in New York. Do you know her?"

With a deliberate show of displeasure, Colleen looked Shylo up and down, and said, "Are you quite certain that *I'm* the woman you're looking for?"

They were not precisely the words Shylo had hoped for during her first conversation with her mother, but at least they were a start. Clearing the enormous frog that had lodged in her throat, she smiled and said, "Y-yes, you're the one all right. I—I have a message from someone you used to know a long time ago."

Shylo thought she saw a flicker of recognition or maybe even suspicion in those eyes, but all Colleen said to that was, "Really?"

"I, um . . . " Her gaze skimmed Josie, then Shylo glanced around, seeking a more isolated spot. Noticing a deserted area near the Pacific Coast Steamship Company building, she suggested, "I think I can explain the reason I'm looking for you a little easier if we can move to a more private place to talk."

Josie, whose nose was already impossibly high, lifted it another notch. "If that's what you want, I'll just go see why these men are so excited, and leave you two alone."

"Thank you," said Shylo, but when she turned back to Colleen, her mother was wearing a frown that suggested this was definitely *not* what she wanted. In spite of that, Shylo persisted. "Would you mind walking up to the steamship office with me for a minute?"

"I would. This is private enough, I believe. Who are you and what is it you want from me?"

Steeling herself against the chill in her mother's voice, Shylo gulped. She was in over her head, the child inside her warned, way over her head. Colleen was dressed to utter perfection in an obviously imported traveling suit of silk and velvet, and a pair of large opal earbobs sparkled out from her lobes, complementing her eyes and the collar of blue stones she wore at her throat.

She reeked of money and all things lofty—but not one comforting aroma touched Shylo's senses. There was nothing to remind her of the love this woman must have bestowed on her as a child. Brazenly presenting herself to Victoria Vanderkellen as the president's niece had been a cinch compared to telling the truth under these circumstances. But she hadn't come all this way to flip coins or let Colleen walk out of her life again—and the woman appeared ready to do just that at any moment.

With another gulp, Shylo said quickly, "Don't leave. I—I just wanted to say hello again. It's me . . . Sh-Shylo."

Something flashed in Colleen's eyes, something that was neither haughty nor cold—it might even have been recognition—but the glimpse she saw beyond that austere facade was nothing more than that—a glimpse. With remarkable speed she restored her previously aloof demeanor, but she did lower her voice so she couldn't be overheard.

"I'm sorry to disappoint you, Miss . . . Shylo, but you must be looking for someone else. I don't know you."

She turned as if to join the Earps and her husband then, and Shylo impulsively reached out and grabbed her elbow. "But you must know me," she said, panic driving her on. "It's Shylo spelled with a 'y' so's I won't get mixed up with a battle. Remember? And I have Cassie with me back at the hotel."

Colleen shuddered slightly, as if taken by a sudden chill, then glanced at Shylo. "Please let go of me. I don't know you, and . . . and I don't want to."

Shylo's heart, her lungs, her entire system, froze at those words. Never, *ever*, had she met a colder person—man or woman. Even Farmer Anderson, who had viewed her as slave labor and nothing else, had been warmer. Cold-hearted or not, this second rejection by the woman who'd given birth to her was more than Shylo could take. Before she knew what she was doing, before she even had a chance to think of the consequences, she exploded inside and completely lost control of herself.

"It's me, *Shylo McBride!*" she shouted. "How in the *hell* could you have forgotten about *me?*"

Colleen blanched and staggered back a step, pressing her hand against the glittering stones at her throat.

Shylo advanced on her with no rational thought as to what she meant to do next, but then suddenly hands were on her, fingers tugging at her, trying to pull her away.

Shylo shrugged off those insistent hands and went after her mother. "I'm not good enough for you, is that it? Take a look at this?" She shoved the finger weighed down by Ari's garish diamond ring in Colleen's face. "My rich Greek husband gave it to me, and if that's not good enough, there's—"

The rest of the sentence was wrested from Shylo's mouth as Dimitri bodily dragged her away to the private corner she'd sought out earlier.

When he was sure they couldn't be overheard, he looked at her as if she'd lost her mind and said, "What is this all about? You are acting like—what is word for *trelli*—crazy. A crazy woman!"

"Let *go* of me!" She kicked at him.

"Shylo!" Dimitri shouted, shaking her. "Get hold of you!"

Turning away from him, she shot an angry gaze over to where she'd last seen her mother. Colleen was standing with her husband, Ari, and the Earps, and all of them were staring at her with such shock in their expressions, for a minute she thought she must have ripped off all her clothes. Then she realized they were not looking at her with shock so much as pity.

Her anger turning to fury—for if indeed she had gone crazy, Colleen would by God share in the blame—Shylo tried to twist out of Dimitri's grip so she could confront the group with the truth.

"Stop this!" he demanded, his grip ever tighter.

"You have made enough fool of yourself. Why?"

"Because, b-because—"

Again she looked to Colleen as the truth formed on her lips, but no one was glancing her way now. They'd walked off the dock to the street, where Niko Pappas was helping his wife into an enclosed carriage that already contained the Earps. Then it drove off, leaving Ari behind.

"Oh . . . it doesn't matter anymore. Nothing matters. Now let me go!"

"But I am not understanding you!" Again he shook her, trying to get her attention and make some sense of her odd behavior. "I cannot help you if you continue this way, *katalaves?* What is so wrong?"

"*Everything*—it's over. All of it. You, me, and my reunion. Over!" Her words surprised him enough that Dimitri relaxed his grip. Taking advantage of the moment, Shylo wrenched out of his arms.

She backed away from him, and immediately Dimitri pursued her. "Don't," she warned, holding up both hands. "There's no point. It's all been a lie, one huge fat lie. I—I just want to be left alone right now."

"But Shylo—"

"I mean it! I can't take any more right now."

Before he could reach her or prevent it, Shylo bolted from the dock, darted into the masses milling around the wharf, and lost herself in the crowd. Then she ran, oblivious of the startled shoppers she brushed against on the boardwalks of Fifth Avenue, deaf to their complaints when contact was more forceful than propriety allowed. She didn't know how long she ran, or where she ran to, but by the time she reached the Horton House Hotel, her lungs were on fire and her legs felt like a pair of quivering reeds.

She leaned against the brick exterior of the hotel long enough to recover a modicum of strength, then dragged herself inside. Although she hadn't given much thought to her destination, she'd been pretty sure that Cassie was the only person she could face at that moment.

When she reached the door to the room she'd once shared with her sister, Shylo realized she was still far too distraught to discuss what had happened. On tiptoes she continued down the hallway to the bridal suite, hoping to God she would not find Dimitri there.

She didn't. Grateful for the first thing that had gone her way today, Shylo tore off her bonnet and went into the bedroom. After closing the drapes, she sank onto the oversize chair near the small table at the bedside. She stayed there an indeterminate amount of time, aching and raw inside as memories of her mother's indifferent eyes and cold, cold words enveloped her. Gradually she succumbed to a quiet pain from which there was no escape.

When Dimitri let himself into their room a short time later, she glanced up long enough to make sure that it was he, then noticed the surprise in his expression at having found her there. She dropped her gaze back down to her lap, listening in utter silence as he lit the wall lamp just inside their bedroom and turned the flame down low. Then she heard his cushioned footfalls as he crossed the thick carpet and sat down at the edge of the bed across from her.

"Will you talk to me now?" he asked, his voice a gentle caress.

How could she speak of her mother's betrayal? She could barely think of it, much less voice the facts of her second rejection. "I—I'm sorry, but I don't think that I can. Besides, there's really nothing I could say of interest to you."

"Perhaps you are wrong. I have many, many questions of you. As your husband, I believe I have a right to some answers."

Her husband. Of course. He wasn't here to find out about Colleen. This was about *them.* With an agonized groan, Shylo let her head fall back against the chair and closed her eyes. "What do you want to know?"

"There is much confusion over your behavior at the dock." Dimitri's voice grew harder. "The woman you sought, the lady you tried to attack, is very upset, I think."

In a voice as hollow as her emotions, she said, "I don't care."

"I think you should, since she is the wife of my father's brother—my uncle Niko."

Shylo's eyes flew open. "Your uncle?"

"Yes. I believe that makes Colleen Pappas, the woman you insulted, my aunt."

"Your . . . *aunt?*" Good God, she thought, would this day of cruel surprises never end? She laughed, the sound desperate, hysterical, even to her own ears. "I won't even discuss who insulted who at the docks today, but why in hell didn't you tell me that Niko Pappas was your uncle before now?"

Dimitri shrugged. "I wasn't sure that he was my uncle until I saw him today. He has changed his family name."

There was nothing she could say to that. She'd done exactly the same thing.

Dimitri leaned forward, rested his forearms on his knees, and let his hands fall between his legs. Then, although she did her best to look away, he captured

Shylo with an intense gaze. "It would seem that we both have kept some secrets. Perhaps it is time we spoke the truth to each other."

Again Shylo's head fell back against the chair. "I wish that I could, Dimitri, but I'm afraid I've had about all the truth I can handle for one day. I wouldn't even know where to begin."

"But I," he said, that smooth, velvet voice a little rough around the edges, "have had more lies than I can handle for my entire life, and need today's truths. Let me decide where to begin. To start, please tell me how can this woman have made you so upset, and is it possible that I heard you call yourself 'Shylo McBride' when you spoke to her?"

Hugging her knees against her chest, Shylo rocked back and forth on the chair. She'd known this was coming, so why not answer him and get everything over with in one day? She was full up with pain already, there couldn't possibly be room for any more. And what did admitting her real identity matter now that Colleen knew who she was? There was no one left to fool.

Releasing her knees, Shylo sat up straight, then smoothed her skirts as if that might somehow make her and the things she'd done more respectable. "Shylo McBride is my true name, the one I was born with."

"McBride?" Dimitri was stunned and, instantly, confused. "But didn't you tell me that your friend Cassie was the McBride? Have you exchanged names?"

"No. Cassie is also a McBride. She's my baby sister." At the look that suddenly shadowed Dimitri's handsome features, an expression not unlike the one Colleen wore earlier, Shylo realized much too late that she was not up to this at all. "I'm sorry," she whispered, unable to do more. "Sorry if I . . . inconvenienced you."

"Inconvenienced?" He laughed harshly. "I'm not understanding what any of this means. Please explain to me."

"What's to explain? I lied to you about everything I am and everything I've done! You're a free man—what else do you need to know?"

He rose from the bed then, moving as if he truly were carved of marble, and said in a dark tone, "Free of what? And what about the Folsoms and the president? Do they know of this?"

She might have dissolved into tears right then had Dimitri not brought up her "ties" to the White House. But her guilt receded a little, and she snapped, "I'm a McBride. I've *always* been a McBride. The Folsoms have no idea who I am, and if Grover Cleveland knew I was running around telling folks I'm the niece he doesn't have, he'd probably toss me into prison and throw away the key. Is that clear enough for you to understand?"

A muscle in Dimitri's jaw twitched as he asked, "You lied to me about your family?"

Miserable again, Shylo nodded. Then she leapt out of her chair and looked him in the eye for the first time since he'd come into the room. "But I'm not the only one who lied, and I'm not going to take the blame for everything. The day you asked me to marry you—when you figured on using me and my link to the president—you led me to believe there would be something in the arrangement for me, but you don't have any more money than I do!"

"It is not the same! We are not talking about money— it is our marriage at issue here."

"It is the same," she insisted, her hands on hips. "You said 'the arrangement' between us was nothing but a business deal. Maybe I didn't quite hold up my end of the bargain, but so what? Neither did you, and business deals go sour every day, don't they?"

Something bright went off inside Dimitri's head, ignited by an instant surge of anger. Not sure what he might do or say to Shylo, he walked a safe distance away and began pacing at the foot of the bed. "Our marriage was a business arrangement, yes, but am I supposed to feel nothing when I learn that my wife has lied about her past? Am I to have no feelings when I find out that I no longer know who she is?"

"Your . . . wife?" His back was to her now, but Shylo didn't have to see his expression to know that he hadn't put all the information together yet. "Who I am and all the lies I've told, none of it makes a damn bit of difference now. It's not as if you're stuck in a business deal you can't get out of, you know. You're as free as you've ever been."

He whirled on her, his expression thunderous. "I *vowed* to you! Business deal or not, do you think I am not a man of my word? You did not think at all, or you might have considered how your lies would affect me. I do not believe in divorce, if that is your suggestion, and I will not seek one."

Her heart already breaking, not knowing how much more of this she could take, Shylo spelled it out in terms he couldn't possibly misunderstand. "You vowed to a woman named Shylo Folsom—she doesn't exist! That means our *marriage* doesn't exist. It wasn't legal." The expression that darkened Dimitri's features now, as comprehension finally sank in, was astonishingly haggard and more murderous than any she'd ever seen. Feeling a trickle of fear, she backed up as she said, "We don't owe each other a thing anymore. You're free to go, so why don't you?"

Dimitri stood rock still, just staring at her as if he'd never seen her before.

"Get out!" she screamed, so devastated, she thought she might collapse at any moment. Too cowardly to face him any longer, frightened of what he might do to her as well, Shylo turned her back to him. "Get out and leave me alone. I . . . I don't want to see you again."

He said nothing, but she heard his footfalls as he strode out of the bedroom and into the foyer of the suite. Her shoulders slumped with both relief and profound sorrow. And then the tears began to fall.

Still standing in the foyer, Dimitri sought but had yet to find whatever it would take for him to just walk out of Shylo's life as if he'd never been a part of it. Icy fury ripped at him, making him angry enough to tear the hotel room apart brick by brick, yet he couldn't quite figure out where to aim that anger or whom to blame. He wanted nothing more than to direct it all at Shylo, but somewhere inside he knew he was at least as much at fault. So why was he so damn angry? He could walk right out the door and be a free man forever if he wanted to. Why couldn't he just do it?

Shylo had been right about their marriage. It had been nothing but a business deal, by God, only business. Had their union lasted longer, she might even have completely bankrupted him! He should be feeling relief now that it was over. But he didn't.

Now that he knew her as Shylo McBride, and realized there was no way that she or her "family connections" could have done him or the import business any good, he should have been happy that she was not his wife. But he wasn't.

Dimitri reached for the doorknob, trying to convince himself that he was better off this way. Shylo would probably have made him miserable had he taken her to Greece as planned—hell, she'd already distracted him so much that he'd practically forgotten about the caryatid and the return of the Elgin marbles! To think that he'd actually considered having her work at his side, this woman who'd deceived him so! It was better that he left now without another word. He would be better off, much better off. But somehow he knew that he wouldn't be.

He knew all this and more, knew for his sake as well as hers that he *had* to go now, but the moment his fingers touched the cold brass knob, Dimitri heard himself mutter, "The hell if I will."

Then he spun on his heel and stormed into the bedroom again. Shylo's back was still to him, her face in her hands. Gripping her trembling shoulders, he spun her around and dragged her into his arms. His jet black eyes glittering with as much passion as fury, he repeated in a low, dark growl, "The *hell* if I will."

Then he flung her onto the center of their bed.

17

Beyond all rational thought, consumed by a driving need to reclaim his woman, perhaps even as a way of denying the truths she'd laid before him, Dimitri threw himself down on the bed beside her, pinning her with his torso, and tore the pins from her hair.

"I'm the one who arranged this business deal," he said, his voice as ragged as his emotions, "and I'll be damned if I let you back out of it until I've gotten a little better return on my investment."

"Dimitri—"

Done with words and explanations, he came down on her mouth with his, the kiss as plundering as it was arousing, and slid his shaking fingers up to the collar of her jacket. He fumbled with the buttons there, releasing some from their lace catches, tearing others from their moorings, until the garment was open. Then he tore his mouth from hers and gazed down at her, eyes blazing in the semidarkness.

"You're mine," he muttered thickly, speaking in Greek. "Understand me? I don't care whose name you signed on our wedding papers, you're mine."

Uncertain of the meaning of his words, but sure of the deep and terrible sense of betrayal behind them, Shylo swallowed a sob as she whispered, "I'm sorry. Please believe that I'm sorry."

"For what?" he asked in English. "A business deal gone wrong? We both had some rewards from it, did we not?"

Dimitri stopped a reply with his lips again, and this time as he kissed her, deeper, harder, and longer, he released the satin ribbon at the neckline of Shylo's chemise, then pulled aside the material, exposing her. He ran his hand across her breasts, rubbing the rough skin at the side of his thumb against her nipples, and when this drew a little cry from her, he took his lips from hers and lowered his head to those offended crowns. Raising his head in response to Shylo's moans of pleasure, he looked into her eyes. Her lids were half closed, and she was panting a little, waiting and eager as she always was when his hands were on her.

He uttered a hoarse laugh. "So you agree our business is not quite finished?"

Shylo's eyes rolled to a complete close and she caught her bottom lip with her teeth, but that was all the answer she gave him. Needing no more permission than that, Dimitri slid his hands down her hips and tugged at her skirts, lifting them above her waist. He was already nearly out of control as he began caressing her in big, bold strokes. When Shylo began to writhe beneath his touch, he muttered,

"You may not need me as your husband any longer, but I think you cannot say that you do not want me as a man!"

"Dimitri, I—I'm sorry," was all she could manage before his hands drove her to madness. In the next instant she came with a tremendous rush and cried out his name as she tumbled down from the throes of passion. "Dimitri! Oh, please, Dimitri—please forgive me!"

Even though he was rock hard with need, an inferno that threatened to ignite him, Dimitri thought he might have regained some measure of control if not for those words and the finality he heard in them. Shylo had given something to him, and while he couldn't put a name to this thing he'd never wanted or expected, he'd accepted what she had to offer. And now she was taking away that unnamed something with no thought to his needs. He fell on top of her anyway, opened his trousers, and filled her slick, hot body with his own.

Just feeling the soft folds of her femininity surrounding him, knowing that he would never experience this exquisite sensation again, nearly sent Dimitri over the edge in that same instant, but he fought for at least that much control of himself. He remained still inside her, kissing her mouth, her hair, and her throat, alternately muttering Greek curses and words of endearment. When he allowed himself to move at last, driving in long, bold thrusts, he continued talking to her in his native language.

"Do not ask me for forgiveness again, my sweet little liar, for you have robbed me as surely as a thief—taken something from me I think I may never find again." Shylo reached around to his back, her fingernails clawing the muscles there, and Dimitri continued to grind his hips against hers. "For what you have done to me, I can never forgive you. Understand me? *Never.*"

He lost all sense of time and place after that, becoming a creature of pure sensation instead. As both the tempo and depth of his thrusts increased, Dimitri slid his hands beneath Shylo's bottom, gripping her with a fierceness he'd never known before, and lifted her hips from the mattress. He was joined with her as closely as humanly possible, driving into her deeper and harder than ever before. When Shylo cried out in ecstasy a few moments later, her body twisting and bucking beneath him, Dimitri let out a roar of anguish as his own release bore down on him. Then he collapsed against the pillow beside her, as profoundly disturbed as he was satisfied.

Later—how much later he couldn't guess—the sound of Shylo's soft sobs finally brought him back to reality. He didn't know why she was crying. He doubted it was remorse, and God help him, he hoped he hadn't hurt her physically, but he knew he couldn't stay. Not if he wanted to regain any of his sanity or pride. Without a word he rolled off the bed, adjusted his clothing, and walked out of the room.

Shylo lay there in the semidarkness, knowing he'd left their room but assuming that he'd gone into the foyer to collect himself. She hated for things to end this way, hated the idea of them ending at all, but knew that now wasn't the time to discuss such matters. Dimitri was still too angry, she thought, and she was too . . . She didn't know exactly what she was. Shylo's emotions were tattered and jumbled, torn apart with unrequited love for both a mother who didn't want her and a man who, she was sure, wished he'd never laid eyes on her.

The door to their suite slammed shut then, leaving

a terrible echo to reverberate in the bedroom, filling her ears over and over with the sounds of good-bye. Dimitri had walked out on her after all. She'd been kidding herself to think that there could be anything more between them, as she had since the day she'd first set this idiotic plan in motion. And what did she have to show for it? A heart as shattered as the wineglass Dimitri had crushed on their wedding night.

After pulling her skirts back down around her ankles, Shylo tucked her pillow beneath her head and curled into a miserable little ball. Just as the tears began to fall, she heard the door to the suite open again. *Dimitri?* Had he come back for her? She sat up in the semidarkness, allowing herself to hope, and when he strode into the bedroom she thought she might burst with joy. He *had* come back for her. He had!

"There's one other thing," he said when he reached the side of the bed. "An asset I cannot allow you to take from our little business deal."

His normally smooth, rich voice was so gruff, Shylo could hardly believe it was he who had spoken the words. She shrugged. "I don't have a dime to my name—I swear."

"I don't want your money—not even that which you still owe me." Leaning over her, he grabbed hold of her left hand. "I believe you have already made your point with this. I hope Colleen was impressed."

Then he ripped Ari's diamond ring off her finger and left, slamming the door again. Out of her life.

Shylo had a headache, her bottom felt bruised, and even though she'd washed up and fixed her hair, she felt like a mess. All she wanted to do was climb back in the bed, pull the covers over herself, and never come up again. But as she'd done all her life, she didn't take the easy way out.

After standing in front of Cassie's door for several minutes, wondering how in the hell she would explain their mother's reaction on the dock without upsetting her too much, Shylo finally knocked.

"Well, it's about time!" Cassie cried after opening the door. She dragged her sister inside the room. "I've been pacing this rug long enough to wear out a pair of new shoes. What happened?" She glanced out into the hallway, found it empty, and closed the door. "Where's our ma?"

"It's a real long story." Avoiding her sister's gaze, Shylo glanced around the room. "You are alone, aren't you?"

"I said I would be, didn't I? Buck is waiting downstairs in the bar until I send someone to go get him. Now what's going on, and—" She cut herself off as she noticed her sister's desolate expression and puffed eyes. "Oh, shit. You mean to tell me she wasn't on *that* packet, either?"

"Oh, she was on it all right. Come sit down with me."

Scared now of both her sister's dark mood and how the events of today might affect her future with Buck, Cassie followed Shylo to the bed and sat next to her. "Ma wasn't real happy to see you again, is that it?"

"That's about it all right!" Shylo tried to laugh, but it came out sounding more like a sob. "In fact, she pretended that she didn't even know who I was. She said it right to my face, too. 'I don't know you, and I don't want to.'"

"Oh . . . Shylo." Cassie wasn't too troubled one

way or another over this news, but she had more than
a fair idea how badly her sister was hurting right now.
Reaching a tentative arm across her shoulders, she
added, "You sure it was her? Maybe we've been
wrong about—"

"It was her." Shylo had spent all her life *not* forgetting that beautiful face, dreaming of the day she'd set
eyes on it again. Now she would have to spend the
rest of her life trying to forget it. "I expect you're pretty upset, sis. I know it's a shock and all, after everything we've been through to find our ma. I've done a
fair amount of carrying on about it myself already, so
don't feel ashamed if you want to cut loose in front of
me. Go ahead, get it over with."

But Cassie's only concerns were for Shylo. "I'm all
right. It's you I'm worried about."

"Well, don't." Shylo took her sister's arm from her
shoulders and faced her squarely. "If we're past all
that, let's get to figuring out what we're going to do
now. Where do you think we ought to go from here?
And how are we going to pay for this hotel room until
we get enough money for train fare out of this town?"

Cassie's eyes crossed as she peered at her sister.
"*We?* As in what are you and me going to do?"

Shylo nodded. "Who else?"

"Well, ah, Dimitri for one." And Buck, she amended silently, for another.

Shifting her gaze toward the window, Shylo said,
"That's over now, too. Dimitri knows my true name,
and that we aren't really married. He's, ah . . . " She
swallowed the terrible ache in her throat. "Gone."

"Oh . . . *Shylo!*" Now Cassie really did want to cry,
and although she tried to hold them back, a couple of
tears rolled down her cheeks. "You loved him, I know

you did. Can't you just tell him that you're awful sorry, and ask him does he want to get married again for real?"

She thought she'd cried herself dry, but had Cassie's naive question not tickled her funny bone, Shylo was pretty sure she'd have dissolved into tears again. Allowing the chuckle instead, she said, "Our marriage was nothing but a business arrangement to Dimitri, and now that I'm not worth anything businesswise, I'm not worth anything to him at all."

"Oh, but Shylo—"

"I don't want to talk about it anymore." She couldn't. "Now how much do you think can you make in a week at the dress shop if you take in a little more sewing?"

Cassie shrugged, then showed her sister an exaggerated pout. "Probably not a heck of a lot more than I made last week, but I'm not gonna go planning our next move until we get something else straightened out. Ain't you forgetting about someone else?"

Keeping her mind busy by calculating their expenses instead of thinking about Dimitri, Shylo asked absently, "Who?"

"Bucky, that's who. I ain't leaving town without him."

Shylo rested her forehead in her hands. "Are you sure you just got to drag him with us? I hate to see you waste your life on a no-good outlaw."

"Buck *is* good," Cassie insisted. "There's lots to him that most folks don't see right off. He's fun, and gentle, and real smart when he has to be, and better than all that, he treats me like I was a queen or something. I love him, Shylo, and there's nothing—not even you—that's gonna keep us apart."

"You know," Shylo said with a weary sigh, "it might just be that you've been reading too many of those silly romance novels. I even read part of that one myself, and while it all sounds real exciting, you can't believe that life is really like that. Life's hard, not some little fairy tale."

"But it can be! It happened to me, didn't it? I knew the minute I saw Buck, he was the one for me. With him, all of my dreams have come true. Don't you want me to be happy?"

Shylo turned to study her sister. There was no denying the love shining deep in Cassie's pale blue eyes, no matter how wrong Buck might be for her or how badly such a union might turn out. Besides, how could she possibly deny her sister the kind of love she herself had just lost? She *knew* firsthand the kind of joy it could bring her—especially if it really was love.

With yet another sigh she said, "Oh, all right, but there's going to be some rules. First off, no more bedding down with that boy until you're married good and proper. Then—"

"Oh, thank you, Shylo!" Cassie threw her arms around her sister's neck and kissed her soundly on the cheek. "You've made me the happiest girl in the whole world!"

Wiping a tear from the corner of her eye, Shylo said, "I'll make you the sorriest if you don't pay attention to the rules. Second, he's got to get some kind of job—something that doesn't involve robbing trains or kidnapping folks. Will he do that?"

"He'll do anything to be with me, I know he will!" She thought a minute, then added, "'Course, I don't know what kind of work he'll be able to find. So far, the only thing he's good at is holding the horses and lighting fires."

Shylo's brows drew together as she tried to make sense of that, but before she could ask for an explanation, a knock sounded at the door. *Dimitri!* she thought instantly, even though she knew it couldn't be him.

Cassie started to rise, but on the off chance Dimitri *had* come for her, Shylo held her sister in place. "I'll get it. You think some more on coming up with a job for Buck."

Her heart in her throat, she rushed across the room and opened the door. It wasn't Dimitri, but the visitor left no less an impact on her than if it had been. It was Colleen.

Shylo's entire system shut down, and her mouth fell open as she stared at the woman who'd given birth to her. She was torn between turbulent conflicting emotions, unable to speak or move until one or the other won out. The first urge that came over her was to slam the door in her mother's face, to let her know what it felt like to be the one rejected. The other, equally as strong as the former, coaxed the child in Shylo to throw herself into her mother's arms, to beg her to hold her and love her—just to love her and nothing more.

"Well?" Colleen said in a quiet voice. "May I come in?"

Dimitri had taken a long brisk walk around San Diego, hoping to somehow bank the fires still burning inside him, but it hadn't helped. In a last effort he went back to the Horton House Hotel and headed straight for the bar. His eyes adjusting to the much dimmer light inside, he didn't look around the crowded room when he entered. He just marched right up to the bartender and said, "I would like raki, please. And leave the bottle."

The bartender laughed. "That's become a mighty requested item, but I'm afraid I still don't have it."

"Ouzo, then? Do you have this?"

As the man slowly shook his head, a voice reached Dimitri from behind. "Excuse me, sir. Are you looking for me?"

Dimitri turned to find Buck standing there. "Why would I do that?"

"I was hoping, wondering, did Cassie send you in here after me? I've been waiting to hear from her for a powerful long time."

"I'm sorry, but I have no message for you." He started to turn back to the bar, then hesitated as he got a good look at Buck. His eye was still swollen, the puffy flesh around it mottled with purplish skin, but the grooves Shylo had carved in his cheek finally seemed to be on the mend.

"Can you tell me please what American cowboys drink to get rid of the thinking?" Dimitri asked him. Buck frowned, so he added, "To make the brain numb, *katalaves?*"

"Oh, that'd be whiskey. Whiskey for sure."

"Would you like to join me?" he asked impulsively. When Buck nodded enthusiastically, Dimitri turned to the bartender and said, "I would like two glasses and a bottle of whiskey, please."

After he paid for the liquor, Dimitri searched the room for a table. Because of a billiard tournament, the dais that circled the entire bar was crowded with

observers and most of the tables in the area seemed to
be filled as well. Then he spotted Ari, Niko, and Wyatt
Earp sitting at a corner table. He hadn't yet found a
chance to confront his uncle Niko yet, and while he
wasn't sure he was physically or mentally up to it
now, his mood was foul enough to do battle with the
devil himself. Thinking a fight might actually do him
some good, he headed straight for the raucous trio,
with Dilly the Kid hot on his heels.

"Dimitri, my son," said Ari as he noticed his nephew's
approach, "come join us! We have much news."

Dimitri pulled out the only empty chair at the table
and slid onto the seat, leaving Buck to fend for himself. Used to helping himself to other's belongings,
Buck pilfered a chair from an adjoining table, then
squeezed it between Dimitri and the man with the
handlebar mustache.

Remembering how protective Shylo had been of
the girl he now knew to be her sister, Dimitri decided
to have a little fun as he prepared to make the introductions, and he actually found himself smiling for
the first time that day. "These are my uncles, Ari and
Niko," he said. Then he pointed to the man on the
kid's left and added, "And this is Wyatt Earp."

Buck's good eye bulged and his Adam's apple began
to bob like a duck on a pond, but the only word to
escape his lips was something between a gulp and a
gasp.

"Meet Buck Dilly everyone," Dimitri went on, his
smile even wider. "Sometimes he's also called Dill—"

"B-Bucky," Buck said, cutting Dimitri off. "N-nice
to make your acquaintance, Mr. Earp, fellas. Could I
have some a' that whiskey now, sir?"

Taking pity on the kid, Dimitri poured him a shot.

Then, purposefully avoiding eye contact with Niko, he turned his full attention to Ari and immediately lapsed into his native language. "I could have sworn I heard you two laughing when I walked up just now, but for the life of me, I can't imagine how anything to do with Niko could be funny. How is that, Ari?"

After glancing at both Earp and Niko, Ari answered his nephew in Greek. "I've learned much about what happened at Adonis Imports, my son, and understand better how the business was lost. Perhaps at another time—"

"Now."

Niko said to his friend Earp, "Forgive our bad manners, but we have much family business to discuss, and English is, I think, too difficult for us all."

"No need to apologize." Earp pushed out of his chair. "I was just thinking I ought to check on my own business before my managers cheat me out of more than I make." And with that he took his leave.

Buck, visibly relieved, seemed to wilt against his chair, but he did have the strength to pour himself another glass of whiskey and toss it down.

The Greeks, unconcerned about the young man or how much he drank, poured their own glasses full and got down to business. "So," Dimitri said to Ari, his mood even blacker, "did Niko tell you if he waited until my father was dead to steal our money, or did he do it while he was dying?"

"I did not know of George's death!" Niko banged his fist against the table. "The first I heard of it was here in this room."

Dimitri looked over to his father's brother. He hadn't seen his uncle in a long time and was surprised to realize how much he resembled the family,

Dimitri's father in particular. Niko was balding now, but the hair he did have was shiny black with very few strands of gray. The telltale little mole at the corner of his lip still peeked out from under his bushy salt-and-pepper mustache, and his body was fit, almost as big as Dimitri's. In spite of his fifty-some years, Niko was still a very handsome man. And he was a thief.

Dimitri turned back to Ari. "Once Niko learned of my father's death, did he agree to return the money he stole from us?"

"I have stolen nothing! Hear me, nothing!"

Tired of lies, Dimitri finally addressed Niko to his face. "You are not to be believed! When you left town, you took everything that was Adonis Imports with you. Everything!"

"I have done nothing wrong, I tell you, nothing!"

"Stop!" Ari raised his arms to intervene. "This will get us nowhere. Both of you be quiet and listen to me."

Because Ari was, above all else, an arbitrator of the highest order, the angry men silently nodded their agreement to this. Pointing to Dimitri, Ari said, "Do not interrupt what I have to say. Just listen and understand."

Dimitri narrowed his eyes but said nothing. He picked up his glass of whiskey instead and used it to seek a little relief from the unrelenting ache inside.

"That your father, George, had a fondness for visiting the *kafeneon* cannot be a surprise to any of us, but I wonder, Dimitri, if you knew how very much he liked to gamble?"

He shrugged. "My father liked backgammon as well as you, I suppose."

"More, I fear, much, much more. I think I knew

that of him a long time ago, but hoped it would not become a problem." Ari clasped his hands together and lowered his voice. "Your father's business was not stolen from him, my son. He lost it."

Dimitri was shocked by this news. "I—I do not understand how that could have happened."

"But it has," said Ari. "I have listened to Niko with both my heart and my mind. I believe he took no more from Adonis Imports than his fair share. I believe also that he took his money in order to keep your father from losing it as well. Those are the things I believe, and there is no reason to doubt them."

Dimitri studied the amber liquid in the shot glass he held and thought of his memories of his father. After their last terrible battle over Dimitri's insistence in going to college rather than taking over the business, his father had had little contact with him, treating him as if he didn't exist. Looking back, he supposed the old man hoped this tactic would make him feel guilty enough to agree to his terms, but in reality the stand only allowed them to drift farther apart. Dimitri knew precious little about his father or his habits after he left Thessaloníki for the University of Athena. Could George Adonis have been so irresponsible as to gamble away the company's capital?

Shifting his gaze back to Niko, Dimitri asked, "If all you took was yours, why did you flee the country and change your name?"

"The day that your father died, as it turns out, we had a terrible argument." Niko's eyes glazed over at the memory. "I had just gone over the books, and discovered a tremendous shortage, one that your father had carefully hidden over a period of time. When I confronted him about it, he became belligerent and denied all, but I knew what had happened to the money. I think your mother did, too."

"My mother knows of this?"

"She must have suspected. Speak to her about this when you return home. I could not, so I did what was best for me." Niko leaned across the table and looked his nephew in the eye. "You have been gone from Thessaloníki for a long time, and do not know many of your family's problems. I have long dreamed of coming to this great country, not to live at first, but to explore. When I made up my mind to quit the business with your father, my first thought was to come to the United States. There is no other reason I came here. I did not flee my country, but left it in search of something new."

"And what of your name? If you were not running away or hiding, could you not have lived as Nikolao Adonis in these United States?"

Niko shook his head sadly. "I could not hope to live for long on what was left of my share of the company. The business was close to ruin. How could I seek investors to start a new enterprise if I represented myself as a partner in a failed business? The only answer was to start fresh, and to do that, a new name was necessary. I have brought no shame to this family, nor shall I."

Although he wasn't entirely sure he believed everything Niko had said, Dimitri sensed that enough of it was true to realize the trip he'd made to California had been a waste of both time and money. Niko wouldn't be returning funds he didn't owe—and he had an idea he wouldn't be too interested in making a loan to the business, either. Adonis Imports—and Dimitri—were losers all around.

Deciding that he'd had enough trauma for one night, Dimitri heaved a sigh and changed the subject. "Your new business must be doing well, Uncle Niko. From the look of you and your new wife, I'd say very well indeed."

Niko caught his nephew with an ardent gaze. "Thank you, Dimitraki, for believing me. I would never harm you or your mother." Dimitri nodded, accepting the truce, and Niko went on with the new subject. "I never had to start a new business. I met Colleen shortly after I arrived in New York, and she and I got on instantly. We were married very soon after that. I'm pleased to say that not only is my wife quite beautiful, but she is a *very* rich woman. I have no need to conduct any business other than overseeing her investments such as the land she owns here in San Diego."

Dimitri allowed a small grin, then remembered some of the things Shylo had told her about the new Mrs. Pappas. A woman, he suddenly realized, who was not just Cassie's mother, but Shylo's as well. Why hadn't he put that together before now? he wondered. And had anyone else—Niko, for instance?

Ari poured new drinks all around and hoisted his glass. "To rich American women and their fondness for foreigners!"

The Greeks' glasses met at the center of the table, and Buck, whom they'd forgotten about, smashed his glass against the others, spilling a good portion of his whiskey. He had no idea what they were talking about, but he gave them a lopsided grin, then settled back on his chair and watched them through half-closed eyelids.

"And," said Ari, raising his drink again, "to our nephew Dimitri, and his new marriage to the beautiful, if not so rich, Shylo Folsom! Did I tell you, Niko, that our nephew is wed to the president's niece?"

"The *president* of these United States?"

"The very one!"

Ari and Niko clinked glasses, but Dimitri just downed his whiskey and refilled his glass. "You celebrate nothing," he said, his voice leaden. "Ari is wrong, as he has been all along. It seems that Shylo is neither the president's niece nor my legal wife."

Ari gasped. "But I was your best man! I was there at the ceremony!"

"You witnessed a phony ceremony." He shot Ari a vicious glance. "Next time you do some matchmaking, be a little more thorough when you examine the bride-to-be's background, will you?"

"But, my son! How can this be?"

"It just is. Her real name is Shylo McBride. She tricked you and me into bringing her here to San Diego to greet her mother, whom, I gather, she hasn't seen in some time." Something else about Shylo and her relationship with her mother nagged him in the back of his mind, but between the whiskey and all he'd been through today, he skipped over the thought. He turned to Niko instead. "The way these American women lie, I wouldn't be surprised to learn that you are not aware Shylo is the daughter of your wife."

Niko choked on his whiskey. "My Colleen . . . a *mother?*"

Dimitri laughed. "You see what I mean? American women are not to be trusted."

Ari, who could hardly believe any of this, said, "Are you *sure* of these facts, my son? You could get Niko in very much trouble with his bride if you are making jokes."

"I assure you that I am not joking. Colleen is not only Shylo's mother, but Cassie's. In fact, I believe the McBride sisters are upstairs as we speak, probably planning more lies so they can find a few more fools to take them back to New York."

Ari went pale.

"Drink up, Uncle," said Dimitri. "But think of something else to celebrate. You really are a terrible matchmaker." He glanced at Niko, who was just recovering from his shock. "Women, huh? The only thing that makes them happy is money—diamonds on their fingers, emeralds at their throats, just give them money and a lofty position in society. That's what Shylo thought she was getting from me." He took another drink.

Niko downed his whiskey. "The only thing Colleen is getting from me, *is* me, since she was very prominent in New York society when me met. As for money"—he laughed and poured drinks for them all—"she has more than she knows what to do with already."

"She may be rich, but apparently your Colleen also has a cruel streak." Dimitri recalled the way she had behaved toward Shylo at the docks. "Is she the cold-hearted woman she appears to be?"

Niko paused a long time, his features looking rubbery. Then he said, "My Colleen is a complicated woman, and sometimes seems to be very cold, yes, but I think she is much like the mountain bear in Macedonia. She burrows deep beneath a winter coat of snow and ice to protect herself, but inside that frigid shell is a warm, slumbering heart that is not always easy to awaken." He cut loose with a boisterous laugh. "And like the hibernating bear, sometimes it is a very big mistake to even try!"

Everyone, including Dimitri, laughed at that. When their chuckles died down, Buck's voice penetrated the foreign conversation, his words a little slurred as he said, "Hey! Are you fellas ever gonna speak Engrish again so's I know what's going on, too?"

"Engrish it is from here on out!" proclaimed Dimitri.

Two rounds of drinks and lots of broken "Engrish" later, Ari, the master arbitrator and matchmaker, decided it would be a good idea for them to round up all the women, straighten out the mixed identities, and properly introduce the mothers and the daughters. Niko, who was still childless after two marriages, rather enjoyed the thought of becoming an instant stepfather to two lovely young women and couldn't wait to put the plan in motion. Buck, who was almost too drunk to think, period, figured this was one hell of a fine time to meet his future mother-in-law and ask for her daughter's hand in marriage—no, to *demand* that she give it to him. And Dimitri, who'd managed to anesthetize quite a lot of the pain inside, thought it would be a fine idea if he just went along to watch the fireworks.

So, after several false starts and a couple of shots of whiskey later, the quartet finally managed to get to their feet and make their way out of the bar. They figured it would be best to start with the sisters upstairs, then worry about where to find Colleen. By the time they reached the second-floor landing, they were traveling in single file, weaving down the hallway like a snake with absolutely no sense of direction.

18

Unaware that all the men had congregated downstairs, Shylo stood back out of her mother's way and showed her into the room. Then, although she'd yet to speak a word to her, she closed the door quietly. What could Colleen possibly want?

A dark silence hung over the room as Shylo watched her mother, resplendent in a Charles Worth suit of rose-, green-, and brown-striped silk, come in and stand near the bed. She was gazing at Cassie with an almost wistful expression, perhaps even a small amount of wonder to finally look upon the fruit of her womb and behold such a lovely young woman. But more likely, Shylo thought with a surge of resentment, her mother was probably horrified right up to her perfectly arched eyebrows to realize that she'd begotten such a pair of "ne'er-do-wells" as these McBride sisters.

Colleen suddenly raised her head to glance at Shylo,

then just as quickly looked back down at Cassie. "I can hardly believe that you're this . . . this grown-up already," she whispered, "but you must be Cassandra."

Cassie nodded dumbly.

Shifting her gaze to the sloppy knot of pink hair piled high on her daughter's head, Colleen pressed her lips together in a faint grin, shook her head slightly, then reached out to touch that hair as if to make certain it was real.

The little show of intimacy put springs in Shylo's feet. "Why did you come here, Mrs. Pappas?" she asked as she crossed the room.

Cassie shot a startled look at Shylo, then stared up at the red-haired woman with awe. "Ma? Is it really you?" she whispered.

"That's Colleen McBride Broussard Pappas," Shylo replied before her mother could answer. "I don't think she'll be wanting you to call her 'Ma.'"

With a sharp glance in Shylo's direction, Colleen stripped off her tan kid gloves and said, "The only reason I came here was to talk to you girls, to explain why I had to leave you when I did, and Shylo—to apologize for the things I said to you at the dock. May I stay long enough to do that? Will you hear me out, or would you rather just stay mad at me?"

Shylo averted her gaze, unable to look into her mother's Irish eyes any longer, but watched instead as she slapped the expensive gloves against her open palm. Shylo wished she had the guts to toss the woman out the door, to reject her as she herself had been rejected, but she'd never been the sort to cut off her nose to spite her face. After all, wasn't this the entire reason she'd come to California in the first place? To find her mother and learn everything she could about her? Of course it was, so why did Colleen's offer suddenly seem anticlimactic, insignificant somehow?

Cassie, edgy and nervous, got up from the bed and stared openly at the mother she'd never known. "I don't know what's got Shylo's tongue, but I'd sure like it if you stayed. I've never really met you before."

"No," said Colleen, again perusing Cassie's hair, "I guess we haven't exactly met, have we."

Shylo hadn't really considered Cassie's curiosity before. For her sister, if not herself, she marched over to the Queen Anne chair, dragged it up by the bed, and gestured toward it. "Why not stay a while, Mrs. Pappas? We'd love to hear what you have to say."

"Thank you."

Once Colleen was seated and the girls had plopped down on the bed in front of her, she drew the pearl-tipped pin from her toque hat, removed the confection of rose velvet and moss green plumes, and set the bonnet in her lap. Then she looked at Shylo and said, "Why don't you girls call me . . . Colleen. I don't see why we can't be at least that friendly with one another."

"All right, *Colleen,*" said Shylo. "We might as well get right to it. I think the main thing the both of us want to know is why you never came back the way you said you would."

Colleen's expression, while carefully guarded, showed just a bit of surprise over Shylo's bluntness, but her voice remained steady as she answered, "I did come back for you, but by then it was too late. I found out that your father had . . . died, and when I asked around about you two, no one seemed to know where you were."

"Did you bother to check the orphanage?"

For the first time Colleen seemed to be at least slightly shocked. With a sharp intake of breath, she clutched the precious stones at her throat and said, "Goodness, no. It never occurred to me that—my goodness . . . "

Fighting against the tears that threatened to choke her, Shylo raised her chin. "We didn't go willingly, mind you. The first time the Children's Aid Society came after us, we took off. Me and Cassie ran the streets with a bunch of other orphaned or abandoned kids for about a year after Pa died, but they finally caught us."

By now Colleen was aghast. "But—but you and Cassie couldn't have been more than, what? Four and—"

"Eight and three when Pa died."

Glancing from daughter to daughter, her eyes huge, Colleen began to tug on the fingers of her empty gloves. "How on earth did you survive? Where did you live, and on what?"

Since she counted memories of that one year as some of her favorites, Shylo was able to shrug them off. "We lived in abandoned buildings and cardboard boxes, mostly. What the other kids didn't give us, we earned as shoe-shiners or beggars, whatever worked best."

"*Lord!*" Colleen's eyes fluttered to a close for a moment before popping open again. "I—I never dreamed . . . "

"I assure you," said Shylo, "most of what happened to us after Pa died was no dream. More of a nightmare, actually, once those do-gooding people got hold of us and put us in a foundling hospital." She closed her eyes and took a breath, amazed that she could still smell the tar soap the hospital always used on her. "Anyway, we didn't stay there long."

"Then you were . . . adopted?"

"Not then," said Cassie, recounting the only part of the story she could remember. "Lots of people wanted to adopt me 'cause I had blond hair, but Shylo always pitched such a fit about splitting us up, the nurses decided it'd be easier to send us away with a whole lot of other orphans."

"Send you away?" Colleen's complexion was pale, and she continued to fiddle with her gloves. "I'm afraid I don't understand."

Shylo was more than happy to elaborate. "They put us on an orphan train. Ever hear of them?" Colleen shook her head. "Cassie was too young to remember much about the trip, but I never forgot a mile of it. They put us on a train with about a hundred other orphans and some church workers who spent all their time telling us how we ought to speak, eat, and behave once we got to Kansas."

"Kansas?" Again she looked from daughter to daughter. "You girls moved to *Kansas?*"

Shylo gave her mother a grim smile. "Not exactly willingly, and once we got there we didn't *stay* willingly, either, but we had no choice." She didn't know how she could explain this final humiliation to her mother, or even if she could put it into words, but she had to try. Maybe, she thought, if Colleen knew this part of her children's lives, it might even melt some of the ice in those cold, cold eyes. "The orphan train made a lot of stops once we hit Kansas. At each town me, Cassie, and the other kids were herded onto the platforms so the fine folks who lived there could look us over. You know, choose the kid they wanted like we were cattle or sacks of seed?"

"I remember that part," said Cassie. "I do, 'cause folks liked my blond hair all over again."

Shylo glanced at Cassie and said, "They may have liked your blond hair better than my dirty brown mop, but you were too little and scrawny for anyone to choose."

"Too little and scrawny for what?" Colleen wanted to know.

Shylo gave a short, bitter laugh. "For why they came to look us orphans over. Most of those folks weren't looking for a family, but for cheap labor. They'd walk right up to us and pinch our arms to see if we had enough muscle to plow a field, open our mouths to make sure our teeth weren't all rotted out, and yes"—she glanced at Cassie again and smiled—"some even seemed to favor the kids with blue eyes and blond hair."

"I told you I remembered," said Cassie with a smug grin.

After chuckling a little at this, Shylo went on. "She's right. Some folks did favor Cassie, but whenever it looked like one of them might be planning to choose her, I just hugged her tight and wouldn't let go unless they took me, too."

"Shylo always looked after me. She was the *best* mama I ever had!" Realizing she'd made a blunder in front of her real mother, Cassie covered her mouth. "Oops, I meant to say—"

"That's all right, Cassie," said Colleen. "Shylo has shouldered an awful lot of responsibility for both of you. I'm—I'm really proud of her for keeping you two together. I'm proud of you both."

"If you're so damn proud of us," Shylo blurted

out, still burning inside with bottled-up anger, "why'd you run off and leave us that way in the first place?"

"Because I *had* to," Colleen snapped, flashing the first display of emotion since she'd walked into the room—anger. Although both girls cringed a little to have this alien mother shouting at them, the outburst did manage to thaw those Irish eyes a little.

Collecting herself a bit, Colleen went on. "I was married to your father when I was just fourteen years old—*fourteen*—and had barely turned fifteen when you were born, Shylo. I wasn't ready for any of it, not marriage or children."

"Then why in the hell did you marry him?" Shylo asked indignantly. "Obviously, it wasn't for love."

"No, it wasn't—I never loved William McBride. I married him to, to escape!" Bright spots of color appeared along Colleen's high cheekbones. "To keep from being old and used up before I was twenty-five the way my mother was! To escape . . . everything."

Not at all happy with the explanation or the way the conversation was going, Shylo jumped off the bed and flounced over to the window. She'd be damned if her mother was going to claim even one drop of the anger she'd stored up all these years.

Seething inside, she said, "How nice for you that you were able to escape your life whenever the mood struck. I'm afraid that orphans like me and Cassie never got the chance."

Colleen stood up, marched over to where her daughter stood, and leveled her with a hot gaze. "I won't bother you with the details. Just believe me when I say that being orphaned *isn't* the worst thing that can happen to a young girl. Sometimes trying to survive among your own family members is much harder. *Much, much harder!"*

Shylo swallowed hard but didn't ask or say a thing. She suddenly did not want all the details of her mother's previous life.

Colleen went on. "William McBride used to deliver fish to the market where I worked as a child. The first time I smiled at him after I began to blossom as a woman, he fell all over himself, so I decided right then and there to set my sights on him. He was a long-shoreman making a decent wage, and since he lived alone, I figured he had enough money to take care of me. I married him the same day he proposed to me."

Shylo thought back to her childhood home, to the tiny one-room apartment in which the McBride family had struggled to pay the bills each month. "If I remember correctly, we pretty much lived hand to mouth. That was your idea of a decent wage?"

Colleen's mouth twisted into a wry grin. "What I didn't know about your father before we married was that he liked to hang around with his Irish cronies. He generally gambled and drank up half his pay before he ever got home. I had to take in wash just to meet the rent."

Shylo didn't remember the part about taking in wash, but she did know her father had had a true Irishman's love for his whiskey. In fact, now that she thought back on it, after her mother left him she couldn't remember a day when William McBride hadn't had a whiskey bottle in his hand. Still, it didn't excuse what Colleen had done. Shylo hardened both her jaw and her heart.

Colleen touched her elbow. "I was young, remember, and couldn't control anything William did. After a while, I figured if I was going to be a slave for some man, at least I'd do it with one who could afford to keep me from taking in wash for the rest of my days."

"So you abandoned your children to avoid the wash? Is that what you're saying?"

"You're simply *not* going to make any of this easy on me, are you?"

"No, ma'am, I'm not."

Shylo and her mother locked gazes for several moments, each one gauging how far the other could be pushed, and then Colleen forged ahead. "All right, if you want it, here it is in a nutshell. I never wanted children at all."

Shylo stumbled back a step as if she'd been struck, though no one had touched her.

Colleen went on, pouring the truth over her like scalding water. "I did everything I could think of to avoid motherhood, up to and including locking my husband out during so-called fertile times. As you're both well aware, it didn't work too well."

Blistered inside and out by her mother's declarations, Shylo wondered for a brief moment if she'd ever hated anyone as much as she hated her mother at that moment. God, but it hurt to hear the truth, to know she'd been unwanted from the moment of conception.

Tears stung her eyes, but she forced them back, ground her teeth together, and swallowed her rage. She would *not* give her mother this last piece of herself. She would not.

When she could speak again, Shylo stared hard at Colleen and muttered, "Sorry to have troubled you so much by being born. Now why don't you get the hell out of here? I can't stand looking at you another minute."

Colleen flinched and drew back her hand, and for a

minute Shylo thought she might have been planning to slap her unwanted daughter across the mouth. She didn't, but when her mother spoke again, her voice had a definite tone of authority about it, a distinct, and somehow dangerous, warning.

"I told you all this in the hopes that you might understand a little of what happened to me." Daring Shylo to rebuff her again, she went on. "After Cassie was born, I just about went crazy thinking about what might be ahead for me in the future, baby after baby, just like my mother all over again. Then I met Charles, and he swept me off my feet with presents and promises. That's when I decided to take up with him."

"So it wasn't the wash, but presents that took you from us?" Shylo couldn't keep the sarcasm out of her tone.

"You aren't listening! The hope for a better life—for us all—took me from you. Charles arranged a divorce for me from your father, and after we married, well, thank God he was unable to . . . well, we never had any children, and that was just fine with me."

Shylo couldn't help but laugh and offer yet another impudent remark. "I believe I have the right to speak for those children when I say that it was just fine with them, too."

Colleen didn't offer a rebuke this time. In fact, she softened her tone, as if just this side of apologizing. "I guess you girls think I did you wrong the day I left your father to marry Charles Broussard, but I really thought I was doing best for us all. I did figure on coming back for you after I got settled in my new life."

Shylo threw her hands in the air. "How do you expect us to believe that when there were three years between the time you left and the time Pa died? *Three years!* Things must really have been 'unsettled' in that Frenchman's mansion."

For the first time since walking into the room, Colleen's cool exterior evaporated. She looked away from Shylo, glanced at Cassie, who was sitting on the edge of the bed, listening with rapt attention, then stared down at the carpet. "I suppose this will be hard for you girls to understand," she said, her voice breaking, "but although I knew Charles had money enough to take good care of me, I was in no way prepared for such wealth, or the many adjustments I would have to make."

"Oh, *God!*" Shylo couldn't bear to hear any more. She stalked over to the bed and stood near Cassie. "Are we supposed to feel *sorry* for you? Is that what you want?" she asked with barely concealed contempt.

"I can certainly understand how terrible this must sound to you, but it really was very difficult for me to fit in with Charles's high-society friends." She stiffened when Shylo's bitterly muttered oath reached her ears, but she went on. "It wasn't as easy as you might think! I knew nothing of life beyond Canal Street! I had to learn how to select the proper clothes, how to staff and run our homes—"

"Did you say *homes?*" Cassie asked from across the room. "Like in more than one place to hang your hat?"

"Yes." Resting her gaze on her younger daughter, Colleen elaborated. "We have a city house in Paris, a country house in a little town near the Swiss Alps called Basel, and, of course, the mansion in New York, along with—"

"You're rich." Above all else, Shylo definitely was not interested in her mother's vast holdings. "I think we get your point."

"Do you?" Colleen directed the question to Shylo and then made sure she understood. "I simply told you about that so you'd know a little about the kind of life I lived with Charles. Now I'm going to ask you both to understand, if you can, what my life was like all those years. With or without money, whether with William or Charles, I was never happy for one moment."

This, Shylo could not believe—*would* not. "Even Cassie, who believes in fairy tales, won't swallow that one. Try another lie."

"But it's the truth," Colleen said. "I was never happy until I met Niko. He's the reason I acted as if I didn't know you at the dock. He, well, I never told him that I had children, and when you surprised me like that, I really didn't know how he'd react if I said I was your mother."

"Oh, I see. Another husband to get settled with before you can 'claim' your daughters, right?"

"It's not like that with Niko." She raised her chin, but it trembled. "I—I love him, and I don't want to lose him or the happiness I've finally found. I was hoping you girls would understand that much, if nothing else."

But Shylo wasn't interested in her mother's love life. She glanced at Cassie, who looked a little confused, and then asked her mother, "Does your precious Niko know about us now?"

"Well." Colleen glanced down at her gloves and held her gaze there. "No, not yet he doesn't. I thought I'd worry about explaining all that to him after I'd talked to you girls. First I thought I'd make sure that you two wanted to claim me as your mother."

Shylo and Cassie looked at each other but said nothing.

Colleen tried another angle. "Shylo . . . I understand that you're married to Niko's nephew. Have you told *him* that I'm your mother?"

She hadn't been expecting either the question or the sharp pain that came with her answer. "There's no need to discuss this with Dimitri," she said, her heart heavy. "He and I aren't really married, and we never will be. He was just an escort me and Cassie used to get us to California."

Shocking both her sister and her mother, Cassie leapt off the bed. "That ain't true! Dimitri *is* her husband, and he's got lots and lots of money. Shylo's done real good for herself, she has!"

Absolutely stunned, Shylo stared at her with disbelief. Cassie, the constant complainer, was backing up lies she'd never wanted to tell in the first place? Cassie, who preferred to remain motherless, was trying to impress Colleen on Shylo's behalf? All this from the pink-haired girl who wanted nothing more out of life than to live out her own private fairy tale with the man she perceived to be Prince Charming. When had she become so bold, so selfless—so grown-up?

After giving Cassie a warm smile, her eyes shining with tears, Shylo turned back to her mother and said, "Cassie means well, but nothing she said is the truth, and I'm about worn out with lies. We've got nothing but the clothes on our backs. We spent every last dime we had." She paused, remembering the train fare they had yet to pay back. "We even spent some borrowed money to get from Kansas to New York to California. We're flat-out broke, but still together—and that's the way we're going to stay."

Colleen looked doubtful. "I don't see how you can be too broke if you've done all that traveling."

Shylo stared hard at her mother, thinking of telling her exactly why they'd been traveling and why they were broke, but something in her wouldn't let her. But Cassie marched right up to their mother and filled in the blanks, again shocking Shylo right down to her toes.

"We was looking for you, Ma—ah, Colleen. Shylo knew you still lived in New York 'cause she saw your picture in the paper, but when we got there, you were gone, so we had to come here."

Glancing from her younger daughter to the older, Colleen asked, "You mean you girls traveled all this way just to find me?"

Again Cassie took control of the conversation. "Shylo's been planning and scheming for us to find you since she was ten years old. Been saving up all our money since then, too."

Shylo was just about ready to gag Cassie to keep her from talking, but then she noticed that an actual tear had formed in the corner of her mother's eye. Colleen quickly brushed it away, but Shylo had seen it for what it was—some kind of miracle. Her own tears threatened to erupt again, and she knew she had to look away or risk exposing herself to more pain. Then her mother's silken voice beckoned, trapping her there, making her watch and listen.

"If—if I had known back then . . . if I'd only known, perhaps things would have been different."

"If you'd known," Shylo managed to say even though her throat was aching, "you'd have done the same damn thing. You'd still have run off with the first rich fella that came along."

"Possibly," Colleen said, still trapping her daughter's gaze in hers. "And even if I'd stayed, maybe things wouldn't have been so much better. Sometimes I think that some of us women really aren't cut out to be mothers. Whether that's true or not, I am sorry I wasn't a better one to you girls. I really am sorry."

I'm sorry. Shylo had said those words a hundred times herself of late, mostly to Dimitri, but never had they held so much meaning as they did coming from her own mother's lips after all these years. Even so, was she expected to forget the past, just like that? She couldn't—she *couldn't!*

Colleen draped a hand across Cassie's shoulders and then, tentatively, across Shylo's. "Do you two think that you can find a way to forgive me? Maybe just a little? I'd really like to get to know you girls better."

"And could we call you Ma, not Colleen?" Cassie asked.

Those Irish eyes sparkled with something close to amusement. "How about Mother? I much prefer that to Ma."

"Mother," Cassie said, testing it. "Yeah. I like that."

"And Shylo?" Colleen met her eldest daughter's eyes. "What do you think? Can we be . . . friends?"

Shylo gulped, knowing she was losing what little restraint she still had left. If she agreed to patch things up with her mother, she would be offering up her heart again, putting herself in jeopardy of being crushed as she had been before. Could she—*should* she take the risk? It wouldn't be a perfect arrangement, and certainly not what Shylo had dreamed of all these years, not by a long shot. But it was a start.

Forgiveness, on the other hand, would be a long, long time in coming. But it would come, she suddenly realized. It *would* come.

Shylo bit her bottom lip, aware that tears had begun

to roll down her cheeks, and nodded slowly. "I—I'd like that . . . Mother."

With a little whoop, Cassie flung herself into Colleen's arms, then dragged Shylo into the clinch. "It worked!" she cried. "I told Shylo when we was planning this reunion that it'd work out just fine, and it did! It worked!"

Blubbering now, Shylo turned away from her mother and sister and wiped her face on the sleeve of her jacket. A change of subject was definitely in order before she broke into uncontrollable sobs.

Picking up where Cassie left off, Shylo said, "That's a bold-faced lie if I ever heard one! You argued with me over these plans every step of the way, and never for one minute thought any of them would work out right."

"Uh-uh." Cassie drew away from her mother. "The only thing I ever got upset about was the day you dyed my hair purple."

Colleen gasped. "Is that what happened to your hair? *Shylo* did that to you?"

Feeling oddly embarrassed, Shylo explained. "I had a little accident with some henna, is all, but it's mostly washed out now."

"You'll notice, Mother," Cassie said, tattling, "that Shylo didn't try the henna out on herself, even though she was the one trying to get all fancied up to go pay Victoria Vanderkellen a little visit."

"Y-you girls went to New York to see *Victoria?*"

"Yes, ma'am." Shylo flashed her mother a sheepish grin. "We found out right off that you weren't in town any longer and figured this Vanderkellen woman might know where you'd gone and when you'd be back."

"Oh . . . goodness." Colleen choked on her thoughts as she searched for the right words to express them. "I don't want to be indelicate, but I know how very . . . *formal* Victoria can be. She probably didn't even let you past the front door, did she?"

Cassie giggled. "I don't think she wanted to, but Shylo had a plan ready to use on her, too."

Colleen's suddenly appreciative gaze slid over to her older daughter as she encouraged the younger one to go on. "Did she now? What did Shylo do?"

"She got all dressed up in the best clothes we could afford, then went knocking on Mrs. Vanderkellen's door and told her that she was Shylo Folsom, the niece of President Grover Cleveland himself!"

Colleen gasped, her hand back at her throat again, and said to Shylo, "You told Victo—*the* Victoria Vanderkellen—that you were the president's niece—and she *believed* you?"

Shylo gave her a broad grin. "She sure as hell did."

"Oh—oh, my!" Colleen burst out in unrestrained laughter, and her daughters joined in. When she caught her breath she added, "I can't *wait* to introduce you properly to that old bag of wind." With movements as natural and automatic as any mother, she took Shylo's hands in hers. "Oh, sweetheart—you're truly priceless. Really, you are."

Priceless? Her very own mother thought of her as priceless? At the thought, the hint of respect, if not love, it suggested, those damnable tears popped back into Shylo's eyes. They were only words, small utterances of admiration, but somehow they soothed her heart and began to heal the wounds to her soul.

If a loud banging hadn't sounded at that exact moment, Shylo had a pretty fair idea that she'd have collapsed about then, making a complete and utter fool of herself.

Grateful for the diversion, she said, "E-excuse me. I'll get it," and rushed to the door, dabbing her nose all the way.

Her tears vanished when she opened the door to discover Ari standing at the threshold. His right arm was bent at the elbow, and his hand was pressed between his wrinkled jacket and his soiled shirt. The odd posture, combined with his general disheveled appearance, made him look as if he were performing a rumpled impression of Napoleon.

"What is it?" she asked, slightly irritated by the intrusion.

"Good afternoon, Miss-sh Sh-Shylo," he sputtered. "I am to represent . . . I am speaking for"—he laughed, sounding a little giddy— "the Greek delegation, who are seeking—"

The door burst open before he could finish his announcement, and a very unstable Buck stumbled past Ari and into the room. "Sugar lips?" he called, brushing by Shylo, then staggering backward a little. "You in here, darlin'?"

"Bucky!" Cassie started for him and met him halfway. "What's wrong? You look . . . Oh, hell, Buck—you're drunk!"

"I'm drunk up with love for you, sugar buns, and I've come for you! I've—I've . . . " He paused, trying to remember what it was he'd been about to say, then caught sight of the red-haired woman standing next to his sweetheart. His good eye blinking as he peered in at her, he said, "Are you Cassie's ma?"

"Oh, my . . . " Colleen grimaced at the sight of Buck's battered face, and then her gaze darted from him to the open door. Shylo backed out of the way to allow the others inside the room. Niko was among them, she noticed with horror. She quickly averted her gaze.

Cassie, thrilled to have her mother meet the man she loved, even if he was a little pie-eyed, said, "This is Buck Dilly, Mother, my own true love."

"That's me all right—Dilly the Kid in the fresh," he said, nearly falling as he turned to Colleen with outstretched arms. "I'm here to tell you that me and Cassie's getting married! I'm gonna kidnap her hand just the way I kidnapped her—whaddya think a' them apples, Ma?"

"Bucky!" said Cassie, appalled.

Colleen backed away, swishing her hands at the young man as if he were a swarm of flies. Then her husband's booming baritone voice reached her from across the room.

"*Matia mou!* You are here! We are all here!" Niko strode over to his shocked wife, took a hard look at Cassie, another quick glance at Shylo, and said, "Are these my girls? They are so beautiful!"

Colleen stared at her husband a moment. "Niko? What are you doing here? And what's wrong with you?"

"I've come to meet my girls." He spread his arms wide as if to welcome them but instantly lost his balance.

"Niko," said Colleen, her voice sharper. "For God's sake. The sun hasn't even gone down and look at you—you're in your cups. This is absolutely inappropriate."

Niko rolled his eyes, looked to both Ari and Dimitri, and said, "What did I tell you? Never disturb a hibernating bear—never, never, never."

"Especially," Ari chimed in, "one protecting a roomful of cubs!"

Shylo, who'd finally closed the door behind the

surprise visitors, had yet to close her mouth. What in *hell* was going on? A three-ring circus? She tried to catch Dimitri's eye, but he'd been careful to avoid her completely. He just leaned against the wall near the door, apparently as fascinated as she was by the scene being played out in the center of the room.

Buck, who'd managed to turn back to where he'd last seen Cassie, pointed himself in her direction and kind of fell toward her. "Give us a little kiss, my pink-haired gal," he said just before tripping over his own feet and landing facedown across the width of the bed.

Colleen took the hand of her inebriated husband and said, "None of this is making any sense. We'd better go now."

Niko roared his laughter and swept Colleen into his arms. "Ah, you are so secrets, *agapi mou,* but I find out. I know of your two beautiful secrets." He winked at her, and she seemed to melt against him. "*Zoei mou, hara mou,* do you not know that you can tell me anything? Do you not?"

Shylo turned to Ari, who'd stayed next to the door. "Is he cussing her or congratulating her?"

Ari laughed. "Is, how you say, love talk—my love, my life, my joy, such as that."

She nodded, turning back to the sight of her mother in the arms of the man she loved, and instantly felt bereft in a way she'd never felt before. Immediately she sought Dimitri's gaze, and this time he met her eyes.

He was still leaning against the wall for support, and now an amused grin was plastered across his handsome face. He raised his free hand then, cocked his index finger, and beckoned Shylo to join him.

Hoping he'd found it in him to forgive her, knowing somehow that he hadn't, Shylo walked over to him on stiff legs. Up close she saw that his grin was more of a silly smirk—and that even his dimples looked intoxicated. "What do you want?" she asked, slightly irritated.

"I am wondering of you," he said quietly, "if you're injuried, if you are well, and I didn't injury to you, did I?"

"W-what? I'm afraid I can't understand you. Why don't you come back later when—"

"Now." Dimitri sighed, sending the faint aroma of whiskey under her nose, and tried again. Brushing her cheek with his free hand, he hesitated, and his features softened for a moment, making him look unguarded as he whispered so no one else could hear, "If I injuried, this morning to your, to the ah . . . nuptials. Did I injury you?"

Aware at last what he'd been trying to say, Shylo blushed from head to toe. "No, you didn't 'injury' me, but thanks for asking. I appreciate your concern."

"Concern, yes." Dimitri took his hand from her cheek. "I must go now."

"But Dimitri—"

"No more." He pressed his finger against her mouth and hardened his expression. "We have no more business, remember? I have no further need for your 'lofty' connections. Ari," he called in a louder voice, "we must go now—our business with Miss McBride is concluded, no?"

Ari shrugged, but Dimitri pushed himself away from the wall and joined him.

As Niko and Colleen headed for the door, too, Niko suddenly planted his feet. "What about my girls? They do not know me yet! I am Niko, my beautiful daughters, your new *baba!*"

Colleen gave him an indulgent smile. "We'll get you properly introduced later when everyone is feeling better. Right now, I think it's best if we were all on our way. Isn't that best, Shylo?"

"Yes, and thanks, Mother. Perhaps we can all visit tomorrow."

Ari opened the door but paused to ask, "Do you ladies need some help getting Buck to his room?"

Shylo glanced at her sister. "Is he staying at this hotel?" Cassie's eyes bulged, and her face turned as pink as her hair. "Uh, he, uh, well, sort of . . . "

Shylo rolled her eyes and sighed. "Never mind, Ari. We'll take care of Buck. Good night."

As everyone filed out of the room, each responded with the same "Good night" except for Dimitri, who was last out the door.

When he stepped into the hallway, he tossed Shylo a grim smile and said, "Good-*bye,* Miss . . . have you picked out a new last name yet?"

Her heart sank, and she quickly looked away.

"I guess not." Dimitri stared at her long and hard, then said, "*Yasas,* Miss Shylo—better luck next time."

Then he was gone.

19

The following morning Shylo woke up out of sorts and disoriented. The window in her room seemed to have moved, and her head was pointing in the wrong direction. Then she remembered that she was no longer sharing the bridal suite with Dimitri but was in bed with her sister. Her heart heavy with that stark realization, she also realized that the lower portion of her body felt as if it were weighed down, too. In fact, her legs were numb.

Rising up to her elbows, Shylo blinked the sleep from her eyes, then focused on the foot of the bed. Buck, whom she and Cassie had carefully positioned on the floor and tucked in for the night, had gotten up at some point and reclaimed his spot on the small mattress. He was curled up at the foot of the bed like a huge puppy dog, his slumbering body resting on both Shylo's and Cassie's legs. Any other time Shylo might have found the sight amusing, if not endearing. On this particular morning, however, it shot a spurt of rage up her spine.

She quickly worked one foot free of her sister's paramour, then gave his backside a fierce kick as she said, "Get the hell off my bed, you stinking, drunken animal!"

Buck rolled off the mattress and hit the floor with a thud. He followed this immediately with a loud groan.

"Bucky?" cried Cassie, instantly awake. "Are you okay, honey?"

He groaned again in response, and Cassie leaped down to the floor beside him. "She kicked me! Your sister went and kicked my ass right off the bed!"

"Shylo!" Cassie popped her head up above the mattress. "How could you have done that to Bucky? His face is still a mess from the last time you lit into him!"

"I'll do it again if he doesn't get on out of here by the count of three. I need some privacy so I can get dressed!"

His head ached, and every bone in his body felt as if it'd been broken, but Buck got to his hands and knees and crawled halfway across the room before he collapsed. "Let me be," he begged, hiding his head beneath his arms as he fell flat on the floor again. "I swear I won't look, but I just cain't face nobody else right now. Don't make me go out in the hall."

Cassie, who'd crawled right along behind him, said, "Please, Shylo? Bucky looks powerful sick, and he sounds just terrible."

"Oh, all right," she grumbled, tearing back the covers, "but I'm warning you now, mister—I catch your one good bloodshot eyeball peeking my way, and I swear to

God, I'll close it up tight like I did the other one!"

A tremor racked Buck's body, prompting Cassie to put her arms around him. She kissed the nape of his neck, then frowned at her sister and said, "Don't worry, grumpy. He ain't interested in anything you got." As Shylo slipped on her stained, torn, and completely rumpled suit of pink sateen, Cassie added, "Why are you so danged ornery this morning, and where are you headed for in such a hurry, anyways?"

"I didn't sleep too good, if it's any of your business, and I thought I'd go down to the bridal suite and get my things before Dimitri sets fire to them." She turned, hands on hips, and faced her sister. "Is that all right with you?"

Cassie studied her sister's costume. "You going to see Dimitri looking like that? Them buttons I sewed back on your jacket yesterday look like they're ready to fall off again, and the whole thing looks like you slept in it. Between that and your sweet disposition, I doubt he'll let you in!"

Shylo glanced down at her ruined outfit, then shrugged and walked over to the vanity. After dragging the brush through her hair a couple of times, she pinned it up hastily and said, "I don't think Dimitri will care one way or another what I look like, and I don't have much choice of attire until I get to his room and collect what's mine. As for my mood, he doesn't have any interest in talking to me anymore, no matter how sweet I am to him."

Satisfied she couldn't do much else to help her raggedy appearance, Shylo stalked over to the door and pulled it open. Just before leaving the room, she glared down at Buck and said to Cassie, "By the time I get back, you'd better have your sweetie cleaned up and ready to face the public. He's got to get himself a job today, or tonight he'll find himself sleeping in the street!"

Then she slammed the door and stormed down the hallway, thinking all the while that what she needed to make her morning truly complete was for a door to open along the way and the wonderfully in love Mr. and Mrs. Niko Pappas to step into her path. Love all around, with nary a drop for her. For a moment Shylo thought she might throw up—or cry. She did neither, but when she reached the bridal suite she'd shared with Dimitri, the reality of why she was there set in.

Her hand was shaking so violently, she curled it into a fist and brought it to the door. As she worked up the courage to knock, Shylo realized that it was already open a crack. Pushing the gap wider, she stuck her head inside the foyer and called out, "Dimitri? Are you in here?"

After a flurry of tiny footsteps, one of the hotel maids appeared from the bedroom. "Yes, miss?"

"Oh, I was looking for my, ah, Mr. Adonis. Is he here?"

"No, ma'am. Mr. Adonis has checked out of the hotel."

"Checked out?" Shylo's heart kind of seized up. "B-but where did he go? And what about my things? Are they here?"

The maid shrugged. "I don't know. There's nothing left in this room."

"Oh." Her breath deflating along with her residual irrational anger, Shylo said, "Sorry to have troubled you." Then she hurried toward the stairs.

Dimitri—*gone?* Gone forever? It couldn't be! Not

yet—not until she'd told him she that was sorry again, whatever good that might do. And definitely not until he looked at her one more time without that horrible expression of disappointment, or whatever it was she'd seen in his dark eyes since yesterday. And what about her clothes? Had he burned them?

All this and more ran through Shylo's mind as she scrambled down the stairs to the lobby below. She headed toward the reception desk to inquire about her belongings, but before she reached it she spotted Ari lounging on a velvet tufted settee near the front window.

Altering her path, Shylo hurried over to greet him. "Hello, Ari. You're still here!"

"Oh, good morning, Miss Shylo," he said, rising slowly to his feet. "I hope you've found the grace to forgive our very bad manners last night. I'm afraid we discovered American whiskey—"

"Forget it," she said, much too anxious to waste time on apologies. "I was just up at the bridal suite, and found out that Dimitri has left the hotel. I was wondering what he did with my clothes. Do you know?"

"Oh, yes, of course. He left them at the reception desk for you, all neatly wrapped in a nice package."

"Oh." Her hopes sinking as she spotted a pair of very familiar traveling bags sitting next to the settee, she glanced around the lobby, then out to the hotel's grand entrance. A few guests were milling around near the horse-drawn cabs parked in the street, but none of them was as tall or handsome as the man she sought. Looking back at Ari, she cleared her throat and asked as calmly as possible, "And Dimitri? Where is he?"

Ari shrugged. "We plan to catch the train to New York today, but first, he said he must go off by himself. To do thinking, I suppose."

Gripped now by an almost desperate need to see Dimitri again, she impulsively grabbed the lapels of Ari's jacket and demanded, "Where did he go? I *have* to talk to him."

Taken aback for a moment, Ari studied the frantic woman, then smiled. "He would not say, but I saw him get on the streetcar heading west. Does this help?"

West—to the ocean. Was it possible he'd gone to their special spot for one last time?

"Ari, I *have* to find him. I've got to try to stop him from leaving things this way, if I can, and I need your help. Will you help me, please?"

Grinning, as the matchmaker in his soul was pretty sure of exactly why Shylo had to stop his nephew, he said, "Of course. What can I do?"

"Money." And a lot of it. She couldn't chance taking the unreliable Ocean Beach Motor Railway. "I need to borrow enough money to hire one of those cabs outside to take me all the way to Ocean Beach. Will you lend it to me?"

His grin spreading ever wider, Ari reached for his wallet, then mimicked one of his nephew's favorite phrases. "But, of course."

Below the high cliffs and deep caves he and Shylo had explored so thoroughly, Dimitri sat perched near the end of one of the fingerlike rock formations jutting several yards into the Pacific Ocean. Behind and to each side of him, other formations, some layered like stacks of phyllo pastry, rose up, then slithered into the sea. An occasional ship heading for San Diego Harbor went by on the horizon, some catching the sun in a way that made them look like ghostly apparitions.

Directly below him, great waves spent themselves against the solid wall of sandstone, filling the air with a thundering roar and showers of salt spray. More often than not, that spray reached Dimitri's perch, splattering his western denims and occasionally his head, but he didn't seem to notice the moisture or the rich panorama before him.

Instead he stared blankly at the dark sapphire blue water, trying desperately to restore some order to his life. All he could think about, in spite of those efforts, was how empty it all seemed without Shylo beside him. Even thoughts of his committee and the upcoming trip to England didn't cheer him up as usual. In fact, they served only to point out that not a single marble statue or even all six caryatids could ever equal the one warm woman who'd somehow become a part of him.

Dimitri thought back to last night and the fact he'd been forced to spend it alone in their bridal bed. Shylo's exquisite scent had saturated the sheets and pillows, nearly driving him wild with wanting her, *needing* her, and he'd tossed and turned until almost dawn. Even then, during those few hours of sleep, he'd been consumed by dreams of Shylo. Surely this attraction, or whatever this hold she had over him could be, was simply a physical obsession—God knew he'd never had such a wildly satisfying relationship with another woman before, so what else could it be? Even now, knowing her for the liar and user that she was, he ached to touch her, to hold her in his arms and kiss her until she cried out from wanting him.

It was physical all right, he decided, trying to convince himself. A physical obsession and nothing more. But even as he pronounced his feelings as such, Dimitri suspected his emotions ran much, much deeper than that—perhaps all the way to love.

Love was a strange and foreign sensation, if that was indeed the thing making him so crazy. Yet if he loved Shylo, how could he have been so cruel to her last night? The answer popped up right on the heels of the question. He hurt. And he wanted her to hurt, too, hurt as badly as he was hurting now. Not that he had the same power over her that she had over him. As far as he knew, the only people who had any power over Shylo were her family.

Dimitri thought back to the train ride west and the first time he saw her hair flowing free, remembering particularly the way the sun drew out those irresistible sparks of red. She'd tricked him into paying her way west to find Colleen Pappas, a woman he now knew to be her mother. Yes, he thought, recalling more, her mother had hurt her, and badly, he suddenly realized.

Dimitri nearly choked when it finally occurred to him that Shylo had been the little girl in her story about the orphan train. *She'd* been the abandoned child he'd felt so sorry for, the pitiful waif who fiercely protected her baby sister at all costs, determined to keep together what was left of her family. Why hadn't he realized that before now? And why the *hell* hadn't he been more supportive of her?

God, he thought, sick inside, the things he'd said and done to her, especially in their room after that ghastly scene with her mother down at the wharf. How could he have been so cruel, so blind? Because, Dimitri thought darkly, he was an idiot. An idiot who'd drive a wagon into a ditch and who couldn't see what was really important, even if it stood before his very own eyes. Had he always been so insensitive toward those he loved? Dimitri's thoughts turned automatically to his father, particularly to memories of the old man's disappointment over his son's chosen career.

Like the giant wave that had just doused him, another sudden realization swept over Dimitri: Was it possible that he had made the trip to San Diego in the first place more to assuage the guilt he felt over letting his father down than to revive the business? It certainly made sense in that light.

Now that he knew Adonis Imports had not failed because of his uncle's misdeeds, and that Niko would not be saving it from ruin, Dimitri felt both robbed and burdened at once. Ari could be of no real help, not now that he'd exhausted his source of contacts in New York. And he really couldn't ask more of the old man. No, only Dimitri could decide how to proceed with the company's future from now on—and that sobering fact offered yet another revelation. He was in the exact position he'd struggled to avoid his entire life.

What now? He could sell what was left of the business, he supposed, and invest the proceeds to see to his mother's needs for as long as the money lasted. Soon after his return to the university, he'd have a full professorship and would be able to take on financial responsibility for both her and himself. She was a simple woman who required little by way of expenses and who preferred living in Thessaloníki with her widowed sisters, and he knew he could make her quite comfortable for the rest of her life. Also, she would not be terribly disappointed in the sale of the family business—not the way his father would have been had he lived to see this day. All in all, selling the company seemed like the perfect solution.

But what about Shylo? How could he ever hope to win her hand again? With sudden clarity Dimitri knew that was exactly what he intended to do. The trouble was, with him as a hardworking professor who cared more about ruined civilizations of long ago than all that glittered in today's world, there would be precious little incentive for her even to think of coming back to him. Looking at it in those terms, he saw another alternative. He could keep the business and run it himself, bringing it back to its former level of respect and profitability. If he were to revive the business successfully, it might be enough of a jewel to again attract the attentions of one Shylo McBride—a woman, like her mother, who seemed to covet money, diamonds, and social position.

But *could* he do it? Could he actually force himself into the role of businessman and then live with that decision? To do so, and without a lifetime of regrets, Dimitri knew he would have to be very sure of his heart. The question was, did he really love Shylo enough to take over the helm of Adonis Imports, knowing that it would cost him his lifelong dream?

Deeply troubled by the impossible decision facing him, Dimitri began to weigh the intellectually fulfilling rewards of pursuing his career in archaeology against the purely emotional compensation he would find in attracting and then pleasing the woman he loved.

At first he thought both burdens to be completely and maddeningly in balance, but as the scale began slowly to tilt, leaning heavily on the side of his heart, Dimitri buried his face in his hands and wept as no man ever wept before.

*　　　*　　　*

As Shylo ran toward the cliffs, praying to God that she'd find Dimitri there, her purpose in going after him became increasingly urgent. How could she have been so wrapped up in finding her mother that she hadn't realized the most important person in her life, the only one who really mattered now, had all but slipped through her fingers? She loved Dimitri, yet she had never bothered to tell him. She loved him enough to throw herself at his feet and admit it, for the alternative—life without ever seeing him again— was too horrible even to think about.

It was a foolhardy plan going after him this way, she figured, one that might cost her a great deal of pride and even bring her more pain, but her dignity suddenly didn't matter. He was well worth the risk. She wouldn't ask anything of him but another chance and a fresh start. Maybe if he knew the *real* Shylo McBride, the basically decent and honest woman, he might still care enough to . . .

No. She wouldn't allow herself to hope past seeing him again. When she reached their usual spot and Dimitri wasn't there, Shylo fell to her knees, exhausted and miserable. Had they crossed paths somehow? Was he already at the Santa Fe station, preparing to board a train that would take him away from her forever? As her heart was breaking, her fading hopes encouraged her to look down at the tidepools, but there was still no sign of Dimitri. Then, as she climbed slowly back to her feet, she spotted a lone figure sitting far out on the moss-slickened rocks.

Dimitri!

Her heart pounding anew, Shylo made her way down the face of the treacherous cliffs, slipping and sliding and nearly falling once. When at last she hit the beach, she ran along the pristine sands, calling out Dimitri's name each time she drew in a lungful of air.

Troubled by a deep and unrelenting sense of loss, but appeased, too, to realize that from the depths of that anguish would come the chance for a lifetime of happiness with Shylo, Dimitri slowly released his doubts and let his mind wander. He realized almost immediately that he was getting wet—and had been getting wet all along. Then he heard the seagulls cry overhead, a strange and mournful song that sounded almost like a woman's voice. One, oddly enough, that seemed to be calling his name.

Dimitri turned toward the sound and saw Shylo running across the sand toward him. At first he thought she was some kind of mirage, because he wanted this sight so badly. Her hair had come loose from its pins, freeing those long strands to bask in a full measure of sunlight. The highlights of red in her hair seemed to catch fire, making her look as if she'd been sprinkled with droplets of sunshine.

His chest swelling with both hope and love, Dimitri wiped his eyes on his shirtsleeve. Then he made his way back down off the rocks and onto dry land. As he ran to meet her, he could see that her arms were outstretched, encouraging him to run harder and faster.

They met in an explosion of hugs, kisses, and garbled mutters, determined to spill the contents of their hearts before it was too late.

"Dimitri," said Shylo, out of breath, "before you go, I have—"

"No, wait—I must to you talk, and I must—"

"But you have to understand that I've been—"

"Please, Shylo, my mind is very important!"

She bit her tongue, knowing that if she didn't let him go on now, she might not be able to understand what he was trying to say. "All right. You first, but then you've got to let me have my say."

Nodding his agreement, Dimitri took a deep breath. "You must first know that I truly am the idiot you said I was in the desert of Winslow."

Shylo opened her mouth to object, but Dimitri silenced her with a finger on her lips. "Promise you will not interrupt me again until I have finished." Pressing her lips together tightly, she nodded, so he went on. "I have not seen or known what you are to me, and what I feel, but now I do."

"Excuse me?" she said, breaking her promise.

Damn, but this proposing marriage was so difficult when it was conducted in the name of love, not business, and he did so want to get it just right. Calming himself, Dimitri took several deep breaths this time and tried again. "I have come to know that you were the little girl on that orphan train, and I cannot tell you how it . . . how I"—he slid his right hand over his heart—"how deeply this knowledge has pained me in here. I cannot say—no, I cannot *express*—"

"Please, stop," Shylo said, cutting him off. "I know I promised not to interrupt you, but please don't go on about that. It doesn't matter anymore—honest it doesn't. The orphanage, the train, none of it matters now that I've found my mother and she knows all about my life. Those days almost seem insignificant to me now."

"But your childhood, it was so—"

"Maybe there is no such thing as a perfect child-hood," she said, thinking not just of her own, but of what her mother must have endured. "I suppose we all burn inside with little embers of the injustices done to us as children, some of us more than others. But the strong ones among us survive, and maybe because of our troubles, we're even stronger."

Dimitri recalled his youth and the opposition he'd met from his father over his dreams of college and an archaeological career. And he recognized that to this day he still burned inside a little over the isolation it had cost him.

Giving her a warm smile, he said, "And so now I know what makes you so strong. Thank you for this— I promise not to talk of your past again."

"I appreciate it." Shylo made a silent vow to herself to try not to interrupt him again no matter what. "You were saying?"

"That I am the idiot, and also the fool who did not see love when it stands in front of me."

He *knew?* Shylo thought with a start. When had he realized that she'd fallen in love with him?

"But I know of that love now," he went on, still having difficulty with the right words, "and I also know that I will do anything to have that love with me for the rest of my life."

To have that love with him? Shylo was a little con-fused.

"What I'm doing," Dimitri finally said, "is the matchmaker job again, and as before, I'm afraid I'm not too good at it."

In spite of her promise, a few words slipped out. *"Matchmaker?* Surely you don't mean that you're—"

"What I mean, Miss Impatient, is that I wonder if

you would consider to marry a businessman—me—if I were head of Adonis Imports? I know that I can have the company making a very nice profit within six months or so, and should make us an excellent living. Will you say yes?"

Shylo felt as if the world had turned upside down, half of her absolutely going wild over Dimitri's proposal of marriage, the other half trying to understand what Adonis Imports had to do with anything. Shaking her head, she said, "I'm afraid you've confused me a little. I don't know what you mean by calling yourself 'head' of Adonis Imports. I thought you would never return to the actual business, and that all you cared about was the university, those marbles, and the trip to the British Museum. Can you actually run the business and carry on with the work you really love all at the same time?"

Something dark and painful shadowed Dimitri's expression for a moment, but in the next instant the cloud was gone. He tried but couldn't quite keep the sadness out of his melodic voice as he said, "No, I cannot. If I am to have the honor of being husband to a woman such as you, running the family business will have to be my only other concern."

"Wait a minute!" Shylo simply could not believe this. "You're not trying to say that you figure on running Adonis Imports on my account, are you?"

"But of course." He chuckled lightly. "I am proposing to you, so who else would I run it for?"

"Well, for you, that's who!"

Again he laughed, this time with a bitter edge to his usually smooth, rich voice. "I care not for the import business. I never have, but I——"

"Wait a minute again!" It couldn't be true—it

couldn't. "You're not saying that you'd give up the career you love—your *dreams*—for me, are you?"

Smiling indulgently, Dimitri took Shylo's sweet face between his hands. "I love you, *kouklitsa,* and my only wish is to vow to the real Shylo McBride. For that privilege and for you, I would give up my very life."

"Oh . . . God, Dimitri." Shylo was stunned, utterly shocked, and tears seemed to spring from every pore in her body. Afraid she might come apart at the seams as the full impact of what Dimitri had told her sank in, she tore away from him and turned her back. "Oh, my God . . . oh, *God!*" she muttered above the ocean's roar. "He'd give it all up for me—*for me?*"

In spite of her efforts to hold them inside, tears squeezed through her eyelids and began running down her cheeks. Shylo pinched herself just to make sure that she was not living in one of Cassie's romantic fantasies, then turned back to Dimitri to be certain that she hadn't dreamed him up or imagined this incredible moment.

He was still standing there in the sand, arms spread wide, his enticing lips still mouthing the words: "Will you marry me?"

Shylo threw herself into his waiting arms, crying, "Oh, Lord, Dimitri, you really *are* an idiot."

"Yes," he agreed, his accent thicker. "I have already accepted that title. What is your answer, *kouklitsa?* Will you marry this idiot?"

Shylo pulled back from Dimitri just far enough to look into his eyes. She did *not* want to miss his expression when she said, "My answer is yes, but there is one condition that must be met." When his brows drew together, she gave him a crooked grin. "I insist that you go back to the university and become a professor.

I simply cannot marry the head of Adonis Imports."

Dimitri tried to smile, but it was a grim expression indeed. "I appreciate your thoughts for me, but life at the university is not very glamours, especially for a woman. Also, while a professor's salary is adequate for my needs, I do not think you would see many diamonds or—"

"Why do you keep talking about diamonds and money? I don't want those things. I want the education you promised me, the journeys to excavation sights, and I'd really love to be with you when you get to England and demand the return of your marble lady. But most of all, my darling idiot, I just want *you.*"

Dimitri felt as if he'd been slapped—hard—and again his English suffered as his pulse raced. "B-but I remember—in our marriage bed, you say to me, 'I married you for your money!' And Ari's ring, you liked it very *big.* I remember all this."

"Yes, and all that's true, but I never wanted any of it for myself. I just wanted to attract my mother, to impress her enough to notice me, and, I suppose, to make her think that I was good enough and rich enough to be her daughter."

As the full realization hit him that he did *not* have to give up one dream to claim the other, Dimitri had to release Shylo and turn away from her to collect himself. After many, many deep breaths, he faced her again, his eyes a little damp, and said, "I am not only an idiot, but you must think me a fool of the highest order."

"Perhaps," she agreed in a throaty whisper, wrapping her arms around his waist and burying her head against his chest. "But you're the fool I love, and the fool I'll always love."

Epilogue

For years after, folks in San Diego talked about the wedding that took place that summer of 1888 as the most colorful, and possibly the strangest, the city had ever played host to.

For the participants, however, it was probably one of the most ordinary events to have happened to any of them in weeks.

The ceremony was held high on the cliffs near Ocean Beach at a location referred to by the bridal party as the "sit a spell" spot and began just before sundown, when the skies looked as if they were painted with fire. There were very few guests, but notable among them were the famous—or infamous, depending on how one viewed the man—Wyatt Earp and his beautiful wife, the former Josephine Sarah Marcus.

The nuptials included not one, but two weeping brides. Much to their mother's chagrin, Cassie wore

Shylo's freshly pressed and mended pink sateen suit because it matched exactly the color of her hair.

Shylo, looking more subdued but still unsuitably gowned for such a special occasion, insisted on donning the organdy and yellow lawn dress, including the hastily added train of cheap lace that she'd worn during her first wedding to Dimitri.

That man, an incredibly handsome groom who almost looked as if he'd just stepped off the top of a wedding cake, wore a proper enough dress suit, sporting tails and satin lapels, but he stubbornly topped the look with his new smoke gray Stetson that set off his pearly black hair even better than the lost hat.

Buck wore denims, a borrowed dress shirt, and a worn rawhide cowboy hat with a misshapen brim. His most prominent adornments were the purplish green bruise covering his right eye and the three scabby furrows running down the length of his cheek. Even if he'd been in tails, he still would have looked as if he'd been dragged beneath a buckboard down the entire length of Fifth Avenue. Midway through the services, this battered groom began to weep right along with his bride-to-be.

To each side of the principals were a pair of best men of Greek descent—Ari for Dimitri, as before, and Niko for Buck. Niko got confused and began answering the questions asked of the grooms—in Greek. The single matron of honor, a woman who also happened to be the mother of both brides, got the giggles when she overheard her husband muttering vows he had no business repeating, and in his native language, no less. By the time the justice of the peace got around to the I-do's, the entire wedding party had become infected by her laughter, and both couples had one hell of a time spitting out their vows well enough to be understood.

At the ceremony's conclusion, after plain gold bands and kisses had been exchanged, the mother of the brides announced the wedding gifts she'd chosen for her daughters. Shylo and Dimitri were given first-class passage to Greece on the luxurious ocean liner, the *City of New York*. She also threw in her country home in Switzerland, which happened to include a working and very profitable vineyard along the Rhine River.

For Cassie and Buck, who had yet to choose their honeymoon destination, first-class tickets were offered as well, along with twenty acres of land and a small hotel in the nearby community of La Jolla, a beachfront block of property that Colleen had been trying—unsuccessfully—to unload since her arrival in San Diego.

After the proper thanks and congratulations were given all around, Dimitri checked the papers he'd just signed to make absolutely certain that he had married the real Shylo McBride this time, then helped himself to two fresh glasses of champagne from the catering wagon Colleen had commissioned for the occasion.

After offering one of the drinks to his new bride, Dimitri took her by the hand and led her away from the group for a quiet moment alone. Standing near the edge of the cliffs so they could watch the crashing surf below, he raised his glass and said, "Here's to you, Mrs. Adonis—to you and your extremely generous mother."

Shylo touched her glass to his. "I'll drink to that! I never dreamed she'd give us so much."

After they'd each taken a sip of champagne, Dimitri said, "Neither did Buck. He almost fainted from shock."

"Actually Mother told us about paying for our honeymoon trips this morning, but made us promise that we wouldn't tell you fellas."

"Ah, so your whole family is sneaky, then."

He winked when he said it, but Shylo knew he was about half serious. And pretty much right, since she was about to put a plan in motion that she and Cassie had cooked up earlier. "Dimitri," she said, her voice suspiciously sweet, "speaking of my sister . . . Cassie was saying just this morning that it might be a real good idea if she and Buck went to Greece with us."

He immediately drew his brows together. "I cannot imagine why. This does not sound like such a good idea to me."

"Well, you know, what with Buck's former job and all, she thinks it might be best if he left the country for a while. Besides, I don't see how that would put us out any. Mother's offered them first-class passage anywhere—might as well be to Greece!"

Dimitri sighed heavily. "And after we arrive? I will be too busy at the university to make certain they stay out of trouble."

"Well, I figured after we got there that maybe you could get him a job with you and they could stay on a while?"

Again Dimitri sighed, this time with resignation, but still he tried to make her see the folly of her suggestion. "What kind of work could I possibly find for this kidnapping train robber at the university, or anywhere else, for that matter? He has no qualifications that I'm aware of."

Shrugging coyly, Shylo dragged the toe of her shoe

along the sandstone. "He's not all that useless. Cassie says that Buck is real good at lighting fires and holding the horses."

"Light—" Dimitri rolled his eyes, then recalled wishing Shylo "better luck next time" the night he thought he'd never see her again. He'd said those words in the most sarcastic of ways, but sarcasm and all, he had a feeling he should have uttered them to himself. He suspected he was going to need all the luck he could get once *both* of the former McBride sisters hit the docks at Piraeus.

"Can they go with us?" she asked again, her eyes aglow.

After raising his glass to Shylo one more time, Dimitri tossed down the last of his champagne. "But, of course."

Then he pitched the glass over the cliff, the exquisitely cut crystal catching a million raindrops of liquid sunshine.

Author's Notes

Sadly enough, the story of my fictional heroine's experience with relation to New York's orphan train program happened all too often. The "experiment," conceived by Reverend Charles Loring Brace of the Children's Aid Society in New York, ran from 1854 to 1929. More than 150,000 orphans, some only infants, were plucked from the streets and over-crowded foundling homes, placed on trains, and sent out west to be adopted by farm families, many of whom did not have the children's best interests in mind. Today there remain around six hundred survivors of this program.

As for the so-called Elgin marbles, the Greek government continues to have an ongoing argument with the British over their return. The legend of the missing caryatid sister and her nightly flow of tears persists to this day. During my visit to the Acropolis, I saw the

Erechtheion, complete with the porch where the six caryatids had originally stood. Because of the heavy air pollution in the Athens area, the statues on the site are replicas, but the five original sisters remaining in Greece are housed in an oxygen-controlled environment at the Acropolis Museum nearby.

COMING SOON

Desert Song by Constance O'Banyon

The enthralling conclusion of the passionate DeWinter legacy. As Lady Mallory Stanhope set sail for Egypt she was drawn to the strikingly handsome Lord Michael DeWinter, who was on a dangerous mission. From fashionable London to the mysterious streets of Cairo, together they risked everything to rescue his father, the Duke of Ravenworth, from treacherous captors.

A Child's Promise by Deborah Bedford

The story of a love that transcends broken dreams. When Johnny asks Lisa to marry him she knows it's the only way to make a new life for herself and her daughter. But what will happen when Johnny finds out she's lied to him? "A tender, uplifting story of family and love...You won't want to miss this one."—Debbie Macomber, bestselling author of *Morning Comes Softly*.

Desert Dreams by Deborah Cox

Alone and destitute after the death of her gambling father, Anne Cameron set out on a quest for buried treasure and met up with handsome and mysterious Rafe Montalvo, an embittered gunfighter. They needed each other in order to make their journey, but could newfound passion triumph over their pasts?

One Bright Morning by Alice Duncan

Young widow Maggie Bright had her hands full raising a baby and running a farm on her own. The last thing she needed was a half-dead stranger riding into her front yard and into her life. As she nursed him back to health, she found herself doing the impossible—falling in love with the magnetic but difficult Jubal Green.

Meadowlark by Carol Lampman

Garrick "Swede" Swensen rescued a beautiful young woman from drowning only to find her alone, penniless, and pregnant. He offered Becky his name with no strings attached, but neither of them dreamed that their marriage of convenience would ever develop into something far more. When Swede's mysterious past caught up with him, he was forced to make the decision of a lifetime.

Oh, Susannah by Leigh Riker

Socialite Susannah Whittaker is devastated by the death of her best friend, Clary, the sister of country music sensation Jeb Stuart Cody. An unlikely pair, Jeb and Susannah grow closer as they work together to unveil the truth behind Clary's untimely death, along the way discovering a passion neither knew could exist.

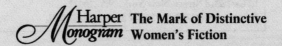

Harper Monogram **The Mark of Distinctive Women's Fiction**

surviving, existing, enduring . . . until he met Kendall. She had revived something in him that he'd thought long dead, and he hadn't wanted to admit it. The past two days with her had been a revelation; she had opened his eyes to all he was missing—all he *had* missed in a relationship with a woman—and the intensity of his feelings for her scared him. It was more than a physical experience; he had found himself watching her when she wasn't looking, loving the way she walked or talked, or gestured. He wanted to share his thoughts with her, his hopes and dreams as well as his nightmares; he wanted to hear those things from her, and yet . . .

Yet he had used the experience in the meadow just now to thrust her away. He had seized it as the perfect excuse to put up a barrier between them. He was becoming too involved, too close to her . . . too near to asking her to share his life, and that scared him most of all.

He wasn't ready for that, not after his marriage to Marie. He felt he had failed his wife in so many ways.

capable of giving her what she

ing to make the

his

gry with himself,

ought, he didn't notice the one still

by his hand.

r hear from Jordan lit another

p from Idaho. The p for several

are, both of them acti plane ride

passionate lovers they like

n them growing with ev had

landed, Kendall was so tau

ke bursting into tears. As

she sat silently on her side

What did he want? Jordan asked himself angrily. He'd just told himself that he couldn't handle another clinging woman like Marie, but perversely, he wished Kendall needed him more.

He didn't know what he wanted, that was the problem. And that was why he had used that incident in the meadow as an excuse. He needed time to think. He had to decide what it was that he really did want.

Except now he probably wouldn't get the chance to decide anything at all. After the way he'd treated Kendall just now, he wouldn't blame her if she never spoke to him again. Dismayed at the thought, he was halfway out of his chair before he made himself sit back again.

He had to give them both time to work things out, he thought. As much as he wanted to straighten out this mess he had made of everything, he couldn't go back to her right now and tell her that he'd been a fool. He couldn't explain how confused he felt, how uncertain, when he couldn't even explain those things to himself.

Depressed and an cigarette. Deep in th burning in the ashtra

Kendall didn't see days after the return t home had been a nighti strangers instead of the been, the distance betwe mile. By the time the plane from nerves hat she felt Jordan drove swiftly home,

He just wanted same

Bu hea hi

the most

of the car, pretending an absorbing interest in the passing scenery, but acutely aware of Jordan beside her, concentrating fiercely on the road.

It seemed impossible to believe that they had been lovers; as she glanced covertly at him, she thought that he was more a stranger to her than he had ever been before. Had she imagined that ecstatic time with him? Had she really dreamed it all—the passion and the delight and the laughter? Looking away from his remote profile, she could almost believe that she had.

On the day the Idaho colt Jordan had bought was due to arrive, she woke earlier than usual. Instead of getting up immediately, as she always did, she lay there thinking, as she had for days, about their estrangement. From the moment he had dropped her off in front of the house with a forced thank-you for having accompanied him and with no mention at all of the disastrous end to their affair, she had run the gamut of emotions from anger to sheer misery. She was still angry, but now, after two days of silence from him, she was even more miserable, and for a moment she actually hated him.

Had she really expected him to call? Yes, she had. She had hoped that some time alone would make him realize how unfair he had been, how cruel to end their affair the way he had with no word of explanation. She had believed that, once he had time to think about it, he would at least be considerate enough to give her a reason she could understand.

That was the worst thing about it, she thought despondently: not knowing why. If he had told her he didn't want to get involved, or that the affair was a mistake, or even that he just wasn't as attracted to her as he had thought, she could have accepted it. She would have been hurt, but she could have dealt with that—eventually. What she couldn't deal with was this cold silence; that hurt most of all. She felt used, betrayed—and sometimes angry enough to want to confront him herself.

She had picked up the phone more than once during the past two days, intending to call and demand an explanation since it was obvious he wasn't going to give one voluntarily. Then she had thought that going to see him would be better. He couldn't ignore a face-to-face confrontation; she would force him to talk to her in person. So she had gone out, keys in hand, determined to have it out with him even if they never spoke to each other again afterward. She had gotten as far as the end of the driveway before she turned around again.

Now the colt was arriving and she would have to call him to tell him it was here. But that was all she was going to tell him, she promised herself. Even if he brought up the subject, she wasn't going to discuss what had happened in Idaho. It was a closed issue as far as she was concerned; he had lost the opportunity to give her an explanation, even a false one. If he didn't care, neither did she.

In fact, she thought defiantly, she was glad now that this had happened. It was obvious that they'd both been carried away by the moment; it had been nothing more than that, and she didn't want it to be. Nice while it lasted, she told herself bitterly, but definitely not meant to be. Their lifestyles were too different. *They* were too different. She had known right from the beginning that he belonged with Kaylene and her crowd, and if she hadn't been such a romantic little fool, she would have remembered that and kept her distance. They led separate lives; they had different goals. And nothing, not even a . . . a *fling* . . . in Idaho during a snowstorm could change that.

Chapter 10

THE COLT ARRIVED ON SCHEDULE. ANOTHER VAN DRIVER came this time, a young man Kendall didn't know. After stopping the huge rig in the middle of the yard, he jumped down and immediately started unbolting the doors, saying, "I'm glad to get rid of this one; he kicked hell out of the stall all the way from Boise."

Kendall was surprised at that; the colt hadn't seemed bad-tempered the day she and Jordan had looked at him. "Maybe he's just not used to trailering," she suggested.

The driver looked sourly at her. "And maybe he's just a mean so-and-so, too. I don't envy you, having to take care of him."

Kendall was about to tell the man that she was sure there wouldn't be any problem; after all, she had seen the horse before, and he hadn't acted spoiled, just high-spirited. But by the time they got the colt down the ramp and into a stall, she was glad she hadn't said anything. The young stallion had tried to rear as they were unhooking the crossties inside the van, and he had struck out with both forefeet, narrowly missing Kendall's head, as she led him forward. Then he had bared his teeth at the driver, and it took both of them to hold him as he scrambled down the ramp and into the yard. He was still fighting them as they led him into the barn, and they both breathed a sigh of relief when they finally reached one of the stalls and got him inside. When Kendall unsnapped the lead rope, prudently leaving the halter on, the colt tried to bite her before she could escape. Slamming the stall door, Kendall wondered what she'd gotten into.

"See what I mean?" the driver said, wiping his forehead with the back of his arm.

"Yes," Kendall said absently. She scribbled her name on the delivery form, her eyes on the colt. He was pacing inside the stall, and his neck and flanks were damp with sweat.

"I'd get rid of him as soon as I could, if I were you. He's a nasty one; he'll hurt somebody if you give him the chance," the man said as he climbed gratefully back into the van.

Kendall couldn't understand it. As the driver jock-eyed the rig around and pulled away, she went back inside the barn to study the colt. For an instant or two, she wondered if this was the same horse, but then she knew it had to be: She remembered the notched blaze and the two white markings on the hind feet. It was the same one, all right—in appearance, if not personality. She wondered then if he had been tranquilized the day she and Jordan had gone to look at him. Some owners were unscrupulous enough to do such things, but she doubted that the Allenbys were that kind. She had been acquainted with them for years; they just wouldn't do something like that, she was sure.

Maybe the colt was just agitated by the long trip, she thought. Some horses didn't travel well; she had seen that herself. The noise of the van, the stops and starts, and the confinement for hours on end could make even the most placid animals mean-tempered and nervous. The horses usually calmed down after a day or two of rest and became themselves again, and she hoped this one would too; she had enough to do here without having to deal with a fractious young colt. She sighed heavily then, remembering that she had to call Jordan and tell him the horse was here. It was the call she had been dreading, but as she reluctantly went into the house, she was still more preoccupied with the horse's behavior than with what she was going to say to the owner.

As she dialed Jordan's number, she wondered if she should call the vet. Then she decided to wait. If the colt didn't settle in by tomorrow, she'd have Dr. Danson stop by. Until then, she would just keep a close eye on him. It was probably nothing, she assured herself, and then became tense all over again when she heard the phone ring at the other end.

An unfamiliar voice answered on the third ring, and when Kendall asked to speak to Jordan, she was told that he wasn't there. Relieved that she didn't have to talk to him after all, she left a message about the arrival of his horse and hung up.

Now *he* can decide what to do, she thought, and she went out to the barn to take another look at the colt. She was still there, finishing the evening feeding, when Jordan arrived. She heard the car and recognized the sound of the engine as his, but there was no escape. She barely had time to take a deep breath to prepare herself before he walked inside, and for a tense moment or two they just stared at each other.

"I got your message," Jordan said finally.

"The colt arrived this afternoon," Kendall said warily. "I thought you'd want to know."

They fell silent again, the tension between them almost palpable. One of the horses snorted just then, and the sound was so loud in the vibrating silence, and Kendall so taut with nerves, that she jumped.

"He's over there," she said, pointing. Her lips were so stiff she had trouble forming the words. She hadn't thought it would be this difficult. She'd been so angry and so disillusioned about the way things had ended between them that she had been sure she'd feel nothing but contempt when she saw him again. Now all she could think about was how much he had hurt her. The pain of his rejection overwhelmed every other emotion; she couldn't even be angry at him anymore.

Jordan didn't look at his horse. His eyes held hers, and he took a step forward. Despite herself, Kendall stepped back. If he came any closer, she knew she would burst into tears, and that would be the final blow to her pride.

Jordan halted when he saw her move away from him. "Have you had dinner yet?" he asked.

Kendall gaped at him. "Dinner?" she echoed blankly, as if she'd never heard the word.

"I haven't either," he said. "Why don't we go somewhere and . . ."

She couldn't believe it. She had moped around the house in sheer misery for the past two days, feeling that her life was over. She had waited for him to call, hoping that he would explain, *praying* that he felt as bad as she did. And now, when he finally deigned to show up, the only thing he could think about was going out to dinner? She was suddenly so furious that she forgot about the hurt and disillusionment she had endured; she wanted to strangle him with her bare hands.

"I'm not going anywhere with you!" she said flatly.

"Kendall . . ." He took another step toward her.

"Stay away from me!" she cried. "Take a look at your horse and get out. I never want to see you again!"

"I don't blame you for being angry."

"Angry! What makes you think I'm *angry!*"

"I'd like to explain."

She was too furious to listen. She had waited days to hear those words from him, but now that he had finally said them, she didn't want to hear any explanations. "It's too late for that. You missed your chance to explain, Jordan. You should have tried that in Idaho. Not that it would have mattered," she added cruelly. "I think we both realized our mistake. It's just too bad that we didn't recognize it sooner!"

"Is that what you think—that it was all a mistake?"

"I think that's obvious, don't you?"

"No, I—"

"Oh, don't tell me you've had second thoughts," she said scathingly. "Not after the way you've behaved!"

He flinched at that, acknowledging the thrust. Kendall was too angry to care. She wanted to hurt him; she wanted to make him feel some of the misery she had endured. Grabbing a broom, she began furiously sweeping the aisleway, turning her back on him. "I think you'd better go," she said. "We don't have anything more to say to each other."

He reached out and took hold of the broom handle. "I think we do."

She tried to jerk the broom away from him. He held it fast, staring down at her, his eyes black as night. "I told you . . . ," she began hotly.

"I know what you told me," he said quietly. "But I haven't spent the past two days despising myself for nothing. I finally got up the courage to face you in person, and I'd appreciate it if you'd listen to me before I lose it again."

Abruptly, she surrendered the broom. She stood there with her fists clenched, longing to tell him that nothing he said now could possibly make any difference, and that she hadn't the slightest interest in anything he had to say. He couldn't despise himself any more than she despised him, and she wanted to tell him again just to go away.

To her horror, she said instead, "Let's go into the house, then."

Hating herself for giving in once more, she tried to tell herself that she was just curious to hear how he was going to explain himself. After all, she told herself angrily, leading the way to the house, he'd had two whole days to think of an excuse. It had better be good. Not that it mattered, she thought with a defiant lift of her head. She had no intention of accepting any excuse, no matter what it was.

In the kitchen, Kendall looked distastefully at the coffee that had been on the stove all day. She wanted something stronger, so she said ungraciously, "I'm going to have some wine. Do you want a glass, or do you want a drink instead?"

They had wine. She was pouring it when Jordan put his hand over hers. He took the bottle from her and set it on the counter. "I'm sorry, Kendall," he said.

He hadn't released her hand. She pulled away from

him, knowing that if she allowed him to touch her she'd never be able to keep her distance. Even that brief contact had set alarm bells ringing in her mind, and she was determined not to weaken this time. It was bad enough that she had agreed to listen to him; she didn't want to complicate things—not when she had spent days telling herself it was all over.

"Sorry isn't good enough," she said.

"I know." He looked so unhappy that, despite all her resolve, despite all her promises to herself and her fierce vow never to forgive him, she felt her anger melting away again. Furiously, she tried to recapture it.

"What you did was unforgivable," she said. Her lip trembled, and she took a shaky breath, trying to get control of herself before she went on. "I think you'd better go after all," she added finally, knowing that as long as he was looking at her like that, she wouldn't be under any sort of control.

"If that's what you want, I will."

That wasn't what she wanted at all. She wanted to throw herself into his arms and tell him that she couldn't manage without him. She wanted to say that she'd spent the past few days longing for him, trying to tell herself that it was all over between them and knowing that it never would be, at least for her. But she couldn't say it, not any of it. The words caught in her throat, and she had to swallow before she could say anything at all.

"That's what I want," she said unsteadily.

He stood there for an endless moment, just staring at her. Then he nodded slightly. "All right. Maybe it is better this way. Good-bye, Kendall."

He turned away, heading for the door. Kendall watched him go, yearning to call him back, willing herself to stand there instead. She wouldn't run after him, not when he was willing to give up so easily. If she meant so little to him as that . . .

The door closed behind him, and still she stood there. In a moment she would hear his car start and he would go away, driving out of her life as easily as he had driven in that first day. She couldn't move; she felt frozen to that spot, every sense tuned to hearing his car. She was holding her breath, her entire body taut, waiting . . . listening . . . hoping.

The back door banged open again, and Jordan paused on the threshold. "I can't leave it like this," he choked.

The hurt and the pain and the longing she had felt were mirrored in the way he said the words. Suddenly she was flying across the kitchen, throwing herself into his arms, lifting her face for his desperate kiss. His arms tightened around her, and he nearly lifted her off the floor, holding her tightly, as if he would never let her go, murmuring her name as he kissed her forehead, her eyes, her throat.

"I'm sorry, Kendall . . . so sorry. . . . Can you forgive me? I was such a fool. . . ."

Tears filled her eyes. The words she had waited to hear filled her heart, and she clung fiercely to him, unable to speak. She murmured something unintelligible, feeling him tremble with emotion, unaware that she was trembling violently herself.

"Oh, Jordan . . ."

He swept her up into his arms, carrying her out of the kitchen and up the stairs. She gestured toward the door to her bedroom, and when they entered, the windows were filled with the last rays of the sunset. Jordan's face looked bronze in the light as Kendall glanced up at him wordlessly, and for a moment they just gazed into one another's eyes.

"I've missed you," he whispered hoarsely.

"I couldn't call . . . ," she choked.

His eyes burned even more deeply into hers. "Did you want to?"

"Yes. Oh, yes! I picked up the phone a dozen times."

"So did I."

They fell on the bed, and as Jordan's weight pressed her down and his mouth covered hers, Kendall wrapped her arms around him, holding him tightly to her. A shudder passed through her; she could feel the heat of his body even through the clothing that separated them, and her desire for him obliterated every other thought. They tore almost frenziedly at their restricting garments, and when they finally moved together again, she uttered a wordless sound of fierce joy. She had thought never to experience this exquisite sensation with him again. She had tried to convince herself that it didn't matter, but it did, it did. No other man had ever aroused her to fever pitch this way; no one else could possibly compare. A single caress from him, just one kiss, and she was lost and didn't care.

In one swift movement Jordan rolled over onto his back, taking her with him, pressing her length along his, pulling her up as his mouth sought first one breast, then the other. Holding her in his hands, he circled his tongue around her achingly erect nipples, and when he began to suck at them, she moaned and arched upward.

The heat of pure passion was already spreading through her; she trembled with the force of it, feeling the longing between her thighs, wanting to engulf him, to draw him deeper and deeper inside her until he touched that explosive core and she found release. She couldn't think; her body was an entity of its own. She was only a physical being whose flesh burned and whose senses screamed for fulfillment. Her pulse was roaring in her ears; she was trembling violently.

She couldn't bear it anymore. Her hips moving without conscious effort, she guided him into her, bracing her hands on his shoulders, gazing down at him unseeingly.

He looked up then, and she bent swiftly, claiming his mouth with her own, taking his tongue deep inside, moving against him, seeking to evoke in him the same blind passion that whirled inside her. Her legs went around him as they rolled to one side; she held him tightly as he began to thrust against her. His hands were all over her body, and everywhere they touched, a new clamor rose inside her, driving her on.

They rolled over again, and now he was on top of her, looking down, his face contorted with the desire she had aroused in him, his eyes glazed with passion. Reaching up, she wound her fingers through his hair, and pulled his head down almost savagely to hers again, pleading hoarsely, "Kiss me . . . please. . . ."

She didn't know what she was saying; she didn't hear what he said. She was aware only of the powerful thrusting of his body, of the trembling of his arms and legs as he drove into her. She met each thrust with a fierce hunger, straining upward, trying to contain that roaring fire, trying to wait, knowing how helpless she was against the force of it.

It was like trying to hold back the wind. The blur of sensation crashed over her, tumbling her, shaking her, sweeping her helplessly along.

"Jordan . . ."

"I can't . . ."

The agonizing pressure exploded inside her just as he cried out. She arched upward again as he stiffened, and for an exquisite endless moment she was filled with such an intensity of pure pleasure that there was nothing else in the world but that feeling of sheer bliss. It came in waves, each more shudderingly ecstatic than the last, and she knew that if it went on she would surely die of that glorious feeling.

"Oh, Jordan . . . ," she gasped at last. Her voice was a faint whisper; she felt utterly drained as they lay, exhausted, side by side.

He couldn't move either. Breathing harshly, he put his arm around her and held her tightly until they became calm again.

"And to think I almost didn't come over here tonight," he said, a long time later.

Kendall smiled, turning to face him. "I hoped you wouldn't. I never wanted to see you again."

He took her hand, bringing it to his lips, kissing her fingers. "I can't blame you for that," he said. Then he laughed softly. "For a while, I thought you were going to attack me with that broom!"

"I might have, if you hadn't grabbed it," Kendall said, smiling too.

"Why do you think I did?"

She laughed at that, raising her head to look at him. Suddenly serious, she said, "I didn't want to call to tell you the colt had arrived. I almost didn't."

"I'm surprised you did. I thought you might tell the transport company to take him right back to Idaho."

"I wouldn't have gone that far."

"No?"

"No. But I was tempted," she confessed with a laugh.

"Well, I'm glad you didn't. Then I wouldn't have had an excuse to come over here tonight."

"Is that what you needed, an excuse?"

He was silent a moment. "I guess I did. I'm not too proud of the way I acted, Kendall. I want you to know that."

It was her turn to hesitate. "Do you want to talk about it?"

He sighed. "No. But I will."

"You don't have to."

He looked down at her. "Yes, I do," he said quietly. "You have a right to an explanation, however feeble."

Suddenly she didn't want him to explain. Not now, when they were so close. She didn't want to spoil this moment; she wanted it to go on forever. Then she sighed too. She sat up and leaned back against the headboard. They had to discuss it, she realized. If they didn't, it would always be between them, overshadowing everything else.

"Do you remember that car accident I told you about, when my wife was killed?" he began.

She nodded, unsure for a moment whether to admit how much she knew. Then she decided he had to tell it his own way. "Yes," she said simply. "I remember."

"I broke my back then," he went on, his voice devoid of emotion. "It goes into spasms every now and then—that's what happened when we went for that walk."

She stared at him. "Why didn't you tell me? Oh, Jordan, I was so scared that day! I didn't know what was wrong!"

"I know," he said unhappily. "And I'm sorry about that. It was stupid, senseless. Especially since I used it as an . . . excuse."

"But why?"

"Because things were getting too complicated. Because I was starting to think that I—"

He stopped again. Kendall waited, but when he didn't speak, she thought she understood. "You didn't want to get involved," she said flatly. "That's it, isn't it?"

He wouldn't look at her. "Yes," he admitted finally, his voice low.

"And now?"

He looked even more unhappy at that, and to her dismay, she felt him draw away from her.

"And now?" she repeated, hearing her voice rise but unable to prevent it. She had the feeling that disaster was coming at her, and she wished futilely that she'd never agreed to this conversation. But there was no turning back now; they had to finish it one way or the other. She had to know. "Answer me, Jordan!" she said sharply.

"I don't know," he said. "I just don't know."

She stared at him. "What do you mean, you don't know?" she demanded. "What kind of an answer is that?"

But instead of replying, he abruptly got out of bed, reaching for his clothes. Kendall followed him, wrapping a robe quickly around her, determined not to let him go until he gave her an answer that made sense. Snapping on the bedside lamp, she glanced at the rumpled bed, and then looked quickly away from it.

"Jordan!" she said sharply.

He was just finishing buttoning his shirt. His hands slowed, then became still as he forced himself to look at her. "You're right," he said in a strange voice. "I do owe you a better explanation than that." He took a deep breath. "No, I didn't want to get involved," he admitted finally. "I never meant for things to go this far. Not then . . . and not tonight."

She gaped at him, feeling the first flush of anger, trying to hold on to her control. "Well, things *did* go this far," she said. "So what are we—"

"I'm sorry, Kendall. It . . . it just isn't going to work."

"You didn't seem to feel that way a few minutes ago!" she pointed out sharply.

He looked unhappy again. "I know. But I wasn't thinking straight. . . ." He met her eyes again, briefly, then looked away. "I can never think straight when I'm around you," he confessed, his voice so low that she almost didn't hear. "But that's no excuse. I can't handle this, Kendall. It's not fair—to you . . . to either of us. I just can't give you what you want. I don't . . . I don't seem to be capable of loving someone anymore. When my wife died in that accident, I—"

She couldn't help it; the anger and hurt she felt burst out of control. "So you're going to spend the rest of your life feeling guilty about it?" she cried. "Do you *enjoy* punishing yourself, Jordan? Because if you do—"

"You don't understand!" he interrupted harshly.

"Oh, don't I?" she replied scathingly. "You're not the only one who's ever had guilt feelings, Jordan! If you weren't so busy feeling sorry for yourself, you might realize that!"

"I'm not feeling sorry for myself!"

"Aren't you? Well, you're doing a damned good job of putting on an act, then!"

"I told you—"

"Oh, I know what you *told* me! I'm just trying to make some sense out of it. But it's a little difficult when you seem to be more confused than I am!"

"I *said* I was wrong!"

"So you did," she said cuttingly. "It's a pity you didn't realize that before! Just tell me one thing, Jordan. Why *did* you come here tonight?"

"I came to apologize."

Her glance flicked toward the bed. "And this was your way of doing it?" she demanded shrilly. "I didn't think even you could stoop so low!"

He looked at her again, his eyes so dark that they appeared almost black. His face flushing with anger, he said, "I'll pretend I didn't hear that."

"Well, that doesn't surprise me!" she cried. "You seem to have a facility for ignoring anything unpleasant!"

"Is that what you think?"

"What else am I supposed to think? You said you never intended this to happen, yet you came here again. You . . . you . . ." She couldn't go on; her anger was strangling her, and in another second she would burst into tears. "Just what should I think?" she choked. "You tell *me*, Jordan—if you can!"

"I think you should forget this ever happened," he said hoarsely. "I told you, it was a mistake."

"A mistake!" she cried.

He started to reach out toward her, but she jerked back violently, a look of such contempt on her face that he cringed and dropped his hand again. "You deserve more, Kendall," he said. "Much more than I can give . . . more than I'm prepared to give. I'm sorry. I wish . . . I wish things were different."

She wished things were different too. She wished he

had never come here tonight; she wished that she had realized how hopeless it was from the start. She wished that she had never met him, and then knew that wasn't true. Even after what he had just said, she still nourished the hope that they could work this out. She wanted to tell him that if he needed time, she would give it to him; she wanted to say that she would wait, that she couldn't—wouldn't—let him go. But she felt the distance between them widening with every passing second, and she knew how futile her hope was. When he grabbed his jacket from the chair, she didn't try to stop him. No matter what she said now, she knew he would walk away from her, and she wasn't going to beg him to stay. She had been humiliated enough tonight; her pride was the only thing she had left.

He turned to look at her as he reached the door. "I . . . ," he began, and stopped, unable for a moment to go on. Finally he said sadly, "It seems like I'm always apologizing to you, doesn't it? But I *am* sorry, Kendall. Truly, I am."

She didn't move, not until she heard him start the car and drive away. Then she sank down slowly onto the edge of the bed, too devastated by what had happened even to cry.

Chapter 11

KENDALL WAS CONCERNED ABOUT JORDAN'S COLT. WHEN she dragged herself out to the barn early the next morning, the young stallion seemed lethargic, in sharp contrast to the wild temper he had displayed when he arrived. When she fed him his hay he ignored it, and she saw that he hadn't eaten much the night before. Her glance went to Cantata, waiting patiently for her breakfast, and she felt a stab of alarm. Trying not to panic at the thought that the colt might have some infectious disease, Kendall dashed back to the house again to call the vet. To her dismay, the answering service told her that the doctor was on an emergency call, and that it would be several hours before he could come to the ranch.

It was more than several hours. The vet hadn't arrived by noon, despite Kendall's increasingly worried calls to his office, and she was about to contact another man when she heard someone outside. She turned in relief toward the doorway, exclaiming, "Dr. Danson, I'm so—," and stopped, the words dying on her lips.

Jordan was standing there—and right beside him was Kaylene Van Zandt.

"What are you doing here?" she demanded, her anxiety making her voice sharp.

Kaylene minced toward her in boots with four-inch heels and designer jeans that were so tight Kendall wondered how she had been able to sit in the car. She wore a flaming red silk blouse with a low V neckline, and her platinum hair glinted artificially in the light. As always, her makeup was skillfully applied, but the thick false eyelashes seemed even more out of place during the day, and Kendall, conscious of the rumpled blouse and jeans she had thrown on this morning, thought nastily that Kaylene looked like an aging Las Vegas showgirl.

"I came to see the colt Jordan bought," Kaylene said, unperturbed by Kendall's rude tone. "When I found out about him, I just had to see for myself."

And just how had Kaylene found out about the colt? Kendall wondered furiously. Her glance went to Jordan, and when their eyes met, hers accusing, his wary, she looked away again. He couldn't wait for her opinion, Kendall thought, infuriated. He'd probably called Kaylene last night, in fact, thinking after their quarrel that she'd duped him into buying the animal in the first place. Oh, she could imagine *that* conversation: Kaylene sweetly offering to come look at the colt; Jordan eagerly agreeing. How dare he do such a thing to her!

It was the last straw. She'd been right about him all along: He had just used her until he could gain entry into Kaylene's good graces. And she had fallen neatly into the trap. What a fool she had been to think that Jordan had really been attracted to her; he'd had this planned from the beginning. All that talk about her being his agent, needing her help to choose his stock. He'd needed her help, all right—to choose the horses in that sale that would bring him the most attention from Kaylene herself. He wasn't really interested in buying her ranch—at least, not right away. He was more concerned with establishing himself with Kaylene and her set first.

And she had helped him, hadn't she? Kendall gritted her teeth at the thought of how easily she'd been taken in. Oh, it was all so clear now, she thought, and she despised herself for not seeing it sooner. Taut with anger and self-loathing, she watched Kaylene and Jordan pause in front of the colt's stall.

Kaylene took one look inside and said to Jordan, "This horse doesn't look well." She turned to Kendall, raising an eyebrow. "Have you called the vet?"

Kendall took a grip on her temper. Did Kaylene actually think that she hadn't noticed the colt's condition? "Dr. Danson is on his way," she said through clenched teeth. "He was supposed to be here hours ago."

Jordan had turned to look at her too. "Why didn't you call me?"

"Because there was nothing you could do until the vet came," Kendall snapped. "Unless you have some unsuspected talent for veterinary diagnosis, I thought it would be better for Dr. Danson to look at him first."

Kaylene smirked at that, glancing quickly from Kendall to Jordan, all too clearly aware of the tension between them. "My, you do seem a little out-of-sorts today, dear," she said, turning to Jordan again before Kendall could reply. To Kendall's fury, she added, "Danson is an adequate man, I suppose, but I really think you should use my veterinarian. Ted Williams has been with me for years; I trust him implicitly."

Jordan glanced quickly at the enraged Kendall. "If this Danson is on his way . . ."

Kaylene made a dismissive gesture. "I can have Ted here in five minutes. Better yet, maybe we should take the colt over to his hospital. He can be monitored much more closely there. You don't mind, do you, Kendall?" she asked, without even looking at her. "After all, this *is* a valuable animal, and we shouldn't take any chances."

Kendall barely suppressed the urge to tell her that Cantata was worth more than all the other horses here combined. Seething, she didn't wait for Jordan's opinion. She wanted them both to leave before she started screaming, so she said, "Why should I mind?" She walked deliberately over to Cantata's stall. "If that colt is infectious, I certainly don't want him here."

"Kendall . . . ," Jordan began.

Kendall shot him a contemptuous look, daring him to object. He had chosen sides, she thought; he could take the consequences.

Jordan flushed angrily at her expression. "All right. If that's the way you want it."

"I'll go cancel the call to Dr. Danson," Kendall said coldly. "You can make your own arrangements about trailering him over there."

"We'll use one of my vehicles," Kaylene said, unable to disguise the triumph in her eyes. "I'll call my driver."

"That won't be necessary," Jordan said curtly, his eyes still on Kendall. "I have my own trailer."

Kendall didn't trust herself to say anything more. She was so furious that she brushed by them without another word, marching into the house without looking back. She made sure she was gone when Jordan came back for the colt, deliberately manufacturing enough errands in town to keep her away most of the day, knowing that if she saw Jordan again, she'd commit murder.

When she finally returned late that afternoon and saw the empty stall where the colt had been, something snapped inside her. She had held herself under a tight rein all day, afraid to give vent to her anger for fear she'd burst into tears instead. But when she saw that Jordan really had followed Kaylene's advice, she lost that last bit of control.

So Jordan thought that his horse would receive better care elsewhere, did he? she thought furiously. Maybe the rest of his horses should be under his own supervision too.

Slamming the door to the empty stall, Kendall turned on her heel and went to get the keys to her stock trailer. Thirty minutes later, a tight-lipped Kendall delivered all of Jordan's horses to his own newly completed barn. The man he had hired to look after the place was astonished when she drove in, but after one look at her face he silently helped her unload. The last stall door was barely closed before she was driving out again, and as she glanced in the rearview mirror, she saw the caretaker standing in the yard, staring after her with a puzzled expression. She lifted her chin defiantly. She didn't care what anyone thought. Jordan was just lucky that she had left the horses in someone's care. The way she felt, she could easily have let them out to fend for themselves

in some empty field, hoping he'd never find them
again.

When the phone rang that night, Kendall knew it had
to be Jordan. For a second or two she was tempted not
to answer, but she had to talk to him sometime, and it
might as well be now, when she was still angry.

"Kendall, this is Jordan," he said without preamble.
"I'd like to know what the hell is going on."

"I assume you're talking about the horses I delivered
this afternoon," she said coolly.

"What else would I be talking about?" he demanded,
exasperated. "You could have told me what you intended to do."

"Like you told me about bringing Kaylene here?"

"I didn't know I needed permission to bring someone
to see one of my horses," he snapped.

"Kaylene Van Zandt isn't just 'someone'!" Kendall
replied sharply. "She and I aren't the best of friends, in
case you hadn't noticed!"

"She just wanted to see the colt."

Kendall didn't ask how Kaylene had found out about
the horse in the first place. "Oh, really? It seemed to
me that she was more interested in establishing the fact
that I wasn't taking proper care of it!"

"Aren't you being a little sensitive? She was only
trying to help!"

"By suggesting that I didn't know what I was doing?"

"She never said that."

"Oh, not in so many words," Kendall said angrily.
"But she certainly implied it—and you obviously
agreed with her!"

"Now wait a minute! You were the one who said you
didn't want the horse to stay."

"And you were the one who couldn't wait to get it out of here!"

"That's not true, and you know it! I said we should wait for Danton, or Danson, or whatever his name is!"

"But you *didn't* wait, did you?"

"No, I didn't wait," Jordan said, obviously trying to control himself. "As soon as you said he might have something infectious, I decided to move him. I didn't want you to have to deal with it."

Kendall was infuriated by the deliberately patient tone he used. "Am I supposed to believe that you humiliated me in front of that woman out of some perverse consideration for me?" she asked sarcastically. "That *is* a novel approach, Jordan. I'll have to remember that when I want to get back at someone myself!"

"It seems you already did that!"

"Because I returned your horses? But I thought you'd be pleased. Since I obviously couldn't be trusted with the colt, I was sure you'd feel the same way about the others. I just saved you the trouble of coming to get them yourself."

"It's not like you to be vindictive, Kendall," he said, angry again, and not bothering to hide it this time.

"Isn't it?" she asked cuttingly. "How would you know? You never wanted to find out *what* I was like, remember? You were the one who didn't want to get involved. Well, we certainly aren't involved now, are we? You've got your horses back, so we don't even have to see each other anymore."

"This really doesn't have anything to do with Kaylene, does it? You're just using her as an excuse because of what happened last night!"

Stung, Kendall said, "You're the one who needs excuses, Jordan—not I!"

He was silent at that, and Kendall closed her eyes against the sudden sting of tears. She didn't want them to be throwing these hateful words at each other. She wanted to say she was sorry; she wanted to hear him say it. But she knew that even if she apologized it wouldn't bring them closer together; nothing would ever heal the breach between them, because Jordan didn't want it to be healed. He had made his feelings perfectly clear last night, and nothing was going to change that.

It wasn't until she hung up that she realized she hadn't asked about the colt. Her hand still on the receiver, she was tempted to call Jordan back just to find out what the vet had said. Then she snatched her hand away. Their good-bye had been final, and she wasn't going to let him think that she had abandoned all pride—or worse, that she was using that as an excuse to talk to him again. Jordan's horses were no longer her responsibility, she reminded herself. She had taken care of that this afternoon. Kaylene could ask after the colt, she thought bitterly; that was what Jordan had wanted all along. She had other things to worry about —chief among them Cantata, who was due to foal this week.

Feeling suddenly alone, Kendall glanced out the kitchen window toward the barn. Picturing her mare, heavy with foal, she sent up a silent prayer that nothing would go wrong. She had waited almost a year for this, and everything depended on it. Her whole future was wrapped up in that foal, and she wasn't going to be distracted by anything else, least of all a hopeless affair with an impossible man like Jordan Craig. She might have lost Jordan, but Cantata wouldn't fail her. She never had. So in a few days all her problems would be over. She'd have a beautiful foal to sell, and she'd finally be out from under this crushing financial burden and able to breathe again.

She hadn't allowed herself to admit it until now, but the strain had been exhausting. She felt more than physically tired; she was emotionally spent, as well. Maybe that was why she'd gone off the deep end with Jordan; she'd just been too vulnerable, too eager to lean on someone else for a while. She had taken a bigger gamble with this foal than Tony ever had with all his bets at the poker tables or wagers at the track, and the thought of failure haunted her.

The irony of it struck her, and she laughed aloud, a sharp, bitter sound. Tony's gambling had gotten her into this; she was risking everything she had to get out of it. But the big difference between them was that Tony always considered everything a game, and she never had. She just wasn't as complacent as Tony had been, even in the face of disaster.

Had Jordan ever risked everything he had on one chance at success? she wondered suddenly, and then deliberately thrust the thought away. She didn't want to think about Jordan; she had promised herself that she wouldn't. It was over between them now, finished before it really even had a chance to begin. She had gambled and lost with him, but that was only one hand. She had another to play, and with this one she was going to win. She might not ever be able to match Kaylene Van Zandt, but she had the one thing that Kaylene could never have: Cantata. And as long as she had that mare, Kendall thought fiercely, she was the equal of anyone.

Lifting her chin at the thought, Kendall grabbed the blankets and pillow she had already set out and went out to the barn. She had spent more nights than she could count over the years sleeping on two hay bales out here while she waited for mares to foal, and her father used to tease her about it. The old saying that a mare could be watched constantly for weeks and then proceed to drop a foal while the attendant absented himself for a few minutes was true. It had happened to her so often that Aaron had tried to convince her to sleep comfortably in her own bed.

"Nature will take care of it," he'd say in his calm way. "You just leave the mare alone and she'll know what to do."

"Yes, but what if nature doesn't cooperate?" Kendall would ask worriedly. "What if the mare *doesn't* know what to do?"

He'd wink at her. "You ever know a mare that didn't?"

"No, but something could go wrong," she'd say, and march out to the barn with her pillow under her arm.

Once or twice a mare *had* been in trouble, and Kendall—and Aaron—had been glad she was there. The possibility of trouble haunted her when she thought about Cantata, and as she arranged the blankets tonight, she didn't care if Cantata went weeks overtime. She'd sleep out here every night until the foal came. Nothing was going to go wrong with this one, not if she could help it.

But Cantata didn't seem in the least interested in producing a baby tonight. She looked up curiously when Kendall peeped over the stall door, and Kendall went back to her makeshift bed again with a sigh. After turning out the lantern she had brought, she pulled the blankets over her, suddenly so tired that she was sure she'd fall instantly asleep.

Fifteen minutes later she opened her eyes again. Staring into the darkness, she listened to the comforting sounds of horses sighing or moving about their stalls, and she knew that sleep was impossible.

Despite her vow not to think about him, her thoughts were filled with Jordan. She saw him in so many ways as she lay there: across the table from her at the hotel; leaning against the fence that day as they watched the colt; his expression when the cat interrupted their dinner that first night. She saw the way he raised his eyebrow, and the way he looked when he laughed, and his eyes as he bent his head to kiss her. She imagined the touch of his lips on hers; she could almost feel the caress of his hands on her body.

Oh, Jordan! she cried silently. Why couldn't you have been honest with me before? Why did you let me learn to love you when you knew you'd never love me in return?

The tears she hadn't cried since last night came in full force now; she pressed a hand against her mouth, trying to hold back her sobs. One of the barn cats came over to investigate the noise; Kendall felt its wet nose against her face, then the rasp of its tongue against her cheek. It seemed to sense her despair, for it arched its back and rubbed against her, mewing softly. Kendall sobbed harder than ever and reached for it, needing comfort from another living creature, even if it was just a scraggly little barn cat. The animal curled up on her chest, purring mightily, and despite her feelings of desolation, Kendall had to smile through her tears at the brave little sound.

The cat, obviously content at this unexpected attention, stayed with her through the long, endless night. Eventually, soothed by the sound of that steady purr, Kendall felt her tears slow and then stop. But she didn't sleep that night, and it wasn't concern for Cantata that kept her awake. A dozen times she decided that she wasn't going to give up on Jordan so easily; as soon as morning came she would call him. But each time she made the decision, she knew she wouldn't call. She couldn't forget her father saying during their roughest times, "We might not have much, Kendall, but we've got our pride. Nobody can take that, not unless you give it away."

Well, she had her pride, foolish as it was, and she couldn't beg Jordan to come back to a place he'd never been. She had begged and pleaded with Tony to reform too many times not to know the futility of trying to change someone. She had learned a bitter lesson from that experience, and she wasn't going to make the same mistake with Jordan.

So, red-eyed and exhausted, Kendall gently put the cat aside at first light. She got up stiffly to look at the sleeping Cantata, and then went into the house to make coffee and take a shower before beginning another day. Her mouth tight, she passed the phone in the kitchen with barely a glance.

Cantata foaled two days later in the early evening, when Kendall had dashed into the house to make a quick sandwich for supper. The only edible thing she had in the refrigerator was a jar of peanut butter, and as she slapped some between two slices of bread she was reminded suddenly of that first dinner with Jordan. They had joked about peanut butter sandwiches then, and looking down at this one now, Kendall lost her appetite. That evening seemed so long ago now, she thought sadly; it was almost as if it had never happened.

Her eyes filled abruptly with tears, and she sat down at the table, her head in her hands. She had to stop crying about him, she thought; she had to stop thinking about him. She was driving herself crazy on this emotional seesaw where one minute she was sure she despised him, and the next everything around her seemed to remind her of him. She'd find herself smiling at some remark she remembered him saying; she'd picture him at odd times—looking at Cantata with an admiring glance, or walking toward her with that long-legged stride of his. She'd think how handsome he looked the night of the sale in his evening clothes; she'd remember the way their eyes met across a room. But most of all she remembered the delight of being in his arms. She ached for him; as tired as she was from this vigil with Cantata and all the other chores she forced herself to do, she still ached for him.

Stop it! she told herself fiercely, wiping her face. Stop thinking about it! It was over, done, finished. The situation wasn't going to change now. She couldn't afford the luxury of pining away for a lost love she'd never even had. Her future was out in the barn, and that was where she should be, too.

She stood up resolutely, looking distastefully at the sandwich she had made and pushing it away. Grabbing a soda instead, she trudged out to look at Cantata again.

The foal lay blinking in the straw, long legs folded under it, its coat still wet. It was too new to notice Kendall's approach, but Cantata nickered softly when

Kendall peeped over the stall door. She felt rooted to the spot when she saw what was inside. She couldn't move; she could hardly breathe. She had waited and hoped for so long, that for a moment she couldn't believe the foal was finally here. Then she laughed aloud in pure delight. The foal was the most beautiful thing she had ever seen.

"We did it, Cantata," she whispered, awed, as she entered the stall. "We really did it!"

It was the filly she had hoped for, a bay with a perfect star in the center of its forehead and two white hind socks. Even at five minutes old, the foal had huge eyes. Its muzzle was so tiny that it fit easily into Kendall's cupped hand. She laughed at its first comical struggles to stand; when she helped steady it, she smiled at the softness of its coat and the silky strands of the ruffled mane. Cantata stood patiently as the baby bumped against her side seeking its first meal, and Kendall laughed again when she had to guide the foal's head to the proper place.

Reluctant to leave even for a few minutes to call the vet, she dashed inside the house and out again, so filled with joy that she felt like shouting. Her gamble had paid off, she thought exultantly. She had won! The foal was perfect in every way. Cantata, with her superb bloodlines and her own exquisite beauty, had passed the same qualities on to her baby. Waiting for the vet, Kendall just stood outside the stall gazing at the two horses, hugging herself in sheer delight.

"You'd be proud of me and this old mare, Dad," she whispered, and couldn't stop herself from dancing around the barn.

Dr. Danson came and pronounced the filly one of the

finest he had seen. He gave her her shots and congratu-
lated the grinning Kendall. "Call me if you need me,"
he said as he left.

"Oh, you can bet on that!" Kendall said gaily. "I'll
probably have you out on an emergency if that baby
even sneezes. If anything happens to her now, I'll die!"

It was only a saying, a phrase that people used
without really meaning it. But that night, when she
went out to check on the foal before going to bed,
Kendall remembered her flippant remark to Dr. Danson and was appalled. To her horror, the filly lay
listlessly on the straw, not even raising her head or
opening her eyes when she entered the stall.

She's asleep, Kendall told herself frantically as she
knelt beside the still form; she's exhausted, that's all.
There's nothing wrong with her; there can't be. Dr.
Danson said she was healthy just a few hours ago. She
can't have gotten sick in such a short time. *There's
nothing wrong with her!*

But the filly didn't move when Kendall gently
touched her, and for a terrified instant Kendall thought
the foal was dead. Fighting panic, she held her palm
against the small ribs, and felt her own heart start again
when the foal took a shallow breath.

It's going to be all right, she told herself fiercely. It
has to be. . . . It has to be . . .

But as she stood again, she noticed Cantata standing
off in the corner of the stall. The mare had turned her
back on her baby, and Kendall felt her heart stop
again. Her alarm increased as she tried to coax Cantata
over to the foal and the mare refused to come. She
could feel hysteria begin to choke her. Horses know
when something is drastically wrong, she thought; they
know better than we do.

Cantata had never rejected one of her foals, not even the filly who had contracted pneumonia. The mare had seemed to know instinctively that that baby would survive, and she had stood over it protectively for weeks until it finally recovered. Cantata's total rejection of this foal was even more ominous to Kendall than the listlessness of the baby itself, and she tried again, grabbing hold of Cantata's halter and pleading tearfully, "Come on, Cantata . . . just come over here. . . ."

But the mare wouldn't budge no matter how Kendall begged, and finally she gave up and ran back to the house. Her hand shook so badly when she dialed Dr. Danson's number that she had to do it again, and she could hardly speak when he finally answered the phone. Stammering, she told him that she didn't know what was wrong. She was trembling so violently when she hung up after his promise to be there right away that she had to sit down.

Dr. Danson took blood samples from both Cantata and the foal and gave antibiotics to the baby. But he offered little hope to the pale-faced Kendall, saying, "The next twenty-four to forty-eight hours will tell. If she . . . survives until then, we might have a chance."

"A chance!" Kendall couldn't keep the despair from her voice, and Danson put his arm around her shoulders, trying to comfort her. She didn't even realize that tears were running down her cheeks until he gave her his handkerchief to wipe them away.

"I'll process these samples as soon as possible," he said quietly. "But blood cultures can take days—time we don't have. I'll do the best I can, Kendall. I know how important this is to you."

Do you? she thought frantically. She made an effort

to speak. "So you think it's some kind of blood infection?" He looked away unhappily, hating to tell her. But she saw the look on his face, and she knew. "It's bacterial septicemia, isn't it?" she said, her voice suddenly flat.

She had seen it before—not here, never here at the ranch, she thought savagely, but at other places. Foals born seemingly healthy, only to sicken after a few hours and then . . . die. Even with the best of treatment and constant care, the odds of survival were almost nonexistent. Dr. Danson knew it, and she did, too.

"I can't be sure. . . ."

"But you think it is."

He hesitated again. But he had too much respect for her to lie or offer false hope, so he finally nodded.

"But how did she get it?" Kendall cried, knowing the futility of the question even as it burst from her. There were so many possible causes: the mare becoming infected and not showing any symptoms; contagion sweeping the barn, leaving older, stronger horses unaffected but striking newborns who had little resistance. It didn't matter how it happened or what the cause was; the only thing that mattered was that this filly—this beautiful filly who had the future of the ranch resting on her survival—had contracted it.

"Try to get some rest," Danson said kindly. "There's nothing more you can do tonight. I'll be back first thing in the morning."

Kendall nodded, not even hearing him go. She sank down slowly onto the straw, cradling the filly's head in her lap, fiercely willing her to survive. She was still there when Dr. Danson returned at seven the next morning; she hadn't moved all night except once, to cover the still body with a blanket she had taken from her own bed.

She looked up at the vet when he came, trying to remember something she had thought about last night, something about Jordan's colt. She wanted to ask him to call Jordan, to find out what was wrong with the stallion, but she never got the words out. She saw the look on Dr. Danson's face, and she knew then that she had lost after all.

Chapter 12

THE FILLY DIED TWO DAYS LATER. KENDALL HAD SPENT
night and day with her, leaving the barn for just
minutes at a time to take care of necessities, ignoring
the constant ringing of the phone in the house. She was
so totally preoccupied that she couldn't even eat; she
made countless pots of coffee on the hot plate in the
tack room to keep her going, trying to coax the foal to
drink from a bottle, keeping her covered, holding her
down when convulsions wracked the small body. Dr.
Danson had come twice a day, his face more grave each
time, but Kendall refused to give up.

But on the morning of the third day even she had to
admit the hopelessness of her vigil. They had done
what they could, but it just wasn't going to be enough.
Kneeling by the still form, she decided that when the
vet came today she'd ask him to put the foal out of her
misery. Kendall couldn't prolong the filly's suffering

anymore; it was too much to ask of such a small creature who lacked even the strength to lift her head.

Kendall was too exhausted even to cry over the decision. Reaching out, she stroked the filly's head, thinking how beautiful she was, how soft and delicate. Just then the filly drew a shuddering breath, and when she exhaled slowly with a sigh, Kendall knew that Dr. Danson wouldn't be needed after all.

"Kendall?"

She looked up slowly, wondering if she had imagined that voice. She glanced around dazedly, and when she saw Jordan standing there she actually thought she was hallucinating. She was so weary she couldn't even react; she just stared blankly at him.

"I've been trying to reach you for two days," he said, his eyes going from her to the foal and back again. "You haven't answered your phone."

She stood up stiffly, feeling like an old woman, muscles and joints protesting. Still she said nothing; she couldn't speak over the lump in her throat.

Jordan glanced uncomfortably again at the still form by her feet. "I . . . I'm sorry," he said.

Kendall looked down at the foal. With its death, all her hopes had died, too. She wondered vaguely why she didn't feel anything at that; it was as if all emotion had vanished, leaving her so empty inside that she couldn't feel anything at all.

"What . . . do you want?" she said, hearing her voice from a distance. She felt faint, dizzy. She looked at Jordan, and he seemed to recede suddenly, becoming a tiny figure that was speeding away from her. Or maybe, she thought absently, she was the one who was going away. There was a blackness around the edges of her vision; she thought with dull surprise that she was going to faint. She wondered what it would feel like, just to drift away, spinning down into darkness. . . .

Alarmed by her white face, Jordan came into the stall. He took her arm to steady her, and she looked at him without really seeing him.

"I think you need some air," he said. "Let's go outside . . . away from this. . . ."

She allowed him to lead her outside. The bright sunlight hurt her eyes, and she winced. There was something she had to do, she thought vaguely, but she couldn't remember what it was. Then she had it. She had to call Dr. Danson. She had to tell him that she wouldn't be needing him today after all.

"I have to call the vet," she mumbled, and started walking away. She hadn't gone two steps before the ground tilted suddenly and she swayed. Jordan caught her as she began to fall; she didn't remember being carried inside. When she became conscious again, she was lying on the living room couch with a cool cloth on her forehead and a concerned Jordan sitting worriedly beside her.

"What happened?" she asked weakly.

"You fainted," he said. "How long has it been since you've eaten anything? Or slept?"

She shook her head. The movement made the room sway slightly, and she closed her eyes against a fresh wave of dizziness. "I . . . don't remember."

"Stay here," he commanded, as if she had the strength to get up. "I'll be right back."

She couldn't have moved if she'd wanted to. Her body felt as if it weighed a ton; her arms and legs were so heavy she couldn't even lift them. The couch seemed softer than a cloud, and she was actually drifting away on it when Jordan returned. He brought a mug of soup with him and a cup of tea.

"I want you to eat this," he said, and helped her carefully to an upright position, holding the mug for her.

The smell of the soup made her faintly nauseous, but she was too weary to fight him when he held the mug to her lips. She felt strength returning after a few sips, and was able to take it from him, finishing the last of it in a few gulps.

"Feel better?" he asked, his expression still concerned.

She nodded. "Yes, I—"

She had started to hand the mug back to him. Their fingers touched as he took it, and for some reason that simple contact unlocked the tight hold her mind had held on her emotions. She looked into his eyes and saw the worry there, and suddenly he was just a blur. Tears filled her eyes, and she cried desolately, "Oh, Jordan!"

In the next instant she was leaning against him, sobbing brokenly, unable to stop herself. He held her until she couldn't cry anymore, murmuring soothing sounds as she wept away the pain and anguish she felt over losing the foal. She'd had such high hopes for it; she'd pinned everything on it, and now all her hopes and dreams were gone. She felt so lost, so filled with despair, that she couldn't stop crying. The feeling of hopelessness was so overwhelming that she knew nothing would ever be right again.

But finally the emotional storm spent itself; she was so exhausted that she just lay weakly against Jordan's chest. He held her tightly, stroking her hair, never saying a word until she moved away of her own accord.

Straightening, she wiped her face with the handkerchief he silently offered, and pushed back her hair. Now that she was calmer, she felt embarrassed at her lack of control, and she couldn't look at him when she muttered, "I'm sorry. I didn't mean to—"

"You don't have to apologize," he said quietly. "I imagine this has been a . . . strain."

"Yes," she said, her voice breaking again before she managed to control it. "It has."

He hesitated. "I'm . . . I'm so sorry about the foal, Kendall. I know how much it meant to you."

She closed her eyes briefly, feeling the tears well up again, and forced them back by sheer will. She couldn't start crying again. She had done enough of that, and it hadn't helped. Nothing was going to help now; she would have to face that. But later, she told herself, when she was alone, she would have to decide what she was going to do.

She made herself look at Jordan again, remembering something he had said—or she thought he had said. "Did you say you'd been trying to call?" she asked. She had to talk about something—anything—just as long as it wasn't about the foal. If she kept her mind occupied, maybe this crushing sense of hopelessness would go away.

Jordan shifted uncomfortably. "Yes," he said unwillingly. "Look, I know this is a bad time to talk about this, but . . ."

He hesitated again, and Kendall said, "I'm all right, really." But they both knew she was holding on to her self-control by a thread, and Jordan looked even more uncomfortable at that.

Finally he asked, "Do you . . . do you know why the foal died?"

She made herself say it. It didn't matter now anyway, she thought dully. The foal was dead; nothing was going to change that. "It was a blood infection," she said emotionlessly. "Septicemia."

Jordan had tensed, staring at her with such an appalled look on his face that Kendall was alarmed. "What . . . what's the matter?" she stammered.

He sprang up then, running an agitated hand through his hair. "The colt . . ." His voice sounded choked. He tried again. "The colt has a bacterial infection," he managed finally. "A mild case of strangles. It was diagnosed yesterday. That's why . . . that's why I was trying to get in touch with you. I wanted to warn you. Oh, I'm sorry, Kendall! When they told me how infectious it was . . ." He stopped and looked at her, his eyes bleak. "If . . . if only I had known sooner."

Kendall stood up slowly. It wasn't his fault, she tried to tell herself; it wasn't anyone's fault. No one could have foreseen that the colt would have contracted an infectious disease and then spread it to the foal even before it was born. If anyone was to blame, she was. She had noticed the colt's strange behavior that first day; that was why she had isolated it in the end stall. But she should have called the vet immediately, even though she couldn't pinpoint anything wrong. She shouldn't have taken a chance. She wouldn't have if she hadn't been so preoccupied with Jordan.

"Get out," she said through stiff lips. "Just—get out."

He didn't move. "I know how you feel, Kendall, but . . ."

She didn't know what was happening to her. Only moments ago she had thought she would never feel anything again. She had been empty, drained of any emotion, her mind once again drawing a protective curtain over the devastating knowledge of all she had lost with the death of that foal. Now she felt a terrible anger rising in her at the injustice of it all; it was sweeping through her entire being, like a prairie fire out of control. She had the fleeting thought that she was hysterical, but she didn't care. She had sacrificed so much this past year; she had worked herself into exhaustion, telling herself that it would all be worth it when Cantata had her foal. She had denied herself everything, even the luxury of feeling sorry for herself, because she knew what had to be done. But it had all been for nothing—all the sacrifices and the hard work and the scraping together of every penny. She hadn't just lost a valuable foal today; she was in danger of losing her home. Now Jordan had the nerve to stand there and tell her he knew how she felt? She thought she would explode with sheer rage.

"You haven't the faintest idea how I feel!" she cried, her hands clenched. "How dare you stand there and tell me that!"

Jordan was taken aback by the fury in her eyes. "I only meant—"

"I know what you meant! You think it's only a foal—that there'll be others! It's a pity, but not the end of the world. Well, let me tell you something, Jordan— it might as well be!"

He tried again. "I know how important that foal was to you, but—"

"You don't have the slightest idea how important it was to me!" she shouted. "So don't stand there and mouth some insipid platitude about how everything is going to be all right. It's not going to be all right. It's never going to be all right! You don't know anything about it!"

"Let me help—"

"Help!" she screeched. "Haven't you done enough? Your horse was the one responsible for this. If it hadn't come here, none of this would have happened!"

Jordan flinched at that, but he somehow refrained from pointing out the unfairness of her accusation.

Even in her fury, Kendall knew how unreasonable she was being, but she couldn't stop herself. It was as if some demon possessed her. She wanted to lash out, hurt someone as deeply as she had been hurt, make someone else pay for all the humiliation she had endured this past year. It wasn't right or fair or just, and if she hadn't been so exhausted, so consumed with anger and despair, she would have realized it and been ashamed.

But she had covered her feelings of rage and pain and injustice for too long; she had kept them bottled up inside, and only now were they reaching the surface.

"Oh, you've done enough, all right!" she flung at him. She hated him in that moment; she despised him for making her feel this way, and she wanted him to know it. "I don't need any more *help* from you!"

Jordan had turned pale beneath his tan. She saw by the stricken look in his eyes that she had succeeded in hurting him, and for an instant she wanted to retract her hateful words. But she was too angry and too devastated at her loss. She felt her world spinning out of control, and for some unaccountable reason he seemed to symbolize everything that was so terribly wrong with it.

"Let me pay you for the foal," Jordan said at last, choking out the words. "It's the least I can do."

The least he could do! Kendall felt anger exploding inside her again. It was all so easy for Jordan and people like him, she thought, enraged. He didn't care about the horses; he never had. Write a check and forget it. There were always more foals; what did one matter, except as a loss on some tax form? He and his kind weren't horse breeders; they were manipulators in some financial game, and she wasn't going to be a pawn. She would lose everything first. Everything!

"Get out!" she said again, her voice shaking.

"Kendall, for God's sake—"

"Get out! You could never pay me for that foal, do you understand? Never!"

He didn't understand. He stared at her, shaken by the pallor of her face and the blazing anger in her eyes. He tried one more time, so unnerved that he hardly knew what he was saying. "I don't care what it costs—" he began, and knew he had made a terrible mistake. The furious light went out of her eyes, replaced by a look of such contempt that he felt it almost as a physical blow.

"The cost of that foal can't be measured in dollars and cents," she said, her voice deadly cold. "But you and Kaylene and all the rest of that crowd don't understand that. You never will. So go play your little games with her; you deserve each other."

Jordan had tried to be calm. He knew how upset Kendall was, how distraught. But her reference to him and Kaylene was too much. He could feel his control slipping away and couldn't stop it. Stung by the contempt in her eyes and the derision in her voice, he was angry enough to say, "Part of your problem is that you think nobody knows anything but you. You may know a

lot about horses and bloodlines, Kendall, but you've
got a lot to learn about people."

"Oh, you don't have to tell me about *people!*"
Kendall said scathingly. "I've seen enough of human
nature this past year to last me a lifetime!"

"I don't think you've seen anything at all," Jordan
said, his voice hard. "You've been so busy trying to
prove you're better than anybody else that—"

"I don't need you to give me a lecture on proving
things!" Kendall cried. "I told you that you didn't
understand! Let's just leave it at that, shall we?"

He started to say something, but the look on her face
changed his mind. "I should have known you wouldn't
listen to anything I had to say!" he said angrily. "I
doubt you've ever listened to anyone in your life! But
maybe you should have, Kendall; maybe you should
have. If you had, you might not be in the position you
are now!"

"And what position is that, Jordan?" she asked, her
voice dangerously low.

"It's no secret that you're in financial trouble," he
snapped, too furious to watch what he was saying.
"And now I see why. If you weren't so damned
stubborn, you'd let somebody help. But no—you're too
proud for that! Well, I hope that pride of yours is a
comfort, because that's all you're going to have unless
you come to your senses!"

He didn't wait for her reply. He turned on his heel
and strode out to his car, so furious that he felt like
smashing something. When he got home, he went
immediately to his study and took out his checkbook.
Grabbing a pen, he didn't even stop to think. He wrote
a check for a huge amount to Kendall Voss, signed his

name in a heavy scrawl, ripped the check from the book and put it in an envelope.

His handyman, Santos, came in just then to ask if he needed anything in town. Still in a rage, Jordan gave him the envelope and asked him to mail it on the way out. As Santos left, Jordan flung himself into a chair, telling himself that he didn't care if she ever cashed it. In fact, he thought savagely, he almost hoped she wouldn't. It would give him great pleasure to haul her down to the bank in person and shove the money right into her stubborn hands. She deserved it, after the way she had acted today.

No, he didn't mean that, he thought. He didn't know what he meant. It was just that she made him so damned angry. He had never met a woman like Kendall; she made him want to strangle her and kiss her at the same time. She was the only woman he had ever known who could make him lose control with a word, or even a look. He hadn't meant to say all those terrible things to her; it was just that she . . . she had *goaded* him into it. She was so determined to do everything on her own. Even in the face of complete disaster, she refused to accept the help he wanted so much to give. It was so frustrating, so infuriating. He felt stymied at every turn, and he didn't know what to do. He couldn't force her to accept his help, and every time he offered, he offended her, and they ended up in a furious argument and he felt even more helpless than he had before.

The phone rang just then, and he grabbed the receiver, hoping it was Kendall. The hope died when he recognized Martin Holbrook's voice.

"Oh," he said. "It's you."

"I'm overwhelmed by your enthusiasm," Martin

said. "Maybe I should have called sooner, since you're so eager to talk to me."

Jordan rubbed his forehead. "I'm sorry, Marty. Things aren't . . . going well here."

His friend sobered immediately. "What's wrong?"

"Nothing I want to talk about."

"Ah . . . problems with Kendall, I take it."

"What makes you say that?" Jordan asked sarcastically.

Martin laughed. "Look, Jordan, why don't you just tell her you love her and get it over with? It would make things a lot easier."

Jordan tensed. "I'm fond of her, I admit, but . . ."

"Oh, come off it, Jordan. This is me, remember?"

Sighing, Jordan gave in. "All right," he admitted. "I'm more than fond of her. . . ."

"You love her," Martin said firmly.

"All right!" Jordan said, exasperated. "I love her. Does that make you happy?"

"I don't know. Does it make *her* happy?"

"I don't know," Jordan said glumly. "Maybe I'm afraid to find out."

Martin was silent for a moment. "Does it have anything to do with Marie?"

Jordan considered that. No, he thought, relieved. It didn't have anything to do with Marie at all. He could think of her now with sadness and regret, but he didn't feel the crushing weight of the guilt he had felt before. "No," he said slowly, "it's not Marie. It's Kendall herself. She's so . . . independent, Martin. I don't think she wants—or needs—anybody in her life."

"Why don't you ask her and find out?"

"It's not that easy. . . ."

"Oh, I see. It's easier to sit there and stew about it."

"I didn't say that!"

"Well then?"

Well then, indeed, Jordan thought as he hung up. Martin didn't understand. How could he, when he didn't understand it himself?

Sitting back, he stared moodily at the phone. Maybe Martin was right, he mused. Why didn't he just tell Kendall how he felt? Was he that afraid of rejection? Was he really as cowardly as that?

Slowly he reached for the phone again. His fingers curled around the receiver, but he just couldn't make himself pick it up. Despising himself, he dropped his hand again.

Maybe there was another way to tell her, he thought. Maybe he could show he loved her in some way that would prove it. But how? He had made so many mistakes so far that he was almost afraid to try again. What could he do that would demonstrate to her how deeply he cared? There had to be a way, but what was it? Bleakly, he had to admit he didn't know.

Yet.

Chapter 13

KENDALL RECEIVED THE CHECK IN THE MAIL THE NEXT day. Recognizing Jordan's bold handwriting on the envelope, she stared at it for a long time, debating whether to open it or not. She was tempted to send it back; she didn't want to know the contents. Even if it was an apology, which she doubted, it was too late. She'd never forgive him for all the horrible things he had said. He had been callous and cruel . . .

And right?

She shut her mind to the question. In an act of defiance, she opened the envelope, telling herself haughtily that she didn't care what he said in this letter. She'd ignore it all.

But when the check fell out and she saw the amount it was written for, her hand actually trembled. This was more, far more, than she had ever dreamed of getting for the foal, and for an instant she was transfixed, imagining herself not only free of debt but having enough left over to—

What was she thinking of? She had to be out of her mind even to imagine cashing this. It was conscience money, she told herself furiously; that was all it was. Jordan was feeling guilty and responsible, and that was the only reason he had sent this. It wasn't because of the foal, or her, or anything else; he was just trying to salve his conscience.

Well, she wasn't going to let him, not this way. He couldn't casually write off their affair by signing a check; she wasn't going to ease his conscience by accepting it. This was an insult. Money didn't mean anything to him. *She* didn't mean anything to him—not if he could do something like this. She had thought she had made it clear to him that she didn't want his money; she had been adamant about it. But oh, no, he had to send this just to prove a point, to show her what a big man he was.

Well, she didn't need anyone's charity, *especially* his.

Infuriated at the thought, she ripped the check in two. Grabbing the envelope again, she put the pieces inside and reglued the flap. Then, in huge angry letters, she wrote "RETURN TO SENDER" across the front. She marched out to the mailbox and stuffed the envelope inside. She slammed the box shut with a clang, muttering, "Take *that,* Mr. Craig!"

Her feeling of satisfaction lasted until she got back to the house. Hearing a car behind her, she turned around angrily and sighed in exasperation when she saw Dennis. Glaring at him, she said rudely, "What are you doing here?"

Dennis swallowed. Then he hesitantly held out a bouquet of daisies. "It's a peace offering," he said, his face turning red.

Feeling ashamed of herself for her rudeness, Kendall accepted the flowers with a muttered thanks. "I'm sorry, Dennis," she said. "It . . . it hasn't been a very good day."

"Oh," he said tentatively. "I—I was hoping I could talk to you for a minute."

She wasn't in the mood to talk to anyone, especially Dennis. But she could hardly refuse after he'd made the gesture with the flowers, so she said reluctantly, "Come inside. I'll put these in water."

He followed her into the kitchen and stood uncomfortably while she hunted for a vase. She couldn't remember the last time anyone had given her flowers, and the sight of the daisies in the center of the table softened her harsh attitude toward Dennis. Maybe he wasn't so bad after all, she thought, and asked, "Would you like some coffee? I just made a fresh pot."

He nodded silently, and as Kendall fetched cups and brought them to the table, she wondered why he was there. Hoping that he wasn't going to make a scene, she gestured for him to sit down, and when he still didn't say anything, she prodded, "What did you want to talk to me about?"

"I . . . uh . . ." He looked down at his cup. "Do you have any sugar?" he asked, stalling.

Sighing, Kendall got up again to find the sugar bowl. "Are you sure you don't want milk, too?" she asked, astonished at the sight of him nervously adding four teaspoons of sugar to his cup.

He shook his head, making a face as he took a sip of

the coffee. Kendall almost laughed, but then she saw how unnerved he still was, and she hid her smile behind her own mug.

"I'm really sorry about Cantata's foal," he said finally.

Her head jerked up. "How did you find out about that?"

"I saw Dr. Danson in town. He told me. You should have called me, Kendall. I would have sat with it for you."

She was surprised at that. Dennis was usually so self-absorbed that he wouldn't have thought of making the offer before. "Thanks," she said quietly. "But it wouldn't have helped."

"No, I guess not," he agreed, looking up at her. "But at least you wouldn't have been alone. It's hard to be by yourself at times like that. I know you hate me, but I would have been somebody to talk to."

Touched, Kendall protested, "I don't hate you, Dennis. . . ."

"Oh, I know I've been a jerk. I wouldn't blame you if you did. It's just . . ."

He stopped, looking so miserable that Kendall said gently, "It's just what?"

"It's just that I care so much for you, Kendall," he blurted. "I always have. I hated it when you married Tony. I knew he wouldn't be any good for you. He was my best friend, but I still knew. And then when he . . . when he died, I thought—I hoped—that if I gave you enough time . . ."

He stopped and shook his head. "But all the time in the world wasn't going to be enough, was it?"

His expression was so woebegone that for an instant

she was tempted to lie to him. This was a Dennis she had never known, and she had the fleeting thought that things might have been different if he had abandoned his swaggering bravado act long ago.

But he was being honest for perhaps the first time since they had met, and she couldn't insult him with a lie now. "No," she said as gently as she could. "I'm sorry, Dennis. I just never felt . . . the same way you did. I thought you knew that."

He sighed and sat back in his chair. His shoulders slumping, he said, "I knew it. I guess I always did." He grimaced. "I should have realized when I saw you with Jordan Craig how hopeless it was, but no, I had to go and make an even bigger jerk of myself that day. Any fool could see how much you love that guy, and I—"

He stopped as Kendall choked violently on her coffee. "Are you all right?" he asked, springing up to thump her on the back.

Coughing, Kendall gasped, "I thought . . . I thought you said . . ."

"What? What did I say?"

Still choking, she gestured wildly. "Something . . . about . . . Jordan."

"What? That you were in love with the guy?" he said, obviously bewildered at her reaction.

She finally succeeded in getting the coughing fit under control. "Who told you that?" she demanded when she caught her breath.

He looked even more perplexed. "Nobody had to tell me. Kendall, all anyone has to do is see you together. I may be dumb, but I'm not blind!"

Kendall closed her eyes, feeling totally humiliated. If Dennis knew, everybody in the world did. She groaned inwardly. She'd never be able to hold her head up again.

"Look, Kendall," Dennis said anxiously. "I didn't mean to make you mad—honest. I was hoping that we . . . that we could still be friends."

She made herself look at him again. "We can still be friends," she said. "And I'm not mad—really. It's just . . ." She swallowed. "It's just that you're not the only one who feels like a fool."

Dennis smiled sadly. "Don't be too sure *you* are," he said. "I think that guy loves you, too."

Kendall felt like laughing hysterically at that. Jordan in love with her? Even the thought was ludicrous. The only person Jordan was in love with was himself. He was so determined to spend the rest of his life feeling guilty and remorseful, that he couldn't see beyond his own nose. He enjoyed his self-enforced martyrdom, and she, for one, wasn't going to indulge him in it. In love with her! Dennis was more blind than he knew!

But at least Dennis had tried to make things right between them, she thought after he had gone. She smiled sadly, remembering his anxious, "Let me know if you need anything, Kendall. I'll be happy to help in any way I can." He had smiled crookedly. "No strings attached. Just as a friend, all right?"

She needed a friend, Kendall thought as she went to her desk and stared down at the pile of unpaid bills. In fact, what she really needed was a miracle. She sat down and pulled the stack toward her, and as she started going through them, she began to feel desperate. No matter how many times she added the figures, she knew bleakly that, without the sale of that foal, she just wasn't going to make it.

Drumming her fingers on the desk, she sat and tried to think calmly about it. But the list she had made of her debts stared back at her, unchanging, and it was impossible to be calm when disaster was rushing at her.

What am I going to do? she wondered frantically. There's nothing left to sell.

But there was. There was one thing left.

Involuntarily, her glance went to the framed picture above the desk. It was a photo of Cantata the year she was named national champion mare, and Kendall closed her eyes in pain. She couldn't do it, she thought despairingly; she couldn't sell Cantata. It would be like selling a part of herself; she'd rather lose the ranch instead.

And if she lost the ranch, then what would she do?

She could go somewhere else and start over, she argued, but without hope. Where would she go? She'd lived here all her life; she'd been born in this house. How could she bear to leave it?

But how could she bear to part with Cantata? She had bred her as a foal. She had raised her and taken her all the way to national champion. How could she sell her now, when so much of their lives were bound together? Was that going to be Cantata's reward for all those years?

Kendall put her hands over her ears, trying vainly to still the voices inside her head. Tears ran down her cheeks, and she rocked back and forth silently in sheer misery.

There has to be another way, she thought desperately; there has to be.

But there wasn't. Before she could change her mind, she reached for the phone. She didn't have to look up the number; she had memorized it sometime during the past few days, knowing deep in her heart that she'd have to use it.

When the voice answered at the other end, Kendall took a deep breath. Then she said dully, "Kaylene, this is Kendall. I've decided to sell Cantata after all."

Kendall only went to the barn during the following two days to feed the few remaining boarders. She couldn't stay longer than a few minutes at a time; Cantata's empty stall filled her with such desolation that she couldn't look at it without tears gathering in her eyes. It seemed impossible to believe that the mare was really gone; she would find herself waiting for Cantata's welcoming nicker in the mornings, expecting to see that exquisite head hanging over the stall door, waiting to be petted when she entered the barn. But Cantata wasn't there; she was with Kaylene Van Zandt now, and every time Kendall thought of that conversation with Kaylene, she felt humiliated all over again. If she hadn't been so desperate that day, she would have slammed the phone down in the woman's ear. Even now, she could hear the condescending smirk in Kaylene's voice when Kendall told her why she had called.

"Selling Cantata!" Kaylene had exclaimed. "But you said—"

"I know what I said," Kendall had interrupted, holding on to her self-control by a thread. "I've changed my mind. Do you want her or not?"

"Well, this is so sudden, my dear. You can't expect me to make a snap decision."

"Why not?" Kendall asked, hating the woman. "I thought you prided yourself on snap decisions. At least, that's what you told me before."

"Well, I know, but . . ."

Kendall almost hoped that Kaylene would refuse. She'd like nothing more than to tell the other woman that someone else was interested and that she couldn't wait for Kaylene to make up her mind. But she didn't have another buyer right now, and even though she knew she could find one, she didn't have the time. Refusing to think about what she would do if Kaylene balked at buying Cantata, Kendall took a tighter grip on herself and decided to use reverse psychology.

"I'm sorry I bothered you," she said. "I thought you still wanted to buy her. My mistake."

"Wait!"

Kendall smiled grimly.

Kaylene sighed. "I can't understand why you're in such a hurry. Surely you want to wait until the mare has her foal."

"She had her foal," Kendall said, willing her voice under control. "It died."

"Oh, I *am* sorry to hear that," Kaylene said.

I'll bet you are, Kendall thought savagely. "So there's no reason to wait," she went on, closing her eyes against the sudden image of that still form in the stall that morning. "And now that I've decided to sell her, I want to do it now."

"I see."

Kendall could almost hear the wheels turning in Kaylene's head. She waited, not realizing she was holding her breath.

"Well, if that's the way you feel," Kaylene said, "I suppose I shouldn't pass up this opportunity. She is a beautiful mare, after all. I've admired her for years."

So have I, Kendall thought sadly, so have I. "Then it's agreed."

"Yes, it's agreed."

"Fine. I'll draw up a contract based on the price you offered before."

"Oh, but that was last year, my dear!" Kaylene protested with a condescending laugh. "I wouldn't think of paying that now!"

Kendall closed her eyes again, this time against a wave of anger. Was there no end to this humiliation? It was only by the fiercest effort that she prevented herself from slamming the phone down on that self-satisfied voice.

"And what would you *think* of paying for her now?" Kendall asked, unable to keep the angry sarcasm from her voice.

"Well . . ."

Kaylene mentioned an amount that both of them knew was barely acceptable. Before Kendall could swallow her anger enough to respond, Kaylene added, "After all, the mare *is* almost twenty. I have to consider how many more foals she'll have before she stops producing."

"*One* would be enough to cover her cost and more!" Kendall said sharply.

"Well, if the offer isn't acceptable, my dear . . ." Kaylene allowed her voice to trail delicately away.

Kendall thought quickly. It wasn't as much as she wanted, but it would be enough. It would have to be, she decided bleakly. If she backed out of the deal now, she didn't doubt that Kaylene would be on the phone the instant she hung up, slyly suggesting to any interested buyers that because Cantata's foal had died, there was something wrong with the mare herself. She'd seen Kaylene do that sort of thing before, and in the horse world, where gossip spread like wildfire, the rumor would soon be accepted as fact, especially if the source was Kaylene. After that, any denial from Kendall would be viewed as some desperate cover-up of the truth.

Trapped, Kendall said, "I'll draw up the contracts today." She thought of loading Cantata into the trailer for the last time and knew she couldn't do it. As cowardly as it was, she just couldn't transport the mare knowing that it would be the last time. "You can pick her up when you like," she said, and didn't care what Kaylene thought.

"Oh, I'll come and get her this afternoon," Kaylene said happily. "I want to breed her back to my stallion on this cycle, now that she's open."

Kendall clenched her fist, willing herself to remain silent. It would be a crime to breed a mare like Cantata to that stallion, she thought. Cantata was so far superior that it was an insult to the mare, a travesty of breeding principles.

"Don't you think that's a good idea?" Kaylene asked.

Kendall swallowed, forcing back tears of anger and humiliation. "She's your horse now," she said flatly, refusing to give Kaylene the satisfaction of knowing how much the admission hurt her. "You can breed her to a donkey for all I care."

The implied insult hadn't fazed Kaylene. Kendall hung up on the woman's laughter, but when Kaylene arrived an hour later to finalize the arrangements and to take Cantata away, Kendall was caught off guard completely by her attitude. Hesitating before she signed the contract, Kaylene looked at the tight-lipped

Kendall with what could only be interpreted as a sympathetic glance and said, "Are you sure you want to do this, Kendall?"

That sympathetic look was nearly Kendall's undoing. She had vowed she wasn't going to cry, especially not in front of Kaylene, but she couldn't help it. Tears came into her eyes, and she had to look away. "I'm sure," she said tightly, wishing Kaylene would just sign the papers and get out.

Kaylene seemed about to say something else. But then she took the pen and signed with a flourish, and it was done. As she placed the papers in a folder, she avoided Kendall's eyes, saying, "You don't have to come out. I brought one of the hands to help me."

If Kendall hadn't been trying so hard to control herself, she would have been grateful for this unexpected kindness. As it was, she could only give a brief nod. She had already said a private, tearful good-bye to Cantata; she had been dreading going out to the barn to load her into the trailer.

But she had watched from an upstairs window instead, her hand pressed hard to her mouth, her shoulders shaking with silent sobs as Cantata stepped elegantly into Kaylene's trailer. Then the man locked the doors, shutting away even the sight of the mare, and the gesture had such a note of awful finality that Kendall had uttered a heart-wrenching cry and turned away. She couldn't watch them go; she couldn't see for the blur of tears in her eyes.

Now, three days later, Kendall woke early, knowing that she had to make another painful decision. She had paid off the last of her debts the day before, but instead of celebrating the occasion, she had wandered around the house in a deep depression, trying not to cry.

She would never be happy here again, she thought sadly. There were too many ugly memories now, too much sense of failure, even though she had finally succeeded in clearing her name. Paying off the money she owed had given her no sense of satisfaction; the way she'd been forced to do it made her feel too empty inside.

So she had to go away, start over someplace else. Leave all this behind . . . leave Jordan behind. The thought of living next to him and never seeing him in the years ahead appalled her. She would always think of what might have been, and she wouldn't be able to bear it. She'd become one of those bitter, lonely old women who were totally wrapped up in their horses, living their lives only for them, and as much as she loved the animals, she couldn't do that to herself. She *wouldn't* do it to herself.

If she stayed, she'd always be aware of how much she had missed, and she'd know that she'd never be able to change it. She didn't want to become lonely and bitter, because whatever else he had done, Jordan had shown her what it was to be a woman. She had despaired over him, fought with him, even almost hated him at times, but she had also experienced the height of passion with him, a desire that went far beyond the physical. He had given her joy, if only for a short time, and she wanted to feel that again—or at least try. She knew in her heart that no man could ever compare with him, and she hoped in time she would accept that. She couldn't accept it now; there were too many memories of him here. Everywhere she turned she was reminded of him; the house seemed filled with his presence, and she knew that if she stayed, she *would* become that bitter old woman, pining forever for a lost love.

So as soon as the chores were done, she went into town to find a real estate office. She stopped at the first one she came to and went inside before she could change her mind. The agent's name was Dan Jenkins, and Kendall disliked him on sight. He had an eager, oily look, and as he rose ponderously from behind his desk to shake her hand, Kendall had to fight the impulse to turn and run.

She forced herself to take a seat. It didn't matter who handled the sale of the ranch, she told herself despondently—just as long as it was done quickly. Her voice emotionless, she answered the man's questions and didn't even care that he looked at her strangely. He didn't know how she had agonized over the decision to sell the ranch, or how difficult it had been to come here, and she wasn't going to tell him. The only way she could handle this at all was to be strictly businesslike, and if he was annoyed that she didn't respond to his blithe assurances that he could sell the place in no time at all, she would go somewhere else.

"I want a fair price, that's all," she said, when he told her he had a list of clients eagerly waiting for property like hers.

He chuckled at that, winking at her as if trying to engage her in some conspiracy against an unsuspecting buyer. "Well, fair means different things to different people," he said slickly, winking at her again.

"It means only one thing to me," she said flatly. "I know what the place is worth."

"Oh, I don't think you do, Miss Voss. The way this area is growing . . ."

She didn't want to discuss it with him anymore. She signed the papers he had put in front of her, and stood. "I'd appreciate it if you would call before you bring anyone out," she said. "I . . . I'd rather not be there when you do."

"Oh, certainly. I understand," he said sympathetically. "It's always hard to sell a house; there are so many memories in it, aren't there?"

She couldn't tell him just how many memories there were. So she nodded instead and quickly went outside before she grabbed the papers she had signed and tore them in two. After climbing into the truck, she sat for a minute with her forehead against the steering wheel, wondering if she had made a mistake. It all seemed so pointless now; what difference did it make how close or far away she was to Jordan? He would be with her always, no matter where she went, and severing all ties here wasn't going to prove anything.

But the thing was done now; she wouldn't change it. As she put the keys in the ignition, she thought hopefully that maybe the ranch wouldn't sell after all. If it didn't, at least she would know she'd tried to make a new start. Feeling more cheerful at the thought, she turned the ignition key.

Nothing happened. Frowning, she tried again. The truck had run perfectly on the way in. What could be wrong with it now? But there was only the faintest of clicks when she tried the key again, and she sat back, trying to be calm.

Drumming her fingers against the steering wheel, she waited a few minutes, wondering what else could go wrong. It wasn't bad enough that she'd put the ranch up for sale; now she wouldn't even be able to get away from it if the truck had to be fixed. Her jaw tight, she tried the key again, and this time the engine turned over enough to start. Praying that it would run long enough for her to limp to the garage Dennis owned, she drove over there slowly, coasting in when it died again in front of the auto shop.

Dennis glanced up in surprise when he saw Kendall. Climbing out from under the car he was working on, he grinned. "You're just in time to take me to lunch."

"Well, we'll have to go in your truck, then," Kendall replied sourly. "Something's wrong with mine."

"Oh? What?"

She looked at him in exasperation. "If I knew, I'd fix it myself. It was running fine; then just now it wouldn't start. I barely made it over here."

"Let's take a look, then," he said, walking with her to where she had left it in the middle of the parking lot. He raised the hood and peered inside, humming to himself as he fiddled with various things in the interior. But it wouldn't start for him, either, and he finally slammed the hood down and gestured to one of the other men working there. "Hey, Charlie, help me move this, will you?"

"What's wrong with it?" Kendall asked after they had all pushed the truck into the garage.

Dennis grinned at her again. "I'm a good mechanic, but even I will have to try a few things before I can tell you."

"But I need it," Kendall said a little desperately. She pictured herself stuck at the ranch when that oily Dan Jenkins came out to show the place. She wouldn't be able to bear watching strangers poke around the place, or listening to them talk about knocking out walls or covering the hardwood floors with carpeting.

"Not to worry," Dennis said cheerfully. "If it takes a couple of days to fix it, you can use mine."

Kendall was immediately ashamed of her earlier tartness. "That's nice of you, Dennis, but I couldn't."

"It's no big deal," he said, trying to speak lightly but unable to disguise the way he still felt about her. "Besides, what are friends for?"

She felt even worse at that, suspecting that she was taking advantage of him but not knowing what else to do. On impulse she said, "Well, at least let me take you to lunch."

"Aw, I was just kidding about that."

"I'm not," she said, suddenly enthusiastic about the idea. "We'll go to . . ." She thought a moment, and then named one of the better places in Scottsdale.

Dennis looked shocked. "But that costs an arm and a leg!" He looked down at his greasy hands. "And I can't go like this!"

"Yes, you can. We both can," she said, suddenly wanting—needing—to be extravagant for once. She'd been depressed for so long that she needed a treat, and she didn't care what it cost. She was tired of juggling every penny, of denying herself even a simple pleasure like going out to lunch. It was time she learned to live again . . . whether she wanted to or not.

Chapter 14

THE PARKING LOT WAS CROWDED WHEN THEY GOT THERE. This restaurant was a popular place for Scottsdale's elite, and Kendall had been there only once or twice in the past with clients. She knew that more business deals were concluded over two- or three-martini lunches here than were settled in air-conditioned offices around town, but today she didn't care if she met anyone she knew. She could hold her head up now, because for the first time since her disastrous marriage to Tony, she was free of debt. She didn't owe anybody anything, and when Dennis hung back for a moment, saying that he wasn't sure they should go in, she grasped his arm firmly and sailed ahead. She was through feeling guilty or ashamed or intimidated; if anyone dared to look askance at her, she'd spit in their eye.

The place was jammed. They had to wait for a table, but even when the elegant hostess looked down at

Kendall's skirt and sandals and at Dennis's jeans and told them it would be an hour's wait, Kendall looked back evenly at the woman and told her blithely that they'd be in the bar.

"You seem different today," Dennis commented after they had ordered their drinks.

Different? Well, she was. Nothing about her seemed the same. She hardly knew who she was anymore, or what she wanted, or even where she was going. She felt rootless and adrift, and the euphoria that had accompanied her into the restaurant faded abruptly. It seemed impossible to believe that she had actually walked into that real estate office and put her home up for sale, and for a panic-stricken moment she wanted to run back there and tell Dan Jenkins that she had changed her mind. She couldn't rid herself of the thought that she had made a terrible mistake, and she was just about to slide out of the booth when the waitress came with their drinks.

Dennis had ordered a beer, but Kendall, who rarely drank, had requested a strawberry concoction that tasted more like a milkshake than a drink. So when Dennis ticked the rim of her glass with his and said, "To friends," she responded with the same, and then proceeded to drain her glass halfway before putting it down again.

Dennis raised an eyebrow when she ordered another a few minutes later; he was still finishing his first beer. The noise in the crowded bar made conversation difficult, but after finishing the second drink in the same record time, Kendall slid closer to him and said, "What did you mean when you said I seemed different today?"

He hesitated. "Well, at first I thought you looked happy . . . relieved. But now . . ." He waited, watching in surprise as Kendall signaled the waitress a third time. "Kendall, is something wrong?" he asked anxiously.

There was a buzzing in her ears that she told herself had to be from the noise in the bar. "Why do you ask?"

"Because I've never seen you like this." He paused again as her third drink was set in front of her, and when she drank half of that, too, he said, "Maybe you'd better go easy on that stuff."

Kendall laughed gaily, feeling the effects of the alcohol she had consumed so quickly. "But this is a celebration, Dennis. It's not every day I put the ranch up for sale!"

He stared at her. "You did *what?*"

Almost defiantly, she finished the last of her third drink. The room swayed a little, she noticed, but that was because it was so stuffy in here. "I put the ranch up for sale," she repeated, and signaled to the watiress again before the transfixed Dennis could stop her.

"Buy why?" he asked. "Why would you—" He stopped and tried again. "I thought you loved that place."

"I do—I did," she said, wondering why it was suddenly so difficult to think. It was so warm in here! she thought, and seized the fourth glass the waitress had just brought, hoping the cool drink would help. "But I need a change," she went on, wondering if she was slurring her words or if she just imagined it. "I want to get away for a while. I need a . . . a vacation."

Dennis was still staring at her with that dismayed expression. "But you could take a vacation without selling the ranch! Kendall, this isn't like you!"

Through a haze, she recalled suddenly that Jordan had said the same thing to her once. Irritated that he had intruded into the wonderful time she was having, she stared back defiantly at Dennis, wondering why these men presumed to know what she was like, when she didn't even know that herself anymore.

"It's time for a change," she repeated stubbornly. "There's nothing to keep me here. Not anymore."

"But where will you go?"

Oh, that was a good question, she thought, and shrugged. "I haven't decided yet."

"But what about the horses?" Dennis pressed. "What are you going to do about them?"

A sudden image of Cantata flashed into her mind. She could remember the night Cantata was born as clearly as if it had been last night instead of so many years ago. She had slept in the barn for weeks, waiting for Cantata's dam to foal, and the night it happened she was so tired from all that interrupted sleep that she almost missed the whole event. It was always an experience watching a foal being born, but that time it was even more miraculous than usual. When she saw how beautiful the filly was, how perfect in every detail, she had felt like singing.

"That's why I named her Cantata," Kendall mumbled now. "Because she was my song . . . ."

"What?"

She looked up blankly at Dennis, still lost in memories of that night. It was so long ago, she thought, and now she had come full circle. It seemed to her now that all those years had been just a wonderful dream. She had only to go home and look at Cantata's empty stall and wonder if it had even happened at all.

"Are you all right?" Dennis asked when she didn't respond.

Kendall looked down at the array of empty glasses in

front of her and wondered for a moment whom they belonged to. She couldn't possibly have drunk that much, she thought blearily; she usually didn't drink at all. Suddenly nauseous, she glanced at Dennis and muttered thickly, "I think we'd better skip lunch. I . . . I don't feel very well."

"I'm not surprised," a familiar voice said. "It's amazing that you can feel anything at all, if that's what you've had to drink."

For a confused moment or two Kendall thought that Dennis was playing a trick on her by mimicking Jordan's voice. She glared at him, intending to tell him the joke wasn't funny, but then she realized that he was staring at something behind her. She turned her head to see what he was looking at and saw Jordan standing there. Appalled, she just stared at him for a minute, wondering if she had somehow conjured him out of her whirling thoughts.

"Hello, Kendall . . . Dennis," Jordan said calmly.

"Hello, Mr. Craig," Dennis replied in the same tone.

"What are you doing here?" Kendall demanded, gripping the swaying table with both hands. It occurred to her that maybe she was the one who was swaying, but she couldn't tell for sure. The entire room seemed to be moving; Jordan was the only one who appeared to be stationary, and she fixed her belligerent gaze on him, trying to summon a little dignity.

"I was going to ask if I could buy you both a drink," Jordan said, sounding amused and exasperated at the same time. He glanced at Dennis, and when their eyes met, some silent communication passed between them that Kendall couldn't understand. He looked at her again and added, "But I see that's not necessary. You seem to be doing enough damage all by yourself."

She glared at him. Straightening haughtily, she was about to tell him that it was none of his business how much—or with whom—she chose to drink. But suddenly the room was spinning again, and she looked uncertainly at Dennis instead. "I . . . I think I'd like to leave now," she said, and tried to stand.

Both men reached for her as she stumbled to her feet, but she shook them off, staring icily at each of them in turn. "I can manage," she said proudly, and then wished she hadn't sounded so confident. The exit seemed miles away, and the tables scattered around the bar were like obstacles deliberately placed in her way. She made it outside somehow, wincing at the brightness of the sun, and wondering how she was going to drive home when she could hardly stand.

Dennis seemed to read her thoughts. "I think I'd better drive you home, Kendall," he said nervously. "You don't look—"

"I'm fine," she insisted, feeling the sidewalk move under her feet. "I'm perfectly capable of driving myself. And besides, you have to get back to work and fix my truck."

"That can wait."

"I'll drive her home," Jordan said.

"You certainly will not!" Kendall declared. She held out an imperious hand. "Give me the keys, Dennis."

"Kendall, I really don't think—"

"If you're worried about your truck, don't be," Kendall said, beginning to get angry. "I've never had an accident in my life!"

"It's not the *truck* I'm worried about," Dennis replied, sounding injured.

"Well, then?"

"Look, this is ridiculous," Jordan said impatiently.

He took a firm grip on Kendall's arm. "I'm taking you home, and that's the end of it."

Kendall tried to jerk her arm away. She didn't want to go anywhere with him, and she certainly didn't want him doing her any favors. She'd walk all the way home first, and she told him so.

Both men ignored her. Their eyes met again in that look of understanding, and they nodded. "Good-bye, Dennis," Jordan said. "And thanks."

Dennis nodded again, and to Kendall's amazement, the two men shook hands. As Jordan began literally propelling Kendall in the direction of his car, she glanced back and saw the sad resignation on Dennis's face as he watched them go. She turned furiously back to Jordan again. "Thanks for what?" she demanded. "What did you mean?"

"You wouldn't understand," Jordan replied, his voice rough. "Especially not in your condition."

"I'm not in *any* condition!" she said, staggering slightly. "And you don't have to drive me home, either! I don't want you to, in fact. I'll take a taxi instead!"

"Just get in the car," Jordan said, holding the door open for her.

She glared at him, barely resisting the urge to brace herself against the car frame. If she weren't so dizzy, she thought, she'd give him a piece of her mind. He couldn't order her around like this, and she was about to tell him so. But then she thought that maybe she'd better sit down after all. Everything was spinning again, and she wondered if she was going to be sick. The thought appalled her, and she plopped down weakly on the car seat, closing her eyes against a wave of nausea. She was *not* going to be sick, she told herself; that would be absolutely the last straw.

Jordan climbed in on the driver's side. She could feel him looking at her, but she didn't dare open her eyes. "Do you think you can make it home?" he asked quietly.

She nodded, gritting her teeth. "I'm *fine*," she insisted, though she had never felt so miserably sick in all her life.

"Tell me if you want me to stop."

"Just . . . drive," she said, and prayed the motion of the car wouldn't make the nausea worse.

"Why don't you lie down on the seat?" he suggested.

She didn't want to, but as he started the car and they moved out of the parking lot, she felt so awful that she had to obey. Barely realizing that he had cradled her head in his lap, or that his arm rested lightly on her shoulder, she huddled in sheer misery, wondering what had ever possessed her to drink so much. Never again, she vowed. If she survived this experience—which she was beginning to doubt—she'd never touch a drop of anything stronger than water.

The next thing she remembered was Jordan gently shaking her awake. When she opened her eyes and saw that they had arrived at her house, she looked up at him bemusedly as he helped her out of the car.

"What happened?"

"You passed out. It happens when you've had too much to drink."

She flushed at that, putting a hand to her aching head. She wanted to thank him for bringing her home, but she couldn't find the words; she was suddenly too aware of his arm about her waist as they went up the steps to the front door, and she didn't know whether to be grateful for his support or not. Confused by the gesture, and wondering if it was that or the alcohol that

made her feel so weak, she couldn't even look at him.
Fumbling in her purse, she finally found her keys, but
her hands was trembling too much to find the lock.

"Here, let me."

He took the key ring from her unresisting fingers and
opened the door for her. "Will you be all right?"

She looked up at him, knowing it was wrong but
unable to deny the sudden desire she felt for him. He
seemed to fill her with his presence; the only thing she
could think about was lying in his arms once more. She
didn't know if that was the effect of the alcohol or not,
but she didn't care. She had thought about him,
dreamed about him, *yearned* for him for so long that
the words were out of her mouth before she could stop
herself.

"Why don't you come in?" she asked, her voice
suddenly husky.

He gazed at her for a long moment without speaking,
his eyes holding hers. A variety of emotions crossed his
face, but she saw the longing in those dark eyes, and
she couldn't wait for his answer. She needed him now.
Passion was welling up inside her; she was so breathless
she couldn't say anything more. She moved toward him
then, winding her arms about his neck, pressing her
body against him as she drew his head down to hers.

"I've missed you so much," she murmured, her lips
against his. "Oh, so much . . ."

He groaned helplessly then, embracing her tightly,
kissing her with a passion that matched her own. They
swayed with the force of it, mouths hungrily seeking,
locked in each other's arms as if they would never let
go. Kendall was instantly swept away, the sheer joy of
being kissed by him again so powerful that it was a few

seconds before she realized he was trying to draw away. Dazed by the intensity of her emotions, she looked up at him blankly as he pulled her arms from around his neck.

"No!" he said hoarsely. "Not this way! You don't know what you're doing."

She blinked, trying to understand what he was saying. She moved toward him again, but he held her away, his face agonized. "No!" he said again, his voice choked. "It's too much to ask of any man! I can't . . . I won't . . . take advantage."

If she hadn't had so much to drink, she might have understood. But the alcohol had befuddled her brain, and all she could hear was his rejection and not the reasons for it. She stiffened, suddenly painfully aware of the fool she had made of herself. She had never thrown herself at a man. Never! And now, to have done so, and to have been repulsed so completely, was so mortifying that she couldn't even speak.

He was still holding her hands, and she jerked them away so violently that she stumbled back. He reached out, trying to catch her, but she evaded him, her face drained of all color, her eyes wide with shocked realization.

"Kendall—please! Try to understand! I didn't mean—"

She couldn't listen to him. Any explanation would only prolong this awful moment when she wanted to die of humiliation. "No!" she cried, putting her hands over her ears. "Don't say it! Don't say anything more! Just—just go!"

"Kendall," Jordan said desperately.

"Please, Jordan!" she cried again. "Just leave!"

He started to say something more, but the stricken look on her face stopped him. As if sensing how futile it was, he dropped his hand.

Kendall didn't wait for him to get in his car and leave. She turned and ran inside, running all the way up to her bedroom. Throwing herself across the bed, she buried her face in the pillow, feeling so sick at heart and in body that she didn't know whether she wanted to cry or die of sheer misery.

Jordan stood outside for a few minutes, fiercely willing himself not to follow Kendall inside. He desperately wanted to explain why he had pushed her away; he wanted her to know that it was the hardest thing he had ever done in his life. But he had meant it when he told her that he couldn't take advantage of her, and he knew he wouldn't be able to restrain himself if he went to her. The effort not to give in to his desire for her was so great that he was actually shaking, and he forced himself to take a deep breath, and then another, until he no longer felt like exploding with helpless frustration.

Cursing himself for a fool, he lit a cigarette with hands that still trembled, and then he slowly walked back to his car. Involuntarily, his eyes sought the upstairs window, and for a moment or two he allowed himself the luxury of picturing them both up there, a willing, passionate Kendall as eager for him as he was for her. He imagined her slender body next to his; he could almost taste her soft lips and feel the smooth silkiness of her skin. So strong was the image, so clear in his mind, that he actually took a step toward the house again before he stopped himself. Shaking his head almost violently, he willed the fantasy away. As much as he wanted her—and he did, he did, he thought, closing his eyes in longing—he couldn't take her. Not this way, and not now, when she didn't even know what she was doing. She'd never forgive him if he did that; he'd never forgive himself if he lost her forever because of one uncontrollable act. When she came to him—*if* she came to him, he amended bleakly —it would have to be because she wanted to, not because her inhibitions had been lifted by some alcoholic daze.

So he climbed into his car, and with a last look at the silent house, he drove slowly away.

Kendall endured the next few days, wandering about the place doing the necessary chores without energy or enthusiasm. She tried to keep busy, but she'd find herself stopped in the middle of something, staring blankly into space, not thinking anything at all—or thinking too much.

Again and again her eyes would seek the sloping ground that separated her ranch from Jordan's property, and she'd wonder what he was doing. She imagined him standing on the terrace, coffee cup in hand; she saw him at the barn, looking at his horses. She wondered if the new swimming pool was completed yet . . . and she wondered if he was entertaining some woman. The thought would fill her with pain, and she'd turn away, vowing for the thousandth time that she wasn't going to think about him.

Dennis brought her truck back, and she asked him to stay for a dinner that seemed to depress him even more than it did her. He didn't linger that night, and she was glad to see him go. It had been an effort trying to dredge up any conversation; she seemed to be in some kind of limbo, waiting for something to happen but not knowing what it was she wanted. She knew she had to make plans, but she couldn't summon the energy even for that. Now that she'd made the decision to sell the ranch, she seemed incapable of deciding anything else.

The realtor brought people out to look at the place, and she absented herself each time, taking long, pointless walks and thinking about nothing at all.

As Jenkins had promised, it didn't take long to find a buyer. He called excitedly at the end of that long endless week and told Kendall that someone had made an offer, but that he felt they should counter and ask for more. She didn't care what he did; she left the matter in his hands, just wishing it would be over soon. She hoped that once the ranch was sold she'd be able to snap out of this debilitating lethargy, but until then she couldn't seem to summon enthusiasm for anything, least of all for making the important decision of what she was going to do next. It was as if she were transfixed in time, able to go neither forward nor back. She didn't care about anything except getting through another day without bursting into tears.

And always, though she had vowed again and again not to, she thought about Jordan, and what a fool she had been.

Jordan had been doing a lot of thinking, too. On the morning that the real estate agent called Kendall with the news that he'd found a buyer for the ranch, he received a call of his own from Kaylene inviting him to a barbeque that afternoon.

"I think you'll find it profitable," Kaylene said persuasively when he declined. "Especially since several of my guests are interested in breeding to that new colt of yours."

Jordan was tempted to tell her that he'd been thinking about selling the colt. In fact, he'd been thinking of selling everything and getting out. He couldn't look at any of the horses without thinking of Kendall; he couldn't go anywhere or do anything without wishing she were there too. He couldn't summon the energy or desire to leave the ranch, even though he knew he was spending too much time alone, brooding like a lost soul. Nothing interested him; all he could think about was what Kendall was doing, or how she was, or if she was managing all right. He'd find himself staring in the direction of her ranch, picturing her all alone—or picturing her not alone at all. He'd wonder if Dennis had come around again, and he'd grit his teeth at the thought.

". . . And the strangest thing happened. She actually called the other day and offered me that mare."

Jordan jerked his attention back to Kaylene. He hadn't been listening, but now he asked sharply, "What mare?"

Kaylene laughed her throaty laugh. "Haven't you been listening? Kendall finally sold me Cantata. I was so surprised I could have—"

"Kendall sold Cantata to you?" Jordan straightened in his chair, completely alert now, wondering if he had heard right.

"Yes, that's what I've been trying to tell you, Jordan. But what's even more astonishing is that she put the ranch up for sale. Can you believe—"

"She did what?"

"Aren't you paying any attention at all?" Kaylene asked, exasperated.

Jordan ran a hand through his hair, trying to get a grip on himself. "But she loves that ranch," he blurted. "I can't believe she'd ever sell it."

"Well, she's going to. I thought I'd tell you just in case you were interested in buying the place yourself."

He didn't hesitate. "I'm more interested in buying that mare," he said.

This time Kaylene's laugh was even more amused. "You're not serious!"

But he was, Jordan thought, the idea quickly taking hold. He had wanted some way to show Kendall how much he cared, and the more he thought about it, the surer he became that this was it. He had to buy that horse; he didn't care what it cost, or what he had to do to get it. He'd think about the problem of Kendall's selling her ranch later. Right now, he had to have that mare!

"Name your price," he said.

"But, Jordan—she's not for sale!"

Jordan had dealt with people like Kaylene before. He knew that under the frills and ruffles she was a shrewd businesswoman. She had to be to run an establishment the size of the Van Zandt stables. So if she was the businesswoman he thought she was, there would be a price she wouldn't refuse. It was all profit and loss for someone like Kaylene; he'd just have to find the profit margin she'd accept.

He decided on a direct approach, knowing instinctively that she would respect that more than a circuitous route. "Come on, Kaylene," he said evenly. "Everything's for sale if the price is right."

She hesitated, and Jordan realized that the conversation had suddenly become serious. Smiling grimly to himself, he knew she was thinking furiously, calculating the odds, wondering just how far he would go. He decided to save them both the trouble of negotiation.

"I want that horse," he said flatly. "I won't haggle over the cost."

"Well, this *is* a surprise," she said. "Do you mind if I ask why?"

"What difference does it make?"

She hesitated again, and then said slowly, "None, I guess. I was just . . . curious."

Jordan waited, refusing to consider what he would do if she refused to sell no matter what he offered her. She was silent again for a few moments, but her response when it came took him completely by surprise.

"You're buying the mare back for Kendall, aren't you?"

He considered denying it, but he knew she was too sharp not to detect a lie. He was about to answer, when she sighed. "I knew it," she said. "You're in love with her, aren't you? Oh, you don't have to answer that, Jordan. It's been obvious for a long time, now that I think about it. I was a fool not to recognize it before."

"I don't know how you could have," Jordan said wryly, "since I wasn't really aware of it myself."

"Well, I wish you luck. The Vosses are a stubborn family. I should know. Aaron was even—"

She stopped so abruptly that Jordan was intrigued. "What about Aaron?"

Kaylene hesitated a fraction too long. "Oh, Aaron was even more stubborn than Kendall," she said, trying to speak lightly. But her voice caught, and when she tried to cover it with a laugh, the sound was even more forced, betraying her.

She had been in love with Kendall's father, Jordan thought incredulously. Suddenly so many things became clear: Kendall's mention of the feud between Aaron and Kaylene; Kaylene's antagonism toward Kendall. Aaron must have rejected Kaylene long ago, Jordan thought, and that rejection still hurt. It was ironic: The woman who seemed to have everything she could possibly want had been denied the one thing she wanted most. For a moment he didn't know what to say.

Then it occurred to him that now he had a lever to force Kaylene into selling him Cantata. She had kept her secret all these years; she wouldn't want it brought to light now. He could say . . .

He couldn't do it. Someone else might be able to use the threat of exposure, but he had never been that ruthless, and he couldn't be now, not even for Kendall.

The silence between them had gone on too long. When Kaylene spoke again, Jordan knew that she was aware he had guessed her secret, and that in her own way she was grateful to him for not mentioning it. Sighing, she said, "Foolish pride. I guess we're all afflicted with it at one time or another, aren't we?"

She didn't wait for a response, but drew another breath. Then, in a brisk tone that made him smile, she said, "Just how badly do you want that mare, Jordan?"

Chapter 15

KENDALL WAS IN THE KITCHEN WHEN SHE HEARD SOME-
one pull into the yard outside. She tensed, sure that it
was the real estate agent who had come to tell her that
the buyers had accepted her counteroffer. She had to
go through with it now; she was committed.

No, she wasn't, she thought in sudden panic. Nothing
was final until she signed the papers. He couldn't force
her to sign; she could tell him that she had changed her
mind.

Had she? She didn't know. She wasn't sure of
anything anymore, except the fact that she didn't want
to leave here. The prospect of going somewhere else
daunted her; she hadn't even decided where to go yet.
And now he was here, and it was too late, and she
wasn't ready. She wasn't ready at all.

A car door slammed, and she bit her lip. She could

pretend she wasn't home, she thought. She wouldn't answer the door.

But the back door was open. He'd know she was inside, and that would be even worse. She had to face him; somehow, in the next few seconds, she had to make up her mind.

She was just starting toward the door when she heard the whinny. She froze. It can't be, she thought, telling herself that she hadn't recognized that sound. She was hearing things. It couldn't be Cantata; she had just dreamed it. But when she saw the truck and trailer outside, she froze again. Jordan was leaning against the side panel of the truck, and for an instant, as their eyes met, Kendall told herself she had to be dreaming that, too.

Jordan straightened as she approached. Her heart was pounding so loud in her ears that she was sure he could hear it too, and she made an effort to control herself. What was he doing here? She was almost afraid to ask for fear that her voice would betray her.

She had told herself that she never wanted to see him again, but she had known all the time that it was a lie. She had tried to forget him, but she had known she never would; she had tried to believe that the ending of their affair was for the best, but she had known that she would never accept that. She loved him; she loved him shamelessly and without reservation, despite all the things he had done. Even the sight of him was enough to make her feel weak; she longed to touch him, to hold him. She ached to be held in his arms; she yearned just for that—to be held by him, so close that she could feel his heart beating in time with her own.

But she could pine for him until the end of her days, and nothing would change the fact that he wouldn't—

couldn't—love her in return. That was the final, harsh
reality, and as she slowly walked up to him, she told
herself that he would never know how she felt. She
wouldn't be able to bear the pity in his eyes if she ever
told him; she wouldn't be able to listen to him say how
sorry he was. That would be worse, far worse, than
never having him at all.

The horse inside the trailer neighed again just then,
and Kendall started violently. Her glance went disbe-
lievingly toward the vehicle, and Jordan smiled.

Even before he unbolted the ramp and led the horse
out, Kendall knew it was Cantata. It had to be; she
would have known that neigh anywhere because she
had heard it so often over the years. Swallowing,
she stood rigidly as Jordan brought the mare over to
her, but as Cantata butted her head against Kendall's
shoulder in greeting, she couldn't help herself. Her
hand trembled as she reached out to stroke the satiny
neck, and when Cantata nuzzled her again, she bent
her head to hide the sudden tears in her eyes.

When she looked up again, the tears were gone. She
didn't know why Jordan was tormenting her like this,
but he wasn't going to see her cry. She had wasted too
many tears on him; she had no more to shed. But when
she spoke, her voice still shook, and it was an effort to
force the words out. "Why did you bring her here?"

"Because she's yours," he answered simply, holding
out the lead rope to her.

Kendall's glance dropped to that rope. She wanted to
take it; she actually trembled with the longing to accept
it. The thought of having Cantata again made her feel
that there was hope for the future after all. She could
succeed anywhere with just this one mare; it didn't
matter where she went, because the foals from Cantata

would continue the breeding program she and her father had designed years ago. She would be Voss Arabians again, she thought blissfully, and . . . .

It was impossible. Her visions of triumph vanished abruptly as reality set in. She couldn't do both, she knew. Even with selling the ranch, she couldn't hope to buy another place and Cantata, too. Oh, why had Jordan done this? she wondered. Did he hate her so much that he had to torture her with the thought of all she had lost?

"She isn't mine," she forced herself to say. "She's Kaylene's now. She bought her."

"I bought her back for you," Jordan said, trying not to be dismayed by the look in Kendall's eyes. He had thought she'd be overjoyed; he couldn't understand why she was acting this way. Why wouldn't she accept Cantata?

"Well, I can't pay for her," Kendall said flatly. "So you might as well—"

"She isn't for sale," Jordan said, trying to thrust away the thought that this wasn't going well at all. "She's a gift. For you."

Kendall stared at him, telling herself that she hadn't heard him right, knowing that she had, and suddenly so angry she could hardly speak.

She had held herself too tightly under control these past weeks. She had agonized over the decision to sell Cantata; she had agonized again before she put the ranch up for sale. Those two decisions had been the most difficult she had ever made, but she had accepted them knowing she couldn't do anything else. She had been devastated at the thought of having to start all over again, and the only thing that had kept her going at all was the idea that she hadn't asked for help from anyone. Everything else had been stripped away from her, but she had held on to that last final scrap of dignity and pride.

And now Jordan was trying to take even that away from her. He knew, he must know, that she would never have sold Cantata if she hadn't been absolutely desperate; he knew, too, that she could never buy her back. So he had bought her himself, and out of some misguided sense of pity or guilt, he had brought her here, magnanimously offering her as a gift, sure that Kendall would have to accept.

Well, she wasn't going to accept. He wasn't going to take away what little pride she had left, not when it meant so little to him and so much to her.

Refusing to acknowledge the pain she felt at the thought of giving up Cantata a second time, Kendall stepped back abruptly from the mare. She couldn't look at Cantata again; if she did, she'd never be able to surrender her.

"I can't accept her," she said through stiff lips. "Put her back in the trailer and take her away."

Jordan looked stricken. "But—"

She couldn't talk about it anymore. She could hardly speak over the lump in her throat, and she choked, "I don't want her, don't you understand? I sold her; she isn't mine anymore!"

"She'll always be yours," Jordan said urgently, trying to make her understand. "You bred her, you raised her—"

"And I sold her!" Kendall shouted suddenly. She was trying desperately to sound convincing. He had to believe her. She had to make him angry enough to go away and take Cantata with him. If he didn't go, she'd beg him to stay, and she wouldn't humiliate herself like that again. She'd asked him to stay once, and he had repulsed her. She couldn't bear that rejection again, not a second time, not ever. Trying frantically to control the ache of tears at the back of her throat, she said, "She doesn't mean anything to me now. She's just an . . . an old mare!"

"You don't mean that!" Jordan said, shocked.

"Yes, I do. I was glad to get rid of her. She's . . . she's outlived her usefulness."

"I can't believe you're saying such things," Jordan said, trying to keep himself under control. What was the matter with her? He didn't understand this at all. He had thought to make her happy. He had wanted so desperately to make her happy.

"Well, you should believe it," Kendall said, making her voice as cold and heartless as she could. Oh, why wouldn't he just leave? She couldn't bear much more of this or she'd break down completely. "There's no room for sentiment in the breeding business," she went on harshly. "If you don't now that now, you'll have to find out the hard way!"

Jordan couldn't believe this was happening. She couldn't mean what she was saying; she couldn't. She didn't believe those things any more than he did. He hadn't been that wrong about her; he knew it. There was something going on here that he didn't understand, and he wasn't going to leave until she told him the truth. "Maybe I don't want to find that out," he said, beginning to get angry from sheer frustration.

"Then you'll just be playing at being something you aren't and never will be!" she flung at him.

"Like you are right now?"

Kendall lifted her head. "What does that mean?"

"I know how much Cantata means to you," he said.

"I don't care how much you deny it. You're the one playing games, Kendall, and I think it's time you admitted it."

"I don't have to admit anything to you!" she cried. She started to turn away, but he grabbed her arm, trying to force her to turn and face him. She closed her eyes, summoning all her control. She had to act angry; she had to make him angry enough himself to storm out of there. It hadn't been difficult at all to do that in the past; why was she failing so miserably now?

"Let go of me!" she cried, facing him. "Why is it so hard for you to understand that I don't want anything from you?"

Jordan had tried to control his temper; he had vowed he would. He had told himself that nothing she said would make him angry enough to leave. But when she looked up at him like that, her eyes blazing, her expression filled with contempt, he knew that things were so wrong now that nothing could make them worse. Barely restraining himself from shaking her, he grated, "You're not going to run away from me this time, Kendall. We're going to settle this once and for all."

"There's nothing to settle! I told you to take Cantata and—"

"This has nothing to do with the horse!" he shouted, feeling the last vestiges of control slipping away. He didn't care now if he lost his temper; he almost welcomed the feeling. He was furious at her stubbornness and enraged at his inability to change it. He had hoped that his gesture with Cantata would tear down the wall between them, but now he realized how wrong he had been. He had made one mistake after another with her, but this time—*this time*—he wasn't going to let her go. Not until he heard from her own lips that she didn't care about him, that she didn't want him—that she didn't love him.

"You're hurting me, Jordan!" Kendall cried, freeing herself at last. She spun around to face him. "What's the matter with you? Are you crazy?"

"Yes. Yes, I guess I am. You make me crazy, do you know that? I thought you'd be happy to get Cantata back, but I should have known better. You seem to think the simplest act is some devious attempt to humiliate you, and I'm tired of it, Kendall. I'm sick to death of it! I know you value your independence, but damn it, there has to be a limit!"

Kendall's face had turned pale. Her eyes were enormous as she gazed at him. She had seen Jordan angry before, but she had never seen him as furious as this. Half-frightened, half-fascinated, she backed away a step. "Are you finished?" she stammered.

"No, I'm not finished!" he shouted. "I said we're going to have this out, and we are. You may never speak to me again, but for once I'm going to tell you how I feel!"

He stopped, breathing heavily, his anger draining away abruptly. He wanted to reach for her, to crush her to him; he wanted to take her in his arms and never let her go. But his hands hung limply at his sides, and he could only gaze helplessly at her as he choked, "I love you . . . I love you. I've tried to deny it and fight it and tell myself it isn't true, but it is. It is. I never wanted it to happen because of the way I failed with Marie. I couldn't bear the thought of failing you, and so I tried to tell myself it wasn't happening. But every time I saw you, or talked to you, or even thought about you, I knew."

Kendall's face had gone even paler. She felt light-headed suddenly, almost dizzy with the joy that was spreading through her. She could hardly speak over the lump in her throat, but she whispered, "I didn't—"

Jordan held up his hand. "Let me finish. I may never have the courage to say these things again. . . ." He took a breath. "I admire you, Kendall. I always have. I love your spirit and your pride and the fierce way you cling to your independence. But you make it so hard, " he said chokingly. "You make it so hard for anyone to help, or even to get close to you. I know you think you don't need anybody—" He couldn't go on. He was strangling on all the things he wanted to say and couldn't; he knew he would never be able to make her understand.

Kendall gazed at him for a long, tense moment. Then, finally, the tension seemed to drain out of her, and she looked very small and delicate and helpless. She took a shaky breath and said, "You're right, Jordan. I don't need anybody—not just anybody. But I . . . I do need you." She looked up at him, tears shining suddenly in her eyes, hardly daring to believe that this was happening, that they were finally saying the things that were in their hearts.

"I told myself I didn't," she went on, her voice shaking with emotion. "I tried to tell myself that you were like all the people I despised. But I knew you weren't. . . ." She smiled a little, remembering the scene. "I guess I knew from that first day when you fixed the pipe." Her smile faded. "But then, in Idaho . . ."

Jordan winced at that. But he had to tell her; the time for equivocation was long past. She had to know; she had a right to know. "I was scared then," he confessed.

"Scared of making the same mistakes in a different way, scared of not being able to give you what you needed. I . . . I didn't, with Marie."

"But I'm not Marie," Kendall said softly.

He met her eyes. "And I'm not Tony."

She flinched at that. "No," she said. "You're not. You're so much more than he ever was. . . ."

He dared to step toward her then, putting his hands on her shoulders. "And I'm not like Kaylene."

She couldn't help herself. She hadn't felt like laughing in so long that she thought she'd forgotten how. Now she felt such happiness bubbling up inside her that she couldn't resist. "I don't know," she said, trying not to smile. "You must have something in common with her if she sold you Cantata. I never thought she'd give up that mare once she had her."

Jordan thought of that conversation with Kaylene, and of the lever he hadn't used, and he was glad. Later he would tell Kendall about Kaylene, but he was too happy to bring it up now. "Maybe she just recognized a fool when she saw one," he said wryly. "Everyone else seemed to know I was—except me."

Kendall thought of her conversation with Dennis that day and grimaced. "You weren't alone," she said. "It's taken me a long time to realize that pride is too high a price to pay for happiness."

"So what are we going to do about Cantata?" he asked solemnly.

Kendall glanced over at the mare, who was placidly grazing the grass by the fence, home once again. "What do you say to joint ownership?"

He grinned, a new light of understanding in his eyes. "How about a partnership instead? I think Jor-dall Arabians has a nice ring to it, don't you?"

Kendall frowned, pretending to consider. "I'd prefer Ken-dan Arabians," she said, returning his grin with a wicked one of her own.

"Independent to the last, is that it?"

"Would you have it any other way?"

He raised an eyebrow in that gesture she loved. His lips twitching, he said, "Well, it might be nice if you let me think I'm in charge—some of the time, anyway."

She smiled. "I'll have to think about it. I wouldn't want you to get bored."

He tilted her head up to his, gazing into her eyes. "I have a feeling," he murmured, "that whatever else I'll be in the future, it won't be bored."

She smiled again. "And I promise, in the future, no more foolish pride."

His eyebrow went even higher at that. "I think that's a little too much to ask of yourself, don't you?"

Her eyes twinkled. "Well, I can *try*."

"We both will," he said softly. "But somehow, I don't think it will take much effort—on my part, anyway."

She gazed at him, her eyes soft. "Nor mine," she said tenderly. "I do love you, Jordan," she said, touching the strong face she held so dear, loving the expression in his eyes that she knew was meant only for her and always would be . . . now.

"I've waited a long time to hear those words," he said with a sigh.

"I've waited a long time to say them," she whispered. "And to hear them from you."

"I'll say them night and day if it will make you happy," he murmured. "All I want is for you to be happy, Kendall. I'll do anything to make sure of that. . . ."

"You already have," she said.

Then, as his lips met hers, she put her hand against his chest. A wave of pure joy swept over her. She felt the hard pounding of his heart under her trembling palm, and she knew that the rhythm matched her own and always would.

ENTER:

Here's your chance to win a fabulous $50,000 diamond jewelry collection, consisting of diamond necklace, bracelet, earrings and ring.

All you have to do to enter is fill out the coupon below and mail it by September 30, 1985.

Send entries to:

In the U.S.	Silhouette Diamond Sweepstakes P.O. Box 779 Madison Square Station New York, NY 10159
In Canada	Silhouette Diamond Sweepstakes Suite 191 238 Davenport Road Toronto, Ontario M5R 1J6

NAME _____

ADDRESS _____

CITY _____ STATE/(PROV.) _____

ZIP/(POSTAL CODE) _____

RULES FOR SILHOUETTE DIAMOND SWEEPSTAKES

OFFICIAL RULES—NO PURCHASE NECESSARY

1. Silhouette Diamond Sweepstakes is open to Canadian (except Quebec) and United States residents 18 years or older at the time of entry. Employees and immediate families of the publishers of Silhouette, their affiliates, retailers, distributors, printers, agencies and RONALD SMILEY INC. are excluded.

2. To enter, print your name and address on the official entry form or on a 3" x 5" slip of paper. You may enter as often as you choose, but each envelope must contain only one entry. Mail entries first class in Canada to Silhouette Diamond Sweepstakes, Suite 191, 238 Davenport Road, Toronto, Ontario M5R 1J6. In the United States, mail to Silhouette Diamond Sweepstakes, P.O. Box 779, Madison Square Station, New York, NY 10159. Entries must be postmarked between February 1 and September 30, 1985. Silhouette is not responsible for lost, late or misdirected mail.

3. First Prize of diamond jewelry, consisting of a necklace, ring, bracelet and earrings will be awarded. Approximate retail value is $50,000 U.S./$62,500 Canadian. Second Prize of 100 Silhouette Home Reader Service Subscriptions will be awarded. Approximate retail value of each is $162.00 U.S./$180.00 Canadian. No substitution, duplication, cash redemption or transfer of prizes will be permitted. Odds of winning depend upon the number of valid entries received. One prize to a family or household. Income taxes, other taxes and insurance on First Prize are the sole responsibility of the winners.

4. Winners will be selected under the supervision of RONALD SMILEY INC., an independent judging organization whose decisions are final, by random drawings from valid entries postmarked by September 30, 1985, and received no later than October 7, 1985. Entry in this sweepstakes indicates your awareness of the Official Rules. Winners who are residents of Canada must answer correctly a time-related arithmetical skill-testing question to qualify. First Prize winner will be notified by certified mail and must submit an Affidavit of Compliance within 10 days of notification. Returned Affidavits or prizes that are refused or undeliverable will result in alternative names being randomly drawn. Winners may be asked for use of their name and photo at no additional compensation.

5. For a First Prize winner list, send a stamped self-addressed envelope postmarked by September 30, 1985. In Canada, mail to Silhouette Diamond Contest Winner, Suite 309, 238 Davenport Road, Toronto, Ontario M5R 1J6. In the United States, mail to Silhouette Diamond Contest Winner, P.O. Box 182, Bowling Green Station, New York, NY 10274. This offer will appear in Silhouette publications and at participating retailers. Offer void in Quebec and subject to all Federal, Provincial, State and Municipal laws and regulations and wherever prohibited or restricted by law.

SDR-A-1

Genuine Silhouette sterling silver bookmark for only $15.95!

What a beautiful way to hold your place in your current romance! This genuine sterling silver bookmark, with the distinctive Silhouette symbol in elegant black, measures 1½″ long and 1″ wide. It makes a beautiful gift for yourself, and for every romantic you know! And, at only $15.95 each, including all postage and handling charges, you'll want to order several now, while supplies last.

Send your name and address with check or money order for $15.95 per bookmark ordered to

Simon & Schuster Enterprises
120 Brighton Rd., P.O. Box 5020
Clifton, N.J. 07012
Attn: Bookmark

Bookmarks can be ordered pre-paid only. No charges will be accepted. Please allow 4-6 weeks for delivery.

She fought for a bold future
until she could no longer
ignore the...

ECHO OF THUNDER

MAURA SEGER

Author of **Eye of the Storm**

ECHO OF THUNDER is the love story of James
Callahan and Alexis Brockton, who forge a union
that must withstand the pressures of their own
desires and the challenge of building a new television
empire.

Author Maura Seger's writing has been described by
Romantic Times as having a "superb blend of
historical perspective, exciting romance and a deep
and abiding passion for the human soul."

**Available at your favorite
retail outlet in SEPTEMBER.**

ECO-B-1

Silhouette Intimate Moments

COMING
NEXT MONTH

VALLEY OF THE SUN
Elizabeth Lowell
Hope Gardener dreamed of finding the water that would
bring her ranch to life. Rio was the one man who could
save her ravaged land, but would he leave her with a
ravaged heart?

THE MALE CHAUVINIST
Alexandra Sellers
Kate Fenton was an ardent feminist. Andreas
Constantinou seemed to epitomize the attitudes Kate had
fought hard to escape, yet his potent sensuality drew her
into his arms again and again.

SOFT TOUCH
Möeth Allison
Chalice York was a Hollywood screenwriter, Joe Dante a
New York playwright. They had nothing in common,
except a fierce competitiveness and an irresistible
passion.

TIGER PRINCE
Erin St. Claire
The island paradise of Jamaica brought vacationers
Caren Blakemore and Derek Allen together in a blissful
fantasy...until Derek's secret life threatened to destroy
their paradise and tear their worlds apart.

AVAILABLE THIS MONTH

DEVIL'S DECEPTION
Doreen Owens Malek

FOOLISH PRIDE
April Thorne

STARDUST AND SAND
Amanda York

COMES A STRANGER
Maura Seger